I0728082

# Maui Winds

## Edie Claire

third of the **Pacific Horizons** novels

Copyright © 2016 by Edie Claire

Cover design by Cormar Covers.

This book is a work of fiction. The names, characters, places, and incidents are products of the writer's imagination or have been used fictitiously and are not to be construed as real. Any resemblance to persons, living or dead, actual events, locales or organizations is entirely coincidental.

All Rights Are Reserved. No part of this book may be used or reproduced in any manner whatsoever without written permission from the author.

# Dedication

For whoever invented chocolate.
Thanks.

# Acknowledgments

The "Foundation for Ocean Mammals" is a fictional organization, but heartfelt thanks go out to the Pacific Whale Foundation, which is a very real non-profit organization based on Maui dedicated to protecting the ocean and its animal life through science and advocacy. I have spent several glorious hours on PWF whale watches leaving from Maui, and the book *Hawaii's Humpback Whales*, co-written by the organization's founder, Gregory D. Kaufman, and Paul H. Forestell is my favorite go-to resource. A special shout-out goes to Michelle Trifari, former PWF intern (and also an Alaskan whale-watch guide!), who patiently answered my bizarre questions about life as a marine biologist, many of which I flung at her while she was trying to take humpback pictures from a moving boat. Thanks, Michelle! Any factual mistakes in this book are my own errors (i.e., don't blame them. These people know their stuff.)

# Prologue


*Moscow, USSR, October 1991*

The door swung open before her, and Julie Sullivan stepped through it. She was doing her best to steady her nerves, but no amount of mental preparation could slow the frantic pounding of her pulse in her ears. This was it. At last. They had waited so, so long.

The room was sparse and square, with a vinyl-tile floor and unadorned, white-painted masonry walls. Sixteen metal cribs lay within, arranged with a military precision that maximized the limited walking space in between. Each crib sported a thin mattress and single white sheet. One attendant sat in a straight-backed chair by a stainless steel sink; she looked up only briefly, then returned to her sewing. The still air smelled mildly of bleach, with only the faintest of more objectionable odors hidden beneath. The floor and linens appeared spotlessly clean, but overall, the room seemed dim. The two windows on the near wall were generous enough in size, but little sun navigated its way through both the cloudy sky and the narrow alleyway outside, and only half the light fixtures in the ceiling had working bulbs. Each of the cribs was occupied, although Julie didn't hear a sound.

The director of the orphanage stopped walking again just a few steps into the room. A stocky, middle-aged woman who managed an engaging smile despite a prominent missing tooth, she turned and said something in Russian to Julie and her husband. The couple smiled back at her, then looked immediately at the thin, elderly man who had been their interpreter and constant companion since they had landed at the Moscow airport the night before.

"All of the babies in this room are between six months and a year old," he explained. "They are all fed and washed on a schedule appropriate for their age. Everything is kept very clean here. The women are proud of their work, and all the babies are healthy."

Julie and Tom exchanged a guarded look. Save for one tiny hiccuping sound while the interpreter was speaking, the infants remained silent. "Yes," Tom replied, turning back to their hostess. "Everything is very clean."

The director smiled and nodded, seeming to need no translation of the compliment. She turned and walked on into the room.

Julie hesitated, looking down to study the two infants in the cribs nearest her. They were awake. Their little eyes were open. One of them turned its head and twisted around to look at her better. The other did not. They were dressed neat and tidy in pastel-colored onesies, with light hair cropped close around their small, pale faces.

*Six to twelve months,* Julie thought with dismay as she struggled to maintain the necessary facade of approval. She was a psychotherapist, not a pediatrician. And she had no experience as a mother. But she had read and studied enough about child development to know that these babies were not acting as they should. By six months they should be sitting up; the older ones should be crawling, pulling up on the bars, maybe even taking their first few steps.

She raised her head and scanned the room. She saw only five babies managing any sort of upright posture. Five of sixteen!

Tom's hand pressed gently into the small of her back. She turned to look at him and realized she had frozen in the aisle and was holding up the group. "Sorry," she whispered, moving on.

*You knew it would be like this,* she reminded herself sternly. Babies growing up under institutional care, with little personal attention and inadequate mental and physical stimulation, were bound to suffer developmental delays. At least in this relatively well-equipped urban facility, she and Tom had been assured that the infants were adequately fed.

The director led them around the center island of cribs, then stopped short again. Her smile, which had been ever-present during the previous session of paperwork, transformed suddenly into a grim line. She reached out and took Julie's ice-cold hands in her own large, calloused ones. Her words were earnest, but hushed.

The interpreter pushed forward. He listened closely, but even after the director stopped speaking, he said nothing.

"What?" Julie asked earnestly. "What did she say?" The director's eyes had scanned the still-open doorway of the room as she spoke, as if afraid that staff outside in the corridor might overhear her. The attendant already in the room did not seem to worry her.

The interpreter hesitated.

Both Julie and Tom turned to the last member of their party, a paralegal who was their adoption agency's local representative. "Yana?" Tom beseeched.

The petite forty-something woman, who understood English fairly well but had difficulty speaking it, nodded and spoke calmly to the interpreter in Russian.

The man frowned in disapproval, but he began to speak. "The director would like to thank you herself, personally, for adopting this particular baby." He looked warily at the paralegal, but she nodded back at him once more, and he continued. "This is a very unusual situation for the orphanage, Mr. and Mrs. Sullivan. You understand that raising this child here... It is not a normal thing. That is, we have very few Negro persons here in Russia." He shot a look at the director of the orphanage that bordered on reproach. "The director seems to feel as if the infant might not be safe here. She says that she worries about her, and she is very glad that the girl will be raised in the United States because life will be better for her there."

Julie looked into the eyes of the orphanage director. She wasn't sure whether to trust the accuracy of the translation, but she had no doubt as to the sincerity in the director's pale blue eyes. She was a caring woman. Caring... and fearful.

*Dear God.* Was the director trying to tell them that the baby wouldn't be safe growing up in Russia, or that the child wasn't safe *here,* in the orphanage this woman herself was in charge of?

"We will make sure that she is safe. Always," Julie said forcefully, although she could hear her own voice shaking as she said it. "Can we see her now?"

The interpreter spoke, and the director smiled at them again. She released Julie's hand and stepped over to the crib tucked in the dimmest corner of the room. Julie and Tom approached together, shoulders touching. Julie held her breath as she leaned over the railing and peered inside.

A baby in a faded yellow onesie squirmed on her back on the mattress, her sticklike arms and legs moving aimlessly in the air. Her tiny little hands grasped at nothing; her toes were bare. Her face — and Julie had never been one to exaggerate — was that of an angel. Her dark eyes sparkled; her light-brown complexion was flawless. Little ringlets of soft black curls covered her head. Her tiny lips were full, still moistened with the faintest bubble of milk from an earlier feeding. For one precious, wondrous second, this beautiful, perfect baby girl turned her face toward Julie, and their gazes locked.

Julie Elizabeth Sullivan fell hopelessly, helplessly, permanently in love.

The baby looked away again.

"Oh, Tom," Julie cried, reaching out to lift up her daughter. "She's... she's..."

Her husband wiped a tear from his eye. "She is very beautiful," he agreed, finishing her thought. "Just like her mother."

Tears filled Julie's own eyes as she gathered her baby to her. *So light,* she thought with a pang of fright. *She's as light as a cat!* She tried not to panic as the calculations ran through her head. An eight-month-old baby should weigh at least sixteen pounds. Could this child weigh twelve pounds, even? Ten? Julie tried to nestle the child against her, but the little body wouldn't cooperate. The baby's back remained stiff, her limbs unyielding. Julie held the infant awkwardly against her chest instead, facing out so that Tom could see her.

The orphanage director was talking again. The interpreter translated as she spoke. "She's a good baby. Very well behaved.

Takes her feedings well. No vomiting."

Tom grinned at the child and attempted to hold her hand, but she avoided his eyes and clenched her fingers shut, staring fixedly over his shoulder.

Julie leaned down to plant a gentle kiss on top of the baby's head. The silky black curls were so soft. They exuded a soapy smell that brought back memories of childhood bubble baths. Julie closed her eyes and tried again to cuddle the infant closer.

The baby stiffened.

"All we've been told is that the child is biracial," Julie heard Tom saying. "Can you ask the director again what she knows of the birthparents? Was the orphanage given specific information about them, or is everyone simply guessing, based on the baby's appearance?"

Julie opened her eyes, and as the interpreter repeated the question, the director shook her head. Her response was a long one.

"She says no one knows," the interpreter explained. "The baby was found at a railway station. She was abandoned. Wrapped in a blanket and left on a bench. The doctors said she had only just been born. But she was not born in any of the *roddoms* — the state maternity hospitals. Such a birth would not go unnoticed."

The director put a hand to her belly with an emphatic gesture and continued to speak rapidly. The interpreter threw her a pained expression, but nodded and continued to translate as she spoke. "Nor was the baby's mother likely attended by any trained midwife, since the cord was not cut properly. But everyone believes the mother must have been white, because the very few dark-skinned people living here either work at an embassy or are exchange students at university, and these will almost certainly be men. A Russian mother with a dark-skinned baby would find her life made very difficult. The child would... not be accepted."

Julie watched her husband's face harden, even as her own teeth clenched. They were both aware of the scarcity of people of color in the Soviet Union, whether African, Asian, or any other ethnicity. Discrimination was prevalent even among the various shades of Soviet nationals. They had not been surprised that a white Russian mother might choose to give up a biracial baby for adoption, particularly in the midst of the present political chaos. But at no point had she and Tom been told that their future daughter had been abandoned in a railway station, much less born without any medical assistance. They knew from the agency only that a biracial baby had been expedited for adoption, and that because the Sullivans had indicated no racial preference, their names had been moved to the top of the list.

Julie caught her husband's eyes and held them. She lifted the stiff, too-tiny body and tucked the baby's head protectively under her chin. Had the birthmother been so afraid of exposure, of public censure, that she had given birth in secret — possibly even alone? How terrified she must have been... and yet, she must have cared for her child. Had she not left the infant wrapped warm and snug in a crowded place where she would be found quickly?

"Please," Julie pleaded, looking at the director, "is there anything else you can tell us about who her mother or father might be? What country her father might have come from? Anything at all? It could be very important."

Julie held her breath as the interpreter began his translation. For her own part, she couldn't care less what part of the world her baby's progenitors hailed from. The warm bundle in her arms was already a permanent appendage of her own body. But she had read enough about adoption to understand that the information could someday matter very much to her daughter.

Julie's hopes were crushed as the director's response came with saddened eyes and a shake of her head.

"She says she has no idea," the interpreter said. "She doubts the police even tried to track down the mother. They just took the baby to hospital and then at two weeks old, she came here. The nurse who brought her from hospital thought she might be half Indian. Most of the staff here believe she is half Negro. But no one knows."

Julie shifted her daughter in her arms, and tears welled up in her eyes again as she gazed into the perfect little face. The baby's cheek bones were high, her lashes thick and long, her eyes bright with awareness even as she insisted on staring out into the room rather than back at Julie. She squiggled again and emitted one brief, gurgling sound of protest.

"That will be the first of many," Tom teased, smiling. He was still attempting, unsuccessfully, to hold the baby's hand.

"Oh! I'm sorry," Julie apologized. "I guess you'd like to hold her too, huh?"

He laughed. "Well, yes, actually. If you don't mind."

Julie handed over the baby, and Tom set her against his chest atop one strong arm, supporting her back with the other. He too dropped a kiss on her precious little head, and Julie wanted to smile at the picture they made, but a biting fear left her with a frown instead.

*So small.* Julie looked around the room again. All of the infants might have some delays, but none looked as small and underdeveloped as their daughter did. At eight months many normal babies were crawling, but this tiny girl could not brace herself to sit on Tom's arm without assistance. Food was in short supply at some orphanages, yes, but they had been told that this one was well provided for. Had they been lied to about that? Or...

A sick feeling churned in Julie's stomach. Was it only *their* baby who had been shorted?

She shot a glance at the attendant who sat by the window, sewing. The woman looked back at her, her face expressionless. Her pale eyes were inscrutable.

Julie's pulse pounded in her ears again. She took a deep breath and tried not to judge. Perhaps this woman was one of the trusted ones. Perhaps that was why the director had spoken openly in front of her. But the director could not be at the orphanage every day and night, could she? If even one of her staff had acted with bigotry toward a dark-skinned baby — had fed her a little less, scowled at her, spoken to her cruelly — who would know? How would anyone ever know?

All at once, Julie felt as if the sterile, white-painted walls were closing in on them. "Tom," she barked, putting out a protective hand to cradle her new daughter's thin, fragile shoulder. "I think we should be leaving now."

Tom's eyes studied hers. He could see her panic. "Are we sure there's nothing else we need from here? We don't want to be sorry later that we forgot anything." He turned to the interpreter. "Please ask if anything was with the baby when she was found. The blanket she was wrapped in, maybe? Did the police bring anything at all with her to the hospital?"

Julie watched as the baby grew increasingly agitated. The child seemed to want down, to be put back into her crib. The sight pierced Julie's heart with a primal pain.

This little girl wasn't used to being held. Wasn't used to being looked at, or talked to, or played with. Wasn't used to being loved. Their little angel baby showed any number of red flags for having attachment problems. She and Tom would have a tough road ahead of them.

*It's all right, sweetie,* Julie's heart pleaded. *Don't worry. We will love you, now. No matter what.*

"The nurse from the hospital brought nothing here with the child," the interpreter reported. "She said the blanket the baby was wrapped in originally was very nice, but that it was 'lost' in the hospital. The nurses thought the mother must not be so poor, or she would never have given up such a fine blanket."

Julie's eyes flashed with ire. *As if the freakin' blanket was the sacrifice!*

"We're leaving now," she said firmly, giving one last nod of thanks to the director as she turned her feet toward the door. "Our daughter is going home."

# Chapter 1



*Near Maui, Hawaii, May 2016*

"Excuse me. Seat in the upright position, please. We'll be landing shortly."

For one long, very confused moment, Ri Sullivan had no idea who was talking to her or where she even was. All she knew was that her back was sore, her neck was sore, her head weighed a couple hundred pounds, and everything was dark.

She pulled off her face mask and rubbed her eyes. The back of an airplane seat swam into focus.

*Landing shortly.*

*Oh my!*

She whipped her brain to attention, pushed the button to fix her seatback, and hastily shoved up the window blind. Immediately her blanket, the face mask, and the worthless inflatable pillow that had deflated hourly since its purchase at LAX slipped off her lap and onto the floor.

Ri ignored all three and looked outside.

*Maui!*

Was she really here? A hint of a greenish-brown mountain peak showed itself briefly, then vanished into a bank of fluffy white clouds.

*Wait. Or was that Moloka'i?*

Ri wasn't sure. She knew that Maui was the biggest in this particular cluster of Hawaiian islands, and that the bi-lobed, lopsided land mass was made up of two volcanoes, the small West Maui mountain, and the much larger East Maui mountain, better known as Haleakala. She had learned that the names of the smaller, older volcanic islands that dotted the ocean nearby were Moloka'i, Lana'i, and Kaho'olawe, but although she could point them out on a map, she couldn't tell which was which from the air when she didn't know which way North was. She also had no idea how to pronounce them, particularly the last one. But she would figure it all out, with time. She had four months.

She sucked in a breath and held it behind her smile. She was as excited as she was terrified. Hopefully, no one would realize the latter. Her apprehension would be difficult to explain. She was twenty-five years old and past due for a grand adventure. She'd spent her entire life in New England, growing up in southern Maine, attending the University of New Hampshire in nearby Durham, and then working her first real job at a small aquarium on the Massachusetts coast. Although she couldn't imagine ever being parted from the ocean, she had never intended to plant herself permanently in the North Atlantic, either. Everyone always said she was the dreamer in the family — the born explorer who would grow up to scale Mount Everest or hike the Sahara or take the first step on Mars. She didn't really care about any of those things anymore, but exploring the other six of the seven seas had been her heart's ambition for as long as she could remember.

She hadn't considered, as a child, that she would have to put thousands of miles between herself and everyone she loved in order to do it. But she was here now. And everything would be fine.

Ri felt the plane drop in altitude, and as she peered out the window, blue sky began to show through the cottony wisps of cloud. She bent her sore neck and looked down, and her eyes widened in wonder. Bright green peaks of mountain. Scalloped, chiseled cliffs. Sandy-brown shores meeting cerulean-blue waters. Long streaks of white where waves broke over underwater reefs. The vivid tableau was so surreal she felt as if she were watching a movie trailer.

The plane turned. It dipped further. Ri's gaze remained glued to the window as the jet neared the airport, which lay in the land bridge between Maui's two mountains. From the shape of the land below, she reasoned out that the peaks she had seen first must be those of the smaller western mountain. She tried to make out more landmarks, but as the plane made its final approach into the city of Kahului, her view was obscured by clouds again.

Ri sat back in her seat with a bounce. No matter. She would have plenty of time to see everything there was to see on the island, even without an airplane. Haleakala was 10,000 feet tall. She'd read that from near the top of it, you could look out towards the other volcano and see the ocean on both sides of the land bridge at once.

She'd definitely be doing that.

Her spirits remained high as the plane touched down and taxied. Her view out the window in the low-lying valley was less dramatic, but if she gazed out over the asphalt and past the bland airport buildings she could see the West Maui Mountain in the distance.

Despite her excitement, her exhaustion caught up with her again as she waited an eternity to deplane, dumped the worthless inflatable pillow in the nearest trashcan, and followed the signs to baggage claim. At some point as she moved through the disappointingly generic airport she must have slipped into autopilot, because as she stood by the luggage carousel sizing up a nearby bench for a nap, she suddenly realized she could remember nothing since leaving the jetway. For a brief moment, she even forgot which airport she was in. Sheesh, she was tired!

Hauling her bag off the carousel caused an unexpected wrench in her back, and she stretched her spine and rotated her shoulders with a grimace. She was in excellent shape physically, and she wasn't used to such bodily protests. Then again, her body wasn't used to spending thirty-six hours straight in airplanes and airports, including trying to sleep with her knees drawn up on a two-seater bench overnight at LAX after her first flight to Maui was cancelled yesterday.

*Ignore it. You're in Hawaii!*

She pulled up the handle on her bag and headed off toward the pickup curb. A cluster of transport people stood near the doors, holding signs. She scanned them, but saw nothing relevant, then jumped when she realized that a person standing not four feet away was looking at her and waving. The woman was about her own age, had a blond ponytail, and wore an aqua-colored polo shirt emblazoned with the Foundation for

Ocean Mammals logo, a breaching humpback whale.

"Sriha?" the woman asked tentatively.

Ri tensed a bit. Then she smiled. "It's Ri. But yes, that's me."

"Nice to meet you!" the woman enthused, shaking her hand. "I'm Kaley. I'm the HR Assistant working with Trish. Did she tell you what the plan is for today?"

Ri's head spun a little. Kaley's voice was high-pitched and she talked at light-speed. A flurry of emails had occurred in the hours since Ri's flight cancellation had kept her from showing up at orientation on time, but for the life of her, she couldn't remember their content. One sleepless night in an airport her brain might be able to tolerate, but she hadn't slept the night before either, thanks to a fun-filled family going away party that had seemed like a great idea at the time.

She greeted Kaley with a smile, hoping to remember "the plan" in the process. But she needn't have worried, as the chatty HR assistant was happy to supply it.

"Can I carry anything for you? Oh, you just have the one suitcase and the backpack? Okay! Well, follow me, then! Trish said for you to just leave your stuff in the van, that I should take you straight to the marina as soon as we get to Ma'alaea. This morning's orientation was all classroom stuff, I guess, but this afternoon all the interns are going out on the boat, and they're going to wait until you get there, so we don't want to hold them up. Oh, no!" Kaley stopped abruptly, and so did Ri. "I forgot! I brought your shirt and everything. You're supposed to go ahead and get changed."

Kaley reversed course and led Ri toward a restroom, then handed her a canvas tote bag which also bore the Foundation for Ocean Mammals logo. "This has a shirt and your nametag," she explained. "You can go ahead and change into shorts and sandals if you want. You'll be going right out onto the boat, Trish said."

Ri blinked. *Right out onto the boat. Onto the Pacific Ocean.*

Her heart pounded with excitement. She had waited forever. Now it was happening so fast! No matter. She took the tote, wheeled her suitcase into the restroom, and changed. It was not until she emerged from the stall and examined herself in the mirror that she noticed the name on her engraved plastic nametag, which had already been attached to her shirt.

Sriha Sullivan. Research Intern.

*Sriha.*

A sinking feeling hit her square in her gut. *No! Oh, no.* She had specifically asked them to put "Ri" on her nametag. She had asked them more than once.

She closed her eyes. Let her breath out slowly. She wished it didn't matter. She'd been trying to *make* it not matter for nearly two years now. But it did.

She opened her eyes. The face that looked back at her in the mirror was sad, exhilarated, and exhausted all at the same time. It was the face of Sriha Mirini Sullivan, daughter of Julie and Tom Sullivan, sister of Mei Lin Sullivan. Holder of a bachelor's degree in marine biology and a minor in psychology. It was a face with light-brown skin, tightly curled dark-brown hair, and big brown eyes. A face that confused people. A face that frequently brought on lingering, quizzical second looks. Where was *she* from? Hmm. She had a high forehead and cheek bones, perhaps from her Russian mother, but for whatever reason, most people seemed to think on first glance that she was Indian. But her lips were full, which didn't quite fit. And she didn't really look African, either, because her hair wasn't right. Then again, her hair wasn't right for anything — it was funky curly, but silky in texture, with such a strange combination of reddish highlights and black lowlights that the color looked fake. Was she Middle Eastern, maybe? Her nose was no help; it looked stereotypical of nothing and was just kind of there. In fact, she had no preponderance of features that pointed to any particular ethnicity. So how to explain her?

How to explain, indeed.

The question of her life.

When she was a child, Ri had reveled in that mystery — the mystery of herself. She had reveled and reveled good, most often at other people's expense. Impudent questions such as "where are you from?" were answered with made-up tales of ever-increasing inanity, featuring foreign royalty, international spy rings, and the occasional injection of magical unicorns. Ri was different, she was special, and she was good with that.

*No problem.*

Adolescence had been rockier. By the time Ri headed off to middle school, knowing the truth about her birthparents and her ethnic origins had become more important to her. But despite her parents' unwavering support, including their willingness to hire a private detective in Russia, the truth she sought could not be found. So, like most muddled tweens, she had simply followed the path of least resistance. Her first name sounded Indian. She looked like she could be half Indian.

Ergo, she was Indian.

*Liar.*

"You ready?" Kaley called into the restroom.

"Just a sec!" Ri swiped at her eyes with a tissue. They were rheumy from lack of sleep, that was all. What way was that to meet her fellow interns? The next four months were going to be fantastic. Most fledgling marine biologists would give their left arm to spend the summer working with the research team at the FOM, but spots were highly competitive and unpaid besides, and living expenses on Maui were killer. She'd had to save for years at her aquarium job to fund this venture and still stay on track for grad school next year, and she was damn well going to enjoy every moment of it.

"Ready!" she announced, popping out of the restroom with a smile. She would ask the HR director, Trish, to make her a new nametag. Problem solved.

They got as far as the exit to the airport parking lot before it started.

"I love your name. It's so pretty! Is it Indian?" Kaley chirped.

Ri steeled herself. The words came out by rote. "Yes, it is. My middle name is Mirini, which is Swahili. You could say my parents are imaginative types."

"Oh, both names are so pretty!" Kaley cooed, as people generally did.

"Thanks," Ri replied with a smile. She didn't disagree. She'd always loved both her names. Not only the sound of them, but the unique heritage each one implied.

Too bad she could no longer claim them.

Kaley opened her mouth to say something else, but Ri was ready to cut off the inevitable next question. She had lots of practice at that. "I prefer to go by Ri, though. Can you tell me something about the other interns? I hate that I'm coming in so late, when they've already had most of a day to get to know each other."

Kaley the speed-talker was easily diverted. As she rattled on about Shelby, Will, and Bryant, Ri found her own attention unexpectedly diverted also. She could not stop looking at the many people who were out and about enjoying the balmy weather in the modernly generic outskirts of Kahului. The local residents looked much like the people in the airport, but what was strange about them hadn't dawned on Ri's foggy brain until now.

She wasn't entirely sure what *their* ethnicity was either.

"What are the demographics here?" she asked, realizing too late that she had interrupted Kaley's current story, which was something about a past intern and a shark in Australia. "I'm sorry. It's just that I thought Maui was mostly white, except for the native Hawaiians... I guess I didn't really think about it." *Which was stupid of me,* she recognized. She had studied the area's geography and natural history, but she knew next to nothing about its people or politics.

Kaley chuckled. "Oh, no. None of Hawaii's mostly white. Maui's about half white. The rest is Asian and Hawaiian. But it's all mixed."

Ri felt butterflies in her stomach. "Asian? What kind of Asian?"

Kaley shrugged. "Oh, people are from a lot of different countries originally. You'll see Japanese, Filipino, Chinese, Korean. But most people aren't just one thing, you know? Like I'm from Indiana and I'm German and Scandinavian and Irish and who knows what else? Well, Hawaii's a melting pot for, like, all the Asian countries and the Polynesian islands and then pretty much anything else you've ever heard of, too."

Ri stared back out the window at the spectrum of skin

colors and wide variety of physical features on display. She could walk down any of these streets, right now, and no one would pay her a shred of attention.

Now that would be bizarre.

"So, what nationality are you?" Kaley asked brightly.

Ri tried not to wince. She had walked right into that one. She could tell the truth, and most likely Kaley would be fine with it. Too bad she herself was not. "I'm Russian, Indian, and African," she answered.

*You are such a damn liar.*

"Oh, that is so cool!" Kaley gushed. "Wow, well, it looks gorgeous on you! I love your eyes."

"Thanks," Ri returned, feeling miserable as usual. "The Germans and Scandinavians and Irish didn't do so bad either."

Kaley laughed. She went on to tell a story about some grandmother of hers who had a strange eye color, but Ri's sleep-deprived brain was unable to concentrate. As the car drove out of the city and on through the old sugarcane fields nestled between the mountains, her conscience continued to bait her.

*Why do you keep lying to everyone? What is it you're so ashamed of?*

Ri squirmed in her seat. She had no good answers for those questions. No way to explain herself, to heal the raw edge of pain and embarrassment that had nagged at her soul ever since the day the fated envelope had arrived.

"Ri! Ri!" her sister Mei Lin had screamed, running in from the mailbox like a third grader instead of a twenty-two-year-old who had just received her nursing diploma two days before. "It *did* come today! Oh, I can't wait! Open it!"

Ri had been just as excited, even though she herself was twenty-three and should have known better than to think that a commercial DNA test would bring clarity and resolution to her life.

Clarity and resolution.

*Right.*

Ri the tween hadn't been happy when all efforts to find more information about her birthparents had failed, but she had eventually made peace with it. If she couldn't know whether her paternal half was Indian *or* African, she would simply claim them both. After all, she didn't know she wasn't both, did she? So for years she had answered the question the same way she had just answered Kaley, and everyone was content. Friends who knew her better might hear the "or" story later, after the risk of awkwardness was gone. No one else needed any more explanation.

Ri's parents had let her know about autosomal DNA testing as soon as it was available, and she could have gone through with it earlier. But by high school, Ri's feelings on the issue had shifted. As an older teen and a college student her focus was squarely on her present life and her future, and any concerns related to parental units — whether birth or adoptive — were secondary. It was only after she graduated from college and had lived on her own for a while that the nagging insecurity began to resurface again.

Who *are* you? Who are your people?

"We're almost there," Kaley chirped. "Whatever you don't want to haul around with you on the boat, just leave in the van. As soon as they cut you guys loose, come up to Trish's office and she'll run you out to the house."

Ri nodded. "Thanks." Officially, interns were responsible for finding their own lodgings. Unofficially, they rented rooms on the cheap from an FOM patron who owned a house fifteen minutes away on the bus line.

"You've never been to Hawaii before, have you?" Kaley asked.

Ri shook her head. "Until yesterday, I've never been farther west than Colorado." She leaned forward to get a better view out the windshield. The landscape was opening up. They were nearing the ocean. The *Pacific* Ocean!

"I have cousins in Colorado," Kaley chatted. "Do you have family there, or were you just sightseeing?"

Ri fought the urge to tense up again. These were perfectly normal, friendly questions. "My sister and I used to go to summer camp out there. It was fabulous. Beautiful scenery. But the view from the plane just now... I mean, wow."

No need to talk about camps. Specifically, heritage camps.

They truly were a fabulous thing for international and transracial adoptees, and she and her sister had been both. Their parents had been all over the heritage thing from day one, so for her and Mei Lin, talking openly about their birth countries and cultures had been as natural as breathing. The Chinese family camps were a staple of the Sullivans' existence, and Ri had as many friends among the regular attendees as did Mei Lin, even if none of the girls believed that young Ri was Chinese, despite her wild assertions that she and Mei Lin were conjoined twins born attached at the pinky toe.

Ri was less enamored of the Russian camps, where despite her legitimate ticket to entry, she had been viewed with suspicion by the children and staff alike, her parents once being asked by a check-in counselor if they had not accidentally registered their daughter for the wrong week. But she had always enjoyed the African and Indian camps, where she could tell people whatever she wanted — which she did, with much dramatic flair — and no one bothered to argue with her. Back then, she could claim either heritage with pride.

Since the damn DNA test, she couldn't claim either.

"I know, it's like, ridiculously gorgeous here, isn't it?" Kaley responded to Ri's flattery of the island. "But it's too expensive to live unless you know somebody. I'm only here because my aunt and uncle retired and bought a little house in Kihei, and I rent a room from them. I swear it's the exact same size as my closet in Indiana. But it's worth it. Here we are!"

Ri looked out. She rolled down her window a few inches, breathed in, and smiled. She had yet to see more than an occasional glimpse of the water ahead, but she could smell it. Brine. Fish. Wind. Seaweed. Water. Shells. A hundred different individual scents, all mingled together to form one unmistakable whole. *The ocean.* This scent differed from that of the familiar bay in Massachusetts, and she studied the aroma with glee, trying to tease out the various new scents within it.

The car weaved around a crowded parking lot. The Foundation for Ocean Mammals was headquartered at a small marina at the opposite end of the island's central neck from the airport, near the base of the West Maui Mountain. This side of the smaller volcano evidently saw little rain, leaving the face that was visible from the marina dry and relatively colorless, except for the bright line of windmills that trailed down its slope. The blades turned as Ri watched, creating energy from the funnel effect caused by Maui's ample winds as they converged onshore and whistled between the mountains.

The car stopped. "We'll park here and I'll walk you over," Kaley offered.

Ri didn't hesitate. She pulled a lightweight sling bag out of her backpack; tossed in her wallet, a water bottle, her eco-safe sunscreen, and a few other boat necessities; then closed the van door behind her. It was all she could do not to jog ahead of Kaley in her eagerness.

*Yes!* This was real. It was finally happening. She would be working with whales and dolphins in the North Pacific. Humpbacks, bottlenoses, spotteds, spinners, and monk seals! They were all here waiting for her. All of that, and her only living genetic relative on the face of the earth, too!

*Whoops.*

Ri's teeth gnashed. She hated it when "the thought" cropped up unbidden like that. She hadn't made up her mind what to do about that little piece of information yet, and with good reason. Besides the fact that the vast majority of people on earth had never taken a DNA test and were therefore not included in the sampling pool — such as virtually the entirety of the former Soviet Union — the technology itself was fraught with limitations. "Moderate confidence" was hardly a guarantee. The supposed "fifth to eighth cousin" identified as a match to herself had only a twenty to fifty percent chance of being even that closely related to her. The link could be more distant. Or the whole thing could be laboratory error. She would never know.

*But you can't totally dismiss the possibility, either. You could at least try to rule it out.*

"That's the research vessel," Kaley announced.

Ri's heart jumped into her throat. There it was! She'd been staring at pictures of it on the website for years now. The fifty-foot-long gleaming silver catamaran was to be her new floating classroom, and her feet itched to climb aboard and feel it pitch and roll on the relatively warm waves. The sun shone hot on Ri's dark curls, and she marveled at the disappearance of the clouds that had surrounded the airplane just minutes ago. As they reached the water's edge by the dock, the beauty that met Ri's eyes was near to overwhelming.

Her view to the left across the wide bay was consumed by the big mountain, Haleakala. It rose from the flat lands through which she had traveled and sailed upwards into a ring of clouds, its middle obscured from view as if it were wearing a life preserver, while its peak gleamed in the sun. Looking out over the ocean, she could see the little boomerang-shaped island of Molokini, famous for its snorkeling, and the larger and now uninhabited Kaho'olawe behind it, which was in the process of being restored after years of use by the military as a bombing range. To her right curved the southern tip of the smaller West Mountain, the bend of which currently hid the nearby islands of Lana'i and Moloka'i from view. Behind her were steep slopes of green and brown, flowering plants and exotic trees, chattering birds, and waving palms. Before her was blue sky and blue water and a beautiful shiny research boat.

Nothing else mattered.

Really, it didn't.

She had wanted to come to Maui long before her supposed relative relocated to the exact same island. She'd had her eye on this particular internship since she was a junior in high school, for heaven's sake!

They reached the boat. Other people in matching shirts were standing around next to it, and Kaley made introductions. Ri's sleepy brain felt addled again as she struggled to commit her co-interns' names to memory.

"What a pretty name!" the brunette with the heavy mascara effused. "Is it Indian?"

"Yes," Ri answered mechanically. The name *was* Indian. That wasn't even a lie. Mirini was really Swahili, too. Her parents had chosen the names with great care, in hopes of covering their bases.

Ri had always been fine with that. She should be fine with a wider field of possibility as well.

"Oh! Are you from India, then?"

But she wasn't okay. She wasn't okay because ever since that day when she and Mei Lin had opened that envelope together and read the results of her ethnicity breakdown, she'd felt like a complete and total fraud.

A sick feeling settled in her stomach. "Russian, Indian, and African," she lied.

"Oh, cool!" the girl replied. Ri had forgotten the speaker's name already.

*Oh, wait.* They were all wearing nametags. Her name was Shelby.

"Well, if everybody's ready, let's head out!" announced her new boss, a jovial fellow with an Australian accent.

Ri felt moisture behind her eyes again, and she fought back a fierce urge to scream and stamp her feet with frustration. What was wrong with her? Everything was *right* now. She had everything she'd been looking forward to!

For a brief moment she felt a flash of panic, a dim memory of a time when everything was scary and nothing made sense and her emotions were not under her control. When screaming and crying and lashing out was her response to any and every kind of pain.

But then she was okay again.

It was sleep deprivation. That was all.

Ri inhaled deeply, then let out a shaky breath. She wasn't going to think about the ancestry thing right now. She just wasn't. Two years ago, she'd made the decision to dig deeper and find out more, and she'd wound up knowing less. The ordeal had caused her so much grief she'd made a vow to forget the DNA results altogether. It was crazy to turn her life upside down over a commercial test with such low specificity. Particularly when she looked all wrong for the part.

*Forget about it,* she resolved again. Failure to be content with what she knew and what she had was what had landed her in this purgatory of insecurity to begin with. Taking another step in that direction now would be idiotic. She would simply have to resist the temptation. The smooth-talking snake could keep his apple. She would embrace the mystery and move on.

*You seriously think you can live on this island for four solid months and not even TRY to look up a possible, honest-to-God blood relative?* she argued with herself. *You are SO full of it!*

A brisk wind kicked up, and fellow intern Shelby groaned as her too-long bangs battered her face around her eyes. "I should have brought a headband," she groused, flattening the offending hair with both hands. "You were smart."

Ri blinked back at her, then produced a second headband from her bag. Her own springy curls, which appeared windblown regardless of the weather, were always safely secured off her forehead when she went out on the water, and she never traveled without a backup band.

Shelby expressed her thanks, and as the two stepped forward to board the boat, Ri looked over her shoulder at the clouds ringing Haleakala. They seemed thinner suddenly. It was amazing how quickly the clouds could move and the weather change as the trade winds swept between the mountains.

*You'll change your mind, Ri. You know you're going to.*

She stepped onto the boat.

"I am Sriha Mirini Sullivan," the bold little preschooler had announced proudly, to anyone and everyone who asked. "I am different, and I am special. There is no one on earth exactly like me. But I am like everyone else in some way or other."

That little girl never flinched, did she? She never shrank from the tough questions. Never once felt like a fraud.

*Maui.*

She was here, now. And for better or for worse, call it coincidence or call it destiny, so was "moderate-confidence" cousin fifth to eighth.

Ri's gaze drifted over the ocean beyond the harbor, and a brilliant smile warmed her insides. It was the first of May, and getting late in the season for humpbacks. But as she watched, the white plume of a whale spout shot up clear as day, then drifted lazily sideways in the wind.

Perhaps it was destiny after all.

# Chapter 2

"Yo, Lach! Hold up!"

Ri turned to see a tall redheaded man jog up to the dock and leap onto the boat. The vessel was already pulling away from the dock at the time, but he took hold of the railing, swung his long legs across the gap, and made it aboard with ease.

"Hey! What's up?" Ri's new boss answered, looking both worried and disgruntled. Lachland Kennedy, to whom she had just been introduced, was the head of the research team on Maui. He was a thirty-something Australian with an impressive CV in the marine biology world, and Ri couldn't wait to work with him. Who the crazy redhead was, she had no idea.

"Nothing bad," the newcomer said, smiling broadly. "But you've got to see this. It's unbelievable." He looked at the assembled crew. "These your new interns? Perfect. They'll love this." The interloper walked over to the bridge, leaned into the doorway, and shouted something up to the research assistant driving the boat, with whom he was obviously also familiar. After a brief conversation, their captain nodded in agreement, and the redhead returned to Lachland with a smug smile on his face.

Lachland raised his hands in disbelief. "What the hell, Parker? You're hijacking my boats, now?"

The man laughed out loud and clapped a hand on Lachland's back. "Trust me. If she's still there, it'll be worth it. But we've got to hurry."

"She?" Lachland asked, looking suddenly interested.

The interns watched the exchange with a mixture of confusion and amusement. Ri studied both men with fascination. She had never considered any career other than marine biology, but her minor in psychology reflected a keen interest in human nature. Although she was a strong introvert, she enjoyed studying interactions between people, watching for subtle clues in facial expression and tone that gave away hidden feelings and motives. She could blame the obsession on growing up with a psychotherapist for a mother — she and her sister were both convinced that such weird parenting had warped their young brains — but in truth, she was proud of the talent. Right now, for example, she was certain that her mentor and the man named Parker were close friends, probably with a long history between them.

Shelby let out a small sound — something between a gasp and a giggle — and Ri didn't need to look at her co-worker's face to understand its meaning. Any woman would have to be either gay or dead not to notice how attractive both of the men were. Lachland was blond and tanned and rugged looking, and his friend was lean and muscular, with a handsome face and sparkling eyes that promised a wicked sense of humor. The two of them standing on a boat together in the Hawaiian sunshine made a provocative eyeful, but Ri quickly noted that both were wearing wedding bands.

"I'm not saying any more," Parker teased. "You'll see her if we find her."

Lachland lowered his bushy eyebrows with a growl. Then he addressed the interns. "Well, everybody, I guess we've had a slight change of itinerary. This is Captain Ben Parker, who used to be a friend of mine."

"Oh, that's cold," Ben interrupted with mock hurt.

Lachland growled again. "He fancies himself an expert on marine mammals, but he's just some shill with a master's in oceanography or pottery or some damn thing."

"I bow to your superior knowledge, as always," Ben admitted, actually bowing, albeit facetiously.

"He knows his stuff, but instead of getting his doctorate and contributing to the academic knowledge that will ultimately save the earth," Lachland continued, "he runs commercial whale watches so he can tell jokes and get rich off tips."

Ben frowned. "Ouch. No subtlety, there."

Lachland smirked. "Hey, I didn't say they weren't *good* jokes, mate."

The men's banter continued privately as the captain steered the boat out of the harbor and on into the open waters of

Ma'alaea Bay. Ignored for the moment, the interns clustered around Ri.

Will, a big guy with loose brown curls and a face full of acne scars, gave her a friendly smile. "So, where are you from, Ri? Where'd you go to school?"

Ri smiled back. He had remembered what she preferred to be called. For that alone, she already liked him. She gave them all an abbreviated resume, and they reciprocated. Will was twenty-two and from central California. He was missing his own graduation ceremony in order to be here, but he didn't seem to mind.

Bryant was slender and medium height, with dark hair and eyes and a quiet nature. He was twenty-six and married with a two-year-old son, and his wife was back in Sarasota, Florida, working a full-time job at a bank. Ri studied his face as he talked, struck by his nonchalant tone of voice. The situation he described, being separated from his wife and child for four solid months, sounded like sheer hell to her. But he spoke of it as more of an inconvenience.

Shelby, like Ri, was petite in stature. But unlike Ri, her skin was pale and her features delicate. She had the kind of exaggerated figure that fashion photographers favored, including both generous curves and sticklike limbs devoid of muscle, and she was meticulous enough with her appearance that she had prepared for day one of her internship with two layers of mascara and a professional manicure. Ri wasn't quite sure what to make of her. Marine biologists tended to be earthy, physically active people.

"Where did you go to school, Shelby?" Ri asked.

"I graduated from UT Austin last year," Shelby replied, sounding like a Texan. "I'm starting on my master's at A&M next fall, at Corpus Christi. Can't wait. I applied *everywhere* for a job last year and wound up working retail."

"Yeah," Will sympathized. "You can't get jack in this field with a bachelor's. You were lucky to get that aquarium job, Ri."

Ri chuckled. "I started out cleaning tanks at minimum wage for fifteen hours a week. And it's a crappy little tourist trap, really. Just fish and turtles and a couple of sharks. But I talked myself into full time eventually."

The others laughed with her. In truth, she'd come on board at a time when half the plants in the giant shark tank were dying, and she'd diagnosed the problem with a few quick tests and was able to turn things around. In three years she'd gone from part-time tank cleaner to Assistant Manager of Aquatics, and the assistant part was a joke because there hadn't been a manager in a year and a half — they just didn't want to pay her any more.

Bryant cleared his throat. "I haven't had any trouble getting work with a bachelor's," he said offhandedly. "But Jen and I really want to move to Hawaii, so I'm hoping something will open up for me here. Shouldn't be too difficult."

Shelby and Will exchanged a dark look, and Ri gathered that in the short time since the others had met yesterday afternoon, Bryant had already made himself unpopular. Which was unfortunate, because the four of them would be spending a whole lot of time together — all summer long.

Ri resolved to try and like Bryant anyway. She was always intentional about relationships, at least the important ones. Another side effect of lifelong, in-home psychotherapy.

Shelby turned to Ri with a smile. "So, we know that Bryant's left his wife behind, Will's crushing on some girl in the gift shop, and I'm on the rebound. What's your story?"

"It's not a crush," Will protested playfully. "I am *in love.*"

Shelby rolled her eyes. "You met her less than twenty-four hours ago."

"So? Don't you believe in love at first sight?" he teased.

"Not hardly," Shelby shot back. "I don't believe in love at all. Ri?"

Ri's gaze moved from one to the other. These people certainly moved fast with the chit chat. "I'm single," she reported with a shrug.

"Good!" Shelby said with a smile. "You and I can go clubbing this weekend. Rebound man is here somewhere, just waiting for me. I can feel it."

Ri smiled noncommittally as she searched her brain for a response. "Clubbing" had never been her idea of a good time, but it was Shelby's unabashed announcement of her quest for a rebound man that left Ri speechless. Shelby's tone had not been serious, but the look in her deep blue eyes left no doubt of her true intent. The woman was wounded. And hurting. And desperate to stop the bleeding.

Sometimes, Ri's talent for seeing deep gave her more information than she wanted to know.

She was saved from responding by Lachland, who returned to his mentees to begin their planned tour of the research vessel. As the boat moved steadily further from shore he walked the four of them from stem to stern, proudly describing its environmentally responsible design and special whale protection features. He had only just begun to explain the use of its gear when his friend Ben interrupted him, pointing eagerly out over the water.

"This had better be good," Lachland complained again.

"Just look, will you?" Ben returned. "You're amazingly lucky, you know. It's been nearly half an hour now, and she's still there! Logging right where we left her."

Ri looked out over the ocean to see the unmistakable dark gray profile of the dorsal fin and back of a humpback whale. The animal was still some distance away but appeared to be resting at the surface, sleeping or "logging." From the length of back that was visible on either side of the fin, the whale seemed to be quite large.

"There's a calf with her," Ben added. "Just saw it a second ago."

"Probably a late season calf," Lachland explained to the interns as the boat approached. "Whale numbers here in May are way down from the peak in February. Most of the whales have headed to the feeding grounds in Alaska already, now that the calving and breeding season is pretty much over. There's no food for them here, and they're hungry. But the females who give birth later in the season tend to stick around Hawaii a little longer, so that their calves have time to put on enough blubber before migrating back to colder waters. And of course, a few mature males will hang around as long as the females are here. Hungry or no, they'll stay as long as they've got a shot. From her length, this female appears—"

Lachland stopped talking. Ri looked over to see his mouth hanging open and his eyes bugged. The boat drew to within the regulation one hundred yards of the whale and stopped. Lachland continued staring at the animal, his lips moving silently with several unfamiliar words that probably rated as profane in Australia.

"What did I tell you?" Ben beamed. "Is that, or is that not, the most beautiful thing you've ever seen?"

Ri turned from the men to look at the whale again. Now that the boat was closer, she could see that the animal wasn't normal. Just off the midline of its back, a few feet in front of its dorsal fin, a huge chunk of flesh was missing. The poor whale had a giant, misshapen divot that looked as if at some point a ragged piece of blubber had been ripped out and cast off by a giant claw. Fortunately for the whale, the gaping hole had somehow managed to heal over completely, and the wound was now covered with smooth, healthy looking skin just like the rest of her back.

"I can't—" Lachland gasped. "Is that her? Is that the one?"

Ben laughed out loud. "It's got to be! Look at the shape of that scar. And the location of it. It's perfect! And her size. Everything's perfect." He put a hand on Lachland's shoulder and gave it a shake. "It's her, my man. And she's A-okay. Even got a new calf this year."

Lachland said nothing. He just kept staring at the whale, dumbstruck.

Ben's voice lowered. "You didn't kill her, Lach. You hear me?" he said gently.

Ri watched, startled, as the Aussie's blue eyes turned misty.

Bryant, who had been studying the whale with binoculars, lowered them and turned to the men. "Looks like a ship strike to me," he declared. "Whale's lucky to be alive."

Ri sighed to herself. She would have a difficult time liking Bryant. The guy was oblivious.

"Yes," Ben answered evenly. "It was a ship strike. Three years ago last February. It wasn't anyone's fault though; it was just a freak accident. She came up underneath a boat Lach was driving for a friend of ours. She surfaced without a blow first, so no one on board saw her, and it's anyone's guess why she didn't see or hear us coming, because it was an old bucket of bolts and plenty loud."

"I thought she was dead for sure," Lachland managed to mumble finally. "There was so much blood in the water... And the poor calf..." He turned to Ben. "How the devil could she keep the sharks off her?"

Ben offered a shrug and a smile. "No idea. But there she is! The scar's healed amazingly well, don't you think?"

Lachland's handsome face finally showed a smile of its own as he looked back out at the still-slumbering whale. "I'll be damned."

They spent a good deal of time taking photographs of the whale before, finally, the animal began to stir. Within a minute, and with one powerful flick of her black and white tail flukes, she and her calf disappeared under the water. Lachland appeared to be doing his best to act reserved and scientific about the find, but his best wasn't good enough to fool Ri. The man nearly teared up three separate times and his face beamed with good humor for the rest of the afternoon. In fact, she was pretty sure he was hurrying through the agenda so that he could cut them loose early and go celebrate someplace private.

After they had learned the vessel's features and capabilities, talked about the current research projects they'd be working on, and stopped for the incidental sightings of another humpback whale and a bottlenose dolphin, the boat headed back to the marina. Ri's fatigue, which had gone into happy remission the second she'd stepped onto the catamaran, came flying back at her full force once Lachland pronounced the interns dismissed. And as she leaned over the railing, admiring the view of southern Maui as the boat approached land, the horizon began to swim before her in the haze of the late afternoon sun.

*Wake up!*

"So, Shelby," she forced herself to ask as the other intern joined her. "Do you like living in Texas? My sister is moving there in a couple weeks. She's a geriatric nurse, and her fiance got a job with Lockheed Martin, so she's going to work for a rehab hospital in Dallas."

Shelby's answer came eagerly, but Ri found herself unable to follow it. She still couldn't talk about Mei Lin's moving away without feeling melancholy, never mind that technically, Ri herself had left New England first. She and her sister had never expected to spend their entire lives together; they'd expected to find significant others and have families of their own, and Ri had always planned to travel. Yet not until Mei Lin made the actual announcement two months ago did the reality of those plans finally sink in. Cell phone communication was a wonderful thing, but it pained Ri to think that for the first time in her life, her sister's warm hugs would no longer be a few hours' drive away. And she could hardly afford a plane ticket whenever she wanted one.

Shelby was looking at her expectantly. *Shoot.* "I'm sorry," Ri apologized. "What were you saying? I'm falling asleep again. I've been up for three days straight now. I think."

"Three days?" Shelby exclaimed. "No! I was hoping you'd want to catch the bus into Lahaina with me later. I'm dying to check out the nightlife!"

Ri pictured her unconscious body sliding down the steps of a public bus and out onto the street in front of a crowded tiki bar. She would probably still be snoring as the bus pulled away.

"Um... sorry. I really just want to settle in and go to sleep. Some other time, maybe?" she offered.

"Fine," Shelby agreed with mock chagrin. "But I'm holding you to that. I am so ready for a hookup. So many surfers... so little time."

Ri smiled back, attempting to cover her lack of enthusiasm. She wanted to get along with Shelby, but she was not on Maui to "hook up" with surfers or any other men. Ri was not a hookup kind of woman. Ri was a "do you want a real, honest, lasting relationship with me or don't you" kind of woman. And as much as she would love to meet someone new, she didn't think she'd find a like-minded man by hanging out in a Lahaina bar.

The boat pulled into the harbor, and Ben stepped over to

talk to the interns. "Good to meet you guys," he said cheerfully. "I'm off to Alaska with the whales in a couple days, so I doubt we'll cross paths again. But just so you know — Lach's the greatest. Learn from him, and you'll go far. Where are you guys coming from?"

"Fresno," said Will.

"Sarasota, Florida," said Bryant.

"Houston, originally," cooed Shelby.

Ben looked at Ri.

"I'm from Maine," she answered.

He looked taken aback. "Maine? Really? I thought you were a local. That's cool. Tell me about your gray seals. What's happening with the population out there?"

Ri blinked. *A local?* She wanted to ask him why he had thought that, but she answered his question about the gray seals first, only to find it followed up with several more related ones. She was musing over his level of knowledge on the topic, and listening to him elaborate on the FOM's research on Hawaiian monk seals, when Lachland reappeared.

"Parker!" he shouted with faux irritation, "Stop lecturing my interns! Do you work here?"

Ben laughed. "Might as well."

"Go get your damn doctorate," Lachland groused. "Then we'll talk."

Ben smirked. "I'm planning on it. Starting next spring, maybe. Next fall, at the latest."

"Well, hallelujah!" Lachland teased.

Ri's mind wandered again as the men traded barbs. Ben lived on Maui — at least during whale season — and he thought she was "a local." Why?

The boat neared the dock. It was now or never.

"Excuse me," she said boldly, catching Ben's attention as soon as Lachland's was diverted. "Why did you think I was a local?"

Ben studied her a moment, then looked embarrassed. "I don't know. You just seemed... Well, your appearance is similar to that of a lot of people who live here. That's all. Sorry if I offended you."

"No, no," she said quickly. "I'm not offended. I was just curious."

He smiled back at her, then waved farewell to all the interns. "I'm off, Lach!" he shouted, vaulting himself off the boat before it reached the dock again, in a perfect reverse execution of his move on the way out. "Gotta get back to the wife!"

Lachland shouted back some nonsensical thing that must have been an inside joke, and Ben laughed loudly as he jogged down the dock and out of sight.

Ri realized, with some disappointment in herself, that her heart was thumping loudly in her chest. *Your appearance is similar to a lot of people who live here.* She had thought the same thing herself. Just looking out the car windows in Kahului had been like nothing she'd ever experienced before. But to hear the words from an actual resident of Maui...

What did it mean?

She wished she didn't care. She really, truly did. But the thumping in her chest was telling her something.

Perhaps that she was sleep deprived?

*Nice try, Ri.*

No. Her heart was making her position clear. She *did* care who she was. Who her people were.

She always would.

And the answer could be right here.

# Chapter 3

Wolf slowed his steps, admiring the sunset with a deep sense of satisfaction. "Vog," a combination of the words "volcano," "smog," and "fog," was technically a form of air pollution. The lake of lava that constantly sizzled and brewed in the caldera of the volcano Kilauea over on the Big Island shot up all sorts of gases and particles into the sky, and when the wind blew just so, that haze drifted over the ocean to Maui. Add sunlight, oxygen, and a little moisture, and voila — you had vog. Since the spooky grayish-white mist carried sulfur products that could irritate the lungs, many people found little to celebrate in the phenomenon.

Sunsets and sunrises were the exception. When sunlight filtered through vog at just the right angle, an amazing array of colors resulted. Fiery oranges. Glowing reds. Warm pinks. Even cool purples. The kind of colors one didn't normally see in the sky. Yet here they were now — in all their glory.

Wolf's steps stopped altogether. He unclipped his water bottle and lifted it for a swig, only to remember he'd emptied it already. *Right.* It was only the beginning of May, and the heat was already getting to him. He'd have to pace himself better tomorrow.

Deciding to relax for a minute, he set down his gear and stretched out on a rock to enjoy the view. He was running terribly late already, but what the hell. He could make it back to his truck before it got totally dark, and dinner at the field station wasn't much to look forward to anyway. But how many more purple sunsets would he get to see in his life? Particularly ones as spectacular as this, playing out over this deserted stretch of mountainside as if for him and him alone?

He'd spent a long, tiring day taking volatile gas measurements on the slope of Haleakala. Performing gas flux sampling solo was proving more time-consuming than anticipated, and he was beginning to worry about his deadlines.

He should have completed the Maui phase of his data collection by now, but a variety of equipment problems had delayed the project, and when the spring semester ended, so had the services of his undergraduate intern. Not that he minded working alone. In fact, he preferred it. Chris had been a nice guy and a promising geophysicist, but the kid's constant chatter about nothing had worn on Wolf's nerves. He much preferred what he was hearing now.

The whir of the wind whistling past his ears. The cluck or chirp of the occasional bird. There was no traffic noise. The nearest dirt track was still a ten-minute hike away, and he was far above the closest thing to a highway.

*Perfect.*

He gazed out over the craggy southern slope of the ancient shield volcano, which in this particular location was on the dry side. The brown and green landscape was dotted with clumpy bushes, short trees, and black rocks as it tumbled down to the ocean. Looking west he could see across Ma'alaea Bay and all around the southern curve of the land bridge to the other mountain. Above his head, the higher regions of Haleakala were engulfed in clouds, but from where he sat, he could look out under them and across the water to a dazzling display of purples and pinks projected off distant cloudbanks on the horizon.

"*Nice,*" he mumbled to himself. Most definitely worth a slightly later dinner.

When the sun slipped beneath the water's edge and the colors began to fade, Wolf shouldered his gear and moved on. He walked briskly, knowing he had a long drive ahead of him. Getting from anywhere to anywhere on Maui was often "a long drive," since all points of interest ringed on roads around the bases of the two mountains, and both rings were effectively impassable at one point or other. Thinking about how close together things actually were "as the crow flies" was a recipe for road rage, so Wolf tried not to dwell on it. At least all the long drives were spectacular ones.

He had almost reached his truck when he heard the dogs barking. He listened a moment, then broke into a jog. Wolf knew dog barks, and these dogs were upset about something. Excited, but also fearful.

He muttered curses under his breath as he neared the pullout where he'd left his truck. He often parked it here, because the location served as a good trailhead for hikes in several directions leading to different parts of the reserve. The road bordered on private property, and there were several small houses — and he used the term "house" generously — clustered nearby. One of them was home to two pit bulls and a bonafide mutt he'd become fond of. Usually all three dogs roamed loose in the yard, but while the pit bulls were occasionally locked up in chain link pens, the mutt was always left to wander.

He reached his truck and peered into the clearing across the road. The master of the house was home, and he was drunk. The man tottered around the small yard with a bottle in one hand and what looked like a mostly eaten whole chicken in the other. He was wearing shorts, sandals, and a bad sunburn. His head was either bald or shaved, but a shaggy red-blond beard trailed onto his chest. "Where're you hiding, Bella?" he shouted angrily, slurring the words.

The pit bulls were barking with agitation, keeping a careful distance from both the man and the food. The skinny, long-haired mutt was no longer barking. She was cowering under a rusted Chevy that sat in the weeds ten feet away.

The man tore off a piece of meat and dropped it on the ground near his feet. The pit bulls were clearly conflicted. One of them darted forward, but then quickly withdrew when the man raised the bottle in the air in a threatening gesture. He laughed out loud.

Wolf's teeth clenched. What sort of sadistic game was this?

"Aw, poor babies, that's all right. Daddy'll feed you," the man said then, pulling off several hunks and throwing them out toward where the pit bulls waited. The dogs grabbed the pieces and ran, gobbling them as they moved. Sensing a change in fortune, the long-haired mutt crept out from her hiding place and approached the man also, her filthy, ratted tail wagging. The man tore off another piece and held it out to her. But just as she came close enough to sniff it, he snaked out a long leg and aimed a kick at her ribs.

"Hey!" Wolf shouted, dropping his gear by the truck and stepping forward.

The man swung toward the sound, swinging a little too far and almost toppling over. "Who the hell are you?" he snarled.

"Someone who reports animal cruelty," Wolf snarled back. He didn't care if he sounded confrontational, but he did stop short of trespassing. The mutt had squealed loudly, but did not appear to be injured. In fact, the second the man's attention was diverted, she dove back in and grabbed the piece of chicken that dangled from his hand, then skittered out of sight. She was a gutsy little thing.

The man threw the remainder of the chicken down in the dirt, then shouted back at Wolf with a muddled stream of profanity best left to a bathroom wall. Wolf watched as the two pit bulls swooped in and whisked the carcass away. Their master was now oblivious to them.

Wolf considered. The threat to the animals was over, for now. All three had disappeared with their booty. The man was blind drunk and could barely stand up. Even if he did deserve to be taught a lesson, odds were he wouldn't remember it tomorrow.

Wolf decided to move on. Ignoring the man's continued verbal tirade, he returned to his truck with an air of nonchalance. He was, of course, listening carefully for the sound of footsteps behind him, as well as the thud of a door slamming, which could mean that the man was fetching a firearm. No self-respecting Alaskan would ever turn his back on an argument without considering that possibility. But since all he heard was continued profanity coming from the same spot in the yard, he didn't even deign to look over his shoulder. He simply loaded his gear in his truck and drove away.

*Way to ruin a perfectly good sunset,* he thought to himself. He loved dogs, and he missed his own terribly. He hadn't seen them since January, when he'd flown down from Fairbanks to begin work on Haleakala. He would have brought them with them if he could, but dogs weren't allowed in the state park because of the risk they posed to the endangered *nene*, Hawaii's state bird. His dogs were reasonably well behaved, but how could he expect them to resist such a primal urge as stirring the feathers on a bunch of fat, slow-waddling geese? Much less turn down a breakfast of fresh eggs sitting on the ground? No, much better if he let his dad spoil the dogs in Anchorage for a while. In the meantime, he'd settled for making some canine friends here on the island, including the long-haired mutt, who now routinely greeted him at his parking spot looking for a kind word and a scratch behind the ears. She was a friendly thing, but too skinny by half. He'd been wondering why she didn't get fed as much as the pit bulls. Now he knew it was because her owner was a drunk — and quite possibly not altogether sane.

As he drove the long way back around the base of the mountain, then caught the single road that headed uphill to the field station, he mulled over his various options. He would report the incident to the Maui County humane authorities. After that, he'd play it by ear. Keep an eye on the dogs. Best case scenario, the man was only mean when he was drunk, and he only mistreated the one dog. Perhaps if the field officers spoke to him, he'd be willing to surrender the mutt for adoption.

Otherwise, the man's unpleasant confrontation with Wolf today would not be his last.

The long, winding drive up the slope grew foggier as the truck climbed, and when Wolf pulled into the Haleakala field station, which sat nearly 7000 feet above sea level, he was completely engulfed in the clouds. He weaved through the cluster of green-painted clapboard buildings — none of which he could actually see at the moment — by memory, then maneuvered the truck into its usual spot beside another equally sorry-looking vehicle from the same leasing outfit. The other truck still had its lights on, its driver having also just arrived.

Both drivers cut their engines, got out, and began unloading their cargo.

"Hey, Maddie."

"Hey, Wolf," the striking woman replied with a smile. "Any

new and exciting gases today?"

He gave a casual shrug, even as his pulse rate shifted into high-alert mode. It always did with Maddie; he couldn't help it and no longer bothered trying. The woman was engaged and strictly off limits, and he respected that. But no matter how grungy her work clothes were or how tightly she braided her long red-gold hair, his fellow researcher was — hands down — the most ridiculously sexy female he'd ever met. He also liked her very much as a friend, which was a damned annoying combination.

"Same old, same old. What's new in cat crap?" he replied.

Maddie grinned. They'd had this same conversation any number of times over the last few months. Despite the fact that a body like hers should rightfully be modeling high fashion on a runway in Milan, Maddie Westover spent her days crawling all over the island of Maui rooting around under bushes collecting samples of feral cat feces. What's more, she appeared to enjoy it.

"Mystery awaits in every baggie," she said with enthusiasm, displaying a handful of plastic specimen containers. Wolf listened with amusement as she went on to describe a frustrating adventure with a particular tomcat as they collected their things and locked up their trucks. "I swear he knows exactly what I'm doing," she mused. "He's probably hiding somewhere while I'm setting up the traps, watching and laughing at me."

Wolf chuckled. Maddie had set out to neuter this particular feral tom months ago, but the wily beast continued to elude her. It was an unusual pale orange color and apparently this made her certain it had fathered dozens of the younger cats that wandered the area.

"That colony will never get a proper caretaker, either," she lamented. "It's too remote. The volunteers will be lucky to round up a third of the new kittens, and the ones they miss will have miserable, unnaturally short lives."

Wolf's thoughts drifted as Maddie restated her views on the devastation feral cats were causing the island ecosystem. He could understand her passion on the issue. She had a PhD in ecology. But she was also a cat lover, which put her in a quandary when it came to accepting best-evidence solutions. He sympathized with her moral dilemma. But right now, hearing her bleak reports of starving, flea-bitten kittens only made him worry more about the long-haired mutt. He needed to make that phone call.

"Something wrong?" Maddie asked, stopping what she was doing. Her beautiful blue-gray eyes bore into his with concern.

He squirmed under her gaze and looked away. "Nope," he answered. "I was just thinking about a call I need to make. Got to stash this. Catch you later." He turned away from her and headed toward the supply closet where he kept his equipment.

"Later," Maddie called after his back, sounding a tad annoyed with him. That happened sometimes, but there was nothing he could do about it. A casual friendship with a co-worker was all well and good, but Maddie was the type that pushed it, sometimes. He didn't need that.

He didn't need anybody.

Wolf groped his way through the fog to the supply room, put away his gear, and headed back toward what was affectionately dubbed "the Hilton," the long, single-story dormitory at the field station in which he rented a room. The Hilton housed six researchers at a time, for a few months to a few years, as they conducted various biological and geological studies. "The Marriott" housed another four scientists next door, in addition to the small permanent staff. The accommodations were sparse, but functional, and most important, they were affordable on a government grant.

Wolf couldn't see the Marriot. Wolf could barely see his hand in front of his face. But as he walked around to the front of the Hilton, he could hear another car pulling up and parking in a space farther out.

Wolf grinned to himself. He heard a car door open and shut, but still could see nothing in the thick fog. "Evening, Kai," he called out.

Footsteps hurried toward him, and the figure of a tall, well-dressed local man around Wolf's own age emerged from the mists. "How did you know it was me?" the guy asked with amusement once he'd recognized Wolf.

"I know the sound of that worthless pile of crap you drive," Wolf teased. He held the door open.

Kai chuckled. "Hey, every time that worthless pile of crap even gets me up this mountain, I say a prayer, man." He hustled on inside the door. "Maddie back yet?"

Wolf didn't have to answer that question. Maddie appeared in the Hilton's "lobby" before the door could shut behind them. In the next second she had launched herself into her fiance's arms. If Wolf wasn't there, he was pretty sure she'd have thrown her legs around Kai's waist, too.

*Retreat.*

The couple remained locked together like teenagers as Wolf skirted around them in the small confines of the shared living area and walked down the hall toward his room. He tried not to hear the various giggling and cooing noises that echoed up the corridor behind him.

They caused an almost physical pain.

He reached his door, went through it, and shut it soundly behind him. *That's better.* He pulled off his work boots, sat down in his comfy desk chair, and pulled up his phone.

He felt lousy. Really lousy.

Seeing Maddie and Kai together always did that to him, and every time it happened, he became more annoyed with himself. Maddie was hot, yes, but it wasn't about his wanting her physically. Volcanologists' work conditions often forced them to live like hermits for months at a time, and that kind of pain, he knew. But this kind of pain made no sense at all. Kai was a genuinely nice guy. The couple seemed good for each other and Wolf wished them the best. So what the hell was his problem?

He didn't want to think about it.

He looked up the number to report animal abuse and called it.

# Chapter 4

Ri signed her name on the line and handed the lease agreement to her new landlady, along with her first rent check. Mrs. Araki, a friendly Japanese-American woman who carried herself with a comfortable air of wealth, smiled and offered Ri a key to the rental house in exchange. The woman's outfit was "put together" in the finest detail from her jeweled earrings to the tips of her pedicured toenails, and according to Shelby she lived in a multi-million dollar spread somewhere northwest of Kahului. Yet not only did she seem at ease checking the new intern into what was probably the smallest — although admittedly not the shabbiest — dwelling in the area's southern outskirts, she was quite chatty about it.

"You have good neighbors on this street," Mrs. Araki praised. "Nice people. The bus stop's just a block away and you can get to the Foodland in no time. Waikapu's close to everything. If you—" Her voice broke off. She studied Ri with a speculative look.

Ri was trying hard to listen politely. Or at least to appear to be listening. But she was so very, very tired she was about to fall asleep on her feet. She wasn't sure what had made Mrs. Araki interrupt herself, but she was afraid that perhaps her eyelids had drifted shut. She must have done something, because up to now most everything her landlady had said had sounded like a rehearsed speech. But what came out of the woman's mouth next was said in a distinctly different tone. "Are you *kama'aina?*"

Ri stared. The question was asked curiously, and in a friendly way, rather than accusingly. But she was embarrassed. The word must mean sleepy. "I'm sorry," she replied. "I don't know what that means."

Mrs. Araki's eyes widened a bit in surprise, but then she laughed lightly. "No, I'm sorry. I just assumed. A *kama'aina* is a long-term resident. I thought maybe you were from one of the other islands and I was about to waste my time telling you things you already knew."

Ri snapped back to alertness again. The tiny kitchen in which she was standing — which was barely big enough to accommodate the spindly card table and chairs in its center, seemed to grow instantly warmer and more confining. "Mrs. Araki," she said earnestly, "please tell me why you thought that. You're the second person today to say so, and I've never had anyone tell me that on the mainland. Is it... I mean..." Her heart pounded as she brought forth the previously ridiculous thought. The thought she never would have dreamed before the DNA test. "Do you think I look Japanese?"

For a long moment, Mrs. Araki seemed to be struck dumb. Then she tossed her pretty head back and laughed out loud.

Ri felt like crumpling into a heap.

"Oh, my dear," Mrs. Araki said quickly, tempering her humor. "No, no. Don't be upset. But, no. No, of course you don't. Why would you think so?"

Ri still felt like crumpling. She *knew* she didn't look Japanese. Her own skin was browner than Mrs. Araki's, and she was half Russian. And whatever it was about a person's eyes that made them look Japanese, or Chinese, or Asian in general, she didn't see it when she looked in the mirror. There was really nothing about her that made her look Asian at all. And yet that's what the damned DNA test had said. Forty-seven percent "East Asian." *East Asian!* Not Indian — that was a whole other gene pool. Not African — that was a continent away. But aside from those two exclusions, which shattered everything she *thought* she knew about her biological father, East Asian was about as broad, as diverse, and as minimally helpful a clue to her identity as possible.

The test results had offered her only one small consolation in exchange for that vagueness. The profile of her supposed fifth to eighth cousin had not included an ethnic breakdown and was not associated with an online family tree. The person did not even have an individual account on the genealogy website, but had been listed by a third party, probably a relative from a different branch of the family. But the listing did have a name. And that name was Japanese.

"I..." Ri began haltingly. But she was too tired to bother with a facade. "I was adopted internationally. I'm not sure why I look the way I look, but I have reason to believe I might have a Japanese ancestor."

Mrs. Araki beamed with delight. "Oh, I see! Well, you should feel very much at home on the islands, then. Many people here are of mixed ancestry, and from a variety of countries. More are mixed than are not!" She reached out, took one of Ri's hands in both of her own, and gave it a squeeze and a pat. "You are fortunate to be part Japanese. You be proud." She gave a wink and a nod, then released Ri's hand and headed for the door. "Now, you go to bed. You look exhausted, my dear."

Ri did not need to be told twice. She locked the door after her landlady and walked through the small, modestly furnished living area and on into the far bedroom. The women's sleeping quarters was barely big enough for twin beds, but Ri was grateful for the relative luxury she and Shelby would be enjoying, since the guys' room on the other side of the kitchen had bunks. She hoped none of the four of them was a slob, but she was in no position to complain. Mrs. Araki was renting the house as a favor to the Foundation and most likely as a tax write-off, since it was questionable whether what the interns were paying would even cover her taxes, utilities, and upkeep.

Ri had no energy left to unpack her suitcase. She didn't even bother with a shower. She changed into some comfortable sleep clothes, brushed her teeth, pulled out the single sheet set she'd brought with her, and made up the thin mattress. Though the house came furnished, there was no pillow or blanket, so she pulled out a jacket and a bathrobe and made do. Tomorrow, she'd go shopping. She'd known she would need bedding, but it seemed silly to waste prime packing space with bulky things. She sank down into her improvised nest, closed her eyes, and fell instantly asleep.

At some point in the haze of hours that followed, she was dimly aware of people coming in, of banging noises and loud voices. She managed to rouse herself to a sufficient level of consciousness to recognize that the intruders were her roommates, and therefore no threat to her, and then she was out again. How many more blissful hours of nothingness passed before the screaming, she had no idea. She only knew there weren't nearly enough of them.

The screaming, in and of itself, was not enough to completely wake her. She'd spent way too many years living on a college campus for that. But somewhere in the middle of her happy darkness, a question mark inserted itself. How to classify the scream? Was it drunken? Stupid? Excited? Terrified? She'd only have to pay attention to the last one.

Ri listened closer.

*Dammit.*

Her heavy-as-lead body waged war with her brain. She tried to open her eyelids, but nothing happened. *It's on TV, probably. Forget about it.*

The high-pitched beeping of a fire alarm pierced her skull. Then a guy's voice shouted. It sounded like Will. "What the hell are you doing! Don't—"

A bang and a splash. Sizzles. More screaming. Now there were two guys shouting.

Ri woke up. The smell of smoke hung thick in the air. She clutched her jacket around her and stumbled out into the living room.

Shelby stood in the doorway to the kitchen, still screaming. In the sink was a sauce pan. Water was running from the tap, hitting the pan and sizzling. Flames seemed to be everywhere. They were coming from the pan, flying upward as the water hissed and sizzled. They were all around the sink, from tiny embers of orange glowing on the countertop to a black cancer forming on the roll of paper towels to wild, licking bursts of light erupting on the folds of the linen curtains. Red specks of fiery grease had attached themselves to the floor. The walls. Even the ceiling.

Ri noticed that the oven exhaust fan was on.

*Good God.*

"Shelby, come out of there!" she ordered. "Come this way!" There were two doors to the house. One was in the center of the living room near Ri, the other in a mud room that connected to both the kitchen and the guys' bedroom. Shelby couldn't use the other door without literally walking over fire to get to it.

The girl didn't move. She had stopped screaming. Her eyes were wide and unblinking.

Ri swore and stepped forward.

Will was standing in the far kitchen doorway holding a fire extinguisher. "Get her out of here, would you?" he shouted to Ri as he struggled to figure out how to use it.

"Never mind!" argued Bryant's voice from somewhere Ri couldn't see. "Let's just get out and call the fire department. That stupid fan is going to carry it everywhere!"

"We've got to try!" Will argued back heatedly. "All my stuff's in here!" He managed to pull out the pin and squirted a small amount of foam on top of his feet. "Get her out of the way!" he shouted to Ri again. Then Ri saw his eyes widen. "Her hand!"

Ri was attempting to pull Shelby out of the kitchen without fully entering it herself by pulling Shelby's nearest hand, but the woman was resisting her, frozen like a statue. Only when Ri looked around Shelby did she see the flames lapping over the cloth oven mitt on her opposite hand.

Gasping with horror, Ri garnered her strength and spun the other woman toward her like a top. Caught off guard, Shelby practically tripped into the living room. Ri flung the jacket off her own shoulders and wrapped it tightly around the flaming mitt, then hustled Shelby out the door.

"You need help?" a man said, nearly bumping into them on the small lawn. "Should we call the fire department?"

"Two guys inside," Ri stammered, trying to think quickly. The man looming over her was shirtless, sweaty, muscular, well over three hundred pounds, covered with tattoos, and smelled of beer, and on any other occasion, he probably would have scared her to death. But right now, she was sure he'd been sent straight from heaven. If he sprouted wings and flew she would not bat an eyelash — she wasn't even completely sure she was awake and out of bed. "They're trying to use a fire extinguisher but they need to get out if it doesn't work," she explained quickly.

The man took off, but his spot at her side was immediately filled by a woman and two teenagers. "Should we call an ambulance?" the teenage girl asked her mother as the group hustled them away from the house.

"Shelby?" Ri said softly. Her fellow intern's eyes were still wide and glassy. "Are you okay?"

There was no response.

"She's in shock," the neighbor woman announced. "Did she get burned? What happened?"

Ri looked down. She was still holding her jacket around Shelby's wrist. She slowly began to unroll it. The oven mitt was blackened on the surface, but did not appear to be burned through anywhere. Ri pulled it off Shelby's hand and saw no obvious injury. But between the dim glow of the neighbor's porch light and the street lamp above them, it was hard to tell.

The teenager whipped out a cell phone and shone a flashlight on Shelby's face. "Oh, Mom," she said fearfully, "Look."

Ri looked, too. Shelby's face was covered with half a dozen angry red spots. So was her neck. And her arms. She must have been spattered with grease when she put the saucepan under the tap. It was a miracle her hair hadn't caught fire.

"Maybe you should call that ambulance," Ri agreed, wrapping her jacket around Shelby's shoulders.

"Sit down over here," the neighbor suggested, leading them both a few yards to a bench on her own front porch. Ri sat, pulling a zombielike Shelby down with her. More people appeared, seemingly an army of them. The neighbor man returned with Will and Bryant in tow, and Ri was relieved to see that both guys appeared unharmed.

"I think it's out," Will announced, even as a siren sounded in the distance. "But we can't be sure with that fan pulling air up in the ductwork. The firemen are going to have to check it out." He smeared a dirty hand across his brow and dropped down on the ground beside the bench.

"What started it?" three or four people asked at once.

Will shot a look at Shelby, but said nothing.

"Grease fire," Bryant announced. "She said she was going to make popcorn, but she didn't know how to do it except in a microwave, so she looked it up online. Then she didn't know how to use a gas stove." He rolled his eyes. "Next thing I know she's screaming her guts out. By the time we got there she was standing there holding this pan in the middle of the room with flames shooting up out of it, and before we could stop her she'd thrown it in the sink and turned the water on full blast."

Winces, along with a few sympathetic groans, rippled throughout the crowd. The wail of a second siren added its song to the first, and Ri felt an unpleasant wave of dizziness. She looked again for signs of normalcy in Shelby's stony, checked-out face, but saw none. She glanced down at the other intern's diamond-studded watch and noted the time.

Half past midnight.

*Midnight? Are you kidding me?*

Ri couldn't have slept more than four hours. It wasn't enough. Not nearly enough. Perhaps, if she was lucky, she had dreamed up this entire scenario and she was actually still in bed, safely and happily asleep.

Shelby's shoulders began to shiver. Only a little at first. Then uncontrollably. "Could somebody bring a blanket?" Ri heard herself ask as she wrapped an arm around the other woman and pulled her closer.

"More smoke's coming out of the roof there!" someone in the crowd declared, pointing.

A fire engine arrived. Some hazy amount of time later, an ambulance pulled up as well.

Everything that was happening to Ri had a certain edginess to it, that unpredictable touch of reality — like the distinct smell of burning plastic, or the nagging pain from a cut she'd acquired on her bare left foot — that should have convinced her she was *not* making this up.

But Ri had always been a dreamer. A dreamer with abundant faith in the power of her own imagination.

And as the hours ticked by through the rest of that endless, miserable night, she never gave up hoping.

# Chapter 5



*Portland, Maine, 1992*

"I didn't come here for you to give *me* therapy," Julie said crossly, sniffling into a tissue. She was angry at herself. She'd never broken down in front of Ri's therapist before. She was a professional herself. It was embarrassing. "It's just that I thought we'd see more progress by now."

"Every child is different," the older woman said calmly, holding Julie's now perfectly content baby daughter on her own lap. The infant sat up straight and tall, alternating banging the stuffed lion she'd been given against her thigh and sticking its head into her mouth. Occasionally she babbled at the therapist and put her hand against the woman's mouth when she was talking, apparently in an effort to attract her attention. But whenever the therapist did look at her, the baby quickly turned away.

"You keep forgetting how much progress she's already made," the therapist reminded. "Physically, you've done wonders with her. She's gained weight, she's sitting up, and she'll be crawling any day now. She *will* catch up altogether, in time. And the way she's taken to babbling, I see no reason to worry about speech deficits. She is having to learn a new language in the midst of all the other upheaval."

"I understand that," Julie said quickly. She didn't need to be told any of this. New sights, new sounds, new smells, new feels, new tastes. Everything in the world, *everything*, had changed for baby Ri when Julie and Tom had ripped her away from that orphanage and flown her thousands of miles to her new home. Even change for the better was still drastic, frightening change. "It's just that..." Julie's eyes grew weepy again, and her face burned with shame. "I knew what could happen, but I didn't know how hard it would be to feel..." Julie knew she should go ahead and say it. "She doesn't even *like* me!"

Julie smashed her whole wad of tissues onto her face, covering her mouth, eyes, and nose. Sobs shook her rib cage, and she decided to let them come. Her tears flowed freely, and she lifted the tissues only enough to breathe and hiccup until the torrent at last came under control.

She took two deep breaths and wiped the mess from her face. She opened her eyes and looked up. The therapist was watching her sympathetically, holding out several more tissues. What was more amazing was that Baby Ri was also watching her. Those gorgeous big brown eyes were, for once, looking fully back into Julie's own. They seemed oddly curious. And then they turned wary.

The baby looked away and stuck the lion's head back in her mouth.

Julie laughed ruefully. "That's the longest she's looked at me in weeks."

The therapist smiled. "Mrs. Sullivan," she said gently. "What you're feeling is completely understandable. No matter if you knew whether to expect it or not. I suspect I would feel the same way in your shoes. And I mean that."

Julie nodded appreciatively.

"You know that this isn't about Ri not liking you," the therapist continued. "It's about a baby who spent the first eight months of her life having no idea what face would appear above her crib next. Who would pick her up. Who would feed her. *If* anyone would feed her. She stopped crying when she wanted to be held or comforted because no one came anyway. She stopped paying attention to people because no one paid attention to her. She was born pre-programmed to bond, yet for the longest time, there was no one she could bond to. So she closed that door in self-defense."

"I understand," Julie mumbled, wiping her eyes again. She did understand. It just didn't help.

"In the months you've had her, you and Tom have worked wonders," the therapist assured. "In *every* way. She's opened up to the world. She's engaging. She's interacting. She's playing. She wasn't making eye contact with anyone at first, and now she's quite sociable, at least with strangers. And you know why that is."

Julie nodded, sniffling again. "She doesn't feel threatened by them. She's pretty good with Tom, too. She'll sit in his lap and look at him. She's even smiled at him a few times."

"I know that hurts, Mrs. Sullivan," the therapist said. "But Ri resists you the most only because she is beginning to feel close to you. By getting inside her heart you are demanding something from her that frightens her. She never learned to trust, and she still doesn't believe she is safe with you. She *will* come to trust you. But in order to do that, she's got believe that you're different from every other person she has ever known, even farther back than she can consciously remember. Once she does believe that you will *always* be there for her, once she feels safe, you are going to see a very different little girl. It just takes time."

"But how much time?"

"You know I can't predict that," the therapist answered. "But I can tell you that I've seen many adopted infants with symptoms similar to Ri's go on to lead perfectly normal, happy lives. And as much progress as she's made so far, I believe you have every reason to be optimistic. Please try to get as much rest as you can, and to keep your spirits up. Have you been sleeping any better?"

"Not really," Julie replied. "Most nights she still cries." *For at least two hours straight. Sometimes four or five. And nothing I do can console her.*

The therapist offered her sympathetic smile again, then rose. "I'm so sorry. Keep up the strategies we talked about, and add in the new ones. I wrote everything down on the sheet. As she improves in other areas, the sleeping problems should gradually diminish, too."

Julie nodded without comment. She'd heard that line for months. There was no change. She didn't see how she could ever sleep when Tom had to work days and she was up every night. Any kind of childcare was out of the question. Part of Ri's therapy was that she should never be separated from Julie, even for an hour. Constant togetherness was critical for their bonding.

The therapist held out the baby, and Julie stretched out her arms and took her. Ri cried out in protest, first stiffening her back and then kicking her feet as Julie tucked the child onto a hip. The lion was cast off onto the floor as Ri's arms began to flail wildly.

"She always does that," Julie said quietly.

The therapist nodded.

Julie started to leave, then turned back again. "These other children who get better," she asked, wincing as a tiny fist struck her ear. "They go on to have normal relationships? I mean, not just with their parents, but with other people, too? Siblings? Friends? They get married? Have kids of their own?"

"The research is young, like I said," the therapist answered. "But yes, we have every reason to believe that, with the right therapy, these infants can go on to have full, normal, healthy relationships. With anyone."

Julie dodged a wild swing at her nose.

"Thank you," she replied.

# Chapter 6



*Maui, Hawaii, 2016*

Ri's eyes opened to a room comfortably darkened by two layers of curtains. Sunlight peeked in only around the edges of the window, which consumed the majority of the wall beside the bed in which she slept. Ri was sure she had never seen either the window or the wall before, but oddly, that thought did not disturb her. She merely lay there staring, mildly curious at best, letting her eyesight and brain slowly adjust to full consciousness before she expended any effort on the matter.

A motel. She was in a motel. *Interesting.* And how had that happened?

*The fire!*

Ri's pulse shot up. *Of course.* There was a reason she didn't want to remember. As long as she was still asleep she could continue to pretend the whole, horrible scene with Shelby had never happened. She stretched her limbs with a groan, then looked around. Her backpack sat on the motel desk. Her suitcase lay on a rack beside it. It hadn't been a dream. The fire had actually happened.

But she was here now, and safe. She should count her blessings. First off, everybody got out okay. Secondly, she still had her stuff. Thank goodness she'd been too tired to bother unpacking. She had no idea how her bags had mysteriously moved themselves from her bedroom to the neighbors' patio last night, considering that no one had been allowed back inside the house after the firefighters left. But she suspected she owed her neighbors a favor. Aside from the clinging smell of smoke, her belongings had come through unscathed.

Her memory of last night was hazy in general, but the part after Shelby left in the ambulance was particularly incoherent. She could remember the arrival of a very upset Mrs. Araki, and a bit later, that of an administrative higher-up from the

Foundation. But all she knew was that the latter had driven the three remaining interns to the motel, checked them in, and told them to take the next day off. Any details beyond those had failed to register. Not only had she no idea of the man's name, she could not pick his face out of a lineup if her life depended on it.

She leaned toward her bedside table and checked the clock. It was three in the afternoon.

*Oh, my.*

Ri pulled herself out of bed and winced as her left foot contacted the floor. *Oh, right. The cut.* She really should take care of that. She located her phone and scrolled through well wishes from Lachland and several others from the Foundation, including an email from HR which provided her with the cell numbers of the other interns. Will and Bryant must have escaped with their phones, too, since they had apparently texted her about breakfast four hours ago.

Ri roused herself to full consciousness, showered, and dressed quickly. She put some ointment on the cut on her heel — which didn't look that bad — applied a bandage, and headed outside. She needed to find something to eat, and she wanted an update on Shelby. She stepped out onto a pathway leading through a green lawn and looked around. It was humbling to realize she had no clue where the hotel was even located.

A flock of spotted doves cooed and pecked in the grass near her feet, and a gusty breeze kicked up. Ri caught a scent on the air and breathed in with a smile. *Ah-ha!* She turned and walked around the corner of the building to where the courtyard opened up. Now she knew where she was. The hotel was on the north end of Kahului, facing the bay on the opposite side of the land bridge from where the Foundation was located. Within this protected harbor, the waves didn't roll into shore with much gusto, which is why she hadn't heard the ocean. But it was here just the same. She had glimpsed this area from the plane yesterday.

*Was it really only yesterday?*

The view was modest, as Maui views went, with the open

ocean being hemmed in by the jetties that arched out to form the harbor. But Ri concentrated on the blue of the water and the intoxicating smell of the sea. Roughly twelve hours' sleep, straight through, had definitely revived her. She had been given an unexpected weekday off, and she still had a few business hours left of it.

*Should I do it? Is this my chance?*

Her fingers itched to pull out her phone and call her mother. She was used to bouncing such major life decisions off her mom. She usually ran them by her dad and Mei Lin as well, although the Mei Lin step in the process was really just for affirmation, since her sister rarely disagreed with anything Ri decided. But this time, Ri resisted her itchy fingers. She'd called her family just last evening to let them know she had arrived okay. But she couldn't call again now without telling them about the fire, and that would only worry them when they should be focused on the business of getting Mei Lin and her fiance moved to Texas. Ri would talk through everything with her family eventually. They were close, and it felt right. But in the end she had always made her own decisions, and she felt confident making this one now. Ri was ready for answers, and she wanted them today.

Her decision made, she got directions and advice from the desk clerk, grabbed a quick fast-food brunch, and set off. She had texted back to Will and Bryant, but neither of them were answering, and Shelby's phone was off the grid — probably still lying somewhere in the burned-out kitchen. Lachland, however, promptly answered her email by reporting that Shelby's injuries were not serious and that they expected her to be released from the hospital sometime today.

Once Ri's angst was relieved on that score, she focused on the matter at hand. Whatever doubts she'd had before about pursuing the DNA connection had been put to rest the moment Mrs. Araki asked if she was *kama'aina*. Ri wanted to meet this possible distant cousin of hers, and she wanted to do it face to face. Ever since she'd located her supposed relative's place of employment, people had been telling her to "just call!" But she had never wanted to do that. Relationships were too important to her. Phones could be hung up and emails could be ignored. If she was going to confront this person with her questions, she wanted to do it in person. To look in his eyes, see his expression, hear his tone of voice. She wanted to make real contact.

As the bus bounced along the Kahului thoroughfare, Ri studied the people sitting around her. She tried not to stare, but the local populace fascinated her. So much diversity of appearance. So many shades of brown. So many eye shapes, and nose types, and bone structures. Most people here had dark hair and eyes. But beyond those similarities, all bets were off. Throw the occasional Caucasian into the mix, and you had a cornucopia of appearances so complex that no one stood out. Least of all Ri, who melted into the crowd like any of a hundred chattering myna birds in the trees outside the bus windows.

Growing up as a biracial child with a Chinese sibling running about an otherwise solidly white, upper middle-class hamlet of Maine, one might think Ri would find the change refreshing. She wasn't sure herself why her first experience with anonymity should feel so disconcerting.

Her stop rolled up all too soon. She disembarked and looked around at the new, boring rectangular buildings of a generic commercial district. If it weren't for the palm trees, some planted hibiscus, and the profile of the West Mountain in the background, she could almost forget she was on Maui. She followed the numbers on the buildings until she arrived at the business she sought. Then, leaving herself no time to reconsider, she marched up to the reception desk, asked to see the employee in question, admitted she did not have an appointment, and even had the gall to claim to be a relative.

"Oh, all right, then," the friendly woman behind the desk said with a smile. "If you'll just have a seat, I'll let him know you're here."

Ri sat.

The lobby of the office building was pleasant enough. The walls were covered with framed prints of natural landscapes and wild animals, and leafy plants hugged the large windows.

She had liked everything she'd read about the law firm, which was a nonprofit that supported environmental causes. But the longer she sat, the more time she had to second-guess herself.

Too late, she realized she had lost the element of surprise. Her name would mean nothing to him. There was a distinct chance she'd be sent away before she ever laid eyes on the man.

Ri's back straightened. *Forget that!* She just wouldn't leave.

Two minutes later, she heard the sound of a door opening down the hallway. A tall, very attractive man wearing a tie and business slacks strode up to her and extended a hand. His hair was dark and wavy, his skin very similar in tone to her own. Liquid brown eyes with long lashes — unfairly beautiful to belong to a man — looked at her quizzically, while a friendly face smiled down at her. "Hello," he greeted. "Are you Ri Sullivan?"

Ri nodded as she rose and shook his hand. "That's me, yes."

"Kai Nakama," he introduced. "Nice to meet you. You want to come back to my office?"

Ri stood baffled for a moment. He didn't recognize her name, did he? How could he? "Sure," she answered mechanically. He gestured for her to precede him the short distance down the hall to an open door, and she walked into a smallish office and sat in the single guest chair opposite the desk.

He closed the door, settled himself in his chair, then looked at her expectantly.

Ri looked back at him. She had never actually planned anything to say. She'd always figured that once she introduced herself as a relative, she would be busy answering his questions. "You don't seem surprised," she stated.

He looked back at her, confused. "About what?"

Ri was confused, too. "About some strange person you've never met before wandering into your office claiming to be related to you."

To her amazement, he chuckled. "Oh, *that*," he replied good-naturedly. "I have lots of relatives. Where are you from, Ri? How is it we're related?"

Ri released a breath and relaxed. He was making this easier

than anticipated. "I'm from Maine. I just got here yesterday. As for how we're related, that's the part I was hoping you could help me with. I don't want to take up a lot of your time, but you see, it's like this. I'm adopted, and I know next to nothing about my birth parents. But I had an autosomal DNA test done with an ancestry search site, and the database identified you as a distant cousin. I know that for most people, that's no big deal. Most people have so many matches show up they don't even bother with a link as remote as fifth to eighth cousin. And the confidence level was only moderate. But—"

Her confidence flagged a bit. He was frowning.

"Wait. How did information about my DNA get on a website?" he asked.

Ri swallowed. "I don't— I mean... I assume someone else put it up for you. Your profile has another person listed as administrator. Their username was EllB123 something."

His brow furrowed for only a second, then he smiled and sat back in his chair. "Oh, I remember. It was Ella! My great aunt. Back when I was a teenager. She was a genealogy buff, and she couldn't wait to see what ethnicities would show up for me. She asked me if I'd take the test if she paid for it, and I said sure, whatever." He looked troubled again. "I had no idea the information would go up online, though."

"Well it didn't, not really," Ri explained. "I'm sure your aunt opted you out of any public display of information. Nothing shows anywhere except your name. Not even your ethnicity breakdown. But the database still matches you with potential relatives. I assumed you were part of her family because you were on her account, and you could tell from her family tree that she tested pretty much everybody else she was related to."

Kai smiled again. "That was Aunt Ella," he said fondly. "Very thorough. And loyal to a fault. She died three years ago. We all miss her."

Ri considered. That explained the sudden absence of activity on the administrator account. She had tried to email the woman once, but the message had bounced. "I'm sorry."

"Thanks. So how did you find me here?" he asked.

Ri squirmed a bit. "Before you write me off as some kind of

stalker, maybe I better explain *why* I found you."

His dark eyes twinkled with curiosity. "Okay."

"First off, I don't want any money," she defended with humor.

Kai smirked. "Well, good. Because I don't have any. I'm getting married this summer. I'm beyond poor."

Ri smirked back. She liked a guy who was committed to a woman and who laid it all out there within a few minutes of meeting another woman. His fiance was lucky to have him. "It's like this," she began, watching him closely. "My entire life, Kai, I've spent looking at this face in the mirror and not knowing who or where I come from. Literally speaking, I came from Russia. The adoption agency believed that my mother was Russian and the DNA test seems to confirm that. But up until I took the test, everyone always thought that my father must be either Indian or African."

She stiffened as Kai sat up straighter in his chair. "Really?" he said with interest.

Her heart thudded against her ribs. "They were only assuming," she continued. "And the DNA test disagreed. It said I was half East Asian."

"Ah," Kai said immediately. He nodded. But then he said no more.

"The thing is," Ri plowed on, "knowing that didn't help me much. It only made me doubt what I thought I knew. And then there was the fact that out of all the thousands of people in the ancestry database, there was only *one* person who showed up as any kind of a match with me, and as far as I could tell until five minutes ago, you were Japanese."

Kai's handsome face first broke into a smile. Then, to Ri's astonishment, he laughed out loud.

"I'm sorry," he apologized, stifling his reaction when he noted her bewildered expression. He cleared his throat and sobered. "Um... I can certainly see why you would think that. But no, I'm not Japanese. My biological father died when I was a baby. I was adopted by my stepfather, who is Japanese, and I took his name."

Ri considered. His being adopted explained a lot. And to

think she'd been twisting herself into a pretzel thinking the test was all wrong because *she* didn't look Japanese! How could the thought of *his* being adopted never have crossed her mind?

"I guess I've been making too many assumptions," she admitted with embarrassment. "I confess I've tried to find out more about you online, but you're like the invisible man. I could tell that you were in school in Utah, but I could never find a picture of you anywhere."

His smile bordered on smug. "I'm not a social media kind of guy," he confessed.

"Obviously," Ri agreed. "I only knew you were here because I got a hit last fall with this law firm. Their website listed you on the staff page as a new intern. I thought that was pretty ironic, since I'd been wanting to do an internship on Maui, too. Yet even when the plane landed yesterday I still hadn't decided for sure whether looking you up would be a smart thing to do. But then I kept seeing..."

She paused a second and collected herself. She didn't want to babble. "Anyway, as far as ethnicity goes, I was able to find information about your family in Utah. Or what would be your family if you were related to the woman who listed you. But nobody else on her tree was a genetic match with me, so I thought—"

"All of my Utah relatives are from my birthfather's family," Kai explained with a knowing smile. "Call me crazy, but I have a sneaking suspicion that if you and I are related, it's going to be on my mother's side."

Ri's eyes met her cousin's. A pang shot deep through her middle as she realized that the two of them *could* be cousins. Feature for feature, she looked as much like him as she looked like anybody, except that she was short and her hair was lighter and curlier. She knew that she was close to an answer, but now that she was here, she grew suddenly afraid.

She sucked in a nervous breath. "You really think so?"

Kai studied her with concern. After a moment he leaned forward toward her. "Finding out about your birthfather — your heritage — it means a lot to you, doesn't it?"

Ri felt hot tears spring up behind her eyes. His voice was so gentle, his eyes so caring. If losing her lodgings in a fire her first night on Maui was bad karma, she was making it up in spades by finding this man today. He was a truly kind person. She had no doubt of that.

Words wouldn't come. She nodded.

He pulled a tissue from a box on the corner of his desk and handed it to her. "Listen," he said softly. "I can't tell you anything for sure. I don't know if the test is right. But if it is right, I'd be happy to give you my best guess, based on my mom's history, and the test results I got, and what I see in your features."

Ri sniffled and nodded again. "Please."

"Did you have any Pacific Islander show up in your profile?" he asked. "Any Native American?"

She shook her head. "Nothing but East Asian and Eastern European."

Kai smiled again. "Well, then. If the test can be trusted and you're related to me, I'd say there is a very high likelihood that your birthfather was Filipino."

Ri blinked at a fresh spate of tears. *Filipino.* The word danced in her brain, tried itself out. She had heard of the Philippines; she'd just never given the country much thought. It was an island in the Pacific... somewhere.

"Filipino?" she repeated stupidly.

"Absolutely," Kai confirmed. "Can't you see it in yourself? The Hawaiian Islands are full of Filipinos. I'm surprised you didn't wonder about the likeness the second you got off the airplane."

"Like I said," Ri defended weakly, "I'm from Maine."

Kai's dark eyes twinkled into hers. He smiled at her slyly. "So you're used to standing out, I take it?"

She smiled slyly back and wiped away more tears. "Maybe."

"Well," he said with a laugh, "you'll have to get over that! How long are you staying on Maui? Did you get that internship you were talking about or are you just here for vacation?"

Ri pulled herself together enough to describe her position with the FOM. She was able to do so mechanically, which was good, because most of her brain was still consumed with the one glorious, glowing word: *Filipino.*

Could it be true? Could she finally know, as of *now*, *today*, who she truly was? Where both her parents had come from?

Kai was looking at her expectantly. He had asked her a question.

"Sorry. Head in the clouds," she admitted. "Could you repeat that?"

Her newfound cousin smiled at her warmly. "I asked if you wanted to come to dinner with me and my fiance. I'd love to hear more about your internship and your plans for the summer, and I know she would, too. Maddie's an ecologist — she loves anything to do with dolphins. I can tell you all about the family history, too, if you care. Or not."

"That sounds... perfectly wonderful," Ri said honestly, rising and heading for the door. "Thank you. But don't let me interrupt your work any more. Should I meet you somewhere later?"

"Did you drive here?"

"I took the bus."

"Give me ten minutes," Kai replied. "I'll drive you."

Ri nodded gratefully. "I'll wait outside." She closed her cousin's office door behind her and practically skipped down the hall to the lobby. She smiled at the receptionist, located a women's room, and rushed straight up to the mirror.

The face that looked back at her glowed with happiness, even around red-rimmed eyes. "I am Sriha Mirini Sullivan," she said out loud, drinking in her own reflection with pride. "I am Russian." Her smile widened and her voice grew bold.

"And I am Filipino."

# Chapter 7

"I am so sorry!" a voice called out.

Ri looked up to see one of the most beautiful women she'd ever seen — a blazing redhead with the body of a supermodel — weaving through the tables in the outdoor restaurant and heading straight towards them. The woman's bushy hair was in a ponytail and she was wearing a simple cotton top and capris, but the ordinary clothes did nothing to mask her extraordinary appearance.

"Traffic was at a crawl the whole way past Ka'anapali," the woman continued as she approached, "or I would have been here ten minutes ago."

Ri watched, intrigued, as her cousin's face lit up like a Christmas tree. He rose from his chair to greet the woman, and the couple came together with a hug and soft kiss on the lips that seemed involuntary. Their eyes met and held as if they were communicating some secret message, and it was with obvious reluctance that they parted and took their separate chairs.

*Wow.* The electricity coming off the two of them was enough to frizz Ri's hair.

"Ri, this is my fiance, Maddie," Kai told her proudly. "And Maddie, this is Ri, a newfound distant cousin of mine. She's here doing a summer internship with the Foundation for Ocean Mammals."

Maddie turned to Ri with a friendly smile. "Oh, cool! Hello."

Ri said hello back, wondering how much Kai had told his fiance about her over the phone. Not much, apparently. Kai had invited a virtual stranger, and a woman at that, to intrude on his fiance's dinner with very little notice. Yet Maddie didn't seem to mind. Ri studied the two of them closely, although she was careful not to show it. She'd learned the hard way that psychological scrutiny, however innocently academic, tended to freak people out. Still, she really couldn't help herself. Unselfish love, particularly the rare romantic kind, fascinated her.

"Did you order for me?" Maddie asked Kai hopefully. "I'm starving!"

"Yes," he said with a smile.

Maddie looked at him expectantly, her stunning gray eyes sparkling. "Did you..."

Kai laughed. "Yes! I ordered your gnarly poi."

Maddie clapped with glee. "You like poi, Ri?" she asked, putting her napkin on her lap.

Ri had no idea what poi was, but before she could ask, Kai broke in. "Did you notice, Ri," he said with a grin, "that Maddie just assumes you know what she's talking about?"

Maddie looked from him to Ri with confusion. "What? Shouldn't I?"

Ri met her cousin's eyes and felt a warmth to the tip of her toes. "I see what you mean," she replied. Maddie had just naturally assumed that Ri was "a local." Not because she was a relative of Kai's, necessarily. But because she looked like she belonged here. Because she looked part Filipino!

She *was* part Filipino.

A rush of emotion swept over Ri, and her eyes began to tear up again.

"What did I *say?*" Maddie asked again, aggrieved.

Kai took pity on both of them and explained the situation himself while Ri used up a few more tissues. She wasn't usually this emotional. Her sister was the crier in the family. Perhaps if Mei Lin was here drowning them all now, Ri would be better able to resist the impulse. She looked out over the view of the 'Au'au Channel visible from their table and breathed in deeply of the soothing sea air. It had been nice of Kai to bring her here. The open-air restaurant was lovely, all casual wooden tables and tropical planted flowers, situated right on the southwest coast just north of the port of Lahaina, with a moderately priced menu of local favorite dishes. She couldn't have asked for a better end to a day that had started out so very horribly.

"Oh, Ri!" Maddie gushed when Kai had finished. "You'll

have to come to Lana'i with us some weekend and meet Kai's mother and grandmother. You want to hear family stories, they'll tell you plenty!"

"I'd love that," Ri said eagerly, happy to hear the invitation come from Maddie, even though Kai had already offered. "As soon as I figure out what my job schedule looks like, anyway." A pang of worry shot through her middle as she realized to what extent her internship was currently at risk. She had managed not to think much about the fire since meeting Kai, but the truth was that if she and the other interns couldn't move back into Mrs. Araki's house, they would be essentially homeless. She presumed that the Foundation would try to help them find someplace else to live. But she was only presuming. The FOM had no budget to subsidize their housing for four months. And her own budget couldn't stretch any tighter than she was already stretching it without jeopardizing her plans for grad school.

If her only option was to suck it up and pay Maui's market rate for housing, she'd have no option at all. She would have to resign the internship and fly back home. Because as important as this experience was to her, grad school mattered more. She needed a master's degree in order to move on in her career.

*Don't think about it.*

Maddie and Kai laughed frequently as they told Ri various anecdotes from when they were growing up together on the island of Lana'i. Apparently Maddie had left when they were still children and the two had only reconnected in the past year, but the couple's degree of simpatico could easily pass for a lifetime project. Studying them, Ri saw any number of similarities between this young couple and her own parents, who had been happily married for well over thirty years. But although she was happy for Kai and Maddie, a niggling sense of disquiet arose in her gut on behalf of Mei Lin, who was also recently engaged but whose interactions with her fiance looked nothing whatsoever like this.

Their dinner was served. Ri had ordered a "mixed plate" of shoyu chicken, fresh fish, and teriyaki beef, all of which looked delicious. Her family had frequently headed for American

Chinese food when they ate out, not because of Mei Lin —
who hated anything spicy and always lobbied for McDonald's
— but because Ri's father was crazy about it. Hawaiian cuisine,
as Kai explained, had its own twists. Barbecued seafood,
chicken, and pork was combined with local vegetables and
fruits and seasoned with Asian flavorings. Kai's plate of *mochiko*
fried chicken looked delicious as well, but Ri could find nothing
positive to say about the assortment of pale, limp things on
Maddie's plate.

"Which one is the poi?" Ri asked, trying not to wrinkle her
nose. The scoops of white rice and yellow macaroni salad she
could identify, but the only other thing that looked even
vaguely familiar on Maddie's "local favorites" plate was a
steaming pile of shredded pinkish-brown meat with yellow
leaves in it, which she was guessing was pork and cabbage.

"This is the kalua pig," Maddie said excitedly, pointing to
the meat. "And this is the *lau lau*." She stabbed her fork at a
rolled up leaf that was square and dark greenish brown. "It's
kind of like a tamale," she explained. "Pork, beef, and taro —
kind of like potato — wrapped up in leaves and steamed. *So
good!* You don't eat the outside leaf though. Just the inside
one."

Ri thought the whole thing looked like something a
fisherman might accidentally get caught on his hook, but she
said nothing. "And that?" she asked, pointing to a chopped
salad in a small dish.

"*Lomi lomi* salmon," Maddie answered. "Fresh salmon and
tomato salad, with onion and peppers." She pointed to the
second of three small bowls. "This little white square is dessert.
It's called *haupia*, a coconut cream custard. Sweet and yummy.
And *this*," she said as she made a little flourish with her fork
over the third bowl, "is poi!"

Kai grimaced. "Otherwise known as pulverized taro. Worse
than baby food."

"Oh hush," Maddie teased, picking up a forkful of kalua pig
and dipping it into the pale, brownish-purple paste. "It's
wonderful."

Kai gestured to Maddie, then shrugged at Ri. "Seriously,

she'll eat anything."

Maddie swallowed, then nodded. "It's true. I will. But I do love this especially. You want to try it?" She pushed her plate to the middle of the table. "Try anything you want!"

Ri decided to be adventurous, trying it all and sharing from her own plate as well. She and Maddie quizzed each other about their scientific backgrounds, and Ri was delighted to find they had so many interests in common. But as splendid a time as Ri was having, the more she watched the happy couple, the more worried she grew about Mei Lin.

She told herself she was overreacting. Her long-married parents were no fair comparison, and for all she knew, Maddie and Kai were really unusual. But the closest Kai had come all evening to saying anything even remotely negative about Maddie was "seriously, she'll eat anything," and he'd even said that like it was a compliment. Ri couldn't imagine Kai coming out with a typical Josh laugh line like "that poi's almost as mushy as your brain, Mei Lin." Or "you keep eating like that and I'll never be able to carry you over the threshold." He always said such things as if they were a joke, and Mei Lin always laughed them off and insisted that she thought it was funny and that his idea of humor really, truly didn't bother her.

But it bothered Ri.

"Oh!" Ri said, jumping in her seat as a blue-gray flash out on the water caught her eye. "Dolphin!"

"Was it a spinner?" Maddie asked.

Ri shook her head. "I couldn't see it well enough. But I'm going to pretend it was. I've been dying to see a spinner or a spotted, neither of which I've ever seen before, and the whole time we were out on the boat yesterday the only dolphin we saw was a bottlenose!"

Maddie laughed. "You'll see plenty of the others, don't worry. Enjoy the humpbacks while you can, though. They'll be getting scarce soon."

Ri grinned. "Oh, I definitely will. I plan to be out on the water every second they'll let us, believe me." Her phone rang in her bag, and she looked down at it with a sense of foreboding. She picked it up and looked at the number. "I'm sorry," she said nervously as she stood and stepped away from the table. "I'd better take this. It's my boss."

Walking instinctively toward the ocean for comfort, she pulled the phone to her ear. "Hello. This is Ri."

"Ri, hey, Lachland here. Just wanted to catch you up on the latest. First off, you're good to stay at the motel another two nights on the Red Cross voucher, and then I talked to the head of the Foundation, and we've got an emergency fund that can carry you through the rest of the weekend. So don't worry about the bill."

Ri froze. The bill? The thought had never occurred to her, but it should have. Although her room was a modest one, the building was technically oceanfront. If she had to pay for even a night or two on her own, she'd wind up camping on a beach somewhere instead.

"As for after this weekend," Lachland continued, sounding uncomfortable, "things get a bit more complicated."

"We can do some of the cleanup at Mrs. Araki's place ourselves, if that will help us get back in faster," Ri suggested.

Lachland sighed. "I'm afraid that's not going to be possible. Mrs. Araki is working through her insurance company and they're saying the restoration will take at least three months. The damage to the kitchen was pretty extensive, and I guess the roof, too."

Ri's heart fell into her shoes. *No.* Everything could *not* fall apart on her! Not now.

"We're putting out some feelers within the Foundation," Lachland continued, "seeing if we can find someone to take you guys in temporarily. We're also looking for somebody who can rent a room for four months at something close to what you were expecting to pay. I'm afraid we can't make any guarantees, though. Most everybody with room to rent is already renting it."

Ri looked out over the gorgeous blue ocean in front of her and tried to calm her fears. Something would work out. It had to.

"It would help if you had somebody you could share rent with," Lachland added.

His words touched off an alarm. "What about Shelby?" Ri asked.

"Oh," Lachland said awkwardly. "I'm sorry. I thought you heard. Shelby's going back to Texas. Her flight should be leaving right around now, actually. I guess the burns on her face were serious enough that she and her parents decided she should be looked at by a specialist back home. She said she wants to come back and finish the term if she can, and I did tell her we'd keep her spot open. But between you and me, I doubt that's going to happen."

Ri's stomach churned. Could she even justify spending money on temporary lodging if a full summer's worth wasn't likely to become available? Without the value a completed internship would add to her resume, she could be throwing that money away.

"I'm really sorry about this, Ri," Lachland commiserated. "Do you think you might be able to pay a little more for housing than you budgeted?"

Ri swallowed. She wanted to say yes with all her heart, but she knew that her head had to rule. Julie and Tom Sullivan had saved very hard to put Ri and Mei Lin through college without student debt, but that gift had come with a clear understanding that graduate school, if desired, would be on their daughters' shoulders. And in Ri's field, not only was competition for assistantships uncommonly fierce, but living expenses — near the ocean, of course — were always high. "No," she answered evenly. "I really can't afford to pay any more than I've already budgeted for the summer."

"Oh," Lachland replied stiffly. He paused a moment. "Well, like I said, we're putting out feelers and we'll see what we can find. In the meantime, somebody'll give you guys a ride down to the Foundation tomorrow morning. Just be in the lobby by seven-thirty. All right?"

Ri assured him that she would be ready and waiting, and then they hung up. She remained standing where she was another few minutes, staring out over the turquoise waves and enjoying the breeze as it ruffled the nearby palms.

Everything here was so perfect. She could *not* go home now.

When she decided that the soothing blues and greens before her eyes had sufficiently mellowed her, she returned to the table. And when Kai and Maddie asked her if anything was wrong, she made the decision in an instant to tell them the truth. They had no way of knowing how unusual such an act of sharing was for Ri. How normally only her nearest and dearest would be privy to any acknowledgment of distress. Her usual MO would be to tell a casual acquaintance that everything was fine, then run back home, pick up the phone, and gush to Mei Lin or to her parents. But Ri felt the thousands of miles of distance between herself and her family acutely. She was here and they were there, and she did not want to be dependent on a phone.

"So that's where things stand," she said as she finished. "Hopefully the FOM can help me find someplace before the weekend is out." She tried to smile, but judging from the looks on her new friends' faces, her attempt was weak.

Maddie looked at Kai thoughtfully. "When is that guy moving into your old room at your uncle's?"

Kai shook his head. "Sometime next week. I can't think of anybody who's got room right now. Not on my dad's side, anyway. I could ask my mom, though. Maybe she knows somebody."

"I'll ask around, too," Maddie offered, turning to Ri. "Kai's related to half the island and I know some people through work. Surely someone's got some space. If you're willing to share a kitchen and a bathroom and you're not picky, people around here are pretty open to bringing in a few extra dollars from a spare bedroom."

"Or closet," Kai added.

"Or closet," Maddie agreed.

"I'll live pretty much anywhere as long as the people are friendly and I can get to a bus line," Ri assured. She gave them her budget constraints and tried not to notice the look of dismay that crossed their faces at the number.

"We'll do our best," Kai promised.

# Chapter 8

Wolf fought down an unaccustomed sense of foreboding as he finished the final leg of his hike. He had no reason to be down today. The weather was magnificent. Unusually clear skies had made visibility on the mountain fantastic since dawn. He'd eaten his lunch while enjoying a view of the Big Island to the east and then watched the late afternoon sun shining around the silhouettes of Kaho'olawe and Lana'i to the west. His equipment had only screwed up twice, and he was pretty sure all of the day's measurements would be usable.

Still, he was uneasy. He had pushed hard all day so that he could knock off a little earlier than usual. If his worries were realized, he wanted to be back in cell phone range before the answering machine took over the animal abuse hotline.

He reached the empty pullout where he usually parked his truck, then stopped and studied the yard where the dogs lived. The pit bulls were in their fenced runs, snoozing. Of the long-haired mutt, he saw no sign. Since the pit bulls were caged and no truck was parked beside the house, Wolf assumed the man was not home. "Bella?" he called out, happy to know the mutt's name, finally.

He heard nothing. One of the pit bulls woke and lifted its head, but after one squirmy movement of the rear — which in another breed would have been a tail thump — the dog lay back down again.

Wolf blew out a worried breath. The mutt hadn't been around this morning, either. She could be wandering. She could even be inside the house. Or maybe animal control had sent a field officer out yesterday and they'd taken the dog into custody. The last option would be a good thing. The mutt was a cutie and would have a good chance of being adopted. But somehow, he doubted all of the above.

He continued down the dirt road, heading around the bend toward the wide spot where he'd pulled off and parked his truck this morning, out of sight of the man's house, as a precaution. Wolf was sometimes accused of being a pessimist, but he preferred to think of himself as being wise. *Not expecting a counterpunch from any man low enough to kick his own dog would be naive.*

Unfortunately, he had underestimated the guy's willingness to travel.

*Dammit.* He should have parked a full half-mile short of the house, up at the crossroads. It would have been safer. There would have been more witnesses about.

Wolf strode toward his truck with a scowl. He should be thankful, really. At least there wasn't any monetary damage. No broken windows. No extra dents. The paint-job wasn't even keyed. Just a solid bucketful of stinking dog crap smeared all over his windshield and door handles.

*Whatever, dude.*

He took care of the worst of the problem with a rag from the bed of the pickup, then drove off toward the field station for a hose to deal with the rest of it. At least one of his questions was answered. Someone from animal welfare had definitely paid The Beard a call yesterday. And clearly, Wolf's days of parking in the highly convenient pullout were ended. But the question disturbing him the most still lingered. Where was Bella?

He stewed over the dog's whereabouts the whole drive around the base of the mountain and back uphill to the field station. The total lack of fog this evening offered rare views from his home base that he ordinarily would revel in, but as he pulled into the lot in the filthy truck he found himself missing the area's usual shroud of mystery.

Ilma, a German botanist in her early fifties who happened to be standing in the parking lot nearby at the time, raised an eyebrow at him. Ilma's command of English was marginal, so she didn't talk much, but she was intelligent and seemed to have a good sense of humor. She sniffed. "What is this?"

Wolf shook his head. "Met up with a *really* big dog," he quipped.

Ilma narrowed her eyes to slits. Then she laughed at him

and moved on.

Wolf would clean the truck eventually. But now he had other priorities. He locked up his gear and then headed for the Hilton's shared living area, which was blissfully unoccupied. He sank straight into his favorite recliner and pulled out his phone.

He was in luck. The humane shelter volunteer who answered, Mario, was someone he knew. Every Saturday that Wolf allowed himself a break, he would check out a shelter dog for a day at the beach. It was part of an ongoing program the shelter ran both to exercise the dogs and to advertise their adoptable pets, but for Wolf it was all guilty pleasure. He missed his own dogs and enjoyed the canine company. He explained to Mario the report he'd made two days ago, and the chatty animal lover was only too happy to dish.

"I heard about that one," Mario said immediately. "But they couldn't do anything about it."

"Why not?" Wolf asked, trying to contain himself. If the answer involved a bunch of silly legal restrictions, so help him, he'd—

"Because the guy denied up and down that the dog in the complaint even belonged to him," Mario said. "He claimed he owned two pit bulls, and the officer confirmed that those two dogs didn't look abused or neglected. But the guy's story is that the other dog is a stray, and that he was only aggressive with it because it was threatening him and his other dogs and he was trying to scare it off. He says it was all self-defense."

*"Are you kidding me?"* Wolf railed. "That dog doesn't have an aggressive bone in her body, and I've seen her at his house every time I've been out there for months! I've seen him call her by name! She's his, all right. He's just trying to get out of a fine!"

Mario let out a sigh. "I believe you, man. Look, if he sticks to that story, they can always pick her up. They would have picked her up right then but I guess she ran off before they'd finished checking it out."

Wolf's teeth gritted. *Or The Beard stuffed her in the shed or in the house.*

"If you find her wandering off his property, you can bring

her in yourself," Mario advised. "But be careful. We never give out names on citizen complaints, but—"

"Oh, he knows it was me," Wolf said. "I told him I'd report him."

The shelter worker did not seem pleased to hear that. Wolf only half listened as the voice on the phone went on to give way more details than necessary about various unpleasant run-ins with abusive dog owners and the inadvisability of Wolf's having any more to do with this particular bully, who in Mario's uninformed opinion was at best an alcoholic and at worst mentally unstable.

"Don't worry about me," Wolf said dismissively. "I can handle myself." He thanked Mario and the shelter's staff for their efforts, then hung up the phone.

Footsteps approached from behind, and he looked around. It was Maddie, looking gorgeous as ever even in nondescript cargo work pants and an orange Auburn University jersey that clashed with her wet, freshly showered hair.

He forced his eyes away. Geez, the woman was easy to stare at.

"Wolf?" she began, her voiced filled with concern. "Not that I was intentionally eavesdropping or anything, but as you happened to be talking on the phone in a public space..." She dropped onto the loveseat across from him and looked at him expectantly.

He made no response.

"Who did you report for what, and what exactly can you handle?" she demanded. "Or if you won't answer any of those questions, which I'm sure you won't, how about this one: Is there anything I can do to help?"

Wolf looked into her genuinely troubled, gorgeous gray eyes and smiled. She was sweet to be concerned, but her offer of assistance was unnecessary. That said, if he were suddenly to find himself outnumbered three to one in a common street brawl and a female of his acquaintance happened upon the scene, he had a sneaking suspicion that Maddie Westover would be more useful than most. Her well-toned biceps and that steely glint in her eye made him suspect she was not above violence when necessary.

"I think you know the answer to all those questions," he replied mildly.

Maddie sighed, loud and long. "Of course," she said sarcastically. "The lone wolf thing. I'd be curious to know your approach to life if your mother had named you Lemming."

"She named my brother Bear," Wolf heard himself say.

"Oh?" Maddie replied with interest. "And does he act accordingly?"

Wolf didn't answer. He was still trying to figure out why he'd said that. He never talked about his mother. His mother didn't exist. The only mother in his little brother's life had been Wolf himself.

"Is your brother older or younger?" Maddie asked lightly, settling back in the loveseat's cushions.

"Younger," Wolf said begrudgingly, his jaw muscles beginning to twitch.

"I'm envisioning a bush pilot," Maddie said playfully. "Six foot two, totally ripped, full brown beard. He got taller than you in the tenth grade and you totally flipped out."

Wolf stared at her. "Wrong." But damn, she was close. Bear wasn't rugged in any sense of the word — he was blond, lanky, and looked more like a swimmer than a weight lifter. But he *was* a pilot. And as for the reference to a certain tenth grade milestone — that was uncanny.

Maddie's head tilted skeptically. "All of it?"

"Okay, so he's taller than me," Wolf said without thinking again. "But only by an inch."

He regretted the words as soon as they were out of his mouth. Conversations with Maddie often left him tongue-tied, but the babbling thing was new, and that made it disturbing. Particularly when it came to talking about family. He was a private person. He and Maddie were not that close. He specifically didn't want them to be.

The front door opened. Ilma stepped in just far enough to reach a pile of bedding and equipment that was lined up along the wall. She offered both of them a smile, then grabbed a handful of stuff and dodged out again.

"Where's she going?" Maddie asked.

"She's starting her pollen collection in the Northwest Islands tomorrow, remember?"

"Oh, right," Maddie replied thoughtfully. Her eyes took on a distant look, and Wolf took advantage. Ilma's entry couldn't have been timed more perfectly if he'd planned it himself. He didn't want to offend Maddie, but like many women of his acquaintance, her company wore thin when she tried to get inside his head.

"If you'll open the door," he said, rising, "I'll grab the last load for her." He made a move toward Ilma's belongings, the remainder of which he could easily sweep into his arms.

"No, don't!" Maddie said, jumping up from the loveseat and inserting herself between him and the pile.

Wolf blinked back at her in surprise. "What?"

Maddie's beautiful lips puckered and her face reddened. "No offense, really, but Wolf — you *reek* of dog crap."

Now his face reddened. "Oh," he said, stepping quickly backwards. "Right."

"As much as Ilma would appreciate fewer trips to her car," Maddie said, laughing out loud now, "I don't think the stench is worth it to her."

Wolf imagined the fastidious Ilma wrinkling her nose all the way to the airport. He laughed along with Maddie and found himself looking straight into her eyes. Her irises were gray, with just a hint of blue. But it wasn't the color of her eyes that got to him, that reached out across the space between them and clamped around his heart like a vise. It was the look. That damnable, liquid look of caring and compassion that said *See me. I'm right here. Do you feel the connection? You can trust me.*

Wolf stopped laughing. He turned away from her and headed for the door. "Well, I'd better hose off that truck," he announced. "And hit the shower."

He was halfway out the door — no, at least three-quarters out — when Maddie tried to stop him. She said his name, and then something like "wait a minute" or some other thing that women say in that tone they use when they want to *talk* talk. He knew that tone like he knew the back of his own hand; he knew it so well he could feel it coming. Which was a good thing, because in most cases, like now, he could avoid it without upsetting the speaker by pretending not to hear her. He didn't want to upset women when they were genuinely trying to be nice to him — particularly Maddie, whom he admired for any number of reasons besides her incredible body. But he couldn't talk to her. She was getting too close.

The smartest, most interesting women always did.

It was beyond annoying.

Wolf closed the door behind him and headed for his truck.

# Chapter 9



*Cape Elizabeth, Maine 1992*

"I can't believe your little girl is walking already! How old is she?"

Julie smiled at the young mother standing beside her in the toddler area of the pool complex. She was terribly proud, even if not for the reason the other woman assumed. "Oh, she's sixteen months," she explained, understanding the confusion. Ri was still so little that she appeared to be under a year old, and the fact that she was walking and even running a bit often startled people. But considering how far behind the child had been in development just eight months ago, Julie considered it a testament to Ri's spunky nature that she was walking at all. "She's small for her age. But very agile."

"I can see that," the other woman said with a laugh. "My Truman hasn't a prayer of keeping up with her."

The women watched indulgently as their offspring, clad in swim diapers and bright new suits, padded around on the soft rubbery surface of the play area, which featured an assortment of differently sized pipes that spit out water at unpredictable intervals. Truman, a bruiser of a boy who was more than twice Ri's size but to Julie's eyes looked no more than two and a half, was intent on stopping the flow by capping the appropriate pipe with his pudgy hands. Ri, however, had other plans. She wanted to stand in the water. Their parallel games ran without conflict for quite some time, partly because Truman moved slowly, partly because he couldn't cover all of the pipe anyway, and partly because every time the water stopped, he was convinced that he was responsible and therefore stood in place gloating well into the next spray. But eventually, when two sprays erupted close together and the second was from a conveniently small pipe, little Ri found herself with no water to stand in.

Julie tensed. This would not go well. Ri's rages were diminishing, but they were still a frightening thing to behold. Although it seemed unlikely that she had any conscious memory of the orphanage, the feelings of helplessness and frustration that she had endured for all those months still seemed to bear heavily on her subconscious. Although she could be charming with strangers and had warmed to Tom, she was still distant with Julie. She mistrusted anyone and everyone and was lightning quick to anger.

"Truman, honey," the other mother called out. "Don't do that. Let the little girl play!"

"Ri!" Julie cried at the same time, knowing it was hopeless and that she was too late, even as she stepped forward. She could tell by the way her daughter's skinny little shoulders were hunching, by the way she bawled up her tiny fists...

*And there it is.*

Never mind that the bigger boy could squash Ri like a bug. Ri never bothered about such trifles as "consequences" when she wanted something. She wanted water, she wanted it now, and the best way to get it — clearly — was to aim a vicious jab at the face of the kid who was standing in her way.

Truman screamed. His mother screamed. Julie swooped in. But she wasn't quick enough to prevent the boy's reaction, which was to shove Ri away from him as hard as he could, laying her flat on the ground.

Both mothers reached their toddlers. A quick glance told Julie that the boy wasn't hurt. Ri had missed his eye (which Julie was sure she'd been aiming for, but couldn't quite reach) and delivered only a glancing blow to his cheek. Nor had Ri been hurt by her tumble onto the rubbery mat. But she had struck her head on one of the pipes as she fell. Julie's first instinct, as always, was to gather her baby in her arms and hold her tight. But of course her little girl never wanted that. Her child didn't want to be held, or even touched. At least not by Julie.

"Are you okay, sweetie?" Julie crooned, holding out her hands and crouching close, touching the child just enough to help her right herself. "Did you hit your head? I'm so sorry."

Ri hadn't uttered a sound yet. She lay on the ground looking dazed until Julie helped her to sit. Then she placed a hand tentatively on the side of her head where the pipe had made contact. Her big brown eyes looked directly into Julie's.

"Mommy," she said clearly. "Boo-boo."

Julie's heart skipped a beat. Ri had never called her Mommy before. "I know, love," she whispered, choking back a sob.

Ri's eyes moved over Julie's shoulder. She stared at the other mother and son as one bawled and the other fussed and cooed. Ri stared and stared as she pressed her hand against her skull, smashing her palm into her hair. Then her beautiful brown eyes flooded with tears. "Mommy!" she said in a frantic tone, her voice cracking.

Julie could say nothing. Her own eyes were overflowing.

Ri began to bawl outright. Her eyes turned back to Julie's. Then she scrambled the rest of the way to her feet.

"It's okay, Truman," the other mother said with a hint of challenge in her voice. "The little girl is going to apologize for hitting for you. Isn't she?"

Julie paid no attention. Ri was wrong to hit the boy, but that wasn't important now. The other mother didn't understand.

Ri stumbled forward into Julie's embrace, wrapped her skinny arms around her mother's neck, and held her tight. Ri's little body shook with sobs.

Julie clutched her daughter back, sobbing harder. Ri had never walked into her arms before. Never held her back before. Never sought any kind of comfort before. But now Ri was hurting, and she wanted her mommy.

Her *mommy!*

"Good Lord, the girl is fine!" the other mother said irritably as Truman continued to scream. "It's my boy who got hit in the face!"

"Sorry about that," Julie said to the other mother between hiccups, her face radiant with a smile. She kept Ri wrapped tightly in her arms, rubbed her back, kissed her cheek, cooed to her.

The other woman gaped in outrage, then stomped off with her son in her arms. She muttered something about assault and

medical bills.
	Julie didn't listen. Julie didn't care.
	Ri wanted her mommy.
	Nothing else mattered.

# Chapter 10



Ri looked carefully through the seemingly endless list of images in the "To Be Screened" folder to which she had been assigned. The Foundation sponsored a massive data collection project that tracked the movements and behaviors of whales and dolphins throughout the Pacific, and amateur photographers and first-time tourists alike were encouraged to assist by sending in good-quality pictures of whale flukes and dolphin dorsal fins. Identifying features on the photos could help the researchers not only pinpoint the species sighted, but in many cases, particularly with the humpbacks, they could identify individual animals. The "good quality" part was the catch.

Ri was lucky to score two usable photographs for every five pics submitted. In most, the flukes were either partially obscured or too poorly lit. And it wasn't surprising that so many shots of the fast-moving dolphin fins — snapped with a cell phone on a rocking boat — were out of focus altogether. But it was inspiring how many concerned people took the time to try and help. And every time she did find a winner, she considered it a triumph.

She was the only intern remaining in the basement office now, as it was past quitting time. The team had spent all day yesterday being trained on the Foundation's marine mammal tracking projects; they had spent all day today buried in the most tedious and least desirable chores those projects entailed. Ri was slightly stir crazy at having been chained to a computer for so many hours, but she was content. While she would prefer to be out on the ocean every minute, she understood the realities of research.

"Shut that thing down," Lachland said, smiling at her cheerfully from his desk across the room. "Don't feel obligated to keep going just because I'm sitting here. I've been playing minesweeper for the last twenty minutes."

Ri laughed and followed instructions. "I do think my eyes are starting to cross," she admitted. "I'll be seeing flukes in my sleep."

"You get used to it," he commiserated. Then his smile faded, and his expression turned serious.

The look on his face hit Ri like a blow. She knew what had been going on behind the scenes. It was Friday, three days since the fire, and HR was still scrambling to find her someplace to live by Monday morning. They'd already been successful with the guys. One of the pursers in the tour division had been wanting to sublet his room and move in with his girlfriend, so Will and Bryant would be borrowing Mrs. Araki's bunk beds and splitting his rent between them. So long as the purser and his girlfriend didn't break up, the male interns were good until the lease ran out at the end of August. But for Ri, there had been no such happy news. All she had received was a copy of the company's standard new employee handout, entitled "Affordable Local Housing," which was delivered by a sheepish looking Kaley from HR, the same Kaley who had previously admitted that she couldn't afford to live on the island herself if she weren't renting from an aunt and uncle. Ri had already looked through it. Nothing it suggested even came close to falling within her budget.

Lachland's look of regretful sympathy did not bode well.

"We haven't found anything yet," he announced gently. "A place for you to stay, I mean. But we're going to keep looking."

Ri swallowed. Her throat felt dry and lumpy. She cast a glance down at the floor, which was covered with thin industrial carpeting. Since the office was at basement level, there was probably nothing under that but concrete. "I could get a sleeping bag," she teased. But not really.

"I wish," Lachland replied, taking her seriously. He ran a sun-tanned hand through his longish blond hair. "But we don't have a kitchen here. Or a shower. And of course the board would never approve it because of the insurance. Believe me. We've had employees ask before."

Ri believed him.

The moment turned awkward, and Ri found herself feeling almost as sorry for her new boss as he seemed to feel for her. The fire wasn't his fault, nor was it his fault that the guys had gotten first dibs on a sublet she'd never really had a shot at. But she could tell that he felt like she'd gotten a raw deal.

"Do you have a ride back to the hotel?" he asked, rising.

Ri had already answered that question once in his hearing, when she declined the ride HR had offered to all three interns earlier, but she gave the man a pass. His thoughts were clearly elsewhere. "A friend is picking me up," she answered, looking at the clock. "She should be here any minute. I suppose I should go wait out—"

"Hey, Lach!" a cheerful voice called out, startling Ri into silence.

"Maddie!" Lachland replied, looking surprised himself. "What are you doing here?"

Maddie smiled at Ri. "I've come to pick up my future cousin-in-law. Didn't you hear?"

Lachland looked from one woman to the other with confusion. "Wait," he asked Ri. "You're related to Kai?"

"Distantly," she answered. She had learned over dinner Wednesday night that Maddie actually knew Lachland, as well as several others on staff at the Foundation. Ri wasn't surprised, since Maui was a small island and the scientific research community even smaller. But she had felt odd telling Lachland about her local connections when she'd said nothing about them right after the fire — explaining that she hadn't known Kai and Maddie *then* would be impossibly complicated.

Lachland's face brightened. He looked back at Maddie and cut right to the chase. "Well, can't you guys find someplace for her to stay this summer, then? Kai knows a lot of people!"

"We're working on it," Maddie said with a mysterious tone. A *hopeful* mysterious tone.

Ri's heart leapt. "Did you find something?"

Maddie smirked. "Get your stuff and come on," she said, tossing her head toward the exit. "We're going for a drive."

Ri managed not to bug her chauffeur with questions all the

way to Kahului. But when they made a turn that was clearly taking them away from any possible path to Ri's hotel, she could stand the suspense no longer. "Okay, I give up. Where are we going?" Maddie had called Ri's cell phone in the middle of the afternoon and said that she happened to be collecting samples nearby, would finish up around five-thirty, and would be happy to give Ri a ride home.

Maddie laughed. "I thought I'd swing you by my place first. Show you around. It's a little out of the way... but I hear there might be an opening."

"Your place?" Ri asked, disbelieving. "You mean, at the field station? All the way up on Haleakala?"

"Hey, don't knock it," Maddie said with mock defensiveness. "I make this drive almost every day. Twice. You get used to it."

As curious as Ri was, Maddie seemed to have said all she wanted to say for now. And since Ri was not one who felt a compulsion to fill silence with empty chatter, she sat back in her seat and enjoyed the view.

The truck began its journey up the mountain by winding through a picturesque small town, where houses and a few tourist-type businesses showed off lush green courtyards and colorful flowers. As the road grew steeper the town thinned, revealing a mishmash of expensive vacation homes mixed in with more modest dwellings, tiny ramshackle cottages, and the occasional goat pen.

As they rose in altitude and the temperature cooled, Maddie turned off the air and cracked the windows of the truck, and Ri could hear a million birds singing in the bushes and trees that bordered the snaking two-lane road. Shortly after they passed a sign declaring an elevation of 4000 feet, the landscape opened up, and they drove over a grated cattle guard and onto grassy fields. To Ri's left, several cows grazed near a cluster of evergreens, and ahead of her up the mountain, she could see that the truck would soon enter a series of sharp switchbacks cut deeply into beds of black rock. But the view to her right was by far the most amazing.

When she looked down toward the valley from which she

had come, Ri was high enough up to view the entire crescent-shaped outline of Ma'alaea Bay. She could see the marina where the Foundation was. She could see the whole land bridge all the way to Kahului. She could even see the Pacific on the other side of the island at her hotel!

"Oh, wow," she breathed.

"Pretty impressive, isn't it?" Maddie said proudly. "Now you see why I don't complain about the commute. As far as I live from Kai, I can always tease him about keeping an eye on him at night."

"Can you?"

Maddie chuckled. "Well, not really. Technically, I could see where he used to live, if I borrowed some good binoculars. But I could only make it out on clear nights, which are pretty rare. And I can't see his new apartment at all. But it makes a good line, anyway."

Ri stared. She could hardly believe that the vista she was seeing now was visible with her naked eyes — and from a car window. It looked like something one could only see from a plane. Or on a travel poster.

Her vision was suddenly obscured by a thick patch of white mist. "Oh, dear."

"Yeah, that happens," Maddie explained. "It gets cloudier the higher you climb. At the very top it usually gets clear again, but that doesn't help the field station. We're at 6800 feet, right in the ring zone. Kind of frustrating, unless you like pretending you're in London. Or if you're into vampires and werewolves."

Within another minute, the truck had passed through the patch of fog, and Ri had trouble believing that anything around her could remind anyone of London, much less gothic beasts. Although a thick bank of clouds hung in the air just above them, the stunning landscape was clear again. It was also now changing rapidly, with every twist in the road bringing on a different palette of color and a more arid feel to the vegetation. Grassy meadows changed first to rocky fields, then to black rocks in red dirt. Dark-green clumpy bushes sprung up amidst the rocks, and thin, oddly-shaped evergreen trees stuck up here and there like bottle brushes, oddly reminiscent of cactuses in a

Western cartoon. But looking seaward, the view was unquestionably tropical, with green slopes swooping down amidst blooming flowers to meet the dark blue of the ocean far below.

"If we were here mid morning, you couldn't drive six feet with passing a bicycle," Maddie said lightly. "Right up above us is where all the adventure tour buses and vans park and let people out. It's especially big for passengers on the cruise ships — everyone loves to bike down the volcano."

Ri looked out the window and down at the incredibly steep and twisting, occasionally without-a-shoulder two-lane highway. "On *this* road?" she asked skeptically. She loved to bike, but the idea of pedaling down a volcano had always brought up images up of a dedicated path through a leafy jungle, not sharing space on an open road with pickup trucks.

Maddie chuckled. "Yeah. It can get pretty dicey sometimes. That's why I always get out of here before the morning rush. But what a view for the bikers, huh?"

Ri could not deny that. But of course, much depended on the weather. On a cloudy day, this entire side of the mountain could be engulfed with fog.

No sooner had the thought occurred to her than the truck climbed into another patch of mist, this one thick enough to obscure her view of anything beyond a few yards. When they popped out of it again, she found herself in a forest of spindly trees. The fog thickened and thinned in turn, and a misty rain coated the truck windows. When, in the next clear spell, Ri saw that giant ferns had materialized on the cut rock walls of the switchbacks, she shook her head in disbelief. "This is so weird," she exclaimed. "Everything changes so fast!"

"Oh, it changes all over again at the top," Maddie assured. "But we'll save that for another day. We're almost home now." The landscape opened up once more, and here Ri saw grass and bushes again, along with a sprinkling of wildflowers by the roadside. The entrance to Haleakala National Park was marked with a guardhouse and a stop sign, but the wood and stone hut was unmanned after hours, and Maddie passed the automated pay station and pulled on through. She drove a little farther uphill through the fog, then turned off on a service road that seemingly led into oblivion.

Ri truly could not see more than a few feet in front of the truck's headlights. "How do you even know where you're going?" she asked.

"Instinct," Maddie replied, even as she crept along at a snail's pace. The lane was heading downhill, and wherever they were going, the fog seemed even thicker ahead. "Although if a *nene* decides to cross here," she said worriedly, pulling up tall in her seat to get the clearest possible view of the asphalt directly before the bumper, "it had better watch out for us."

"Maddie!" Ri shouted. Perhaps now she was thinking *too* much about London and werewolves... but she was ninety percent certain that the figure she'd seen skulking in the mist ahead of them was real. "Stop!"

Maddie slammed on the brakes so hard the truck bounced. "What is it?"

"I saw someone," Ri insisted, pointing. "A man. Right over there."

Maddie looked. "I don't see anyone." She shifted the truck into park, popped open her door, and leaned out. "Who's there? Wolf, is that you?"

A man's voice called back, deep and grumbly. No figure was visible now; all Ri could make out was a small light bobbing along as it moved away from the road. "Yeah, it's me."

Maddie growled in exasperation. "Are you suicidal or something? I can't see!"

"Then why'd you stop?"

"Smartass," Maddie mumbled to Ri. Then she raised her voice again. "Where are you going? I need to talk to you about something."

The voice returned from an even further distance. "Camping. See you tomorrow!"

Maddie plopped back in her seat and shut the truck door with a slam. Her eyes turned to Ri. "That was Wolf," she said with annoyance. "I was going to introduce you to him, but apparently, he's gone feral again."

Ri lifted an eyebrow. She'd gotten only the briefest glimpse of a man wearing a hoodie underneath a bulky hunting jacket, his square jaw unshaven and long, light brown wisps of hair curling around his ears and neck. She'd seen his eyes, though. They'd looked a bit odd the way they reflected in the truck's headlamps, but she could swear they were a piercing, cool ice blue.

"Feral?" she repeated, unable to get the image of a white-coated arctic wolf out of her head, even though she was pretty sure that wolf eyes were amber.

"Well, I don't know what else you'd call it," Maddie said, her voice edged with frustration as she shifted the truck back into drive and carefully steered it around a bend and into a parking lot. "Most of the time he's perfectly civilized, even fun to be around. But that's when you keep it strictly co-worker. The second you try and make an actual *friend* out of the man, he snarls and slinks off into the woods and won't come out again for a week."

"Snarls?" Ri asked. The man's appearance in the fog had startled her, but she didn't detect any hostility in his voice. He had sounded rather good-humored, actually.

Maddie sighed. "I don't mean it like that," she admitted. "He's a great guy. I like him a lot. It's just that..." She seemed to struggle with the words. "There's something about him that draws a woman in. And I don't mean physically, although that's another subject. And it's not just me that's noticed it, either. Over the winter, there was a woman here named Sam, and she and Wolf were pretty good friends. Or at least I thought they were. They both liked Mexican food and they used to cook together and make all kinds of spicy stuff. Sam was in her forties and married with two kids and there was nothing romantic about it. But she told me there was something about him that always seemed kind of sad to her. She wanted to help, and she kept trying to get him to talk to her so she could figure it out. She said she thought he'd be a happier person if she could just draw him out of his shell a little bit."

Ri made a noncommittal "hmm" sound. She knew nothing about Sam and shouldn't judge. Most likely, the woman's motivations were good. But Ri was biased. In her own history she'd dealt with way too many extroverts who looked at introverts like herself as needing to be "fixed." Some people preferred a smaller circle of close friends and weren't as into sharing about themselves. That was hardly pathological.

"I've always gotten along well with him, too," Maddie continued. "He knew I wasn't on the market when he met me and he's never hassled me, but he hasn't shunned me, either, and that means a lot. Making guy friends is actually easier now that I'm with Kai, but it's still..." Her voice drifted off. She looked back at Ri and shook her head. "Never mind. Anyway, I've had the same experience Sam had. He's friendly enough, but he'll only let you get so close."

Ri got out of the parked truck and followed her hostess blindly through the fog. No buildings were visible.

"I wouldn't describe him as 'sad' like Sam did," Maddie went on. "But I wouldn't call him content, either. Personally, I think his work makes him lonelier than he's willing to admit. But there's something else that's been bugging him the last couple days — something specific. He seems really worried, and because I cared enough to ask him what was wrong, he's literally run for the hills."

Ri looked over her shoulder in the direction in which the voice had disappeared. It was a stupid thing for her to do, since all she could see was fog. "He's really going camping?" she asked. "In this?"

"Oh, yeah," Maddie answered as they approached a green-painted building. "He pitches a tent out at Hosmer Grove and communes with the wild things. Like living here isn't rustic enough." She opened a wooden door and gestured Ri inside. "Welcome to the Hilton!"

Ri's mind bubbled over with questions as Maddie gave her an enthusiastic tour of the modest shared living area and kitchen, then walked her down the hall to show off the tenants' quarters, which consisted of decent-sized private rooms furnished with a bed, dresser, desk, sink, and closet.

"It's dorm living, I won't lie," Maddie admitted, taking a seat on her mattress and waving Ri toward the desk chair. "But for those of us eking out a living off of grants, it's affordable. And peaceful, too. So here's the deal. I know you'd rather live in the valley if something comes up, but until then, I've worked out a possible option for you. The woman two doors down, Ilma, will be working in the field for the next three weeks. I talked to her about your situation before she left yesterday, and she said she's fine with you staying in her room while she's gone as long as you don't mess with her stuff — which was kind of a joke, because the only things she left behind were a couple of books on botany and one wool coat hanging in her closet."

"Oh! How much would it cost?" Ri asked, unable to contain herself any longer. "And what would I do after three weeks?"

Maddie shrugged. "The rent's already paid by Ilma's grant," she explained. "She said if you want to, you can make a donation to the nonprofit that's sponsoring her research, but that's up to you. As for later, well, something else might turn up by then, and what have you lost? And there's another possibility."

Ri held her breath. It was crazy, the thought of her living all the way up here on Haleakala. But it was also exciting. When the place wasn't shrouded in fog, she could walk around and see the whole bay stretched out below her! "But," she wondered out loud, "how would I even get to work?"

"I drive down the hill every morning," Maddie said. "I can at least get you to a bus stop if I'm not going all the way to Ma'alaea. It will eat into your sleep, I won't argue that. And it will take some coordination to get you home. But if you don't mind taking the bus part way, half the people here drive up that road every evening. I'm sure somebody can give you a lift back if I can't."

Ri felt her cheeks redden. The idea filled her with a budding joy well out of proportion to the cause. Living up here would be a supreme inconvenience. She'd spend hours on the road commuting every day. But what a road! And when she got here, where would she be? She'd be near the top of a volcano, that's where. Hanging with her almost cousin-in-law Maddie. And that guy with the ice blue eyes.

"There's a possibility," Maddie went on, "that you might be able to legitimately rent a room here for the rest of the summer within your budget. It's just a possibility, now, because you're not a typical candidate to reserve a spot at the field station. But you *are* doing biological research. And if there's a vacancy that wouldn't otherwise get filled, I'd say there's a good chance Kenneth might cut you a break."

Ri smiled broadly. She stepped forward and gave her new friend a hug. "Thank you so much. I love this place already. I'm not completely sure why, to be honest, but I do."

Maddie laughed. "It does have that effect on people." She rose and started packing a bag. "Well, let's get you back to your hotel for tonight. Kai and I can help you move into Ilma's room tomorrow if you want. And Kenneth's supposed to get back to me about an opening here for the summer. Wolf's supposed to be out of his room by June first and we don't think anybody's booked it yet — so that's a distinct possibility."

Maddie smiled at her encouragingly, and Ri smiled back. But somewhere, in the depths of her unfathomable psyche, she felt a sharp pang of disappointment.

# Chapter 11

Wolf woke early. How early, he wasn't sure. Nor did he care. The eucalyptus trees in the grove were bursting with raucous bird calls, and the inside of his tent was stuffy. As long as there was enough sunlight to see by, it was time to get up.

He peeled himself out of his mummy-like sleeping bag, opened the tent flaps, and crawled out. The dawn air on the mountain was crisp and cold, just the way he liked it. He lay on his back on the wet grass, stretched out his limbs, looked up at the relatively clear sky, and took a full breath into his lungs. Up here, with no one and nobody in sight, he could almost pretend he was home.

Except that if he were back in Alaska, his dogs would be licking his face right now, hassling him to get up and feed them.

He grinned at the thought. But his happy reminiscence didn't last long. *The dog*, he remembered, his smile fading quickly. What had happened to her?

He knew that logically, reporting what he'd seen to the abuse hotline was the right thing to do. But he also felt partially responsible for whatever fate had befallen the dog afterwards. The Beard had been annoyed enough at being hassled that he had messed up Wolf's truck — had he exacted some revenge on the dog, too? Had he given her away or maybe just dumped her somewhere? In his gut, Wolf feared even worse. His every instinct told him that The Beard, who appeared to live alone, had a history of making this long-haired mutt his whipping girl. That whenever he got mad and got drunk, he took it out on her.

Wolf couldn't let it go.

Where was she?

He rose from the ground and inhaled another lungful of air. Today, he would find out exactly where she was. *How* she was. One way or the other.

He packed up his gear, hauled it back to a deathly quiet and half-deserted Hilton, took a quick shower, and left again in his truck. He could feel the air getting hotter and clammier as he descended the mountain, and he shed layers of clothing accordingly. It would be a hot one down in the valley today. The vanloads of bikers he kept passing on their way up would appreciate their time at the higher elevation, and the early start.

It took him nearly an hour to wind around the base of the mountain, then head uphill again to the spot where the dog lived. But this time he didn't drive on the dirt road that ran behind the house. This time he drove down the lane in front, then searched the yard for the dogs. He saw the two pit bulls lolling in the grass. There was no sign of the long-haired mutt.

He parked directly in front of the house. The dogs rose and began barking, but when he spoke to them through the windows of the truck they quieted immediately, and when he got out they came right up and greeted him like an old friend. "Where's your buddy, Bella?" he asked.

All he received in response were yawns and squeals. He looked around the yard from where he stood, then walked up to the front door and knocked. It was a Saturday morning, and it was still early.

*Too freakin' bad.*

No one answered. Wolf waited a minute, then knocked again. After three more minutes had passed, he considered his duty discharged. Trespassing on another man's property wasn't a crime that he considered lightly. That didn't mean he wouldn't consider it at all.

He stepped around the shack of a house to where he could see all of the backyard, and the pit bulls, vicious guard dogs that they were, trotted happily at his side. "Bella?" he called loudly, knowing full well that The Beard, if he happened to be awake, could hear him from inside. "You here, girl?"

Wolf listened. He thought he heard something. A scratching sound.

"Bella?" he called again.

This time he heard a whine. His heart began to pound as he turned in the direction of the dilapidated shed beside the patio. One of the pit bulls ran ahead of him, nosed its way under the shed and disappeared up to the shoulders. When Wolf reached the shed the dog backed out again, then jumped up at him with an anxious, excited whine.

*Good God.*

Wolf dropped to his knees and peered under the shed. It was too dingy underneath to see anything. "Bella?" he called, more softly this time.

A tail thumped once. Then twice. It began to beat a steady rhythm.

"Hey there, girl. Can you come out?" he cajoled, feeling both relieved and sick with worry. She sounded like she was probably within reach, but if she was hurt he didn't want to injure her further by pulling at her. "Come on out, Bella. Come on, girl!"

More scratching. The dog was clearly trying to move. A few times she stopped altogether, but Wolf kept up a steady stream of encouragement, worrying more about her condition the longer it took. He had to get her out of there. The ground all around the shed was littered with trash and a variety of foul odors mingled in the air. She had to be lying in filth. "You can do it, Bella!"

He could see a paw now. And another. *No.* The second paw was swollen and bloodied. "Come on, girl," he said softly. It took another minute for the dog to completely scoot herself out from under the rough edge of the rotting wooden shed, but Wolf refrained from touching her until he had some idea of what he was dealing with.

None of her legs appeared to be broken. But he could not say the same for her ribs. The light-colored shaggy coat on the side of her chest was completely matted with a nasty, suppurating wound. The fur all over her body was dotted with remnants of dried blood, her tongue was red and swollen, and her gums were pale and dry. Very gently, Wolf reached out a hand and smoothed the hair on the back of her neck. He lifted a patch of skin, then released it. But rather than slipping back into place, the skin remained tented.

Red-hot anger swelled within Wolf's chest. The dog was badly dehydrated. Whatever had happened to cause her injuries, she had probably crawled under here immediately afterwards... and might not have moved since. If The Beard had kicked or struck her on Wednesday, the same day he messed up Wolf's car, that meant the dog must have lain here, suffering, for three nights and two days.

Heat spread through Wolf's veins like liquid fire. It was a good thing The Beard hadn't answered his door. "It's okay, girl," he told the dog, studying her position to see how he could lift her in his arms with the least amount of discomfort. "It's going to be all right now. I'm taking you with me."

"The hell you are," a low voice growled.

Wolf shouldn't have been glad to have company. Really, he shouldn't. He had never been one to spoil for a fight. While the other boys on his hockey teams had jumped into the occasional melee with glee, he had always been the one frowning from the bench, waiting for them to get it over with so the game could restart.

But as he glanced covertly to the side to scope out his adversary, he was extraordinarily pleased to see that The Beard was both unarmed and suffering a probable hangover. The man was standing about ten feet away.

"I was told this dog isn't yours," Wolf said calmly, rising. He didn't turn around. That would dignify the man's presence. "So you won't have any objection if I turn her over to the humane shelter. She'll need medical treatment first, obviously."

"You're trespassing," the man said coldly, stepping closer.

"Am I?" Wolf asked in a deadpan, still looking only at the dog. "I did knock on the door."

The man stepped directly behind him. "Get off my property," he growled. His breath stank of stale beer.

Wolf turned around. "I'll be happy to," he said, staring straight into the man's bloodshot eyes. "Just as long as the dog goes with me."

The man's eyes narrowed, and Wolf prepared. The Beard was not what you'd call a stealthy fighter. He transmitted his intentions like a neon sign, and when the clumsy blow finally arrived, Wolf was nowhere near its airspace. The Beard was taller and heavier than Wolf, and relatively sober, but because missing his mark had put him off balance, Wolf's single, well-placed clip to the chin was able to topple him. He fell onto a half-rotted step next to the shed door and tumbled to the ground in a shower of splintered wood, swearing as he went.

Wolf wasted no time. He scooped up the mutt as gently as he could, raced her out to the pickup, laid her on the passenger seat, and jumped in the driver side. Looking in his rear view mirror as he took off down the street, he could just make out the Beard stumbling around the corner of the house, waving a fist in the air, nearly tripping over one of his own dogs. The pit bulls, whose presence Wolf had entirely forgotten, were barking wildly, circling their owner's heels in confusion.

*Smart dogs,* Wolf thought with relief. He'd been lucky their loyalties were divided. They could have torn him to ribbons.

He looked at the bedraggled mutt, and despite her obvious misery and confusion, she managed to muster up a tail thump for him. His heart warmed. "Don't you worry, Bella," he said cheerfully. "Your life's about to get a whole lot better from here, I promise."

His heart felt wonderfully light, and he was considering whistling a tune when it occurred to him that steering was difficult. He looked down at his hand and flexed his fingers.

*Oh, right.*

It had been a very, very long time since Wolf's fist had connected with another man's face. He remembered one of the many excellent reasons why he avoided such nonsense.

His hand hurt like hell.

He flexed his fingers gingerly, looked down at the dog again, and began to whistle.

It had been worth it.

# Chapter 12

"But nobody goes to Maui to live on the top of a mountain!" Mei Lin chided good-naturedly. "You're supposed to be shooting for an oceanfront condo!"

Ri laughed and rolled back on her bed, wishing it had more than just the one pillow, but she was too cheap to indulge herself. Her sister's face was distorted in the small screen of Ri's laptop, but the familiar, sunny smile warmed her heart. "Oh, that's so cliché," she teased back. "The truly savvy — and by that I mean Russian-Filipino New Englanders — know that living in the middle of a cloudbank on the side of a volcano is totally in."

Mei Lin chortled, and Ri cracked up along with her. It felt good to laugh with someone who understood. The evening after Ri had met Kai she'd gotten her whole family up on one screen and gushed with excitement for half an hour over her newly discovered heritage. Since then, the amount of her limited free time she'd spent online searching for images of other people who were Russian and Filipino, reading up on the cultural history and geography of the Philippines, investigating the history of the country's embassy in Russia, and staring suspiciously at anyone walking around Maui who looked anything at all like herself could be considered excessive. But she couldn't help it. She was excited. She felt wonderful. Her head was in the clouds in more ways than one.

Now that Kai and Maddie had helped her move into Ilma's rent-free room in the sky, she'd even come clean with her family about the fire, although she had downplayed both the drama and danger of it significantly. She was determined not to make her parents worry about her. They'd already done enough of that to last a lifetime.

"Well, I'm jealous," Mei Lin admitted, referring to Ri's physical location. "And to think that Josh and I will be living in a boring little two-bedroom apartment in Dallas with a view of another apartment building in Dallas!"

Ri's mood deflated a little. Her sister was clearly teasing; Mei Lin was ecstatic about the prospect of setting up house with her fiance and couldn't care less where they lived. What depressed Ri was how truly horrible the idea sounded to herself. She didn't understand how Mei Lin could be happy with Josh. But Mei Lin *was* happy... so what right did Ri have to interfere with that? "You won't be the least bit bored," Ri predicted.

"I will not," Mei Lin agreed with a giggle. "So what about you? Meet any cute surfers yet?"

A flash of scruffy dark blond hair and swirling fog intruded into Ri's brain. "Nope," she replied. She hadn't seen *any* surfers yet, actually. Since she'd moved in this afternoon, she also hadn't seen the elusive researcher whose face she couldn't get out of her mind. It was Saturday, but there was no sign of him anywhere at the field station. Maddie hadn't known where he was, but she guessed that he was probably working. Ri wondered if he had slept well last night in a tent pitched on the cold ground in the fog...

"Oh, you are such a liar!" Mei Lin screeched. "Look at you! There is a guy! Who is he?"

Ri jumped. "What?"

Mei Lin cackled. "Who were you thinking about?"

"Nobody," Ri replied with a smile. No sooner were the words out of her mouth than she heard a man's voice calling from elsewhere in the building, "Hey, Kenneth!"

"Yo!" came a response from the hallway outside her door. Kenneth was the field station's resident manager, who lived alone in a small cabin directly behind the Hilton. Ri wasn't certain, but she thought she recognized the other voice as Wolf, and his footsteps were approaching.

"Listen, I've got to go," she told her sister at a reduced volume. "I'll catch up with you again later, okay?" Mei Lin's strident protests met deaf ears. Ri stifled the conversation with a rudeness only sisters can get away with, then shut down her computer. She didn't intend to eavesdrop on the men. But Maddie had warned her that the Hilton's walls were thin as cardboard, and she didn't fancy completing her current conversation with these two standing mere feet away.

The footsteps stopped. "Need to ask you a favor."

*Yes*, Ri thought to herself. It was definitely the same voice as the man on the road last night. She wished she could see him.

"What's up?" Kenneth asked.

"Would you mind if I made use of that pen out by your place for a week or so?"

There was a pause. "The dog pen?" Kenneth asked stiffly.

"Yes," Wolf answered. His voice held a hint of a smile, Ri thought. Would it show on his face?

"For a dog?" Kenneth asked with disbelief.

Ri stifled a giggle. The resident manager, whom she had just met a few hours ago, was a nice man, but a bit of a character. He was a geologist in his early seventies, he had lived at the field station for at least thirty years, and he had his own way of doing things. Part of that way was to pretend to be a hardass when everyone knew he was a pushover.

"Yes, for a dog," Wolf answered.

"You know you can't have a dog running around up here!" Kenneth exclaimed harshly.

Ri wondered why the manager had a dog pen at his cabin in the first place, but now was hardly the time to open her door and ask.

"This dog won't be running anywhere," Wolf explained. "She's injured. I found her and took her in to the vet this morning and they're keeping her overnight. She's got no home, so she'll have to go to the shelter eventually, but I was hoping to foster her up here until she's well enough to be adopted. I've been friendly with her for months now, and she's a good dog, Kenneth. An outdoor dog, used to roaming. If I don't take her she'll be stuck in a stainless-steel cage for weeks. Maybe months. I had a feeling you'd understand just how miserable that would be for her."

Kenneth growled and grumbled under his breath. Ri could hear his boots scraping on the tile floor of the hallway.

"You wouldn't have to do a thing with her," Wolf continued. "She'll either be in that pen or on a lead with me at all times."

Kenneth grumbled some more and swore under his breath. "Doghouse roof leaks," he said finally.

"I'll fix it."

"Aw, hell. You young people think you can just do any damn thing around here! Dogs and elephants and trick ponies and who knows what the hell else..." His grumbling faded away along with his footsteps, and Ri heard the door at the end of the hall open and slam shut.

She wondered if Wolf took that as a "yes." His footsteps followed Kenneth's and the door opened and closed again. When she popped open her own door a few seconds later, both men were out of sight.

Ri was intrigued. She was way more intrigued than she had any business being, and although that thought excited her, it also brought mixed feelings. Mei Lin had her pegged, of course. There was definitely something about Wolf that had instantly snagged her attention and inspired her imagination. Unfortunately, that was a bad sign. One downside of her dreamy nature was that she was prone to baseless infatuation. She had a history of similar, giddy, near-instantaneous attractions stretching all the way back to middle school, and to date not a single one of them had ended well.

That really should tell her something.

Ri sighed and pulled a jacket out of her closet. Maddie and Kai had been wonderful to her today, taking her shopping for bedding and groceries and other necessities, then helping her get moved in. They had even walked her around and introduced her to everyone they could find at the Hilton and the Marriot — which did not include the mysterious Wolf — before leaving her alone to settle in. It hadn't taken her long to unpack, though, and she was already itching to explore the grounds. They'd offered to give her a grand tour of the whole field station and take her out to dinner, too, but Ri was no idiot. Although their offer had been sincere, it was obvious that the couple would implode if not allowed sufficient time to jump on each other, and judging by the tension Ri felt arcing in the air by late afternoon, two-thirds of a Saturday's worth of restraint was their limit. Knocking on Maddie's door now to redeem the guided tour offer was not an option.

Ri tied the arms of her jacket around her waist, put on her one good pair of hiking shoes, and headed outside alone.

Wolf looked down at the roof of the ancient doghouse with a scowl. The patch job would keep the rain out, yes. But he wasn't proud of it. In fact, if his dad ever got a look at it, Wolf would never live it down. Never mind that he'd thrown it together with whatever scraps Kenneth had lying around in his workshop, and never mind that he'd done it mostly left-handed. It was still an unforgivable crap job.

He flexed the fingers of his right hand again, gritting his teeth. He didn't care for the way his knuckles were looking. The swelling was worse and some of his fingers were going numb. He should probably get more ice. Or something.

He had just returned Kenneth's tools and was walking back around the cabin and up toward the Hilton when he saw her. She was further down on the slope, sitting atop one of his own favorite rocks with her legs drawn up and her arms wrapped around her shins. Her chin rested on her knees as she rocked peacefully back and forth, enjoying the view.

Wolf was too far away to discern much about the woman except that she was small, she had bushy dark hair, and she had appropriated his personal rock. But he knew who she must be. Maddie had asked him not five minutes ago if he had seen the field station's newest resident, who was apparently AWOL. Maddie hadn't been overly worried, since the weather seemed clear, but she did wish she had warned her friend earlier not to wander too far away, since one never knew when the clouds might roll in and the visibility drop to nothing.

Wolf knew Maddie's concern to be valid. He shifted direction and walked down the hill toward the stranger. As he drew closer, he could see that she looked like a local, and he remembered Maddie mentioning that she was related to Kai. He was wondering which island she might have come from when she moved from her sitting position to stand straight up on the rock. She stretched her arms high above her head, reaching out toward the sky. Clearly, she was relishing the moment.

He smiled. He liked a woman who could appreciate a spectacular view... not to mention a deep breath of mountain air. He also liked a woman who was built like she was. Petite, but muscular, and curvy in all the right places. Vibrant and dynamic looking, she practically bristled with athletic energy.

She heard him coming and turned.

*Whoa.*

The mop of tight curls had been hiding the face of an angel. Her large, dark eyes with their lovely thick lashes fixed on him and twinkled with delight. Her beautiful full lips drew into a smile, showing off perfect white teeth and making cute little dimples in her smooth bronze cheeks.

Then she seemed to get a hold of herself. She pursed her lips to staunch the smile, and she averted her eyes.

How interesting. "Are you Ri?" he called out casually as he continued toward her.

She looked up at him again. "Yes." Her smile was back now, although this one seemed more guarded. "And you're Wolf. I saw you out in the fog yesterday when Maddie first brought me up here. Nice to meet you officially."

Wolf thought about that. He hadn't realized anyone else was in Maddie's truck last night, but it was no wonder, with the headlamps shining in his eyes. "Same here," he greeted, smiling back at her.

She jumped off the rock in one swift movement, which his gaze eagerly followed. She was an agile creature, but not like a cat. Somehow she reminded him more of a fox. Fleet rather than stealthy. Earthier. Sexier.

What was he saying again?

"This rock has a great view, but it's not the most comfortable thing," she said with a laugh, pointing to the sharp ridge that ran along its downhill edge.

Wolf chuckled. He'd been tempted to dangle his legs off the edge of that rock himself, but it was too brutal on the thighs. No wonder she'd been perched with her legs drawn up. "You noticed that, too? I usually sit toward the back on that hump there and swing my legs over the side."

The angel eyes glittered at him. "You sit on this rock?"

He grinned back. "This *is* my rock."

She laughed. It was a low, melodious sound. Not at all girlish or silly. He liked it. "My apologies," she said sarcastically. "Your rent check is in the mail."

He chuckled. The little minx had a sense of humor, too. "Maddie's been looking for you," he explained. "She said she forgot to warn you how quickly the clouds can roll in up here. She didn't want you to lose your way in the fog."

"Oh, please," Ri said dismissively, pulling her phone out of a zipped jacket pocket. "It's sweet of her, but seriously. I'm from *Maine*."

Wolf supposed she was used to fog. Now that he thought about it, her voice did have an odd ring to it. The disconnect between her New England accent and typically Hawaiian appearance was bizarre, yet refreshing somehow.

Ri checked her phone and quickly fired off a message. "She did text," she said apologetically. "Shoot. I turned the sound off. I was enjoying listening to the birds. And not much else."

Wolf wondered suddenly if he was the victim of a setup. Not only was this woman physically alluring, but the lines she was feeding him sounded custom-made to appeal. Was Maddie playing some kind of game with him?

Ri tilted her head and gave him a smirk. "Until the hammering and cursing started anyway."

Wolf withdrew his suspicion. He was pretty sure he'd just been accused of doing something annoying, which fit much better with his past experience of regular, non-perfect women telling him what was on their minds. "I was fixing the roof of the doghouse," he explained without apologizing. "But I don't remember cursing."

Her sly smile widened, but she let the issue drop. She began to walk up the hill. "I have a confession to make."

Wolf fell into step beside her. A confession?

"I was in my room earlier when you and Kenneth were talking in the hall, so I couldn't help but overhear your conversation," she admitted. "And I saw you working on the doghouse when I walked down the hill earlier, but I don't think you saw me. You were pretty engrossed in the project."

Wolf fought back a sinking feeling as he digested her comments. There was nothing wrong with anything she said, but he knew this would only be the beginning. She was interested in him; he could divine her attraction the second their eyes met. But as flattered as he was to have attracted her attention so effortlessly, her keen awareness of his activities did not bode well. He knew what would happen next. Next would be the questions. *Where did you find the dog? How did she get hurt? Why couldn't someone else take care of her?*

And then, inevitably, she would notice his own injury, and that would start a whole other line of intrusive questioning, complete with implied judgment. *What did you do to your hand? Are you crazy hitting a guy like that? What if he comes after her? What if he comes after you? What are you going to do now?*

He waited. They continued walking up the hill towards the Hilton, but Ri said nothing more.

That was odd.

After a moment, it seemed a little awkward. "I didn't see you," he acknowledged finally. "And if I *was* cursing — and I'm not saying I was," he added wryly, stealing a sideways glance at her, "it's only because I was frustrated at the lousy job I was doing."

He watched as her eyes darted covertly toward his swollen knuckles. So. She *had* noticed. Still, she said nothing.

After another few steps, he surprised himself. "I hurt my hand earlier," he offered, "and now it's nearly useless. But the roof's fixed, anyway."

*There,* he thought with pride. That had been unusually forthcoming of him, hadn't it? She deserved as much, since she hadn't asked. Now they could move on to safer topics. Like the weather. And what kind of food she liked. And exactly how long she'd be staying at the Hilton.

But Ri had stopped walking. He'd made the mistake of lifting his hand and attempting to flex his fingers as he mentioned his injury. Now she was staring openly at his swollen knuckles, her pretty brow furrowed, those large doe eyes of hers wide and troubled. "Can I see?" she asked.

Wolf could think of no polite way to refuse. He lifted his hand. Ri took it, ever so gently, in both of hers, and he fought back a primal urge to flinch. Not because his hand hurt — although it did, and abominably — but because her touch gave him a jolt he was wholly unprepared for. Her eyes did not meet his but focused on his hand as she tenderly traced the swelling with a fingertip. "How long ago did you hurt it?" she asked.

Wolf couldn't answer for a moment. He was too distracted. The fact that a woman could affect him this much merely by stroking the back of his hand was a sad comment on his current lifestyle. He needed to get down into the valley more. "This morning," he choked out.

Ri looked up and studied him a moment. She had heard the strangled note in his voice, but fortunately she seemed to interpret it as pain from his injury. "I'm sorry," she said, releasing his hand. She held his gaze a few more seconds as she contemplated something. "I don't pretend to have a huge amount of medical experience," she said finally. "But if you did ask me, I'd put the odds of you having a fracture in there somewhere at about sixty:forty. What odds are you giving it?"

Wolf let his hand drop to his side. At the mere sound of the word "fracture" a piercing ache had shot through the bones of his palm, but the pain proved a welcome diversion. As Ri waited for an answer with no obvious sign of either censure or pity on her face, he began to notice a few things about her that he hadn't before. First off, her hair wasn't one color. It was mostly dark brown, but with the sun shining in her ringlets at just the right angle he could see highlights that shone auburn, even chestnut in places. And second, she was damned clever.

"Eighty:twenty," he answered. He'd had no intention of fussing with his stupid hand tonight. All he'd wanted to do was ice it up, take two acetaminophen, and go to sleep. But it was probably broken and he knew it and he was just being stupid. And this tantalizing woman he'd never met before had known it, too. She'd also known that almost anything she said about it in either an accusatory or a motherly way would almost certainly cause him to puff out his chest and insist that he was perfectly fine.

Everything except posing a straight-faced scientific question that required a numerical answer.

Perhaps she really was an angel. Either that, or she was a witch.

He started walking again. "I'm driving down to urgent care as soon as I get something to eat," he said matter-of-factly, as if it had been his plan all along. She wouldn't buy that. But he had a feeling she'd let him save face.

She did. They walked another few paces in blissful silence. Invisible birds chirped softly from somewhere under the bushes nearby, while others chattered loudly in the distant trees.

Wolf felt like he was dreaming again. This female was way too agreeable to be true. "Maddie said you were staying in Ilma's room. Do you know how long you'll be here?" he asked. He considered his co-workers at the field station, like his fellow researchers anywhere else, to be strictly off-limits for anything but a friendly business relationship. But Ri was not technically a co-worker.

"Until Ilma gets back, most likely," she answered. "Unless by some miracle I can find a place closer to Ma'alaea before then. But it's more likely I won't find another place at all, in which case Maddie said she would talk to Kenneth. If there's anything here that would go empty otherwise, I might be able to stay. But I'm afraid to count on that."

Wolf kept a straight face, but on the inside he was smiling. His last few weeks on Maui were looking up.

"Kenneth's bark is worse than his bite," he remarked. "I'm sure if he can help you out, he will. Maddie said you were here for some kind of internship?"

Ri's face lit up at the question, and Wolf found himself genuinely interested in her answer. Perhaps she would eat a quick dinner with him in the Hilton kitchen before he headed down the mountain. He was anxious to get to know her better.

He had a feeling he would enjoy her company very much.

# Chapter 13

"I was going to make a box of mac and cheese," Ri told Wolf as they reached the Hilton. "You can have half if you want. It'll only cost you eighty-four cents." She kept her tone teasing, guessing that Wolf was the type who hated asking for help. But he obviously needed some. The man's hand looked like it could barely hold a spoon. How he'd managed to repair a doghouse she had no idea, but she wondered if his condition hadn't worsened in the process. Had he dislocated a fracture that wasn't dislocated before, maybe?

Wolf raised an eyebrow at her. "Can I get a price cut if we use my milk?" he bargained.

"I was already going to steal Maddie's milk," Ri confessed.

He cracked a grin. "So was I."

They shared a laugh as they walked into the kitchen. Ri dropped some ice cubes into a plastic baggie and handed it to him without comment, then put a pot of water on the stove. Wolf sat down at the small table and relaxed with the ice on his hand. As Ri began exploring the rest of the kitchen's wares, she could feel his eyes following her every move, and her cheeks burned with heat from the attention. He was attracted to her. How cool was that? She wasn't wearing anything special or doing anything special. She was used to receiving some attention from the opposite sex, but no one had ever considered her a knockout. Odd or interesting or even exotic, sometimes, but she was never the hottest girl in a room. And naturally, the guys most attracted to her "exoticness" were the first to lose interest when they met the real "girl next door." She had always supposed the study-in-contrasts thing didn't translate as particularly sexy.

She stole a glance in Wolf's direction as she reached up to fetch a spaghetti strainer from a high shelf.

*Maybe not to New England men, anyway,* she thought with satisfaction.

Wolf appeared mesmerized.

"Tell me about your research," she suggested, sounding nearly as cheerful as she felt. "Maddie said you were a volcanologist. Can't say I've met one of those before."

He smiled. His smile was beyond sexy, just like the rest of him. He wasn't overly tall for a man, but he was muscular, with a broad chest and strong limbs that made him seem solid as a boulder. Ri wouldn't have guessed that the rugged, half-tamed type would appeal, but she had the feeling that he wasn't exactly what he appeared. With his longish hair, unshaven face, cargo-style work pants, and dirty hiking boots, he looked like the prototypical mountain man — a stalwart recluse. But on closer inspection, his mass of wavy dark blond hair framed a face that was too handsome to be rough, and his intelligent blue eyes shone with too much awareness to be insensitive. Furthermore, no smile as charming as his could come from some gruff loner with no use for the human race. Ri thought, rather, that it came from a man determined to stay on his guard and remain private.

"I'm working on my doctorate," he answered. "I'll spare you the formal name of my thesis, but the upshot is that I hike around various volcanoes collecting gas flux measurements. I did my master's work on Mount Wrangell, up in Alaska, and I found something unexpected. I'm trying to chase down the source of it now, by making comparisons between it and two similar volcanoes."

Ri felt her cheeks burning as the "arctic wolf" image reappeared in her mind. It didn't help her runaway imagination to know that he'd come from Alaska. Picturing him roughing it on a snowy mountaintop was all too easy, as was picturing him taking off his boots before a roaring fire in a stone fireplace in a snug little cabin. She wouldn't mind being in such a place, herself. There would be a giant featherbed with homemade quilts piled high. And every evening they would roast s'mores...

*Stop that!*

"Similar how?" she asked, trying to engage the analytical side of her brain. "You think Mount Wrangell is in danger of erupting again soon, or is this more academic?"

Her interest seemed to please him. "It's too early to tell. First we need to see what's causing the anomaly in the first place. That's why I'm doing the comparisons. Haleakala and Wrangell are both shield volcanoes, whereas Frosty Peak in the Aleutian Islands is a stratovolcano. But Wrangell and Frosty Peak were both formed the same way geologically, different from Haleakala. Have I lost you yet?"

"Terminology-wise, yes," Ri admitted. "But I get the gist. You want to see where else the anomaly shows up, then try to link it to certain characteristics of the different type volcanoes."

He flashed her the sexy smile again. Fortunately the water began to boil, giving her an excuse to tear her eyes away before her knees weakened. She opened the macaroni box and dumped in the shells. "So have you worked on the volcano in the Aleutians yet?" she asked.

"Yes, but I'm not finished there," he answered, his voice taking on a new angst. "Everything at Frosty has to be done in the summer. I should be getting ready to go there now, but I'm behind schedule because my equipment broke down here on Maui. It's going to be tough getting all the measurements I need before the weather turns again."

He stared at the bag of ice on his hand, and Ri could feel his tension. She hadn't thought about what an injury to his hand could mean to Wolf's research. But she could tell by his face that the consequences must be serious.

She hadn't asked him how he had broken his knuckles, and she wasn't going to. She'd seen hands like that on guys before, in college. Such injuries generally showed up on Saturday or Sunday mornings along with hangovers, black eyes, and pathetic excuses. Wolf had no hangover, nor did he have bruises. What he did have was the custody of an injured dog, a dog he claimed to have "found" somewhere but which he had been friendly with "for some time."

Ri could assume the worst. She could assume that Wolf was a troublemaker and that he had beaten some guy up. Maybe he'd taken the guy's dog because it had gotten injured in the process of the fight and Wolf felt responsible. But even then, he could have just paid the rightful owner's vet bill — no one was making him patch up a doghouse with a broken hand.

No, Ri would not assume the worst. Assuming the worst was never her habit. Her habit was to make up a story that suited her. As far as she was concerned, Wolf had rescued the dog from some horrible situation and gotten *himself* injured in the process. And she was sticking to that theory until proven otherwise.

She hated seeing him look so miserable. "You're a dog lover, aren't you?" she asked, changing the subject as she stirred the macaroni. Whatever he was worried about with regard to his research, he could do nothing about it at the moment.

His expression softened, and he nodded. "I love dogs. I haven't seen mine since January. I miss them."

The wistful tone in his voice was so poorly concealed, Ri had to stop herself from sighing. Good Lord, this infatuation was going to be terrible. Who could resist a man who pined for his pets? He could pretend aloofness to the rest of the world, but he couldn't hide a tender heart from Sriha Mirini Sullivan. She hoped its favors extended beyond canines.

"What breed?" she asked, guessing this was one line of questioning he'd be happy to answer. She was correct. His eyes twinkled at her. Ri was fascinated by the color of his irises. Such a light shade of blue, yet without a hint of gray.

"Suka's pure Husky, and her son, Tog, is a mix. His dad ran the Iditarod, but Tog didn't quite have the drive. Failed out of training as a pup, and I was happy to keep him. Suka had a lot of promise when she was young, but she lost a toe in an argument with a wolverine and had to be retired early."

"Poor thing!" Ri sympathized.

"You'd never know it to watch her run. She's forgotten she ever had that toe. But she has backed off a bit when it comes to debating wolverines."

"There you are!" a woman's voice cried out happily. Maddie and Kai popped through the doorway and Maddie saw that Ri was cooking. "I guess you were serious about not wanting to go out with us?"

"Some other time," Ri answered. "I really appreciate the offer, but you two have done more than enough for me today.

Now go out and have fun. And thanks again."

"It was our pleasure," Kai told her. "And we will."

When Maddie noticed that Wolf was sitting in the kitchen also, her face practically glowed with delight. Ri was surprised that Maddie didn't comment on Wolf's obviously injured hand, until Ri realized that he was hiding it under the table. Before Maddie could say anything else, Kai slipped an arm around his fiance's waist and wrangled her back out the doorway. "Later, Wolf," he called over his shoulder. "See you, Ri. Text us if you need anything!"

"Will do!" Ri replied. No sooner were the couple out of sight than Wolf pulled his hand back up onto the table and repositioned the ice over his knuckles, wincing as he did so. He looked slightly pale.

Ri stirred the macaroni thoughtfully. Wolf's desire for privacy must be strong indeed. Hiding his injury had seemed like a kneejerk reaction. He'd obviously hurt himself just by messing with it. "This will be ready in two minutes," she announced. "Are you sure you want to eat first?"

"Yes," he snapped. A beat passed. "Thanks," he said genuinely.

Oh, he was so busted, Ri thought with satisfaction. He only pretended to be crusty when it suited his purposes. Now how to get his pride to allow her to accompany him to urgent care? He could drive down the mountain with one good hand, but if the bones were dislocated he might require sedation to set them. Even with no more than an awkward splint and painkillers, his driving himself back home again left-handed would be uncomfortable, potentially unsafe, and completely unnecessary.

She didn't want him to feel manipulated. That was not what she was about. Perhaps he would prefer a direct approach.

She walked over to the table and sat down. "I'm sure you'd rather drive yourself," she said frankly. "But if they give you anything that makes you drowsy, either you or your truck — or both — are going to wind up stuck down there. I've got nothing to do tonight and I don't mind going with you if you want. It might even be fun to drive up and down all those switchbacks in the clouds. As long as it's not my truck I'd be totaling."

Wolf's lips drew into a slow, smug smile. He had nice lips. What made nice lips in a man, Ri wasn't sure, but she was certain that she liked his.

He spoke in a low, gravelly voice that caused a flutter in her stomach. "If anybody totals my truck, it's going to be me." The words didn't sound good, but he was still smiling. "You have a point, though. How about I drive down, and then *if* I'm incapacitated on the way back, we'll decide then who's the greater threat?"

Ri smirked. "Deal."

His blue eyes sparkled warmly at her. "Thanks, Ri. I appreciate it."

*No*, she reconsidered. Not warmly. The look in his eyes was hot.

She rose — on uncharacteristically shaky legs — and returned to the stove. Had everything in the past hour really happened to her? She was beginning to doubt that it had. Because stuff like this *didn't* happen to her. She got crushes on cute guys, sure. But they were taken. Or they weren't interested. Or they were very interested, just not in her sparkling personality. This business of her liking someone who liked her back was way too simple and way too fast to be real. In fact, everything that had happened to her since her plane landed — meeting Kai, finding out that she was part Filipino, waking up to a house fire, becoming homeless, finding an amazing place to stay, having a gorgeous guy look at her the way Wolf was looking at her... It had all happened at light speed, in a matter of days. After slogging away at a third-rate aquarium with not much changing in her world for three solid years, in the past five days her new universe had been upending at every shift of the winds.

Lucky thing she was the adventurer in the family.

# Chapter 14


*Anchorage, Alaska, 1995*

Wolf was halfway to his little brother's bed before he even knew what he was doing. His response to the wailing and snuffling had become so rote that he didn't even have to wake up all the way to drag himself out from under his own covers and walk across the room.

"It's okay, Bear," he said with a yawn, crawling up onto the other bed and yanking at the covers that were — as always — knotted up into a useless ball at his brother's feet. "I'm here."

"Mama," his brother whined pitifully, half asleep himself. "I want Mama."

Wolf gathered his brother into his arms and pulled the covers up around them. He'd drop dead of embarrassment if his friends could see him now. He was a big kid, after all. He was six years old and he was in school now. But Bear was only three. He was just a baby, still. And Wolf had to do what he had to do. It was the only thing that made Bear stop crying. "Mama's not here right now," he recited. "But she'll be back."

Bear snuffled. His nose was running all over his face, like always. His eyes opened and he stared at Wolf resentfully. "Says you!" he retorted, his small voice suddenly angry. Usually he cuddled in and settled down. But this time he'd gotten himself so worked up he was fully awake. "Daddy says no. Daddy says she's not coming back!"

Reluctantly, Wolf woke up the rest of the way himself. A choking heat flushed across his face. "Dad doesn't know," he said sternly. "I told you. Mama promised *me*. She promised!"

Bear blinked back at him with eyes that were huge and innocent. Wounded and mistrustful. "Daddy wouldn't lie," he said uncertainly. Pitifully.

"No," Wolf agreed gently. His gut felt like it was on fire. He hated going against his dad. He hated not believing his dad. But his dad was wrong this time. He had to be. "Dad ain't lying. He just doesn't know. But I know. Because she *promised* me."

Bear's giant blue eyes stared up at Wolf, the long lashes still flecked with tears. He said nothing. Wolf could see the doubt, and the fire in his gut stoked all the hotter. His own little brother didn't believe him. Bear had always worshipped the ground Wolf walked on, but he didn't believe Wolf now. Couldn't believe him.

Their mother had left six months ago. She'd walked out the door with two suitcases and an open bottle and gotten into another man's car. They hadn't heard a word from her since.

But she would come back. Wolf knew his mother. He remembered what she was like before. His dad said that the bottles were the problem, that when she was drinking, she became a different person. Wolf could see that, but she was still his mom, and he knew she still loved him. No matter how crazy the bottles made her act, she would never just up and leave him. She had told him so. Last year when his friend Mike's mother had died, he had asked her if she would ever leave him, and she had squeezed him tight and kissed him on the cheek and promised him that no, she would never leave him and Bear, not ever in a million jillion years.

And he had believed her.

And he still did.

"Listen, Bear," he said firmly, readjusting the blankets to wrap his brother in a cocoon. Bear always seemed to like that, at least until he kicked them all off again. "Mama will come back. But until she does, you're *my* cub. Remember? You and me. Law of the jungle." He reached up a hand and tousled his brother's wild mass of white-blond hair and was rewarded with the tiniest of smiles. It was kind of dumb, the cub thing. But Bear liked it. "Now let's go back to sleep. Okay?"

"Okay," Bear whispered, holding onto his brother as he snuggled down onto the mattress and closed his eyes.

Wolf tried to get comfortable. He wouldn't be getting back to his own bed until Bear fell asleep. But that was okay. Sometimes he wished that his dad would wake up when Bear cried, but their dad slept like a log, and Wolf would never wake him. His dad worked hard and always dropped into bed exhausted. When he wasn't working, though, he spent every minute he could with the two of them. He was a great dad.

She shouldn't have left them.

She must have had some reason.

*She'll be back*, Wolf told himself as own eyes closed.

*She promised me.*

# Chapter 15



*Maui, Hawaii, 2016*

"Have a good brunch," Ri heard Wolf say as she stepped out of his truck at the marina the next morning. The Foundation for Ocean Mammals' founder was hosting a Sunday champagne brunch for all the biggest donors — *on a boat!* — and as a special thank you, all the interns had been invited. "Go easy on the champagne, though. Remember you have to work with these people the rest of the summer."

Ri chuckled merrily. She couldn't help it, even if Wolf's own good humor this morning was entirely for show. She knew that he was upset. The x-rays had shown a fractured metacarpal bone, his hand was in a splint, and although he wouldn't know anything for sure until he got in to see an actual orthopedist, he would most likely stay in a splint for at least a month. He had told her little else on their drive back up the mountain last night, but his sober mood made clear that his sustaining this injury now was more than an inconvenience. She suspected that it would put his research in jeopardy, but he hadn't elaborated and she hadn't asked. She had, nevertheless, enjoyed driving his truck up the mountain. In fact, she had enjoyed every second of his decidedly masculine company so much that she felt guilty for taking such pleasure in what must have been a miserable evening for him.

She also felt guilty for the way her brain worked. Maybe other people with less imaginative minds could meet someone interesting and not spend the whole next night of REM sleep spinning fanciful scenarios of moonlit walks on deserted beaches and stunning white gowns and honeymoons in exotic locations and quiet evenings in front of roaring fires and long nights under fluffy down comforters with an adorable dog snoozing on the rug nearby. But she wasn't one of them. Lucky for her, he couldn't read her mind. And she had at least learned to be practical about it. She understood perfectly well that while something might happen with Wolf, it was more likely that nothing would. Her crazy fantasies were for entertainment purposes only.

But hoping was another matter. And this gorgeous Sunday morning, she'd been hoping only that she and Wolf would have a chance to get to know each other better. She'd been fortunate already in being able to hitch a ride down the mountain with him, since he was already making the trip to pick up the dog from the vet clinic. He'd been quiet the whole way, and obviously preoccupied, but when he looked at her, the light of interest in his ice blue eyes burned brightly as ever.

It was all the encouragement Ri needed. Wandering around the strip mall alone last night for an hour and a half (after he shooed her out of the waiting room at urgent care) hadn't exactly made for the world's greatest first date. But there was always tonight.

"Don't worry about me," Ri returned with a grin. "You just take care of that dog of yours. I look forward to meeting her later."

His smile was sincere this time. "Likewise, I'm sure."

Ri thanked him again for the ride, said goodbye, shut the door behind her, and took off with a spring in her step. She was excited about the cruise, and excited about after the cruise. She was excited about life in general. She noticed the utility trucks, but their presence didn't alarm her. The sprawling marina complex housed not only the Foundation headquarters but also a variety of shops and restaurants, and there was always something going on. The computer lab where Ri spent most of her time was located in a windowless corner of the basement, but today Lachland had told them to meet with the other passengers up in the tour assembly area beside the gift shop, and Ri enjoyed strutting through the main entrance like a tourist.

Her high spirits were soon squelched by the obvious vibe of tension in the air. People were standing in clumps all about the courtyard, not chatting and laughing in anticipation of a lovely brunch on the water, but speaking in hushed tones as they shot covert glances about, then stared at their feet.

*What the heck?*

Ri looked around the complex, thinking about the possible significance of the utility trucks outside. Yellow tape was strung across the door to the elevator. Orange cones sat on the floor near the stairs. Some people in tan coveralls milled about, although who they worked for, Ri wasn't sure. She felt as if she had stepped into some sort of disaster zone, but as far as she could tell, the buildings all looked fine. At least on this level. One of the restaurants had its windows shuttered, but it had looked the same all week — it was closed for remodeling. Did the cones by the stairs mean that something had happened on the lower level? The Foundation's level?

*No*, Ri answered herself. *No, it's not that.*

As she watched, the door to the restaurant in question opened, and two workmen and one nicely dressed man and a woman stepped out. The latter two were carrying clipboards. Ri sighed with relief. The problem *was* with the restaurant. Maybe the remodelers had screwed up somehow. Put a hole in a wall. Cracked a beam. Sliced a cable, and now the power was shut off. Thank goodness it was a weekend. As long as it didn't affect—

"Ri, there you are," Lachland's voice called out. She turned to find him approaching from behind her with a grim-looking Will and Bryant in tow.

Grim-looking?

Lachland gestured for Ri to follow, then led the three of them out of the crowd and off to a more private area of the courtyard. They stood in silence a moment as he ran a hand through his hair, seemingly searching for the right words to say.

Ri's heart fell further with each painful second that ticked by.

"There's no easy way to say this," he began with a sardonic smile, "except that I hope you guys aren't superstitious. Because I really don't want to believe that disasters come in threes."

Ri's teeth clenched. Could he possibly be less comforting?

None of the interns cracked a smile, and Lachland blew out

a breath. "The construction crew working in the restaurant damaged a pipe somehow yesterday. Nobody knows exactly how it happened, but at some point overnight there was a water line break, and the building flooded."

*Flooded.* It was a disaster Ri hadn't considered. Her mind quickly sketched out the layout of the complex and the downstairs floorplan, and her gaze met Lachland's. "The computer lab," she breathed.

The Aussie's bloodshot blue eyes said it all. "Right underneath," he confirmed. "We've got nearly six inches of water down there at the moment. It looks like at one point there was ten."

Both Will and Bryant swore. Ri felt numb. Their computers were all desktop units with the towers stored on the floor. Those would be a lost cause for sure. If the water had come through the ceiling splashing everywhere, it most likely had ruined all the electronics.

"It's not as bad as it could be," Lachland assured. "We won't lose any data. Everything is backed up off-site. The paper records in that room are only copies for the most part. The really important stuff was in the locked vault, and it's above the water line. I already rescued the whale bones and baleen and the other samples in the supply closet — they're fine. Most of what we stored at floor level was brochures and handouts and stuff — all of which can be replaced. Same with the computers and equipment. It'll cost a fortune, but the insurance should cover it. It'll just be a matter of time."

He paused and took a breath. He ran a hand through his hair again.

Ri wondered, suddenly, how much of the night Lachland had spent here. He looked exhausted.

"How much time?" Bryant demanded hotly.

Ri's fingers twitched. She'd been trying all week not to dislike Bryant, but he was not cooperating, and she was having a very vivid fantasy of watching her fist fly into his face. It was disturbingly satisfying.

"I'm not sure," Lachland admitted, ignoring the insolent pup's tone. "But I've been thinking about the situation a lot this morning, and I just got off the phone with the director, and here's what we've worked out. I'm damned sorry, guys, to lay this on you when you've already gotten burned out of the intern house — I know it's a terrible welcome. But we're going to have to suspend the internship program temporarily."

Ri's blood began to freeze, but Lachland went on swiftly.

"It may only be for a week. We're looking into renting some computers, and as soon as they're up and running, you guys are back on the job. But until then, the problem is my time. There's not enough work for you guys to do right now that wouldn't require training first, and I'm going to have my hands full just getting the office back up and running."

Ri's spirits plummeted. *Only a week,* she told herself. It could be worse. Surely they could dry out the room and rent a handful of computer stations in that amount of time. Couldn't they?

"Will we still get full credit for the internship?" Bryant snapped.

"Absolutely," Lachland answered.

"Surely we could help haul out the mess or something," Will offered.

Lachland shook his head. "Thanks for the offer, mate, but you didn't sign on for that, and we'll have plenty of salaried people with nothing better to do with themselves this week. Anyway, I have a better idea. Something I think might put a bit of a smile back on your faces."

Ri looked up.

"I'm renting a car for the three of you," Lachland announced. "I want you to take the time off and explore the island. Do the tourist thing. Drive the road to Hana. Go see the top of Haleakala. Do a beach hop up the West Side. Whatever the devil you want. Just be nice and share. The rental will go through Saturday, and then we'll see where we are. Most likely by then we'll have a few computers up and running and we can get you back on the tracking project. Oh, and if you want to jump on any of the Foundation boat tours this week, you can — as long as they're not sold out. Sound good?"

Bryant and Will looked at each other, and real smiles did

light up their faces. "Hey, that's great, man," Will said. "Thanks."

Bryant nodded.

"Thanks, Lachland," Ri added appreciatively. At least she could spend extra time on the water. "Will the brunch cruise still be going out today?"

"Of course!" Lachland answered, seeming relieved to have this particular unpleasantness dispatched with. He huffed out a rueful laugh. "I'm sure no one would miss this golden opportunity to hit up the benefactors for extra donations." He clapped Will on the back. "Go and have a good time. Eat hearty. Just go easy on the booze as long as you're wearing those nametags. As soon as you get back, I'll drive you to Kihei and we'll pick up the car."

As Lachland walked away, Will and Bryant exchanged a sly glance. "This could turn out to be a good thing after all," Will proposed.

"A *good* thing?" Ri questioned. She was as anxious as anyone to drive the road to Hana, but hardly at such a cost. She'd experienced one complete IT meltdown already, at the aquarium, and she knew perfectly well how much agonizingly tedious grunt work it took to get things back in working order, even with appropriate data backup. And that was just the IT part. The Foundation was losing office furniture, carpeting, supplies, and who knew what personal items besides.

"Oh, yeah!" Will confirmed. "We can do this island *right*, now. Only question is, which bar do we hit first?"

Bryant laughed. "Maybe you better let me drive."

Ri looked from one fellow intern to the other, speechless. They were marine biologists. With a car. On Maui. They would have a free Sunday afternoon. They would have a whole freakin' *week*. And all Will could think about was going to a bar? Which he could easily get to at any time — and more safely — by bus? The guy was over twenty-one, but the goofy gleam in his eye made him seem more like a teenager just escaped from his parents' house.

"I want to spend some time up at Ka'anapali or Kihei near the resorts," Bryant said offhandedly. "Hang with my own crowd for a while."

Ri studied Bryant's suntanned, stoic face and could not make out his meaning. She decided they might both be better off that way.

A loud voice called the assembled crowd together. The brunch cruise was about to begin.

Ri returned with her fellow interns to the center of the courtyard, trying hard to conjure the happy mood with which she'd stepped out of Wolf's truck just minutes ago. *Everything's going to be fine*, she told herself. Will and Bryant weren't bad guys. She would get to see different parts of the island she wouldn't otherwise see. She would get to drive herself, some. And she was getting out on the water — right now!

Ri lifted her chin and breathed in the myriad scents of ocean on the air. *Yes, there was that.* She would be out on the blue Pacific for hours today, and she would enjoy every single second of it.

She envisioned being on a boat in a different part of the Pacific, with Wolf. On the rocky coasts of Alaska they'd see Steller sea lions and harbor seals and sea otters and orcas. He would be in his element in a dashing windbreaker with his hair ruffling in the wind, and in the distance behind him she would see snow-capped mountains with bald eagles soaring and puffins swooping about. His eyes would sparkle and he would lean down close with those fantastically kissable lips of his...

Ri smirked. Her mother always said she was good at entertaining herself.

# Chapter 16

Wolf sat on the grass in the chain link enclosure with his back braced against the doghouse. The mutt lay sprawled contentedly on her side with her muzzle draped across his thigh, and as depressed as Wolf felt at the moment, he couldn't help but smile. Kenneth had truly outdone himself. Not only had the station manager weed-eated the overgrown grass and donated his own late dog's food and water bowls, he had laid a clean rubber pad over part of the grass as well as outfitted the doghouse with a door flap and a blanket.

"You know what, Bella," Wolf said as he scratched the dozing dog's ears with his good hand. "I'm thinking that maybe Mr. Kenneth might just miss having a dog around this place."

Bella did not respond. The poor thing seemed utterly exhausted. Wolf doubted that she'd slept at all in the veterinary hospital. She had the look of a dog who'd spent her entire life outside, being around relatively few people or other dogs. The shock of being suddenly confined indoors in a strange-smelling cage with dozens of noisy mammals bustling about must have been intense. Thank goodness the vet had released her to Wolf's care. Wolf was lucky the folks from the shelter had vouched for him.

At least he knew she was relaxed now. She had been rehydrated and she was eating well, and the antibiotics and time should do the rest. But she had to feel like hell, even with the painkillers. The wound in the side of her chest was open and draining still, as was her injured paw. And he didn't see how she could eat with her tongue so swollen, but one sniff of that canned dog food, and somehow she had managed. She was a trouper, his Bella.

He sighed as he smoothed a hand down her back. He wished he could take her home with him, but she would never make it in Alaska. She wasn't bred for it. She had no undercoat for insulation, and her long, shaggy beige hair would only mat with snow and ice. He had a strange suspicion that The Beard had acquired her as a pup believing she was half pit bull — perhaps the offspring of his male. She could be half pittie... but only if the other half was Afghan hound. Her muzzle was long and thin, and her chest was narrow and deep rather than broad. If The Beard had been expecting a pit bull pup, he would have been sorely disappointed.

Wolf's jaws clenched. He didn't know why The Beard had done what he'd done, and it was probably best if Wolf didn't think about it. Both the humane society and the police were on the case now, and one broken hand was causing him enough trouble. The dog was safe now, and she would recover. Wolf was glad that Kenneth was showing interest in her, because she would likely need care longer than Wolf himself would be around.

He stared down at the bulky splint with a scowl. He might as well admit it to himself. His right hand was useless. The data collection he needed to complete — his sole reason for being on Haleakala — had been difficult enough to do solo after he'd lost his undergrad assistant. There was no way he could finish it now. The equipment took two good hands just to carry and set up, and he needed his right hand in particular to adjust and fine-tune the controls.

If his hand had to stay splinted for even three weeks, there was no point in his staying here at all. He *had* to start on Frosty Peak by the first of June; the weather window was too short to take chances with. Up there the splint wouldn't matter so much — he had an intern for the summer who could make up the difference. He'd simply have to delay finishing his data collection here on Maui until the fall, when he could work his instruments solo again. Of course, in order to get back here, he'd have to scrape together extra funds that weren't in the budget. Enough for a second round-trip airfare for himself and the gear, living expenses for the time extension...

He sighed again, leaning his head back against the doghouse roof. He didn't know how he would find the money, and he hated that he'd brought such an expensive inconvenience on the project. What's more, he didn't want to leave yet. An image flashed in his mind of sparkling dark eyes and sexy dimples, and he chuckled sadly. Three days ago he would have been happy to get back to Alaska anytime. Maui had been a fun diversion, but it was getting too hot for his tastes, and despite the island's reputation as a singles' playground, he'd been here four months without meeting any women who really interested him. But then he'd met Ri, and she interested him very much, dammit. He'd been looking forward to spending a few weeks with her.

Now all he'd get were a few lousy days.

Wolf opened his eyes, and his head jerked up when he saw a figure approaching through the early evening haze. Speak of the devil... It was her. She was wearing the same eye-catching shorts and scoop-necked top she'd been wearing when he drove her down the mountain this morning — and which he'd had emblazoned on his brain ever since. Only a woman from Maine would stroll around at this elevation in the cool of the evening and not even bother to don the jacket that was tied around her waist.

"Hello," he called out with a sly smile, feeling as if he'd been caught. "How was the champagne?" As she stepped closer, he could see that her shoulders were sagging. And although she smiled back at him, her brow was furrowed and her eyes showed no sign of their usual sparkle.

In short, she looked as depressed as he felt.

"The cruise was nice," she answered, opening the gate and stepping into the run. She looked down at Bella, who had not even lifted her head. Wolf saw the dog's eyes flutter, but she was way too relaxed to bother with greeting a stranger.

"Will she be okay if I sit down in here, too?" Ri asked.

"She'd love it," Wolf answered, smiling as Ri plopped down to sit cross-legged on the grass beside them. Ri stretched out a hand to let Bella sniff her fingers, but Bella was already asleep again.

"Poor thing," Ri said quietly, looking at the dog's wounds. "What happened to her?"

Wolf followed her eyes to the shaved patch on the side of the dog's chest. The wound was still grisly looking. The vet had decided against continuing with the bandages, since Bella kept chewing them off and the cone had completely freaked her out. But Wolf would make sure her wounds stayed clean. "Her 'owner,' if you want to call him that, broke a beer bottle over her ribs," he answered.

Ri made a quick, horrified intake of breath. "No!"

Wolf nodded, his expression grim. "Cracked two ribs and shattered the bottle. She had shards of glass embedded in her side, and she cut up her tongue trying to get them out."

Ri looked mildly ill. Her eyes took in Bella's swollen paw. "She cut her foot on the glass, too?" she asked quietly.

"Most likely," Wolf answered. A wave of guilt washed over him. "She holed herself up under his shed afterward and stayed there for two days. I didn't know what had happened to her. I wondered where she was, but I thought maybe he'd given her away to someone or that she'd wandered off." He shook his head in annoyance with himself. "I should have searched for her sooner."

Ri's doe eyes fixed on him. "Don't blame yourself," she said firmly. "How could you have known?"

Wolf held her gaze a moment, saying nothing. The woman had a gift for saying what he needed to hear.

Somehow, that only depressed him more.

"You don't look like someone who just got back from a carefree day of cruising on the ocean sipping champagne and watching dolphins," he said, anxious to change the subject from himself. He was also curious to know what had happened to her. She looked exhausted — emotionally, if not physically.

Ri's response was to blow out a breath, straighten her shapely legs, and brace her hands behind her. She dropped her head back and stared up at the sky — or where the sky would have been if the slope weren't socked in by clouds. "The cruise was fine," she said in a gravelly deadpan. "It was wonderful, actually. The food was good. I've discovered a love of passion fruit and mango smoothies that isn't going away any time soon. I even got to see my first spinner dolphins. We saw a couple whale spouts in the distance and I met a whole bunch of really nice people."

She went quiet for a moment. Her words were pleasant but her face was drawn into a scowl. A really adorable scowl. Wolf had never known a woman who could look sexy while she was scowling, but he was beginning to think that Ri Sullivan could look sexy no matter what she was doing. That perfect little body of hers was so solid, yet so agile, so lean, and yet so wonderfully, deliciously curvy...

*Down, Boy.* Wolf forced his gaze back to her face. He didn't have time. Ri wasn't a one-night-stand kind of girl.

"But?" he prompted, trying to keep his tone light. "You can't tell me there isn't a 'but' coming in this story. What's got you so down?"

Ri's eyes slid his direction without her head moving. It was a comical expression. "Down?" she said sarcastically. "Me? Sriha Mirini Sullivan is never down. She gets knocks sideways, occasionally. But that is all."

"So sorry," Wolf said with amusement, wondering how she got such a bizarre name. "So what's knocked you sideways?"

Ri dropped fully on the ground — ironically, sideways — and faced him. "My, you have a lot of questions today."

Wolf was taken aback. Him, asking too many questions? He'd never been accused of that before. How terribly hypocritical of him.

Before he could respond, Ri cracked up laughing. "Just kidding. I don't mind. In fact, I probably should vent to someone before I break something. So congratulations, you're elected."

She spun around and sat up again, and Wolf's head nearly spun in kind at her contortions, both physical and verbal. The verbal were amusing, but the physical were torturous — to him.

"So I get there," she began with animation, "and the first thing I see are a bunch of utility trucks..."

Wolf found himself captivated as Ri recounted the events of her day, beginning with a flooded office, a suspended internship, and the dreamlike champagne cruise. She was a talented storyteller, using not only a wide variety of voices and facial expressions to engage her audience, but throwing her entire body into her act. Not only did she have Wolf in the palm of her hand, but she even woke up the dog. Bella lifted her head and watched Ri curiously, thumping her tail in approval whenever Ri's antics made Wolf chuckle aloud.

"So Lachland is nice enough to get the three of us this car for the week, and it's still just the middle of the afternoon, so we could go pretty much anywhere and do anything and where do you think these guys want to go?"

Wolf had had enough of an introduction to the characters of Will and Bryant to see where her story was headed. "A bar," he guessed.

"Yes, of course," she confirmed sarcastically. "So we end up at this dive in Lahaina — some boring little hole with nothing special about it except that they've got this particular kind of draft that Will wants to try — and by the end of his first beer the guy starts turning into this totally different person."

"Uh-oh," Wolf commiserated. He kept his tone joking in concert with hers, but the topic wasn't one he took lightly. It reminded him too much of the mother he'd never had.

"He wasn't drunk exactly," Ri qualified, "I don't think. The stuff just turned him into an immature buffoon. I swear it was like he regressed to middle school before our eyes. All of a sudden he was giddy and goofy and awkward... his voice even got an octave higher!"

She shook her head with exasperation. "I tried to get them to talk about where we could take the car, what we might *all* like to do together, but once Will got pre-pubertal, I couldn't get them to commit to anything other than driving the road to Hana one day. So then I suggested we take separate days with the car, so they could do whatever they wanted on their days, and they both flipped out on me and said they didn't want to go *any* days without the car and they wanted to stay together and it was all going to be great."

Wolf watched as a devious sparkle lit up her eyes. "And you agreed to that?"

She smirked. "I appeared to. Then I lifted the keys from Will and drove us to Ho'okipa Beach Park to look for the monk seal."

Wolf laughed. "Did you see it?"

"No," Ri replied with a pout. It was a cute pout, coming from those luscious lips of hers, but Wolf wasn't supposed to be thinking about that.

"The resident seal was not in residence," she continued. Then she smiled. "We did see at least a dozen green sea turtles, which was fabulous. And it was exciting to watch the windsurfers. We were actually managing to have a pretty good time, acting like adult marine biologist people, until I went back to check for the seal one more time and they decided to stay down where the surfing action was."

Wolf waited. He could tell by the way her perfectly formed little eyebrows were slanting that whatever happened next had made her furious.

"So I'm waiting by the car at the agreed-upon time," she went on, her voice dropping to a dramatic drawl, "and fifteen minutes after that, the jerks arrive. *With dates.*"

Wolf tried not to laugh out loud at the expression of disgust on her face.

"These girls say they're locals just hanging out for the day," she continued. "They're wearing bikini tops and jean short-shorts and carrying practically nothing with them. And for some reason which doesn't appear at all mysterious to anyone but me, these women are fawning all over Will and Bryant like they're the most gorgeous men they've ever seen. Now keep in mind — Will's liver still hasn't processed all his beer, so he has the social acumen of an eleven-year-old. And Bryant is wearing a wedding ring! So at first I'm thinking these girls are either out to pick their pockets or steal our rental car, but after five minutes of listening to them giggle over Will's attempts to pronounce *Ho'okipa* while 'accidentally' making a belching sound, I'm really not sure they're smart enough to be thieves."

Now Wolf was laughing out loud. Bella, seeming to want in on the action, scootched up to his chest and licked at his face with her swollen tongue. "Easy girl," he said, giving her an enthusiastic rub. "Don't hurt yourself."

Ri smiled at them both a moment before continuing. "But the girls didn't waste too much time before they got around to what they were really after. Guess what? They've been out surfing all day — without boards, I guess, or getting their hair wet — and now they're ever so hungry. Next thing I know, all five of us are in the car heading towards some great little restaurant in Pa'ia that they just *love*."

"Now, see there!" Wolf teased. "And you thought those girls weren't smart. They had those guys pegged. Everyone knows Maui tourists are loaded."

Ri humphed and planted her hands on her hips. Her beautifully curvaceous little hips.

"Tourists may be loaded, but interns are not," she argued. "Neither of them has a dime to spare, but the idiots put the bill on their credit cards anyway. And this place was not cheap. I had to order a frickin' *side salad*. With water! And then I had to sit there staring at an empty plate for half an hour while the girls kept ordering drinks!"

Wolf couldn't stop chuckling. "Sounds like a great time."

"That was just in the restaurant!" Ri insisted, her voice rising. "When we finally got out of there, I kept hinting that it was time to take the girls back to the beach and the guys flat out ignored me. Bryant had the keys then and I couldn't get them away from him — he hadn't driven yet and he hadn't been drinking, either, so I had no excuse. But no one could decide where to go, so for the next forty-five minutes he's just randomly driving around while Will is playing octopus with this girl in the back seat next to me — and this is not a big car. It's a Nissan Sentra. A *compact*. Will couldn't even tell where she stopped and I started!"

Wolf was practically rolling on the grass now. As horrible as Ri's day sounded, he loved that she was able to see the humor in it.

"Well, *that* did it for me," Ri declared. "I told Bryant I was ready for them to drop me off at home and then they could go do whatever the hell they wanted. But then he got mad and said that wasn't fair, that *he* hadn't gotten to drink yet and that they were going to need a designated driver to get them and the girls back to their place."

In a blink, Ri's good humor vanished. "He told me this to my face," she went on in a low voice. "A man with a wife and two-year-old son back in Florida, who he left behind barely a week ago. Even as he was saying it, he had his hand stretched across the front seat of the car stroking this girl's thigh."

Wolf sympathized with her disgust. Her eyes shot a wary glance at him, then she drew in a deep breath and rallied her spirits.

"So, being the easily bullied little lamb that I am, I said that of course he had a point, and that under the circumstances he and Will really should go for broke and take the girls to the hottest spot on the island. Which I happened to know all about, since my swinging local cousin had just let me in on the secret."

Wolf cocked an eyebrow skeptically. "Kai? Said what now?"

Ri chuckled. "You know, the revolving bar in the clouds? I'm surprised you haven't heard of it. It's at the top of Haleakala."

A smile spread slowly over Wolf's face. There was no bar at the top of Haleakala. The entire area was a national park. The only thing at the summit was an overlook for visitors and a scientific observatory that was closed to the public.

"So I directed Bryant up the mountain to the park entrance," Ri continued mischievously, "but darn the luck — when I got out to pay the entrance fee, wouldn't you know I saw a note posted there announcing that the bar was temporarily closed?"

"Shocking," Wolf deadpanned.

"It was," Ri agreed. "But only to the guys. The girls had been saying all along that there was no bar up here, but they were tipsy, so naturally Will and Bryant paid no attention to them. And then, sadly, the evening's designated driver bailed on foot, and poor Bryant had to drive all the way back down the mountain sober."

"You mean you deserted them?" Wolf joked. "In their time of need?"

Ri sighed, even as she grinned. "I've probably just ruined any chance of carrying on a decent working relationship with either of them the rest of the summer." She fell flat on her back on the grass, then reached out a hand and offered to let Bella sniff her fingers again. "But seriously. Enough was enough. Maybe the girls were actually having fun. Maybe they were just seeing how many freebies they could rack up before they ditched the idiots. I don't know and I don't care — more power to them. But as for Bryant," her face darkened. "No way was I going to help that asshole cheat on his wife."

Bella finished sniffing. Ri's expression softened as she began to stroke the dog's head. Bella responded by closing her eyes.

Wolf watched Ri pet the mutt with a queer, unsteady feeling in his center. "Do you have dogs?" he asked before he could stop himself. What kind of off-the-subject question was that?

Ri didn't seem taken aback. She didn't even look up at him, but continued smiling serenely at Bella. "We used to. Bernese Mountain Dogs. We had Callie first, when I was little. Then we had Dorie. She died a couple years ago, but my parents were empty nesters then and they wanted to travel, so we didn't get another one. I've missed having a dog around."

They were quiet for a moment. Ri's creative energy seemed temporarily spent, now that she'd gotten her anger off her chest, and Wolf felt a sudden, fierce urge to lift her spirits. "What will you do now? Are you going to demand at least one day with the car by yourself?"

The second sentence hadn't left his mouth before the idea came to him. It was a terrible idea, or at least a terribly self-serving idea. He had nothing of value to offer in return. Did he?

She was answering his question. But his thoughts were elsewhere. When he tuned back in, she seemed to be finishing a paragraph. "...not worth it. Just take the bus."

Wolf sat up straight. "Ri," he said earnestly, "I have a business proposition for you."

She stared at him a second, then sat up herself. She said nothing. She just seemed surprised.

He held up his splinted hand. "I can't work my equipment with this. It's not physically possible. And if I can't finish up the data collection in the next couple weeks, I'll have to make a separate trip back here later, which my current budget won't cover. I *could* finish now if I had an assistant, but my budget won't cover that either, not even at minimum wage." He paused a minute and swallowed. Damn, this sounded insulting. Ri was a professional, not some kid, and not a geologist either — even the experience on a resume would be useless to her.

He studied her face. She blinked back at him, her expression unreadable. He should stop while he was ahead.

But it would be so much fun.

"You know you can say no. I'm just throwing this out there." He took a breath, having a sudden, uncomfortable flashback to the time he'd asked Mary Lynne Proust to the homecoming dance when she was a senior and he was only a sophomore. "But if you could work as my assistant, even for just this week, I might be able to finish up this job, which would be huge for me. And although I can't pay you any money, I can loan you the truck — if that's what you want — anytime you're not working between now and the minute I have to leave."

Seconds passed. He watched, breath held, as little lights began to twinkle in her eyes. Her lips curved slowly up into a smile.

*Yes!*

"I can drive the truck?" she asked cautiously. "By myself?"

"Of course!"

"And I can take it on the road to Hana, or wherever else I want to go?"

"Yes. Anywhere. Just don't total it, please."

She frowned. "Oh, now you're adding conditions?"

She cracked up laughing before he could reply. Her liquid brown eyes held his like a magnet and the joy he saw shining in them mirrored his own. This was going a hell of a lot better than it had with Mary Lynne Proust.

"Well?" Wolf asked hopefully.

Ri held out her right hand, glanced at his splint, then switched and held out her left instead. "I accept," she replied.

# Chapter 17

Ri looked out to the east to see the sun shining down on top of the clouds. Off to her right, a mountain peak poked through the cottony tufts to claim its own share of the morning light. It was the Big Island of Hawaii, eighty miles away. She smiled to herself, and an inner warmth began to counteract the chill of the frosty morning air. "It must be amazing to watch the sunrise from here," she mused.

"It is," Wolf said, his own voice full of reverence as he paused a moment to admire the view from beside her. "You should check it out sometime when we're not lugging all this gear. I would have started out earlier today, but if you drive up to the summit before dawn, it's impossible to get a parking spot."

Ri laughed. Indeed, as they had started their drive from the field station up toward the summit of Haleakala at just after seven this morning, she had been amazed at the number of cars and busses streaming down in the opposite direction. Now, she could understand. Watching the sun set over the ocean was fabulous, but watching the golden orb rise from a viewpoint above the clouds must be magical. Even now, with the sun already up in the sky, she had trouble believing that what she was seeing was real. Her feet were planted firmly in the soil at around nine thousand feet above sea level, and she was surrounded by an arid landscape of red earth and black rocks and clumpy green plants. Spread out below and beyond her was an endless horizon of the topside of clouds.

"It's a breathtaking view, any time of day," she praised. She indulged herself a moment longer, inhaling deeply of the thin, crisp air. She could hardly believe that anything she was seeing or feeling was real anymore. It was all entirely too amazing.

She had wanted to call her sister or her mother again last night, but she was afraid they would see too much. Her elation at solving the mystery of her biological heritage, at meeting a relative who had already become a good friend, and simply at basking in the natural splendor of the island was enough to make her giddy with happiness, never mind all the strife with the internship. But Wolf's asking her to work with him was really over the top.

The feelings she was experiencing for the man were infatuation, pure and simple, and she knew that. She didn't know him well enough for it to be anything else. Still, her playful impulses would not be reined in. She was having *way* too much fun.

She was playing with fire, of course, and she knew that, too. Wolf's time in her company was limited, and that alone should give her pause. Her analytical mind realized that if she wasn't content with a mere hookup, she should set the "just friends" boundary now and make sure that both their expectations were clear. Unfortunately, her creative mind was having none of that.

Creative mind wanted it all.

Why not?

She wasn't sure why she should feel so optimistic. But when she had seen Wolf cuddling that scraggly mutt — his seemingly aloof appearance so at odds with his obviously tender heart — the sight had unleashed a feeling of connectedness that was all out of proportion to the situation. And along with it, a yearning of such maddening ferocity she couldn't easily call it to heel again.

She could only hope she was hiding the worst of it. So far, she'd been able to behave herself. Last night, far from having a "second date," she had insisted that Wolf teach her everything she needed to know to get started with his work first thing this morning. She'd spent the entire evening familiarizing herself with his equipment and practicing taking measurements, while Wolf had sketched out a plan of how much ground they would need to cover each day in order to collect all the data he needed. He seemed optimistic that they could finish in time for Ri to have the truck for the weekend. But Ri had higher goals. She planned to be so amazingly efficient that they finished in record time each day, knocked off by mid-afternoon, and spent the rest of the evening goofing off at sea level. The more time they had to get know each other outside of work, the better.

She grinned to herself as she recalled another moment in which she'd gotten a glimpse of his true character. Yesterday, when she'd mentioned her own revulsion at Bryant's treatment of his absent wife and child, she had made a point of noting Wolf's reaction. Men's responses to other men's bad behavior were usually telling, and the flare of righteous anger she had seen in Wolf's eyes had not disappointed her. It had made her soul leap. In fact, it had seemed so pointed and so personal she wondered whether Bryant's transgression had reminded him of something else.

Or she could be guilty of wishful thinking. She wanted to believe that Wolf possessed the kind of loyalty she most admired — not just in a prospective boyfriend, but in anyone.

Her grin slipped away as she was reminded of the end of her hopes for a real friendship with either of her fellow interns. She could continue to deal with Bryant just fine as a co-worker, but after what she'd seen yesterday she knew they could never be friends. And as much as she liked Will when he was sober, his willingness to waive all self-regulation for the sake of a particular draft was worrying. Ri prided herself on being able to get along with almost anyone, and she had no interest in making moral judgments about others. But when it came to forming close bonds, only the truly dependable made the cut. Her mother would say that had something to do with what Ri went through as a baby, and maybe it did. She couldn't remember any of that. She only knew that being able to trust was important to her.

She turned to Wolf and picked up the equipment she'd helped to lug out from the truck. "All right," she said, her tone all business. "Let's get started!"

As the next hours passed, Ri spoke nothing but data. Her tasks were relatively simple, and her resolve to be efficient was firm. All she had to do was move the equipment along Wolf's predetermined path, set it up, adjust the instruments as he'd shown her, and read out the results. He was able to record them well enough with his left hand and free right thumb, and after they'd fallen into a routine, the process went smoothly.

The landscape wasn't the easiest to navigate, but thanks to her hiking shoes and experience scrambling around in the White Mountains, she was reasonably sure-footed. Wolf, not too surprisingly, moved up and down the boulder-strewn slopes as nimbly as a mountain goat.

"Why don't we take a break here and have lunch?" he suggested when their course took them within easy reach of the visitors' overlook near the summit. "You haven't seen the so-called crater yet."

Ri made no argument. Having restrooms with running water available at midday was a definite perk. "Did you save the easiest sections of the volcano for last, or am I just lucky?" she asked as they hiked up into the parking lot and merged with the tourists.

Wolf grinned. "Both, I guess. I always do the least accessible areas first. It helps with time management, since you can't predict your progress as well working off-road. Chris and I had to camp out in some of the remote sites. But don't worry, those are all taken care of now."

Ri fought back a smile, glad that her Filipino heritage helped hide the flush in her cheeks. Evidently, he thought that the idea of camping out at a remote site would seem either daunting or unpleasant to her. If he knew what ideas sprung into her mind when she envisioned the two of them crawling into a pup tent together on a foggy mountainside, he might very well be the one blushing.

A few minutes later she emerged from the restroom to find him waiting for her on the walkway outside. He had a twinkle of anticipation in his eye. "You're going to love this," he said confidently. "Follow me."

Ri walked around the piled reddish-black rocks. Here near the summit, the landscape had changed yet again. There was very little vegetation, but the Haleakala silverswords were an exception, and they made their presence known. The rare plant was a shiny ball of curved spikes that shone a pale, metallic green in the sunlight. The disconnect between the plants' striking appearance and the desolation around them was so jarring that they looked like leftover props from the filming of a space movie.

"Now," Wolf said in warm, husky whisper that had way too much effect on Ri, "take a look at *that*."

Ri looked. Yet again, a new angle brought a whole different element of the massive volcano to light. She was looking over a crater-like sunken valley in between several taller peaks of the mountain. Gone was any hint of grass, much less scrubby bushes or trees. There were not even any silverswords in view. Within the vast cauldron was nothing but rocks and dirt — a colorful plain filled with sweeping veins of dark gray, red, and black lava sands as far as the eye could see. Traversing the windswept surface were the pale lines of foot trails, and as Ri watched, she saw a group of intrepid hikers moving slowly along one of them. The people were ant-sized.

"I can't believe all of this is hiding up here," she gushed. The bottom of the valley was low enough in elevation that it fell below the cloud line, and as they stood and enjoyed the view, white wisps blew in and out of the crater, alternately obscuring and exposing its various reaches. "Did you have to do any measurements down there?" Ri asked.

Wolf shook his head. "It wasn't necessary. But I've hiked down there anyway."

Ri chuckled to herself. Of course he had. He was a volcanologist. "It's beautiful," she affirmed. "I have to say, I prefer lush green jungles and sparkling blue waters to dry stretches of lava that look like the surface of the moon. It looks so forbidding. So unwelcoming. But still, there's a beauty to it. An awesomeness all its own."

He turned his head toward hers, and those enticing lips of his curved into a smile.

Ri felt her body flush with warmth. They were standing quite close together, and for a moment, she was certain he would make a move. He was attracted to her. He had to know she was attracted to him.

He took a step back. "So where do you want to eat?" he asked, pointing to two areas beside the parking lot. "We should stick to the public areas for picnicking. I don't want to set a bad example. Too often tourists see me traipsing around with my equipment and think it must be okay for them to wander off the trails, too, even though it should be obvious I'm working."

Ri pointed without paying much attention. She was disappointed. Did Wolf have a thing about not dating co-workers? If he did, she had made a serious miscalculation.

Not that the week still wouldn't be fun.

On second thought, no, it would not be fun. It would drive her frickin' bonkers.

"So when you do this kind of work in Alaska, do you take your dogs with you?" she asked matter-of-factly as they settled onto a rock pile and opened their lunches. She didn't have to think about the question. It was one of a list of nonthreatening conversation starters she'd worked out while trying to fall asleep last night.

His face brightened with a smile, as she had noticed it always did when he was reminded of his canine companions. "Whenever I can," he answered. "Unfortunately, a lot of the places I survey are only accessible by plane, and Suka and Tog aren't what you'd call easily portable. Although I do know plenty of bush pilots who cart their own dogs around."

He looked back at her thoughtfully, and Ri decided that his eyes were aquamarine... the color of clear, shallow ocean on a white sand beach in the Caribbean.

"I hope you don't mind me asking," he said gently, tentatively. "But I'm curious. Maddie said you were related to Kai, but you grew up in Maine? Have you spent time on the islands before?"

Ri felt a beaming smile spread slowly across her face. Oh, he had *so* stepped in it, now. Her answering this was good for all kinds of personal questions in return!

"I don't know exactly how Kai and I are related," she answered. "I only know the odds are good that we share a Filipino ancestor back in the family tree somewhere. You see, I was adopted. From an orphanage in Russia..."

Ri gave him the short version of her story. The shortest version that still made sense, anyway, which was not too terribly short. She explained her background without suffering a moment's angst or embarrassment, and without feeling the slightest bit like either a fraud or a freak. Instead she used strong words that came from her newfound confidence and pride in her dual heritage, and as she took a step back and listened to herself, she recognized the change. It was the first time since the DNA results had arrived two years ago that she once again felt comfortably at peace with her own identity.

It felt good.

*Really* good.

She looked over at Wolf — whose presence she had momentarily forgotten — and found him studying her thoughtfully. He had been attracted to her appearance without having any idea of the specifics of her heritage, which was a point in his favor. The fact that he showed more than a polite interest now was earning him another point. She felt as though he wanted to ask her more questions, but was refraining, and she gave him credit for that, too.

"So how about you?" she asked cheerfully, knowing she was entitled. "I would make a guess about your family background, but I'm at a disadvantage, since I don't even know your last name."

His expression told her that he accepted his fate. He had brought up the subject. "It's Markov," he answered with a begrudging hint of a smile. "The name is Russian, and yes, I'm mostly Russian, too. So it appears we have something in common."

Ri felt a flush of goose pimples. An orphanage in twentieth-century Moscow was pretty far removed — in every way — from the historic fur-trading scene in which his ancestors probably participated, but still, it was something. She grinned. "Well, what do you know? And I suppose in Alaska there's still some cultural influence remaining. Still... I bet you never experienced a Russian heritage camp, did you?"

He raised an eyebrow. "A what?"

Ri chuckled to herself. "Can you do a round dance in a sarafan while eating babka?"

He stared at her.

She laughed out loud. "Clearly you've never experienced a heritage camp," she teased. "Boys don't wear sarafans. And it would be pretty hard to eat anything while you were doing a round dance. Not that I haven't tried." She smiled at him. "Have you always lived in Alaska?"

He nodded. "Born and bred. And I do know what babka is," he defended. "But I can't say I've ever made much of a study of Russian culture." His eyes met hers for a moment, and she had the unsettling feeling that he could see more than she wanted to show. "I can see how important the whole idea of heritage is to you. Listening to you makes me feel like I should care more about my own."

Ri gave a small shrug. "It doesn't have to matter to everyone. It mattered to me because strangers would ask me about it — for the obvious reason." She smiled to let him know she was comfortable with her appearance.

He smiled back. "I've got native blood as well as Russian. Tlingit from my mother and Yup'ik from my dad. But I don't know much about my family's background otherwise."

"What are Tlingit and Yup'ik?" Ri asked with interest.

"Indigenous people. There are a lot of Yup'ik tribes scattered across the western part of Alaska. Two of my dad's grandparents were full-blooded, but I never knew either of them. The Tlingits are just in the southeast." He broke off and looked away.

Ri wanted to keep him talking. "Does your mother know who her Tlingit ancestors were?"

Wolf's head snapped back. For an instant his blue eyes looked at her with a kind of wounded bewilderment, almost as if she had struck him. He stood. "It's just my dad and my brother and me," he said offhandedly, wadding his trash into a ball. He stepped to the nearest waste can and tossed it inside.

Ri cursed silently. She had known from the set of his shoulders that he was tensing up... why hadn't she heeded the warning? He didn't want to talk about his mother. Never mind that he had brought the subject up himself, however absently. There was something wrong there. Something very wrong.

"We've made fantastic time this morning, Ri," he announced, forcing a change of mood. "You're very efficient. I hate to say it, but if Chris had worked as hard as you, I doubt

I'd still be here."

Ri appreciated the compliment, but her answering smile was fake. For her own selfish purposes, she was glad that Chris was a slacker. She didn't want their lunch to end, since it had marked their first real conversation about anything besides dogs, gas flux measurements, and drunken interns. But there was always dinner.

Ri got up and threw away her own trash, then shouldered her share of the equipment. Their break had taken all of fifteen minutes, which was actually good. They had a goal to hit. "Where to next?" she asked.

She turned and found Wolf watching her. She would not have guessed that the mere motions of jumping off a rock, throwing away trash, rotating her shoulders, and donning gear would come across as particularly beguiling.

The look in his eyes said otherwise. Ri's heart thumped in her chest. She met his gaze and smiled back.

"We've got two more sets of readings near here," he answered, his gaze still holding hers. "Then we'll head to another location further down."

There was nothing in his words or tone that was anything less than businesslike. But Ri knew lust when she saw it. She also knew that he was making no attempt to hide it from her. That, at least, was progress. Maybe he had a thing about not dating coworkers, and maybe he didn't.

Maybe he was still trying to decide.

"I was going to drive back down and check on Bella in between sites," he continued, breaking eye contact at last as he stooped to pick up his own gear. "But I got a text from Kenneth earlier telling me not to bother. He says he's 'got it under control.'"

"Sounds like if Bella plays her cards right, she might parlay her stay at the Doggie Hilton into something a little more permanent," Ri suggested.

"That's what I've been hoping, too. From what I understand, his last dog died a couple years ago. But before that, he always had at least one."

Ri stepped up beside Wolf, and they began walking again.

"Maddie told me that Kenneth lost his wife last year," she said. "If he's always had dogs, and now his wife's gone too, he must be feeling pretty alone. Bella could be just what he needs. And vice versa."

Wolf said nothing else. But as they walked, Ri could feel his eyes studying her again. And as they reached the next designated site and began to set up their equipment, it seemed that he hovered a bit more than before. Ri remained intent on her work. They didn't speak other than the data readings, and Wolf's manner remained professional. And yet, he did stand closer to her. So close that, once or twice, their arms brushed.

She wondered if he'd made up his mind.

# Chapter 18



*Anchorage, Alaska 1997*

Wolf knew something was wrong as soon as he stepped off the school bus and saw his dad's truck parked outside the duplex. His sneakers crunched in the dirty, day-old snow as he made his way to the front door. They'd been fighting lately, his dad and Shanna. He'd wake up at night and hear them through the wall. Whether the sounds were muted and tense or loud and angry didn't matter. Any kind of fighting made his gut ache.

Bear loved Shanna. Bear called Shanna "Mama" now. He'd called Tori his mom, too, but Tori wasn't around anymore. She'd left after Wolf started hearing those same kind of sounds coming through the wall at night.

Wolf opened the door and walked inside. His dad was slumped on the couch, his hand draped over his forehead.

Nels Markov pulled his hand away and sat up a little bit, then tried to smile at his son. The effort was pretty weak. "Well, hello there. How was your day?"

Wolf stared his dad down. He might only be eight years old, but he wasn't stupid. His dad was never home from work this early. "Where's Shanna?"

Nels sighed. His eyes were bloodshot and red-rimmed. "Listen," he said gently, "Wolfie—"

"Don't say it!" Wolf shouted, dropping his backpack on the floor with a thud. "She can't have left!" *Not her, too.*

His father said nothing. Just sat there looking miserable.

Wolf's vision got blurry. "No, Dad! Bear's gonna hurt so bad. You know he'll cry and cry and—"

Nels rose. "Wolfie, please listen. This isn't about you or Bear. Shanna cared about you very much. It's just that—"

"She did not!" Wolf argued, his voice beginning to crack as emotions long held in check exploded to the surface. "She didn't give a crap about us! None of them did! They all lied! They're all just a bunch of lying—"

"Wolf!" Nels took his son firmly by the arms. "That's not fair. I told you that Tori and Shanna were *not* replacing your mother. They were never moving in to stay. They were just here for a little while. I thought you understood—"

"I understand they *lie!*" Wolf screamed. "Bear called her *Mama*, Dad! You heard him!"

Nels let go of his son's arms. His lower jaw began to tremble. "I never should have allowed that. You're right."

"He'll be up every night again!" Wolf raged on. "Just like when Tori left!"

Nels looked away. He swiped at his eyes.

"Where is he?" Wolf demanded.

"In his room," Nels said quietly. Wolf took a step in that direction, but his father stopped him with a hand on the shoulder. "He's asleep, finally. At least he was. He... he didn't take it well. Please don't wake him."

Wolf couldn't imagine what else his father expected would happen. He glared at his dad resentfully and shook off the hand, but stopped walking. "Why do you always fight with them?" he asked accusingly.

Nels took a deep breath. "Son," he said quietly. "It's all very complicated. I can't explain it to you. But I'm sorry. I'm sorry I always seem to pick such... Well, what I mean is I'm sorry you guys have to suffer for my bad choices. I'm just sorry, period. It's my fault, son. Not yours. And not theirs, either. You're my boys, and you're my responsibility."

Wolf looked up into his father's watering eyes and saw a man whose spirit had been broken. His usually strong, gentle, happy father had been crushed, bruised, and humiliated. Again. Wolf had seen his father like this too many times. And every time had been because of a woman.

*Come on, Bear, honey!* Shanna had said just this morning as she got his brother ready for kindergarten. She had been a little gushy, now that Wolf thought about it. *I'll miss you, squirt,* she had told Wolf as she sent him out the door to the bus. She'd even given him a kiss on the top of the head. *You be good.* Then she'd turned back to Bear and hugged him tight. *Come on, love, let's not be late!*

And she had known then, Wolf thought to himself, his insides aching again. She'd known then that they would never see her again. Just like his mother, Shanna didn't even have the guts to say goodbye. At least Tori had said something. She'd said, "I can't live with your Daddy anymore. But I'll never forget you two. Be good, now. Have nice lives. Bye-bye!"

*Have a nice life. Bye-bye.*

Wolf stared back at his dad and words wouldn't come. He wanted to scream. He wanted to kick something. He wanted to yell and to curse and to pound. And more than anything, he wanted to haul off and just plain cry.

But third graders didn't do that.

"I won't wake him up," he said, his choking, gravelly voice barely understandable. He moved quickly towards the bedroom he shared with his brother, seeking nothing beyond the privacy of a dark place with covers he could hide his head under for a while.

Maybe, if he were lucky, he could stay there.

# Chapter 19



*Maui, Hawaii, 2016*

Wolf looked at the position of the sun in the sky. He couldn't believe they were done already. Ri was a data-collecting machine. She took to the equipment and the instruments like any technogeek and the hiking posed no problem for her, even when the terrain got steep. But what was most amazing was her willingness to do it all in virtual silence, speaking only when she needed to read out data or ask a question. Otherwise, they just listened to the birds.

Now it was barely midafternoon, they had finished everything he'd expected would take them until seven, and he was the one who was speechless.

"So," Ri said brightly as she adjusted her headband over her glorious curls. The grassy field in which they were standing was at a lower elevation on the mountain, and as the sun beamed down on them, beads of moisture welled up on her forehead. "I suppose we could start into tomorrow's work if you insist. But unless you think the other jobs will go slower for some reason, I'd prefer to stop now and plan for five shorter days, rather than finish a day early."

Wolf watched as a trickle of sweat ran down the side of her neck and disappeared under the collar of her shirt. The sight of her was driving him crazy. If he'd had any doubts before, working beside her all day had erased them. For a long list of reasons, not least of which was that she was both angelically pretty and unbelievably sexy at the same time, Ri Sullivan enticed him as much as any woman he had ever known. And whether he had the pleasure of her company for one day or twenty, there was no longer any question of his not making the most of it.

"If you're sure you can keep up this pace," he heard himself say in a voice far more calm and distant than what he was feeling, "then it doesn't matter to me. You'd like the truck this afternoon, then?"

Ri threw him a mischievous smile and nodded.

"Where will you go?" he asked, suddenly regretting his offer. Cooling his heels alone at the field station wasn't holding its usual appeal. He'd been trying to transmit his interest in her all afternoon, but he was attempting to be reasonably subtle about it. Their work arrangement was informal and he wasn't her boss, but still, it seemed boorish for him to make the first move, particularly on the job. If she was interested in more, it was on her to make that clear.

He hadn't thought it would take her so long. Perhaps he was misreading?

"I want to see that monk seal," Ri answered with determination. "I am *going* to see that monk seal if it's the last thing I do. I am going to see that monk seal if I have to camp out on the beach the whole rest of the summer waiting for it to come back."

Wolf chuckled at her. Given her chosen profession, such an obsession was understandable. He knew that Hawaiian monk seals were rare and highly endangered, and that most of them lived off the remote northwestern islands. But the waters of Maui happened to host one that routinely flopped onto Ho'okipa beach for a snooze. The seal's visits had become so routine that the county had put up a sign warning people not to harass him — never mind the fact that the unusual seal didn't seem at all bothered by the crowds of people and dogs that regularly stopped to gawk at him.

Wolf nodded at her, his mind teeming with images of Ri camping on a beach... with him. If only she were serious. He would crawl into a tent with her anywhere, anytime. "Good luck," he managed.

The angel face smiled at him guilelessly. "Want to come?"

His pulse picked up. This was all going splendidly. "Do I get to drive?" he asked.

"Oh, hell, no," she answered, still smiling.

Wolf laughed. "Will you buy me drinks at my favorite little place in Pa'ia?"

Ri shook her head. "Negatory. All you get is a chauffeured trip down the mountain." Her brown eyes held his with a twinkle. "And the pleasure of my sparkling personality."

Wolf suspected his eyes were twinkling back.

"Sold."

Ri could barely contain her enthusiasm. So many years she'd being dying to check "monk seal" off her marine mammal checklist, and there it was. A dozen feet away from her. Out like a light.

"She's so cute!" she gushed. The giant, tawny colored seal lay on its back on the sand, flippers up and flopping to the side, looking just as relaxed as the Sullivan's family dog, Dorie, used to look when napping on the couch with her paws in the air. The earless seal had a muzzle full of whiskers, a lighter-colored belly, and a streamlined but funny-shaped body that was plumpish in the middle and tapered at either end.

"Is it a she?" Wolf asked. "I always thought of it as a him."

He was leaning against the railing next to her, close enough for their arms to touch. They had changed from their warmer clothes into shorts and tee shirts, which for him had caused quite a transformation. Switching out his work boots for sandals had cost him points in the rugged department, but Ri decided that exposing more of his sexy calves made up for it. And the shorter sleeves enabled skin-to-skin contact on their arms, which was distracting even with a monk seal in the picture.

"Truthfully, I can't tell," Ri confessed. "But I choose to believe it's a girl. Oh, look! Her flipper moved!"

Wolf chuckled, but Ri made no effort to hide her enthusiasm. "This is my second new species in two days," she gushed. "I am *so* stoked."

They stood and watched the slumbering seal for a long while. Sometimes they chatted quietly, sometimes they didn't talk at all. Ri kept expecting Wolf to get bored and go for a walk on his own, but he seemed content. She asked him about the wildlife in Alaska, and he asked her about hiking and camping in Maine. Their arms were touching almost the entire time.

Ri didn't know if she would ever get tired of watching the furry pinniped, particularly when there were a dozen sea turtles roaming in and out of the water just a few paces down the beach. But the seal made the decision for her. With no warning, the giant animal suddenly lifted its head and swung its forebody around until it was upright. Then it trundled awkwardly the short distance across the sand, plunged into the breaking waves, and within seconds had disappeared from view.

"Come back," Ri called sadly.

Wolf chuckled at her again. "I'm sure you'll have other chances. Right now, what do you say we get something to eat? I'm starving."

Ri looked up. He had stepped away from her. "What's cheap?" she asked.

His brow creased. "Nothing. This is Maui. What exactly does your budget allow?"

She shrugged. "Probably enough to stop at a grocery store and buy a deli sandwich."

Wolf frowned. Ri watched the muscles in his jaw tighten, and she figured she had a pretty good idea what he was thinking. He wanted real food, and although he didn't mind helping her pay for hers, he was uncertain how the gesture would be taken. If he paid for her meal, would that make it a date? If they made it a date, would that screw up their work arrangement?

"However," she continued, thinking fast. "I am allowing myself one meal out a week. I can do that tonight, I'll just have to eat in all weekend. Tell me what you have in mind and I'll see if I'm tempted. Because you look like you have something in mind."

He grinned at her. "I do. I'm just afraid to say it."

"Say what?" she wondered.

"Well, you see, there's this little place in Pa'ia that I just *love*."

Ri cracked up laughing. A few minutes later she found herself back in the exact same restaurant she'd spent the miserable evening before.

This evening, however, she was not at all miserable. They settled down at a wooden pub table in the quirky little cafe, and she ordered the duck salad she had wanted last night while Wolf requested the hot fish and chips he'd been craving. The food did not disappoint, and being seated across a table from Wolf gave Ri the perfect opportunity to run through a few more of her non-threatening conversation starters. She asked more about his research and where he'd gone to college, and he asked her the same. The conversation drifted to where she could comfortably ask about his brother and what Bear was doing now, and he asked her about Mei Lin. Somehow they got off on the topic of dangerous animals and argued about whether a walrus was inherently more likely to attack a human — when threatened — than was a moose. They did not settle the issue, but as Wolf tried to illustrate his point by telling the story of a friend who had been forced to flee screaming in his underwear from an irate female moose after he stumbled onto a calf in the bushes while taking a leak in the middle of the night, Ri laughed so hard she nearly rolled off her chair and under the table.

Neither one of them ordered any alcohol, but by the time they left the restaurant, Ri was flying high. She had been attracted to Wolf from that first glimpse of him in the fog. But what she was feeling now went far beyond the physical. Maybe it was his quiet intelligence, coupled with his dry sense of humor. Maybe it was some of the other desirable traits she suspected he had, but couldn't quite prove yet, because he kept so much of himself hidden. Maybe she just liked the mystery of him. Whatever it was, she couldn't remember enjoying any man's company more.

They left the cafe and strolled the streets of Pa'ia. It was a touristy little town on Maui's north central side, the last commercial outpost before one began the long, winding drive to Hana along the cliffs on the northeast edge of the island. They walked aimlessly as Ri window-shopped and people-watched in turn. The little town gave new meaning to the term "local color," with its bizarre mishmash of everything from dumpy bars to upscale art boutiques and everybody from shoeless surfers to women wearing diamonds and dogs riding motorcycles.

Ri laughed some more as Wolf gave an amusing account of the culture shock he'd experienced when he first arrived from Alaska. Though he would never be a chatterbox, she felt gratified that he seemed relaxed enough with her now to share a little more about himself.

Yet still, he made no move.

The sun began to set, and although Ri wished they could catch the spectacle from up on the mountain, she could hardly regret being where she was. The colors in the sky were still surreal — a little too purple to be normal, thanks to the vog — and she was thoroughly enjoying their long, lazy walk in the balmy air. As they fell back into another comfortable silence, she found herself glancing at him surreptitiously, wondering what he was thinking.

He was attracted to her, yet he was clearly restraining himself. Why? Ri assumed the most likely stumbling block for him would be concern over dating a co-worker, or any woman who lived at the Hilton. Technically, she was both, but neither reason was good enough. Ri could take care of that.

The second possibility was trickier. What if he was looking at the amount of time available to them and thinking, "what's the point?" Most men would be fine with a short-term fling, of course, but she was betting Wolf wasn't like that. Everything about him implied a man who was steady and solid. A man who appreciated things that lasted.

Obviously, he didn't know her well. If he did, he would know that when Sriha Mirini Sullivan pursued a dream, she did not let mere circumstances get in her way. The perfect internship, the perfect grad school, the perfect career. All in good order, with patience and time. If she had to leave her family and fly thousands of miles and eat ramen noodles for four months to get the internship her heart desired, then that's what she would do. Wherever she had to work to save money for grad school — to get the degree that would make her ultimate dream job possible down the road — she would do that, too.

She felt the same way about the perfect relationship. There were no perfect people and there was no perfect guy; she was certainly not perfect herself. But if she ever found a man with whom she was convinced she could share her life — a life that would be filled with as much love and laughter as her parents enjoyed... Well, there would be no stopping her. She would move heaven and earth to make that happen.

Whether Wolf was perfect for her remained to be seen. But until she ruled that out, the door between them would stay open. And no little thing like the Pacific Ocean was going to close it. Not on her end, anyway.

"Is there anywhere else you want to drive tonight?" Wolf asked lightly.

Ri considered. Could she counter the man's stumbling blocks — or at least her best guesses at them — without flipping him out? She had to try. Time was slipping away, and he looked entirely too delicious in that athletic-fitting tee.

They reached the truck. "Let's head back up the mountain before it gets any darker," Ri suggested. "I'd like to catch as much of the sunset as we can. Then maybe you can show me wherever it is you like to go camping up there."

His eyebrows lifted in surprise. "Hosmer Grove? It'll be dark by then."

They got in and buckled up. Ri looked out the window in the direction of Haleakala. "Is it spooky in the dark and the fog?" she asked.

Wolf grinned at her. "It's... atmospheric."

Ri started up the truck with a smirk. "Perfect."

Brilliant purples, oranges, and reds mixed, shifted, and lingered over the horizon as Ri drove the truck uphill. They fell quiet again, enjoying the view, as the sky slowly darkened. All the while, Ri planned how she might explain herself, deciding to impart the necessary information in reverse order. If Wolf didn't connect the dots immediately, he'd be better off. She was a big believer in honesty, but when you were as prone to elaborate fantasy as she was, there were parts of your brain fruit you really should keep to yourself.

"I've heard people from home say they wouldn't like living

in Hawaii because they'd miss the changing of the seasons too much," she mused. "I can see that. Spring and fall in Maine are truly amazing. They're explosions of color, and the change in weather is refreshing. But people don't realize you can go from summer to fall just by driving an hour up Haleakala, either!"

Wolf chuckled. "True enough. I liked working closer to sea level in the winter when it was in the seventies, but now that it's in the eighties every day, it gets to me. If I were going to stay here, I'd rather live higher up on the mountain."

"I'd live anywhere on the islands if I could afford it," Ri slipped in smoothly. "I was hoping to find some kind of job here after the summer ended. But now, that's not looking too realistic. I need to save enough in the next year to cap off the grad school fund."

She could feel Wolf's eyes on her. "You're not going back to Maine?" he asked.

She shook her head. "My plan is to start grad school a year from this fall. But until then, I'm a free agent. I'll go wherever the winds take me. Assuming the winds take me someplace I can work in the field and still save enough money without starving to death."

"Want it all, do you?" he asked facetiously.

Ri grinned. "I strive for perfection."

"Well, best of luck to you," he said. "I admire your chutzpah."

Ri fought back a queer sense of disappointment. If he hadn't said that in his alluring husky whisper, it would almost have seemed dismissive. Perhaps she was imagining it.

"What about you?" she asked. "Do you picture yourself living in Alaska for the rest of your life?"

He was quiet for a moment. "Not necessarily," he answered, his tone somewhat wistful. "I'm happy there. But I'd like to travel. I'd like to work on different volcanoes around the world."

He went silent again, and Ri asked nothing more. So far, so good. She had parried potential stumbling block number two, and it was the hardest. Getting rid of number one was child's play; she just had to wait a while.

She slowed the truck down as they entered a thick patch of fog. They were up into the cloud zone now. The sky was totally dark, and cottony white wisps floated across the road before her headlights, alternately hiding and revealing close outcroppings of black rock mere feet from the truck's bumpers.

A hole in the fog opened suddenly, and a tall tree sprang up from an otherwise barren knoll right before them — a scraggly evergreen shaped like a candelabra. "This is so eerie," Ri enthused, having to restrain herself from slamming on the brake. She half expected the Phantom of the Opera to show up next, plunking away on an organ carved out of the black rock. "I love it."

Wolf chuckled at her again. "Then you're really going to love Hosmer Grove."

Ri slid her eyes toward him with a smirk.

She would indeed.

# Chapter 20



*Acadia National Park, Maine, Labor Day, 1995*

"They're all playing so well together, aren't they?" Julie Sullivan heard her older sister say. Julie replied by making a shushing sound and rapping her knuckles on the wooden bench seat.

Karen laughed and sat down beside her. "Oh, don't give me that. As far as I'm concerned, you're a miracle worker. I still can't believe how far Ri's come. And now, seeing the two of them... My God, Jules. We all thought you were crazy, adopting again. You know that, don't you?"

Julie looked at the half-dozen young children, all related through her extended family, that were buzzing happily around the playground by the picnic pavilion. Her eyes focused, as always, on the two little girls who were her heart and soul. She smiled to herself. "Oh, I know," she said wryly.

"Well, you *were* crazy," Karen insisted. "We couldn't imagine you putting yourself through everything you went through with Ri all over again. And even if a second one was easier, it seemed like bringing another child into the family was sure to upset the apple cart. Ri had gotten so clingy with you — we were all sure she'd go mad with jealousy."

Julie kept smiling. Her big sister had never been one to reserve her opinions, but at least she admitted when she was wrong. In this case, Julie couldn't fault Karen's logic. Julie and Tom had taken an incredible risk in adopting Mei Lin, with the statistics weighted so heavily against smooth sailing. Yet here they were, six months later, and Julie had never been happier.

She felt she could take no credit for that. Sometimes, you just got lucky.

Ri picked something out of the rubber mulch and carried it hurriedly toward the bench. "Mommy," she announced, laying the wrapper from a package of cheese crackers on Julie's lap.

"This is trash. You should throw it away so Taylor doesn't choke on it."

Julie fought back a laugh. "I will do that. Thank you, Ri."

The child scuttled back to the others. "She speaks so well for her age," Karen praised. "Mom and I were just talking about that. So clearly, and what a vocabulary! I know she's four. But when she looks no more than two and a half..."

"I know," Julie agreed with a chuckle. "It freaks people out."

They watched as Ri returned to the play area, where a second little girl stood waiting for her. The two were almost the same height, but Mei Lin was rounder and chubbier. The younger sister's dark, straight hair was pulled into a pony tail with a pink ribbon, and her face was bright with a smile of relief. The second Ri stepped back into the mulch, Mei Lin dove forward and enveloped her sister in a bear hug.

"Oh my," Karen gushed, her hands flying to her mouth. "I can't believe Ri lets her do that!"

They watched as Ri clasped Mei Lin back, briefly, then set her aside in order to return to the important business of rearranging X's and O's on the giant flip board.

"We can't believe it, either," Julie admitted. "It took so long to get her to accept any kind of affectionate touch. But now she laps it up, as long as she trusts whoever it's coming from. And with Mei Lin... Well, it's funny, Karen. There was something between those two girls from the very beginning. Mei Lin is such a loving soul, you can feel warmth just radiating from her. I believe it's simply who she is. And somehow, Ri sensed that. She's never seemed to feel threatened by Mei Lin. The jealousy we expected just isn't there. They do squabble sometimes, but with Ri it's more a matter of control, and Mei Lin always gives in eventually, so that takes care of itself."

"Interesting," Karen remarked. "I wonder what will happen when Mei Lin realizes that even though she's a year younger, she'll probably always be bigger than Ri?"

Julie laughed and pointed at the playset. "You seriously think that will make a difference?"

Ri and her cousin Daniel, who was six years old, were

having a disagreement over the placement of the X's. Ri was standing with her hands on her little hips, scolding him. Daniel jumped off the platform and walked away.

Karen lifted an eyebrow. "Better keep an eye on that one, sis."

"Oh, don't worry," Julie laughed. "At least we've got the hitting stopped, thank God. She hasn't socked any kid in the face for almost a year. Now *that* was scary. What child does that? I mean, with preschoolers, I can see kicking or biting or even punching in the stomach or something, but seriously... what drives such an otherwise sweet little slip of a girl to ball up her fist and swing like Muhammed Ali?"

Karen cracked up. "It is pretty funny."

"Not when you're living it, it's not!" Julie retorted. "I used to have nightmares of her being arrested for assault as an elementary schooler. Anyway, she's over it now. She can be moody, and she still has occasional 'rages,' so to speak, but they're much less frequent, and she's learned how to channel her anger better. And her bad dreams are much less frequent, too. I'm really starting to believe that by the time she's an adult, those awful memories of her first months of life will stop haunting her. They'll always be in her subconscious, of course. She may always be 'hypervigilant,' when it comes to protecting herself. But she's showing real empathy, now. And she knows how to love, and to be loved."

"Like I said," Karen repeated, smiling indulgently. "You're a miracle worker."

"No," Julie insisted, shaking her head. "It wasn't us, much less just me. We adopted her at a young enough age, and we knew what we were dealing with and were able to get help quickly. Children adopted at older ages can have much more serious problems. And so many parents aren't told what to expect and then either don't know how to get the right help or can't afford it. Plus, some children are just naturally more resilient than others, for reasons no one understands. Every child is different. Tom and I were blessed, plain and simple. *Twice.*"

They watched as Ri tired of the tic-tac-toe board and came

down to join Mei Lin and their younger cousin Taylor, who were making roads in the rubber mulch and driving large plastic trucks along the trails.

"Ri does still have some social problems," Julie continued. "She tends to isolate herself. She doesn't like meeting new people, and her preschool teacher says it seems hard for her to make friends."

"I'm sure that's just a matter of time, like everything else," Karen assured. "Remember how long it took for her to bond with you, and now look at her! It shouldn't be any surprise if she's slow to make other friends; sometimes the kids who are closest to their parents are like that. She's probably just an introvert by nature. Good Lord, my Katie hung on my legs and wouldn't say 'boo!' to a goose until kindergarten!"

Mei Lin came running up. She barreled straight into Julie's knees and fell forward into her mother's lap, giggling. "What's up, love?" Julie asked, hugging her.

Mei Lin said nothing; she merely kept on giggling. She rolled around in Julie's lap a moment, smiled at her aunt, then bounded off again.

"She's such a dear," Karen gushed. "She certainly doesn't seem to have any bonding problems."

Julie shook her head. "Not really, no. But she was never in an orphanage. We're watching her for PTSD because she's suffered so much loss and so many abrupt changes, but so far she seems amazingly resilient. Being with her biological family the first two years of her life made all the difference, I think. Her birth family must have been very loving. Her foster family, too."

Julie's voice cracked a little. She didn't like to think of what Mei Lin had gone through. The agency had explained that Mei Lin's parents, who lived in a remote, rural region of China, had been essentially destitute when they had been killed together in a bus accident. An older brother had been taken in by extended family. Two-year-old Mei Lin had been surrendered to the state.

Mei Lin scampered over to pick up a truck and started moving it along a road next to her cousin Taylor. Ri pointed to a different road, and Mei Lin obediently moved her truck to that one.

"Uh-oh," Karen said ominously, making Julie look up. "Here comes trouble."

Their younger brother's two hellion sons, Tad and Kade, were running over from the pavilion. Julie sighed. Her brother had been divorced for years and hadn't disciplined his kids when he was married. Now their time with Dad was a free-for-all.

The women tensed. At seven and nine years old the boys weren't evil, but they delighted in pushing hot buttons — like dropping F-bombs around "uptight" people and making fart sounds during large group prayers. Aside from irritating adults, they easily made themselves unpopular with their cousins, too.

"Tad and Kade!" called out Taylor's mother, who was sitting on a bench on the opposite side of the playground, nursing a newborn. "You behave yourselves over here!"

The boys looked over at their aunt briefly, dismissively, as if they had no idea who she was. Then they strolled up to the children playing with the trucks.

Julie watched, unsurprised, as Ri immediately withdrew from the boys' vicinity. Ri took a long time to warm up to other children. She rarely saw these two cousins and hence took no interest in them. Kade, the nine year old, watched the trucks moving along the roads for all of about five seconds. Then he reached down and snatched Mei Lin's truck from her hands.

"Oh, no," Julie sighed, preparing to intercede.

Mei Lin jumped up and held out her arms to the boy. She wanted her truck back. The boy moved it out of her reach, and Mei Lin made a jump for it.

"Kade!" Julie called evenly. "Mei Lin was playing with that truck first."

The boy completely ignored Julie. Seeing that Mei Lin was far too short to reach the truck when he held it high, he lowered it just enough to give her a sporting chance. Mei Lin made another jump, this time grabbing onto it fast and managing to hook her elbow around it. Unprepared for such an effective attack, Kade responded by pressing his palm square in the middle of Mei Lin's face and shoving her off the truck and onto the ground.

Mei Lin fell flat on her back and burst into tears, and Julie started running. But Julie didn't get there first. She was still a good ten feet away when a miniature whirlwind of frizzy dark curls and red polka dots suddenly appeared between the figure lying on the ground and the boy looming above. Before Julie even had time to shout, a tiny tan fist smashed into the third grader's slack-hanging jaw.

# Chapter 21



"Welcome to Hosmer Grove," Wolf announced with amusement. "What do you think?"

Ri looked through the windshield of the parked truck. Beyond the end of the bumper she could see maybe six feet of soggy grass at the edge of the parking lot. Everything else was completely obscured by fog. "It exceeds my wildest expectations," she answered, reaching for the door handle. "Let's go."

Wolf laughed. "Go where, exactly?"

Ri popped open the door. "Well, how should I know? You're the tour guide, aren't you?"

He stared at her a moment. Then he opened the glove compartment, pulled out a flashlight, and got out of the truck.

Ri reached back into the cab and turned out the headlights. Blackness surrounded her so suddenly she froze in surprise. "Wow," she said, feeling foolish. "I'm not used to this much darkness."

"Most people aren't," Wolf said, his voice startling her as it moved quickly to her side of the truck. "Most places, there's always light coming from somewhere. But Haleakala's known for its dark skies. That's why the summit's so good for stargazing. Not this particular campground, so much. Most of the time, it looks exactly like it does right now."

Wolf sounded like he was standing only three feet away, but Ri couldn't see his face. "I don't suppose you could turn that flashlight on?" she asked.

He lit it up, directly under his chin and aiming skyward, illuminating his disembodied head like something out of a horror movie.

Ri laughed. Ah, so he *could* be goofy. She knew it! But if he thought he could frighten her into a scream that easily, he had a great deal more to learn about her.

He frowned at her in disappointment. "Tough crowd. All right, um... you really want a tour?"

"Absolutely."

"Follow me, then."

He shone the flashlight on the ground and walked ahead of Ri along the edge of the parking lot. "I could feel my way around here with a bag over my head," he told her. "So if the flashlight dies, I'll be fine. But if the flashlight and I both fall into a sinkhole or something, just follow the curb around the edge of the parking lot till you get back to the truck. We're not going far."

"Aw, darn," Ri lamented.

Wolf chuckled at her. "Why do I get the feeling that back in Maine you had a thing for haunted houses and abandoned graveyards? I can just see you running around ghost hunting as a teenager. I bet you used to scare Mei Lin and make her scream her head off."

A bolt of warmth shot through her Ri's chest. How could he know that? "I would never intentionally terrorize my sister," she clarified. "Mei Lin wasn't really scared. She just liked getting the guys' attention."

Wolf turned and shone the light around. He seemed to want to see her face, but what he was looking for, she couldn't imagine. His own face was behind the light.

He moved the beam to the side and swept it out over the campground. "This is where I usually pitch my tent," he explained. There were no tents in view, but they could only see a few yards in any direction. "It's not usually crowded out here this time of year, not midweek, anyway. But there could be tents farther out tonight and we'd never know."

Ri could see that. Somebody could be laying in a sleeping bag out there right now, listening to every word they said.

Wolf continued to lead her along the curb until they turned a corner where the grass ended and a thicket of brush and trees began. The curb disappeared, replaced with a series of square wooden posts, and Ri found herself on a trailhead. "We'll just go a little ways into the grove where the trail is obvious," Wolf told her. "I have a feeling you may like the ambience."

Ri could tell from the sound of his voice that he was smiling. And she suspected that he was right. She followed the flashlight beam and his sandaled feet as they moved along the trail, which quickly turned from paved to mulched as it headed downhill and back up again. Just as Wolf reached a stopping point and turned around, Ri noticed something odd.

"That smell!" she cried. "Am I crazy or does it smell like mint?"

"Peppermint," Wolf replied. "Peppermint eucalyptus, to be exact. You're standing in a eucalyptus grove." He shone the flashlight up in the air, and Ri was shocked to see giant tree trunks towering all around them. They were so tall that in the wispy denseness of the fog, she could not even see their tops! She hadn't seen trees so large anywhere else on Haleakala.

"A guy named Hosmer planted them here in the twenties," Wolf explained. "The trees aren't native species for Hawaii, though, and if you want to know how well that worked out from an environmental perspective, you can ask Maddie. But I wouldn't recommend it unless you've got at least an hour to kill. As an ecologist she has strong opinions on the subject."

Ri could imagine. But at the moment, her interests lay elsewhere. "Can I borrow the flashlight?" She allowed her teeth to rattle. They were both still wearing shorts and sandals, and the temperature had dropped dramatically since they'd left both sun and sea level behind.

Wolf handed her the light. The ground around her feet was largely bare of vegetation under the canopy overhead. The tree trunks were broad and stark. They were several feet across at eye level, with pale, vertically grooved bark. She shone the flashlight upward, but could see few horizontal limbs branching out, just the straight, solid trunks standing like soldiers in the choking fog. The only noises she could hear were occasional bird calls in the distance.

It was spooky as hell.

"I'm feeling like I want to turn the light off," she admitted in a whisper.

Wolf laughed. It was a warm, husky, indulgent laugh, and it

sent a little shock wave of anticipation up Ri's spine. It was dark and creepy and spooky and cold. She wanted the man's arms around her.

She shifted the light to see that he had moved to lean against a tree trunk a few feet away. His arms were crossed casually across his chest. "Suit yourself," he said.

Ri switched off the light. Darkness fell like a blanket. She feared that with all her exposed skin she would be eaten alive by bugs, but she disciplined herself not to move. She listened for the sound of Wolf's breathing, and for the tiniest rubbing or scratching sound that would indicate he was shifting position against the tree. He'd tried to scare her once already. There was no way he'd be able to resist. Any second now... *aha!*

Wolf's fingers flew out of the darkness to snatch briefly at Ri's waist.

She laughed.

"Oh, come on!" he complained loudly, standing close. "That's not human!"

Ri laughed harder. She took a step back from him, then turned on the flashlight. He watched her, smiling and yet clearly baffled, as she moved around, scouting for something on the forest floor. She leaned down and picked up a thick stick about two feet long. Then she smiled at him and turned the light off again.

"Ri?" he asked after a moment. "What are you doing?"

She giggled.

"You know," he said dryly, "when a girl picks up a club, gives you a dirty look, and then turns out the light, a guy could get paranoid."

Ri staunched any more laughter. With careful precision, she leaned down and quietly lofted the stick so that it would land on the ground about three feet to Wolf's right. Just as the stick landed and he pivoted toward the sound, Ri leapt nimbly to his opposite side and clutched his waist from behind.

"Gah!" he bellowed, jumping in his tracks.

Ri doubled over in hysterics.

"You are evil!" Wolf reprimanded, spinning around. He wrested the flashlight from her grip, then threw an arm around her waist and pulled her toward him.

The darkness was still complete. Ri could see nothing. They were standing toe to toe, with his left hand holding her around the waist. His other arm was also behind her back, his elbow holding her close, his splinted hand presumably still holding the flashlight somehow. She lifted her own arms over his shoulders. He felt so solid. So warm. So steady. She wanted him to kiss her, but just as much she longed to bury her head in his shoulder and simply be held. She wanted to be close enough to him emotionally that doing so would make her feel safe and comforted and blissfully secure. She and Wolf didn't have that yet. She'd never had it with a man. It was part of the dream.

Nothing happened. Seconds ticked by.

Ri began to curse the darkness. She couldn't see his eyes. She couldn't tell what he was thinking.

But he really should be kissing her by now.

"If you're thinking of me as a co-worker," she said quietly, "don't. I consider my work to be more of a barter arrangement. And as for my staying at the Hilton, I'm really just a temporary guest, not a renter." She cleared her throat. "Just saying."

She could hear him huff out a breath. Their faces were very close.

"She's evil, and she can read my mind," he said in a throaty whisper. "Now *that* should scare me."

But apparently it did not. Because in the next moment, those warm, tantalizingly kissable lips of his pressed over hers.

She heard a thud as he dropped the flashlight.


Sometime later, it occurred to Wolf that his toes were numb with cold. The fact was of no great concern to him; in his line of work, anything short of amputation-risking frostbite was a mere nuisance. But he remembered that Ri was also wearing sandals, and that her lovely lightweight, scooped-neck top and boy shorts were doubtless leaving her more vulnerable to the plummeting temperature than he was. He should stop this now and get them back to someplace warmer. He needed to explain things to her, anyway, before...

Wolf lost his train of thought. He regained it only after a breeze blowing through the grove drew a fresh crop of goosebumps on Ri's wonderfully soft, previously smooth upper arms.

"You're cold," he said, drawing back sharply, albeit reluctantly. It was the only way he could let go of her at all. He rubbed his good hand briskly over her arm a moment to warm her. "Actually, I'm cold, too. I've just been ignoring it. We'd better go." He released her and looked around him in the dark. Something was missing.

Oh, right. The flashlight.

He stooped down and felt around on the ground. He shouldn't have dropped the thing. Then again, he thought with a smile, he'd needed that hand.

He heard what sounded like a muted giggle coming from Ri. Then she joined him in feeling around for the flashlight. Three seconds later, he was nearly blinded. "Stop that!" he chided, reaching out and taking the flashlight away from her again. "I'll be seeing spots for an hour."

"I'm sorry," Ri said, sounding genuine even as she laughed. "I really am. I didn't know where you were exactly."

Wolf turned the beam onto the trail in front of his feet. He really did have spots in front of his eyes. "Right," he said sarcastically. "Follow me."

"Wait," Ri said, reaching out and touching his arm.

Wolf stopped and turned. She sounded upset.

"I really didn't mean to shine the light in your eyes," she said, her voice serious. "Do you believe me?"

Wolf moved the beam so that he could make out her expression. What a puzzle she was. So deliciously mischievous and fun loving... yet when she spoke plainly, there was no guile in her. Her large, dark eyes showed genuine concern. "Yes, of course," he answered truthfully.

Ri's face brightened. She dropped her hand and started walking again. Wolf picked up his own pace, lest the vixen actually pass him on the trail, and they soon found themselves back at the truck.

The fog hadn't let up in the slightest, but it did seem at least five degrees colder than when they'd arrived. They got in the truck and Ri started the ignition, but when she began to put the truck into gear, Wolf stopped her with a hand and shut off the headlights instead. Then he turned on the dome lights, cranked up the heater, and relaxed in his seat. "Let's just warm up here a minute," he suggested.

Ri didn't argue. Instead she kicked off her sandals, twisted her knees, and tucked her bare feet up underneath her. She had cute little feet. And sexy legs. Everything about her was cute and sexy. She scooted closer to him.

Wolf's teeth clenched. It was time again. Time for the talk. The talk he hated, but could not avoid. It was the only way to manage things, to keep things honest. He wasn't a teenager and he didn't play games.

Ri held her hands over the heating vents. She had lovely fingers. Short nails, no polish. Earthy and practical, perfect for a woman who worked with fish and muck, he thought with amusement. A real woman.

A woman who deserved honesty.

"Ri," he began, leaving himself no room to procrastinate, "there's something we need to talk about."

Her brown eyes looked up at him with surprise. He supposed she didn't consider him much of a talker. That was fair enough. "You know I'm not going to be on Maui much longer," he said softly. "A week and a half, maybe. Two weeks, max."

Ri's eyes studied his keenly. "I'm aware."

Wolf had no idea what she was thinking. Hopefully she was thinking that this horribly awkward conversation was unnecessary.

"I don't want to make a big deal out of nothing," he threw in optimistically. "But I also don't like misunderstandings." Almost involuntarily, he reached out his left hand and laid it on Ri's perfect, satiny smooth shoulder. His fingers toyed with her soft, bouncy curls while she watched him, motionless and curious.

He wanted her. He wanted to pick up right where they left off, but his saying what he had to say often killed the mood, at least for a little while.

His fingers moved to trace her angular cheekbone, her perfectly curved jawline...

*Dammit.*

He dropped his hand. "Ri," he said quickly. "It's like this. I'm a solitary kind of guy, and I plan to stay that way. I like you very much, but I don't do relationships. When I get involved, it's... casual, and its temporary, and that's understood."

God, how he hated this. Ri's eyes were wide, but her expression was inscrutable.

"I don't want to hurt anybody," he said more gently. "That's why I'm saying all this now. I'm just trying to be honest with you."

Still, she said nothing. Her face didn't change. She didn't move.

He swallowed and shifted in his seat. "I enjoy your company tremendously," he said with a smile, trying to finish things on an upbeat. "And I think you're incredibly, amazingly sexy. But with me, it's no strings or nothing." He let out a final breath of relief. *There.* He had said it. He was relieved of all moral responsibility. The ball was in her court.

She made no response. After an awkward second, he broke eye contact and gazed out the front windshield.

Ri let out what sounded like a gulp. Wolf looked back to find her staring out the side window. Her face was thoughtful; her eyes no longer wide, but narrowed in contemplation. Even when she was in such a tense posture, he found his gaze lingering over her with fascination. The way her curls drifted over the curve of her shoulders, the profile of her adorable nose, her pert chin, those full, sensuous lips...

"Ri?" he exclaimed without thinking. He couldn't stand not touching her anymore. He needed her answer.

She jumped in her seat a little, startled. Her eyes met his again, and she gazed at him for a long moment, seeming to plumb some depths of his soul so deep and dark that he didn't know he had them. He wanted to ask her what she was thinking, what she was seeing, but he felt like he had no right. He had already asked her a question, and her answer was still hanging out there.

Finally, her face warmed into a smile. It was a small, sad smile, but a smile nevertheless. Wolf's heart leapt as she reached up a hand toward him. She ran her fingertips lightly, tenderly along his bearded jawbone, and her touch ignited him like a lightning bolt. She would accept him with no strings.

"If those are my choices," she said softly, sweetly. "I choose nothing."

# Chapter 22



*Anchorage, Alaska, 2000*

Wolf wasn't sure what had woken him up until he heard it a second time. A short wail, following by a kind of a choking sound. He glanced over at his brother, but knew that an eight-year-old couldn't make his voice that deep, even if he wanted to. Besides, Bear was sound asleep. Wolf looked at the clock on their dresser. It was 2:05 AM.

Wolf swung his feet out of bed and sat up. It had to be his dad making that noise. He walked to the door of his bedroom, opened it as quietly as he could, and walked around the corner into the main room. His father was slumped on the couch, listing to one side. His face was buried in his hands. He was sobbing.

Wolf stood frozen for a moment, staring. Never in his life had he seen his dad cry. He'd seen his eyes get wet once or twice, but this was something different. The man was blubbering like a baby.

Wolf didn't know what to say. He didn't know what to do. All he could think was that the worst thing in the world must have happened. But he couldn't imagine what that might be. His dad looked okay — he didn't look hurt. Wolf knew that Bear was fine, and they'd just talked to their grandpa on the phone a few hours ago. Their dog, Chaga, was lying by his dad's feet, and she looked okay, too. That pretty much covered what mattered most in the world to Wolf. So what was the problem?

"Dad?" he asked finally, tentatively.

Nels Markov shot up off the couch as if he'd been struck. He turned away from his son and wiped his face hastily with his hands, then strode into the kitchen and finished the job with a splash in the sink and a dish towel.

Wolf followed. "Are you okay?"

"Yeah," Nels forced out unconvincingly, his voice full of gravel. He cleared his throat. "Sorry if I woke you up. Everything's fine. You go on back to bed, now."

Wolf stood where he was, staring back at his father. He smelled that smell again. Flowery. He wanted to say grape, but he knew that wasn't a flower. He didn't know flowers. He just knew that when his dad went out on the weekends, he usually came back smelling like that.

Wolf wasn't stupid. He knew his dad had been seeing a woman again. The signs were pretty obvious, at least to him. Bear never caught on, but that was a good thing. And Nels never brought the women home anymore, which Wolf was glad about. He thought his dad was being smart. The three of them got along just fine without a woman in the house.

His dad did still hire a babysitter when he went out late, though, which was a bone of contention between them. Wolf was eleven years old now, in middle school, and he didn't need a babysitter. He could take care of Bear just fine by himself. He'd been doing it for years already. But if nothing else, the regular appearance of babysitters on the weekends was a sure signal that his dad was shacking up again. And this time, Wolf knew who he was doing it with.

"Is this about Ms. French?" he asked with contempt. Until this minute, he'd had nothing against the woman. But he was beginning to think this was all her fault, and "this" was seriously embarrassing. Real men didn't *cry*.

Nels' eyes widened in shock. "How the—" He shook his head and cut himself off. "Never mind. Sit down, son." He put a hand on Wolf's shoulder and steered him to a seat at the kitchen table. They both sat down, stiffly. Nels rubbed his face in his hands again, then let out a long, frustrated sigh.

"I saw your truck parked near her house once," Wolf answered the unspoken question. "And I saw the two of you talking at the art show. I'm not dumb." The evidence was admittedly scant. The truck was actually parked one house down from where Bear's favorite teacher lived, which was hardly a smoking gun. And the couple hadn't been doing anything at the elementary school art show except talking. But

Wolf figured he had an eye for these things. Whenever his dad had a thing for a woman, he started acting all chipper and giddy and weird. And then a few months later, he'd go through the crash. He'd be all mopey and glum and tired, and he would swear up and down that absolutely nothing was wrong with him. And then it would start all over again.

Wolf loved his dad more than anything. But when it came to women, the man was nuts.

"I know you're not 'dumb.'" Nels replied. "Far from it, Wolfie. I just don't think my social life needs to be any concern of you and your brother, that's all."

"No," Wolf agreed. "Unless..." He felt awkward. "Well, unless it's waking me up in the middle of the night."

Nels sighed again. "I'm sorry about that. I'm fine, son. Really. You don't need to worry about me."

But Wolf did worry. He didn't understand his father at all. "So... are you still seeing Ms. French?"

His father's eyes started to look watery again. "No," he said softly. So softly, Wolf could barely hear him. "That's over."

"I see," Wolf replied. He felt very grown-up having this conversation about women with his father. But he still didn't "see" anything. "Why do you keep doing it, Dad?" he asked finally. "Why do you keep falling for these women, and getting yourself all wound up, when you know that every time it ends up like... well, like this?"

His father stared at him. Then, to Wolf's surprise, he chuckled. "That's a very good question."

Wolf was encouraged. Maybe he could straighten the man out, after all. "I mean," Wolf said, sitting up straighter in his chair, "I get that you want women. But why can't you just have sex with them and let that be the end of it?"

Nels froze in place with his hands halfway between his face and the table. First he stared at his son with a flabbergasted expression. Then he rose swiftly and turned away. But before he turned away, Wolf was pretty sure he caught his dad fighting back a laugh, which did not seem at all appropriate.

"Wolfie," Nels said, turning back a moment later with a perfectly straight face. "There is much, much more to life, and to women, than just sex. Now go to bed. It's late."

Wolf frowned. Just when he thought they were getting somewhere, man to man, he was being dismissed. Like he was a kid again.

He scooted his chair back with a scowl, saying nothing. He supposed he should be pleased with himself. At least his father wasn't bawling anymore. But the victory didn't feel good. Somehow, Wolf got the idea that he was being made fun of.

"Goodnight, son," Nels said gently. "Thanks for getting up to check on me."

Wolf felt better. Slightly. He nodded at his dad. "Night." He turned and walked back to his bedroom, feeling every bit as confused as when he'd left it. His dad would always be a puzzle to him. Nels was a mechanical engineer. He was a smart guy, a really smart guy. But when it came to women, he sure acted dumb.

# Chapter 23



"Hi, Mom," Ri said tentatively, speaking into her laptop. "You're sure it's not too late to talk? You look tired."

She watched as her mother frowned into the webcam. "I'm old. I always look this way." Julie readjusted her own laptop so that the camera showed the back of a couch and part of a wall.

"Don't do that," Ri admonished. "You look fine. I just didn't want to keep you up. I know it's late there."

"Are you calling me from inside a truck?"

Ri sighed. She felt ridiculous lugging her laptop outside and balancing it on her lap in the truck's passenger seat, but she couldn't bring herself to have an honest conversation in her room when she knew that she could be overheard from the hallway. The irony of the fact that she was having this conversation in Wolf's truck was not lost on her, but she had his keys, and she'd earned them, so she didn't care. She was just glad the Hilton's wireless carried this far into the parking lot.

"Long story," Ri replied. "But yes."

"What's wrong?"

Ri collected herself for a moment. There was no fooling her psychotherapist mother in a face to face — or even a couch to face — conversation. She'd given up trying a very long time ago. "When was the last time I told you I really, seriously, almost-sorta came close to planting somebody a facer?" she asked.

The picture on the monitor swung back to her mother's head and shoulders. Julie was wearing a fuzzy robe, her hair was a fright, and her brow was furrowed. "Middle school," she said harshly. "Why?"

"I didn't *do* it," Ri defended. "I didn't even clench my fingers. But it wasn't like a fantasy scenario designed to release frustration, either. I was... well... I was angry. Really angry. In fact, for about three seconds, I can't remember ever being angrier."

Julie said nothing. Ri didn't look at the face in the monitor. She knew every nuance of her mother's practiced, concerned, neutral, non-judging face. She didn't need to see it to appreciate its being there.

"And yet," she went on, her tone turning tongue-in-cheek, "because you screwed me up so much with all those childhood psycho-tricks, the first thing that popped into my head wasn't 'Hit him, it will make you feel better.' Oh, no. The first reaction of *my* brain was 'Disproportionate anger response! Identify trigger! Reframe!'"

Julie chuckled softly. "And did that work for you?"

Ri blew out a breath. "Yes and no. I got the anger under control. But that left 'humiliation' hanging out there all by itself. Which totally sucked. And then I got mad about that."

"Ri, honey," Julie said softly. "Would you like to be more specific?"

"No," she answered shortly. "Not at the moment." The wound was still too fresh. The details, too embarrassing. It was bad enough to be told you were only worth a casual fling. It was another level of mortification altogether to have so spectacularly misjudged where someone else was coming from. She still could not wrap her head around it.

"Well, are you happy with the way you handled it, at least?" Julie asked.

Ri thought about that, then nodded. She'd waged a heated war in her head for a while, but her better instincts had won out. She had stayed calm and given Wolf the benefit of the doubt. "There were all kinds of unflattering conclusions I could have leaped to. On both sides," she said, clarifying her thoughts as she talked. That's often how discussions went with her mom, whether Julie said anything or not. Ri wondered sometimes if a life-sized picture of her mother's "concerned listening face" would have the same effect on her psyche, but the very idea of such a photo's existence creeped her out.

"But all along, I couldn't help thinking that something wasn't right," Ri finished. "And it wasn't just that I was surprised, or that I didn't *want* to hear it. There was a fundamental disconnect between what I knew to be true and what I was hearing. And when I calmed down enough to try and reframe it from another point of view, I thought maybe I could see an explanation."

"Good work," Julie praised.

"I think it's coming from fear," Ri said, becoming more convinced herself as she heard the words out loud. In truth, she was making her thought process sound far more organized than it had been at the time. When she had turned away from Wolf to look out the window she'd been in such a fury of temper she hadn't been thinking straight at all. It was only when she'd turned back to face him that the transparent look in his eyes had shocked her brain back into gear.

He was genuinely worried about her feelings. That was what was so mysterious about it all. As crass and as boorish as his proclamation had sounded, only a man with integrity — and real, honest to God compassion — would bother to say anything at all. He hadn't wanted to mislead her. He was going out of his way *not* to hurt her.

She'd practically choked on her own emotion. How could she *not* fall for a man so unflinchingly honest and empathetic both? And how cruel was the cosmos to pair such a pure heart with such an utterly moronic view of sex? Seriously, what was wrong with the man? She had reached out for him with all the pity she would extend to a cute, fluffy kitten dragging two mangled rear legs. And she had answered his question the only way she possibly could. It was already too late for her. There was no halfway. She could and would accept no compromise.

"From fear?" Julie repeated. "Fear of what, do you think?"

Ri was lost in thought until reminded of her mother's existence. But she considered the question rhetorical. "Well, I guess that's what I need to figure out, isn't it?"

"Sounds like it," Julie agreed gently.

Ri smiled. "Thanks, Mom. Listen, I don't want to keep you up all night. But can I ask you one more question?"

"Sure."

"Without getting a whole psychoanalysis thing with it?"

Silence.

"Mom?"

"You know I don't do that," Julie argued. "What's your question?"

Ri had been wondering idly for days, but now the issue had taken on greater importance. Figuring Wolf out would be hard enough; she should at least be confident in what she herself was feeling. "When you and Dad started dating, how long did it take before... well, at what point did you start feeling like you had a connection that could last? Did both of you see it at the same time?"

Julie's eyes flashed with curiosity, but Ri appreciated her mother's efforts to restrain herself. "In our case," Julie answered, "once we started getting close, we both knew we had something special. There wasn't any drama. We connected almost immediately and we've been together ever since."

*Of course... the fairy tale.* Ri tried to squelch a sigh of frustration, but realized she was too late.

"But that's just us," Julie said sharply. "And we're not typical. Like I say about every process in life, there is no *one right way* to build a relationship."

"Thanks, Mom," Ri said quickly, sensing another thera-speech on the way. She wasn't up to it tonight. Her brain was tired. She needed to ponder the question some more, but she needed to do it after a good night's sleep. And maybe after asking Maddie a similar set of questions. Maddie and Kai were definitely one of those couples that...

A fresh wave of foreboding drifted through her already roiling gut. "Oh, and Mom?" she asked, sitting up a bit. "I'm worried about Mei Lin."

Julie's brow furrowed. "Oh?"

Ri nodded. "Maybe I'm just imagining things, but... Well, up to now I've haven't known too many engaged couples. But now that I've gotten to know Kai and Maddie, it's made me think about Mei Lin and Josh, and I don't like the contrast."

Julie was quiet a moment. "Meaning?"

Ri scowled. "Meaning I don't think he treats her right! It didn't used to be that way, did it? I swear, when they were first dating, he was different. He was nicer. But doesn't it seem like gradually, he's gotten more self-centered? More complacent? Ever since they got engaged, it seems like it's all about him. Sometimes he acts like he doesn't respect her at all. He should be *cherishing* her. You know?"

Julie stared straight into the monitor with a frown. "Oh, I know."

Ri's shoulders slumped. She had been hoping that she was imagining it. But the grim look on her mother's face left no doubt.

"I've already spoken to your sister," Julie said soberly. "Several times. And so has your father. But she won't listen to us. She thinks we're 'overanalyzing.'"

Ri cringed. She was no better than Mei Lin, of course. Ever since the girls hit adolescence, their mother's professional credentials had counted against her. A normal mother, they were sure, would not point out pathology every time they crushed on a guy. Ri knew now that they had been unfairly sensitive on the issue, but old habits were hard to break.

"Maybe it would help if you talked to your sister?" Julie suggested.

"I don't know," Ri replied. Mei Lin would be devastated if she felt like her whole family was ganging up against her fiance. "I'll think about it."

"Ri?"

"Yes?"

"You want to tell me about this guy you've met?"

"Sorry, Mom," Ri said with a rueful smile. "Not yet."

Her mother offered a coy smirk. "Maybe when it's going better?"

Ri snorted with amusement. "Yeah, that would definitely improve the conversation."

She thanked her mother for the late-night advice, said a heartfelt good-bye, and shut down the laptop. Her mind was still racing with confusion as she locked up the truck and strode through the fog toward the hazy glow of the Hilton's porch light. Now that she was properly dressed for the weather, the cool, moist air felt good in her lungs, and she felt an urge to clear her head with a good, brisk walk. Heading out onto the mountain in the fog would be foolish, of course, but she could at least circle the building a few times. Otherwise, she might never sleep.

She tucked the laptop under her arm and headed off, walking at as rapid a pace as she could while keeping the lights of the Hilton safely in sight. She was moving around the back corner by Kenneth's place when a light in an unexpected location distracted her.

It was a small, linear beam. A flashlight, almost certainly, even though it was stationary. It was coming from the dog run. Ri decided to walk closer. Was there a problem with Bella? As awful as the dog's wounds still looked, she certainly seemed to be feeling better. When they'd checked on her before dinner she was up on her feet and walking around the pen anxious to be petted, despite her broken ribs. Ri heard something and stopped walking. It was a canine sound of contentment, somewhere between a yawn and a yowl. It was followed by a low, human chuckling noise, then words in a deep, mumbling voice that she couldn't understand.

Ri stood still a minute, absorbing a scene she still couldn't see. Wolf had given the dog her evening medication already. It was the excuse he'd given for jumping out of the truck the second she'd driven them back from Hosmer Grove. He'd taken off into the fog and she hadn't seen him since. So what was he still doing out here now? Was he just hanging out, keeping the dog company?

Or perhaps vice versa?

Ri returned to her original path circling the building, and Wolf's words came back to haunt her already tortured brain. *I don't do relationships,* he'd said. And he didn't mean just on Maui. He'd meant everywhere, anywhere. Not that sex for its own sake wasn't all well and good, but why would he choose to deprive himself of everything else that was positive and rewarding and wonderful about a healthy, loving relationship?

It made no sense. He had to be afraid of something.

She stomped around the far corner of the Hilton, then realized she was heading straight out into the fog. She gritted her teeth and changed course. Wolf had to have a reason. Whatever it was, it was misguided, obviously. He would have to understand that. But first, *she* would have to understand it.

"Ouch!" Her knees banged into the bumper of a parked car. She clutched the laptop closer to her chest, muttered curses under her breath, and moved on. Perhaps it was just as well Wolf had removed himself from her company tonight, because she needed some time to be mad at him. Sriha Mirini Sullivan was very particular about men. She didn't find prospects that excited her very often, and no man had ever struck a chord in her the way Wolf had. To have the rug jerked out from under her now was not only maddening, it was intolerable. If he seriously thought that *she* believed that any man she'd watched coddle a scraggly, wounded mutt — a man who showed such tenderness and quiet strength — had no capacity to have a "relationship" with a woman that was anything but "casual and temporary..."

Was he *insane?* Did he think she was?

Ri tripped over a curb. Desperate to preserve the valued laptop, she drew up both arms to protect it and wound up landing knees-first on the pavement. She shouted curses into the fog and scrambled up, then felt along the legs of her thin capris, where two giant holes over her kneecaps revealed tender, scratched skin.

*Frickin' fabulous.*

Ri gave up her walk and headed toward the porch light. She needed a long, hot shower and a good night's sleep.

She had work to do tomorrow.


Wolf awoke to a familiar, pleasantly unpleasant feeling. His face was wet. And sticky.

"Suka! Stop it!" he mumbled, rolling over and hiding his head under the damp, cold fabric.

A paw scraped his head and trapped a shock of his hair. A dog whined.

Wolf's eyes opened. He peeked out at green grass. The air stank of dog poo.

He shook the paw off his hair and turned back over again. For a moment, he couldn't figure out where he was. The fog had cleared overnight, and in the dim, pre-dawn glow he could just make out the sight of Bella's scruffy long muzzle and the chain link fence surrounding them, which clued him in on his location. The rest of it took longer to fathom. Evidently, he had hauled his sleeping bag out to the dog run. Why in hell had he done that?

*Oh, right.*

*Ri.*

Wolf groaned and closed his eyes. Not that what happened with Ri last night actually explained his waking up next to a steaming pile of dog crap. Connecting all those dots would require more brain cells than he currently had functioning. But at least he knew he wasn't sleep walking. He'd just had a rotten, miserable night.

Bella whined and licked his face again.

"Fine," Wolf said with a groan. "I'll feed you. I've got to get up anyway. If you're lucky maybe I'll forget to tell Kenneth and you'll get breakfast twice."

The dog thumped her tail.

Wolf rose, cleaned up the run, fed and pilled the dog, left a note for Kenneth, hauled his bedding back inside, and took a shower. He was running late. It was well past first light when he unlocked his gear from the storage closet and met Ri at the truck.

Now that his brain had filled in all the missing blanks from last night, he felt anxious about seeing her again. And the fact that he felt anxious annoyed him.

She was leaning up against the driver's door, waiting. She was wearing lightweight cargo pants that were ankle-length now, but which he knew could be rolled up as the day grew warmer. Her voluminous hair was drawn off her forehead with a zany orange band, and she wore a bright teal jacket with the Foundation for Ocean Mammals logo emblazoned on it. Most likely, underneath it, she wore a tank that showed off her generous curves and exposed those gorgeous bronze shoulders of hers. Maybe if they finished early again today, they could go back down to the valley and she would take off the jacket and change into shorts again—

"Good morning," she said cheerfully, smiling at him.

Wolf blinked. For a second, he was lost in fantasyland. He was in yesterday. Ri wouldn't be running around the beaches with him in a tank top this afternoon. Not today, or any day. She'd said *no. Nada. Nothing. I choose nothing.*

They were going out for a day of freaking gas flux measurements. That was it. Her choice. Not his. Why she was pretending to be excited about that, he had no idea.

"Morning," he returned tonelessly.

Ri smirked. Her eyes sparkled at him like they shared some intimate secret.

*What the hell?*

He averted his gaze and got into the passenger side. He hated not driving, but a deal was a deal. He supposed he was lucky she was still working for him at all. Nothing had gone the way he'd expected it to with her, and he had no clue what came next. Up to now, these things had always followed a pattern. He got a lot of interest from women. He was fortunate that way. But he was careful to avoid the ones who were fishing for husbands. He limited himself to women who wanted something as temporary as he did, even if — damn it all — the really interesting women always seemed to be in the first group.

But Ri was supposed to be in the second. She knew that he was leaving Maui. She knew that he was going and never coming back. Yet she'd lured him into that foggy, dark grove and she'd laughed and she'd turned out the light and she'd put her arms around his neck and she'd kissed him like...

His jaw muscles clenched. He remembered very well, now, why he couldn't sleep last night.

After the way Ri had responded to him in the grove, he had every reason to believe they were on exactly the same page. He'd thought that the little speech he gave would be no more than a formality in her case. It was always awkward, but he'd learned that it was worth a few moments' awkwardness to avoid the nightmarish emotional drama that came with mismatched intentions. Besides which, inexplicably, there were some girls the speech really turned on. And yet, at the crucial green-light moment of consent, what had this intelligent, provocative, diabolically evil, angel-faced woman said to him?

*I choose nothing.*

That's what she'd said to him.

*Nada. Nothing at all.*

"Wolf?"

"What?" he snapped.

Ri jumped.

"Sorry," he said quickly. "What is it?"

"I don't know where we're going," she said. The truck was paused at the field station's exit. "Uphill or down?" Her voice was still upbeat. If she noticed his foul mood, she seemed to be ignoring it.

"Uphill," he answered more politely. He gave her the precise directions, then lapsed into silence. He needed to get hold of himself. Their misunderstanding, whatever it had been, was mutual. He'd just have to figure out how to deal with it.

He took a few long, slow breaths. The problem was that he didn't know how to deal with it. He'd been giving the "no strings or nothing" speech since college, but this was uncharted territory. Women differed in their immediate reactions to it, yes. But he had never been turned down flat.

They drove to the research site in silence, set up in silence, and worked in silence. It could have been uncomfortable for them both, but in truth it wasn't much different from the day before. Ri hadn't chit-chatted yesterday either, and she didn't act like there was anything wrong between them now. She was upbeat and smiley and didn't react one way or the other to the occasional accidental brush of their arms or legs or shoulders. If there was any change in her today, it was that she went about her work with such forceful determination that Wolf felt like his own steady pace was holding them up. They didn't even have a real lunch break. She ate her sandwich at the Hilton while he checked on Bella, and he ate his in the truck while she drove to the next site. By 1:30 PM they had finished all the measurements on his schedule, and Wolf decided right then and there that he would purchase an airline ticket home for the upcoming weekend. There was no reason left for him to stick around.

"You are amazing, Ri," he said genuinely after he'd recorded the last data reading. "Shall we move along to the next site on tomorrow's schedule? At this rate, we can stop a little early each day and you can still probably get Friday off. Or at least most of it."

Ri's lovely brow furrowed, shifting her orange band. She glared at him a moment as she took a swig from her water bottle. Then, still studying him thoughtfully, she recapped the bottle and smiled.

"I think not," she said smoothly. "I worked fast today for a reason. I have plans."

Wolf's heart sank. He wanted to finish a day early. He wanted to get away from this vision of delectable sexiness and go home. Well, actually, that wasn't at all what he *wanted*. "Plans?"

She grinned at him. The doe eyes held that same, maddening look of "knowing" again. Like she and Wolf shared some wonderful, exciting secret. Except it was a secret he didn't know about.

"Come with me," she invited.

Wolf's heart skipped a beat. Wait. Was he missing something? Had her answer changed?

"I want to drive around the west side and see the cliffs," she announced with childlike excitement. "I want to pack a picnic and eat it at a beach park somewhere. And I want to see Honolua Bay, where the longboard surfers go, and I want to watch the sun set at Ka'anapali, where all the snazzy resorts are."

"Sounds fun," he said automatically. She would probably wear a swimsuit for that. A two piece. What would her hair look like when it was wet?

Her face lit up. "So you'll come?"

Wolf blinked. She seemed to be waiting for an answer about something. His mind was still on the swimsuit. "What?"

"Let's get going, then!" she said cheerfully. "We'll have to stop and pack the food."

Wolf sensed he was being railroaded. He shook his head to clear the haze, and the bad news came roaring back.

*Nothing. I choose nothing.*

"Why do you even want me to go?" he blurted.

Ri, who had already turned and started walking toward the truck, swung around and stared at him. "Because I enjoy your company," she answered simply.

Wolf stared at her. For the life of him, he had no response to that.

"Come on!" she said, tossing her head. Her brown-black curls bounced in the sun, and a brilliant smile drew her cheeks into two perfectly round, dimpled cherries.

Wolf went.

# Chapter 24

"It's so much greener here than it is on Haleakala!" Ri gushed. She drew in a breath of the warm ocean air as it rushed past her face, whipped her dark ringlets around her neck and shoulders, and buffeted her skin. The scent of it was intoxicating.

She was standing on a cliff high above Honolua Bay, watching with awe as wave after blue wave broke into a feathery line of white over the reefs far below. The volcanic peaks behind her were tall and emerald in color, sheer and sharply angled, unlike the smoother, more gradual and drier heights of Haleakala. Lush vegetation bordered the streams flowing down from the mountains, and the trees in the valley to her left were tall and dense with leaves and vines. She had driven the truck in a wide circle all around the base of the West Mountain and up its far side, and from where she stood now she could look across the ocean and see the island of Moloka'i.

She could hear Wolf's soft chuckle behind her. "You haven't seen the greenest part of Maui yet. That would be the northeast section."

Ri smiled without turning around. *All in good time, my friend... and with luck, you'll be right there with me.* "The road to Hana is on Saturday's agenda," she said.

"Ah," Wolf commented.

Ri breathed the air and absorbed the view in silence for several more minutes. She saw no surfers out this afternoon, but she could see a few people walking on the beaches below. "Is there any place to picnic down by the water?" she asked.

Wolf stepped up beside her. "I think I remember a picnic table or two, yes." He pointed out over the valley that stretched inward from the bay. From the cliff on which they were standing, they could look out over the tops of the trees that filled it. "There's a trailhead off a little parking area down there," he explained, pointing. "I checked it out once. I bet you'd like it."

He was standing close. Ri wanted to reach out, wrap her arms around his waist, and hug him for no particular reason. She wanted the kind of relationship where she could do that, confident that her gesture would be eagerly returned. But they didn't have that. She decided to catch his gaze instead, and as soon as his pure, ice blue eyes looked into hers, she poured every ounce of her telepathic energy into them, trying to show how very much she wanted to touch him, to show him affection. And how sad she was that she couldn't.

He looked back at her with puzzlement.

It was a start. She stepped away from him and towards the truck. "Let's eat, then," she said with enthusiasm. "I'm so ready for that exciting peanut butter sandwich of mine."

She parked the truck in a small dirt lot next to a row of portable restrooms, an overflowing trash can, and a dozen wild chickens. "Welcome to Hawaii," Wolf teased as they hopped out. He grabbed the cooler from the back of the truck. "Some people think the chicken should be the state bird instead of the *nene*. I can see their point."

Ri chuckled as a red hen and her family of mostly grown chicks scuttled along the path in front of them. She and Wolf walked further into the trees and quickly found themselves in the depths of a jungle. "Oh, my," she exclaimed. The canopy of broad leaves high above her head let only dappled beams of sunlight through to the cool, shady floor, where a carpet of tropical greenery grew over exposed roots, twisted branches, and mossy stones. The treetops were alive with the sound of chattering birds, and a splashing stream rushed along through the valley over tumbled lava rocks and fallen limbs. Long, shaggy vines rained down from the uppermost tree branches while giant elephant ears sprang upward to meet them. And all along the moist dirt path, hens clucked and roosters strutted — a few of the more obstinate males being disinclined to step out of the way.

"I don't see your name on this path, Red," Ri said to one of them after a lengthy staring match. "Now move along. I'm bigger than you."

The rooster gave her a dirty look and moved ever-so-slightly to the side.

"Attitude!" Ri complained, sidling by him.

Wolf laughed.

Ri laughed, too. His humor had improved, gradually, once she had gotten him in the truck and on the road. A couple times while they were making sandwiches at the field station she was afraid that he would back out of the venture, but something — perhaps inability to come up with a plausible excuse quick enough — had prevented that tragedy. He had agreed to come with her, and here they were. She had kept the talk on the way over light and breezy, focused on his work and hers, which was appropriate. You couldn't look at someone properly when you were driving, and good eye contact was essential for more in-depth conversation.

*The kind of conversation Wolf avoided,* Ri thought to herself. But no matter. She was up for the challenge. Her spirits remained high as they strolled along the path through the idyllic jungle toward a sun-soaked opening in the distance that promised to reveal a beach. The spot was obviously a popular one with both locals and tourists alike, and they passed several people and a few more chickens before reaching a partly shaded clearing near the forest's edge.

Ri looked out to see a line of trees at the edge of the clearing, with two picnic tables nestled beneath. Beyond the trees, the ground was covered with large, smooth boulders as it sloped down to the water. Two paved lanes ran through a break in the trees and off into the bay to form a small boat ramp, but no boats were in view on the water today. Just a dozen or so people sitting on the rocks and walking along the beach to either side, enjoying the view and the breeze.

Ri was dying to kick off her sandals and get her feet wet, but Wolf had already set their cooler on an unoccupied picnic table. She decided she could wait. Delayed gratification might not have been her forte as a child, but she had learned to appreciate its charms.

Her eyes were drawn to Wolf's well-toned arms and shoulders, even as he performed such a mundane task as unpacking their dinner. His dark blond hair ruffled slightly in the breeze, making stray curls pummel his ears and dance about his sun-browned neck. *Case in point,* she thought ruefully. Wolf might try to hide his classic good looks behind a few days' worth of beard and some dirty boots, but he still had the face and body of a Greek statue.

She smirked to herself. Well, a Greek that worked out, anyway.

Wolf sat down facing the ocean, and Ri sat down opposite him. He looked up at her in surprise. "Don't you want to see the view?" he asked.

"I would," she answered honestly. "But it's more important to me to see the person I'm talking to."

Wolf frowned. "Well, let's switch then," he said, getting up. "I've been enjoying the ocean for four months already."

Ri smiled and consented. They dug into their hastily prepared sandwiches, fruit, and snacks, and she gave them both a few minutes of quiet to take the edge off their hunger before the main event began. She'd thought long and hard about how best to go about her task, but she had never come up with a failsafe plan. Sometimes, when the stakes were highest, she was better off winging it.

"Tell me about growing up in Alaska," she said offhandedly. "Forgive me if this sounds like stereotyping, but did you hunt and fish? Did your dad take you and your brother out with him?"

To her relief, Wolf smiled. "I suppose you could call that stereotyping, but it's a valid question. Hunting and fishing isn't a hobby up there so much as a part of life. Not everybody does it, but pretty much everybody has given it a try. My dad went out with his dad when he was young, but he never cared for it. So Bear and I only got to go fishing or hunting when we visited our grandpa. But those were good times."

"So, your dad was morally opposed to shooting Bambi?" Ri teased.

Wolf chuckled. "That's not how my dad would explain it. He would tell you he was just a bad shot. But I think he didn't have the heart for it. He doesn't even like baiting hooks."

"What about you?" Ri's heart beat hopefully. So far, so

good. He was talking about family, and he was still at ease.

He looked away from her with a shrug. "It's okay."

*Careful, now.* "Baiting hooks or shooting Bambi? I don't think I could look a deer in the eyes and kill it. That really doesn't bother you? Not a tiny little bit?"

He looked at her, then. He looked annoyed. Like she was making him think about something he didn't want to think about. She gave him her most playful smile. "And if you lie to me," she said coyly, hoping her eyes were transmitting her affection. "I'll *so* know."

When his blue eyes smiled back at her, she almost cheered out loud.

"I have killed Bambi," he said with amusement. "More than once. And if I was hungry enough, I would do it again. But, no. Unlike some people, I don't enjoy hunting."

"Knew that!" Ri said smugly. Another risk. At any point, the man could bite her hand and slink off into the wild again.

But thankfully, he still smiled at her. "How did you know that?"

"I see the way you are with Bella," she answered. "A lot of hunters love their dogs, I'm not saying they don't. But there's a quality about you..." She broke off and let a hint of mischief into her smile. "Well, I probably shouldn't use the particular word I'm thinking of. Men don't like it. Not manly men, anyway."

He made a pretend angry-face. "What word?"

*Fished in!* "Oh, now I'm in trouble," she said with an exaggerated sigh. "I was going to say, you have a very 'nurturing' quality about you. I bet you were a wonderful big brother."

Wolf's cheeks flamed. He looked distinctly uncomfortable as he chose that particular moment to toss back his cola and hunt for the last few, nonexistent drops in his already emptied can.

*Say something, Wolf.* Ri waited hopefully. If he said anything at all, it would be a major breakthrough. Most likely he'd change the topic or just walk off. She knew she was digging perilously close to "mother" territory. But she also knew it was the obvious starting point. Not to be too Freudian, but as far as she could tell, the man didn't have a single significant female in his life right now. He held both female friends and intimate partners at bay, and it was just "my dad and my brother and me." Linking one to the other wasn't brain surgery.

"You'd have to ask Bear about that," he said finally, crushing the can with one hand.

His expression was extremely strange. He almost looked angry. But at the same time he seemed sad. Ri thought fast. "Does he still feel like a 'little' brother to you, even now that you're both adults? Mei Lin is a year younger than me, but we were always the same size, and we pretty much always thought of ourselves as twins. Even if I had thought of her as a baby sister back then, I probably wouldn't anymore. After all, she's been the first one to be fully employed as a professional in her field. And she'll be the first one to get married."

Wolf's color returned to normal, and his voice softened. "I think he'll always feel like my kid brother, even when we're old and gray."

"That's interesting. Do you feel like you helped raise him?"

Wolf's gaze shot to Ri, who tried her best to look innocent. All kids helped raise younger siblings to some degree, didn't they? Even when both parents were in the home? Never mind that she was pretty sure that wasn't the case with Wolf and Bear. She watched, continuing to feign innocence, as he breathed in deeply and released a slow breath.

"I did raise him," he said steadily, his eyes holding hers. "Me and my dad, anyway." Then his gaze moved off into the trees. "Our mother died when I was six. Bear was only three."

Ri made a split-second decision. "No, she didn't," she said quietly. "You were lying just then. I could tell. What happened to her, Wolf?"

His head whipped back around. He stared at her resentfully.

*Too far.*

*Dammit!*

"Never mind," Ri said gently. She gave a casual shrug and kept her smile warm. "You don't have to tell me anything."

***

Wolf's hand brushed against Ri's as they strolled along the Ka'anapali boardwalk, and the urge he felt to curl his fingers around her own small, delicate ones surprised him. Fortunately, the splint prevented him from doing anything so colossally stupid, even accidentally.

*Especially* accidentally.

Everything disturbing that happened with Ri seemed to be happening accidentally. It was an accident that he was here, walking with her on a beach at sunset, to begin with. Why was he doing it? What had he been thinking in coming along with her at all?

Damned if he knew.

When Ri told him she enjoyed his company, there was a challenge in her voice that dared him to refuse her invitation, to come up with a good reason why they shouldn't spend time together. And of course they were having fun, as he knew they would. He couldn't remember enjoying any woman's company as much as he enjoyed Ri's... or for that matter, any man's. She just seemed to *get* him. She enjoyed the same things, including the quiet. She knew when to talk and when to listen. She didn't push.

Well, not usually. She'd come close to it earlier when she'd asked about his mother, but after she'd realized he didn't want to go there, she'd backed off. He appreciated that. Something about that conversation still bugged him, but he didn't want to think about that now. He wanted to think about Ri. He wanted to figure out why he couldn't stop his splinted fingers from reflexively reaching out for hers.

He told himself it was because he wanted her. But as strong as his attraction might be, he couldn't buy lust as the sole reason for such an odd impulse. He'd never been a hand-holder. Perhaps he was merely picking up on the fact that Ri would like it?

He did feel like he was getting to know her better. Starting to *get* her, too. She felt the same passion for the ocean that he felt for the earth. He couldn't walk a new trail without looking down at the rocks, and she couldn't be near a body of water without wanting to get her feet wet and check out the algae and the fish. Watching her kick off her sandals and frolic on the beach at Honolua Bay was a delight for more reasons than admiring the figure beneath her skintight yellow cami. There was an innate joy in Ri that made him feel joyful as well. He knew other people, other scientists, who were just as enthusiastic about the natural world and about their work. But the rest of them were always so loud about it. So overwhelming. Ri, like him, wasn't a person who chattered just to fill the air. But nor was she uncommunicative. She had other ways of expressing her feelings.

Like now. The sun was beginning to set over the ocean, and she was looking up at him with those big brown doe eyes of hers as if she wanted to lure him into one of the nearby hammocks and make out like a couple of teenagers. Or perhaps he was projecting?

"Have you had fun this afternoon?" she asked, her low voice silky.

Wolf wondered if she knew how alluring that voice was. His instincts told him she did, but since she was the one who'd chosen "nothing," perhaps she didn't.

"Sure," he answered noncommittally. He was good at that.

"I have, too," she said with a more innocent smile. "Thanks for coming with me."

Wolf was baffled again. As much progress as he felt he was making in getting to know Ri as a person, her actions toward him were still maddeningly obtuse. "Thanks for inviting me," he said in return. What else could he say?

She glanced up from the stone-cobbled path on which they walked toward one of the towering resorts that contributed to the posh Ka'anapali lineup. Here along this sunbaked section of the western coast of Maui, hotel after gleaming hotel stood shoulder to shoulder, joined together by a long, paved walk that gave all their patrons shared access to the public beach as well as upscale restaurants and shops. Many of the resorts were giants of glass and steel, with meticulously manicured lawns and elaborate pools with bridges and waterfalls. "So how much you think a room in this place goes for per night?" she asked, looking at one of the swankier ones.

Wolf looked up with her. He shrugged. "I'd guess at least four hundred and some change."

Ri made a face. "I don't guess you'll ever catch me staying here, then."

Wolf chuckled. "Me neither. Not if I wind up with the Geological Service. But I'm perfectly happy with our own version of the Hilton. It's even got an ocean view, on a clear day."

Ri smiled. "Actually, I like our place fine, too. Even if it is a tiny bit farther from the water." She looked back towards where the sun was setting, then her eyes scanned the beach. The sun was beginning its rapid descent and would drop below the horizon in a matter of minutes. "This is a nice walkway," she muttered. "But I can't believe how crowded it gets."

Wolf nodded in agreement. They had been trying to walk side by side, but every few seconds they had to drop back to single file to let someone else pass. The path was only wide enough for three abreast, and the resorts held thousands of people. It hadn't been so clogged earlier when they first started walking the length of it, but sunset was a popular time.

"Over there," Ri said finally, pointing off the path toward a relatively unoccupied stretch of the public beach. "Let's go sit." She made her way toward it, and Wolf followed. Every hammock, beach chair, and inch of sea wall nearby was taken, but Ri plopped down in the dry sand, drew up her knees, and circled her arms around them. Wolf sat down beside her and threw his hands out behind him. The splint made everything awkward, but he could still put some weight on the heel of his hand.

"This is so exciting for me," Ri said reverently, her voice a whisper. "Rising at dawn to see the reverse in Maine just isn't the same. It's beautiful. But it's cold. And it's always precipitating somehow or other. Here it's so warm and pleasant. And the colors... they're just amazing."

Wolf said nothing in response. He didn't need to. The brilliant pinks and oranges reflecting off both the thin layers of clouds in the sky and the shimmering waters of the ocean spoke a language of their own. The giant ball of sun was bathed in fiery color that blazed in all directions, extending high into the sky and seeming to wrap around Wolf and Ri. For a few glorious moments the beauty of that color seemed to block out all the problems of the world, until the bottom of the orb was abruptly cut off by the leading edge of the dark water. Then, way too fast, the ocean simply gobbled it up. The orb disappeared into the moving blackness, and only a dim legacy of color was left behind in the sky.

Ri sighed with contentment. Only then did Wolf realize that she must have moved gradually closer to him. Because as she sighed, she also leaned back on her hands, with the result being that her side was now pressed up against his.

The effect of her contact was immediate. And beyond frustrating. The woman's actions were incomprehensible. She had made her position clear enough in the grove, hadn't she? She'd said she wouldn't sleep with him without some kind of commitment on his part. Fine. He could respect that. But what the hell kind of commitment could she possibly expect when she knew he was leaving Maui in a matter of days? Just last night he'd booked a flight for Sunday!

Had she changed her mind?

His heart skipped a beat. He sat up a little, testing the waters. Ri immediately snuggled closer into the crook of his arm. She said nothing to him, just continued to watch the sky with a dreamy, contented look on her face.

She *must* have changed her mind.

His hands practically wobbled beneath him. He couldn't believe it. He could drive her back to the Hilton right now...

No, actually, he didn't believe it. "Ri?" he whispered softly into her ear.

"Hmm?" she murmured back, still cuddling.

"What are you doing?" he asked. "Have you changed your mind?"

She didn't move, but he thought he could feel her stiffen slightly. "About what?"

"You know about what," he said firmly. "About wanting 'nothing.' That's not the message you're sending me right now."

Ri sat up. She turned around and looked him in the eyes. He expected to see some guilt there. He wanted her, and she knew it. He was in no position to dole out friendly affection, and she knew that, too. And if she made some lame attempt to pretend ignorance, he intended to call her on it.

But Ri's eyes held no guilt whatsoever. The first emotion he saw in them was irritation. Frank irritation, like she was about to tell him off. The second emotion, the sight of which nearly bowled him over, was desire so powerful it damn near equaled his own.

"I never said that's what I *want*," she said sharply.

Wolf stared at her. Dear God, he was lost. He didn't even know if this was good news or bad. "What do you mean?" he asked, shaking his head.

Ri's brown eyes flashed fire. She took a quick breath before she spoke, and her voice turned softer. "What I *want* is a relationship, Wolf. And everything that comes with it." She shifted and raised a hand to his face. Her finger traced slowly along his jawline. "You think you're not driving *me* crazy?"

Wolf was perilously close to grabbing her around the waist and rolling her on her back on the sand in front of hundreds of people. Some principle or other stopped him, but the funny thing was, he couldn't immediately remember it. It had something to do with protecting himself. Keeping things simple. Avoiding female drama...

Oh, right. *No strings or nothing.* He felt strongly about that. It was his mantra. It had always made perfect sense in the past. Why it was failing him so spectacularly now, he wasn't sure. But he was hardly an unreasonable person. Surely they could come to some compromise?

"Ri," he said gently, "I have a plane ticket for Sunday. I don't know what you want from me."

"Sunday?" The word was little more than a squeak. The sparkle drained from her eyes. The corners of her beautiful full lips, almost always tilted slightly up, dropped to a straight line. He felt as if he'd punched her in the gut with a fist. He felt as if he'd punched himself.

He wanted desperately to make her smile again. He brushed a shock of hair over her shoulder, then let his hand linger over the softness of her neck. "It doesn't have to be 'nothing,'" he suggested mildly.

Her eyes brightened again. Just a little bit. She leaned forward towards him. His pulse began to race, but she stopped short of kissing him. She spoke instead. "I see. So if 'nothing' becomes 'something,' then 'no strings' becomes 'some strings.' Is that right?"

Wolf tried to process her logic. He hadn't meant that at all. She was being way too lawyerly with his words.

Ri pulled away from him. "I can see that's not what you meant," she answered herself. "So as much as it pains me on such a gorgeous evening, I'm afraid I'll have to stick to my original answer." She rose and dusted the sand off her shapely rear end.

Wolf wanted to help with that. He also wanted to throw things and yell.

Ri offered him a hand up. He stared at it stupidly for a moment, then realized it was a sort of peace offering. He put his left hand in hers and stood. The touch of her fingers was electrifying. He tried to let go of her hand and was surprised when she wouldn't let him.

"Wolf," she said in a more normal voice. "If you should change your mind about that policy, be sure to let me know."

Her fingers were shooting liquid desire through his veins. He found it difficult to look at her. "I'll only be here four more days," he said gruffly, extracting his hand from hers. "Even if I wanted 'a relationship,' what's the point?"

She said nothing. He still hesitated to look at her, but curiosity eventually got the best of him, and he raised his gaze to her face. She stood still and without expression, studying him almost as if he were a museum exhibit. He looked back at her a long time before she seemed to notice his staring. She startled a little, then smiled at him. The seductress was gone. Her expression was subdued, but not defeated. Rather, she was back to the fully self-possessed, confident woman he was accustomed to being around.

"Well, I guess we'd better hit the road," she said pleasantly. "It's a long way home, and I want to get an early start again tomorrow."

She turned and began walking toward the public garage where they'd parked the truck.

He accompanied her without comment.

# Chapter 25



*Anchorage, Alaska 2005*

"Wolf? Can you come here a minute? There's something I want to talk to you about," Nels called from the kitchen.

Wolf looked in his father's direction with suspicion. It was ten o'clock on a school night, and Bear was sprawled on the couch watching some screwball comedy and laughing his head off. Wolf had just gotten back from a friend's hockey game, so he had an excuse for being out late. But Bear was only twelve. He was supposed to be in bed by now. "What does Dad want?" he asked in a whisper, poking his little brother in the shoulder.

"Go ask him yourself," Bear answered between chuckles, his eyes never leaving the show.

Wolf dragged his feet into the kitchen. He didn't think he was in trouble for anything. His grades were fine. He'd been doing his share of the chores, as always. Things had been getting a lot more interesting with the opposite sex since his extreme growth spurt last year — not to mention the cool new beard he'd acquired over the summer — but his dad wouldn't know about those ventures. So what was the deal?

"Yeah, Dad?" he asked, standing in the doorway.

"Sit down, Wolf," his dad replied, gesturing to a kitchen chair beside him.

*Not good.*

Wolf sat.

"I'm hoping this won't come as too much of a shock to you," Nels said, smiling. "But I've asked Frieda to move in with us."

Wolf's mouth dropped open with shock.

Nels looked amused. "I... uh... I guess I've miscalculated. Sorry if I caught you off guard, son. But we've been dating for nearly a year, now. Your brother wasn't at all surprised." Nels' cheeks reddened a bit. His smile returned, then broadened. "In fact, he asked me why I didn't go ahead and propose."

"Propose!" Wolf scooted his chair back and stood up. "Dad, are you—" His heart was racing. His mind was reeling. He didn't want to call his father crazy. He wasn't even sure what grounds he'd be basing that accusation on. Of course his father dated. He always had, although he used to hide the fact from Bear. Nels had been more open about seeing Frieda, but then she owned the barbecue place near the hockey rink, so she was harder to hide. But moving her in? To *their* house?

"She has her own place, Dad!" Wolf complained, thinking even as he said it how stupid he sounded. But he had to say something. His dad had no sense of self-protection when it came to women. He was a lamb to the slaughter. "Why do you keep doing this to yourself? You know how it always turns out!"

Nels frowned. "Wolf," he said sternly. "I appreciate your concern. But that's enough of that."

Wolf frowned back. His dad didn't sound the least bit appreciative. "But it's true!" he pressed. "Every single one of those women you fell for — they all just turned around and stabbed you in the back! If you move Frieda in here the exact same thing's going to happen, and Bear's going to get hurt, too! How can you do that to him? Again? And for what?"

Nels' eyes flashed fire. He scooted his own chair back, and as the wooden legs scraped on the vinyl floor Wolf felt a quiver of fear shoot up his spine. His father had never been the physically aggressive type. But still.

Nels stood stiffly. He took a deep breath. Then another. "Sit down, Wolf," he said finally, his voice strained.

Wolf sat.

Nels sat back down himself. "Now, you listen to me," he said evenly. "I understand where this is coming from. I do. But you're out of line. What you're talking about is ancient history. Frieda and I have been together for nearly a year now, and we've known each other a lot longer than that. We want to live together, but there's not enough room for the four of us over the restaurant, so I've invited her to move in here."

His voice lowered and his eyes caught Wolf's. "I love her,

son. And as hard as this may be for you to believe, she loves me, too."

Wolf tore his gaze away. His dad was killing him. Nobody had to tell Wolf how crazy his father was about Frieda. Nels always wore his heart on his sleeve. But he'd "loved" all the others, too. There was nothing different about this one that Wolf could see. She'd lasted the longest so far, but what did that prove? It would only make the fall harder when it came.

And yet, what could Wolf do? Nothing, that's what. Bear wasn't a baby anymore; he made his own decisions. Never mind all the crap they'd gone through together — Bear didn't even seem to remember that. He'd run right out and made friends with Frieda, despite all Wolf's warnings. The damage was already done.

"Whatever, Dad," Wolf forced out, avoiding further eye contact. "I hope you're happy."

Nels blew out a frustrated breath. "I will be, Wolf," he said uncertainly.

Wolf's eyes darted back to his father's, despite himself. There was a "but" somewhere in that statement.

"I want you to be happy too, son," Nels continued.

Wolf thought about that a moment. Then he smiled sadly, knowing the statement was heartfelt. If only his dad could see the truth. Wolf might only be fifteen, but he had a better understanding of women than his father would ever have. "Don't worry about me, Dad," he said confidently, getting up again. "I'll be fine."

# Chapter 26



*Maui, Hawaii 2016*

Ri's heart felt wonderfully light. She laughed out loud as the brisk winds of Ma'alaea Bay grabbed hold of Wolf's shaggy locks and battered him about the face. "Want to borrow a headband?" she teased. "I always carry an extra."

He grinned back at her, wincing as a gale from the side caused a fierce attack on his left eye. He swore and attempted again to stuff all his longish hair up under his cap. But the wind was having none of it. In a matter of seconds, the whole hat came off his head and he only barely managed to recapture it before it flew off over the Pacific.

Ri laughed until her sides ached.

"Hey, I made that save left-handed!" he admonished.

Ri could hardly believe her good fortune. Their conversation on the beach last night had left them at a seeming stalemate, and she'd been afraid that Wolf would take off as soon as their work was done today. She'd tossed and turned all night wondering whether the appeal of her company alone would be enough to overcome his frustrations with her. Either it was or it wasn't — that was the crux of the matter. She had no desire to "win" any man by being scheming or manipulative, no matter how good she believed they could be together. There would be no bait and switch, no allowing him to believe she was okay with "casual" only to trap him into something more. Ri allowed herself only one point of orchestration where Wolf was concerned, and that was trying to maximize the amount of time they had to spend together before he left Maui. Beyond that, she was committed to letting nature take its course.

Even if it meant her heart would take a battering in the process. Last night had been her second swing and a miss, and it had hurt like hell. She'd been honest, as she promised herself she would be. She'd told him flat out how she felt and what she wanted. And what had he said? He'd said, "What's the point?"

*Ouch.*

He still didn't see what she saw. He already knew, because she had told him before, that she was free to move anywhere after the end of August. But that factoid still meant nothing to him. While Ri's fanciful brain had started spinning happily-ever-after scenarios three seconds into their acquaintance, Wolf's disabled neurons still hadn't gone there, and Ri could get seriously depressed about that. But difficult as it was not to take the snub personally, she had made the decision to do just that. Whatever the source of his mental block, it had clearly preceded her. No other woman might have managed to conquer it yet, but no other woman was Sriha Mirini Sullivan.

She *was* making progress. Wolf's brain might still not be able to envision a future that included her, but his heart could not entirely resist her, either. He was smiling at her right this second, admitting defeat as he held his hat in his hands and let the wind whip his hair wildly about his face. And he was here because he wanted to be — no "orchestration" necessary. He had mentioned himself, over their brief lunch break and mid-day hangout with Bella, that one thing he regretted about his time on Maui was that he had never managed to get out on a whale-watching tour.

Now seriously, Ri wondered with glee, how did he think she would respond to that?

"Here," she said with a chuckle, pulling down her ponytail and handing him the tie. "Try this. Then put it up under your hat."

He looked at her skeptically, but took both the hair tie and the suggestion. "I guess it would be nice to actually see the dolphins," he joked.

Ri pulled her extra headband out of her pack and wound it around her own hair. Just as she finished with a funky improvised bun, her eyes widened and she pointed starboard. A two-toned dolphin with a dark gray cape had burst out of the water in a spectacular leap. "Look! A *spotted!* Yes! Finally!"

Wolf looked and laughed with pleasure right along with her as a pod of dolphins performed several more impressive acrobatics. The two-hour cruise was standard tourist fare rather than a research trip, but Ri was delighted that Wolf got to see a breaching humpback as well as two different species of dolphins. He told her about wildlife-watching cruises he'd been on in Alaska, and she mentioned — as she would have anyway — how much she hoped to see an arctic Beluga whale someday. He asked her intelligent questions about the Hawaiian marine life they encountered and she was thrilled to answer, even as they both ignored the highly competent commentary already offered through the PA system. The late afternoon winds were strong and the waters so choppy that several passengers got seasick, but for Ri the time flew by in a haze of bliss. She was in a good mood and Wolf was in a good mood and they always had fun when they were together... and for the moment that was all she wanted to think about.

"Would you mind if we drop by my office?" she asked when they disembarked at the marina. "It's still a mess, I'm sure, but I'd like to see how the cleanup is coming along. And maybe check in with Lachland, if he's around."

Wolf shrugged amicably. He had pulled the hair tie out the moment the boat slowed down outside the harbor, which didn't surprise Ri. Even wearing shorts and sandals instead of his regular work boots seemed to put the mountain man slightly off his game. Ri loved it when he showed more skin, but she couldn't help but chuckle to notice how pale his feet were compared to his darkly tanned arms.

Ri led Wolf through the Foundation building and down a musty-smelling hallway into the research team's computer lab. Or rather, what had been their computer lab. It was now a square room full of jumbled junk. Most of the electronics and furniture were gone. The desks were still in place, but they'd been made of particle board, and their bottoms were bloated and warped. Their desktops were completely covered by cardboard boxes overflowing with office supplies, and the whole place smelled like a locker room at a pool, minus the chlorine.

"It was slightly more impressive before the flood," Ri explained.

Wolf had no chance to reply. Lachland walked through the door with a start, clearly surprised to find anyone there. "Ri," he said, catching his breath.

"I'm sorry," she apologized. She introduced the two men, who exchanged a nod and a handshake. "We just got back from a dolphin tour, and I wanted to see how the recovery effort was going. Are you sure you can't use any of the interns' help with this?"

Lachland's eyes flashed with an aggrieved expression Ri didn't understand. "No, thank you," he said heavily.

Ri suspected that something else was wrong. Something new. She debated whether she should ask him about it and decided probably not. Her day was going entirely too well to spoil now. "Well, if you're sure we can't help," she repeated, keeping her voice cheerful. "Should I plan on coming in Monday, or would you rather I call to check first?"

Lachland's keen gaze studied her a moment. His eyes looked bloodshot. The last time he'd looked like that, he'd gotten no sleep the night before. "Listen, Ri," he began with a sigh, his shoulders slumping. "I was going to call you later, but since you're here, I might as well get it over with."

Ri's blood froze. He could *not* be cancelling her internship. He could not! She felt her knees weaken beneath her.

"You know that joke I made about disasters coming in threes?" Lachland asked.

*This could not be happening.* Ri had waited too long, saved too long. *No, no, no.* She tried to control her nerves but she could feel her limbs trembling. In her peripheral vision, she saw Wolf move closer to her side. He made no attempt to touch her, but she could feel his warmth radiating towards her just the same.

"Will and Bryant took the rental car out for a little joyride last night and wound up in a fender bender," Lachland announced. "Nobody was hurt, but there was significant damage to the rental and a parked car, too. Both guys were drunk. Will's been arrested on a DUI. They've both been suspended from the program."

Ri stopped breathing for a moment. Then she snapped out of it and shook her head. "Wait, what? Will... and Bryant..."

"Immature reprobates," Lachland muttered. "Or rather, one of each, respectively." He looked at her and cleared his throat. "Sorry. I shouldn't have said that."

"No," Ri replied weakly, "I'd say one of each is accurate. But what does... I mean, what does this mean for me?"

Lachland looked confused. But then he stepped toward Ri with a smile. "Nothing!" he insisted. "Your internship will go on as planned, of course. Don't worry about that!"

Ri's breath let out with a whoosh. "Thank goodness," she gushed. "I just thought, with three out of four missing in action—"

"Good God, no!" Lachland declared. Then he threw back his head and laughed ruefully. "I swear, Ri, if it hadn't been for you, I would have cancelled the whole damn thing before orientation was out."

Ri's heart thumped painfully. "What?"

He shook his head. "I swore I'd never tell anybody this. But I don't want you to think we don't have great interns here. We usually do, because I pick the best. But unfortunately, I procrastinate. This spring I put it off till the last minute, then wound up with a GI virus so bad I— Well, it was bad. I went back to work the next week only to find out that Trish had 'taken care of it' for me." His eyes rolled. "I don't know if she threw darts at the applications or just called the first four she picked up, but she couldn't have done a worse job if she'd been blindfolded."

Ri felt like crumpling, but Wolf's solid presence bucked her up, even without a touch.

"She did get one out of four right," Lachland added quickly. "I was going to pick you anyway, Ri. I swear. Your application was at the top of the stack. So I certainly hope you'll stay on, even though when we finally get up and running again, you may be a bit busier than you expected."

"That sounds wonderful," Ri answered honestly. "I can't wait. Thank you."

They said their goodbyes, and Ri led Wolf back to the truck in silent contemplation, her mood brightening with every step. Although it was a shame that Will's internship had come to such an unfortunate end, he had brought it on himself, and Bryant was equally complicit in the deed. Both had shown such blatant disregard for Lachland's generosity, she found it difficult to feel sorry for either of them. What mattered was that no one had been injured in the debacle and that her own internship was safe. She felt gratified that Lachland thought that she was doing a good job and wanted her to continue. She believed him when he said she'd been his first choice. But most encouraging of all, when her fear of bad news had made her genuinely upset, what had Wolf done? He had picked up on her distress and acted protectively toward her. And he probably didn't even realize he'd done it.

Now *that* was something worth smiling about.

"So, dinner back at the Hilton?" Wolf asked uncertainly as they stepped up into the truck. He was probably getting hungry, and he knew that Ri couldn't afford to eat out.

She hesitated. "Actually, we have another option." She'd been debating with herself all afternoon over how to bring up the issue. Kai had texted her earlier in the day saying that he had some information about Filipino relatives he wanted to share with her. He'd made clear that it was nothing particularly exciting, but that he did want to talk to her in person. He'd invited her to dinner at his new apartment with himself and Maddie, and Ri had very much wanted to join them. But she didn't want to give up an evening with Wolf to do it. Luckily for her, Kai had made an alternative suggestion.

"Kai has something he wants to tell me, and he's invited both of us to come over and have some noodles or something. Maddie will be there, too. You want to go? We don't have to stay long."

Wolf shrugged again. "Sure," he agreed. "Sounds like fun."

"Great! Thanks," Ri said with astonishment. Her pulse pounded with excitement, even as she warned herself not to read too much into his response. She didn't know what to expect from him, but after the emotional ups and downs of last evening, he did seem surprisingly placid. He wasn't pressing her, but nor was he actively resisting her.

She wished she knew what he was thinking.

Wolf had no idea what he was thinking. He had no idea why he was sitting at a kitchen table in Kai Nakama's apartment eating some weird spaghetti dish made with spam and cheese and talking and laughing and acting like he and Ri were on a double date with an engaged couple. The optics were like some kind of bizarre greeting card. First, because the picture of mundane domesticity was everything he did not want to be accidentally, circumstantially associated with, because it gave all the wrong impressions about what he was doing with Ri and what he wanted for his own life. And second, because no matter how much he enjoyed Ri's company in the platonic sense, any man who would choose to spend all day admiring such a hot little body when he knew his prospects were nil was a masochistic idiot.

Much to his surprise, he was having a great time anyway.

Hanging with Kai and Maddie together was usually a downer, but the dynamic was different with Ri around, and he found that he'd missed the simple pleasure of having a family-type dinner in a regular home. He especially enjoyed getting a chance to talk with Kai when the women were otherwise occupied. At the field station Maddie was always hanging all over the man, and her presence tended to be overpowering. But by the end of dinner Wolf could see that his positive impressions of the mild-mannered lawyer were justified. Not only was the Lana'ian smart, honest, and blessed with a good sense of humor, the firm he worked for was currently engaged in a legal battle to get the air pollution cleaned up in Fairbanks — a subject which happened to be near and dear to Wolf's lungs.

He also couldn't help noticing that Kai was happy. Not just upbeat, like some people are by nature. The man sitting across from Wolf sipping at a generic root beer was fully, deeply, genuinely, ecstatically, *content* with his life. And as much as Wolf would like to write that off as a byproduct of sleeping in the same bed as a woman like Maddie, he knew that would be naive. There was obviously more to it.

Good for them.

"Okay, Kai," Ri said, breaking into Wolf's thoughts as she bounced a little in her chair and drummed her palms on the table. "You've kept me in suspense long enough. What is it you want to tell me?"

Kai smiled at her. "Like I said, it's nothing to get excited about," he explained gently. "But Nana"— he threw an apologetic glance at Wolf— "that's my grandmother on Lana'i, was very interested in your story, and she made some phone calls."

Ri's eyes lit up. Wolf watched as a smile brightened the angel face he'd become so familiar with. In a few short days, he'd memorized its every feature. She was so proud of her Filipino heritage. So glad to know anything about her biological background. And yet it occurred to him that he'd never once heard her talk about wanting to find her actual birthparents. Was that a secret wish?

"Nana was pretty sure we had some relatives who were into genealogy," Kai continued. "So she decided to give them a call. Turns out she found two who'd done the ancestry DNA testing."

Ri sat up, and her arm pressed against Wolf's. Her touch affected him so strongly he nearly groaned aloud, but with an effort he managed to stifle both the sound and the urge to recoil in self-defense. This wasn't about him. She probably didn't even notice. "And?" she asked.

"One was the daughter of a cousin of hers on the Big Island," Kai answered. "They're related through Nana's father, who came to Lana'i from the Philippines after World War II. That woman checked the database, but although I showed up as a relative match, you did not. And yes, I gave her the ID you used."

"Which proves we're not related through that particular ancestor," Ri stated.

"Right," Kai agreed. "The other relative who tested was a direct descendant of Nana's, a cousin of mine from right here on Maui. She found the same thing, I'm afraid. I was a match, but you were not."

Wolf could feel Ri deflating beside him. She was upset. He watched like an innocent bystander as his arm reached out and hugged her around the shoulders.

*Dammit!* Why had he done that? He hadn't thought. He was sending messages she would misinterpret. Besides which, he was torturing himself. But as Ri melted into his side, he had to acknowledge that the feel of her warm body against his wasn't *all* torture.

"There is still another possibility, though," Kai said, his voice encouraging. "You and I could be related through my grandfather, Nana's husband. He was second-generation Lana'ian, mixed Filipino and Puerto Rican. Nana said that three of his grandparents were born in the Philippines. Our common ancestor could be a few generations above any of those people. It's still completely possible."

"Of course. I see," Ri said, seeming more chipper again. Gradually, Wolf forced himself to ease down his arm, then remove it. He caught a quick dart of Ri's eyes toward him. She had definitely noticed. She hadn't seemed to mind him putting his arm around her, but she didn't care for his taking it away. She was sending that signal again.

*I want you, too, you know.*

Wolf shifted in his chair. Now he was definitely uncomfortable.

"Nana doesn't have many contacts with my grandfather's family anymore," Kai explained. "But she said she'd give it a try, see if anyone knows anyone who's ever done a DNA test. Or if anyone in the family knows of anyone in the Philippines who might have been a diplomat or an exchange student in Russia. But that would be a long shot, of course."

Ri shook her head. "Please, thank your grandmother for me," she said with a smile. "Profusely. I'd love to have some other evidence that you and I are related, however distantly. But to be honest..." She looked wistful as her voice trailed off.

"What is it?" Maddie asked finally.

Ri blew out a breath. "I go through phases," she confessed. "Sometimes I've felt an urge to find my birthparents. To try and meet them and even get to know them. But other times...

well, most of the time, I don't really care about them. I know that sounds callous, but it's true. I used to have a lot of anger bottled up against my birthmother, but I got over that a long time ago. She dumped me in a train station the day I was born, yes, but if she hadn't, I wouldn't have had the parents I love and the life I've got." Her pretty brow furrowed with thought. "I've never known enough about my birthfather's situation to have any opinion about his actions, and sometimes I think that's for the best. I can do without the burden of knowing things I would need to forgive. I'm glad my birthparents created me, but the fact is, I don't need them in my life now any more than they needed a baby in their lives then."

Her features relaxed, and she offered a shrug. "All I've ever really wanted was to know who I am biologically, why I look the way I look, and what people's heritage I share. I have all that now." She smiled around the table at everyone in turn. "So, hey! I'm good!"

Maddie and Kai gave a smile and a laugh of relief, and the conversation soon turned to Kai's family on Lana'i, and how they would all love to meet Ri regardless of the DNA factor.

Wolf's attempts to listen got sidetracked. He was still trying to understand everything that Ri had said. Not so much the content of her speech, but the fact that she had said it at all. Whether Kai was technically a relative or not, Ri had not known any of them a week ago. He knew her to be a thoughtful, relatively private person, yet she had just shared something extremely personal. And she had done so without an ounce of embarrassment. Or shame.

*She dumped me in a train station the day I was born.*

Ri had said that of her own mother without batting an eyelash. She hadn't seemed to think it reflected badly on her. Which of course it did not. Why should it?

Wolf's own words came back to him with a flash of red-hot anger.

*Our mother died when I was six.*

His mother. Dead. That's what he'd told Ri. She had been brave enough and honest enough to admit the ugly truth of her own bio-parental shortcomings, but what had happened when he was asked?

He had lied, that's what. He'd lied because he was a coward, because he hadn't wanted to admit that his own mother had left him. He'd been ashamed to admit it because he'd taken that shame on himself. But he'd been thinking all these years like a child would think. He'd *been* a child back then, dammit — his mother had been the adult. The fault was all hers!

He had nothing whatsoever to be ashamed of. And certainly no reason to lie about it.

By the time Wolf and Ri said their goodbyes to their hosts and stepped up into the truck to begin the long drive home, it was well after nine. Wolf hadn't intended to hang around so long. But Kai had tempted them all with a quick game of cards, and after everyone's competitive streak kicked in, the time flew by. All in all, despite the near-constant physical frustration Ri caused him, he had enjoyed their ocean cruise and mundane domestic evening immensely.

But there was something he had to clear up. "Ri?"

"Yes?" she asked hesitantly, seeming to sense the import of his tone.

"I lied to you yesterday."

"About what?" she asked. She did not sound particularly surprised, and he had no right to be offended by that. But her easy acceptance of duplicity on his part did bother him. He would prefer to have her trust.

"My mother isn't dead," he announced. "The last I heard, she was alive and in Montana. But I wouldn't say she's 'well.' She's an alcoholic and has been since she was a teenager. She had a dry spell in her twenties, when she married my father and had me and Bear. But she walked out on all three of us when I was in the first grade, and I haven't seen or heard from her since."

Wolf looked out the windshield at the passing lights of Kahului.

"I'm sorry," Ri said softly.

Wolf shrugged without looking at her. He wasn't telling her this to elicit any particular reaction. He was telling her because he shouldn't have lied to her in the first place. He needed to get the words out, and he'd done that. It hadn't been all that difficult, really.

"You did me a favor, talking about your own birthmother," he admitted. "It made me realize that lying about mine was an automatic reaction. I started doing it when I was a kid, and then I guess I never bothered to rethink. But I've got no reason to lie. What happened wasn't my fault. So, hey—" he threw up his hands and gave her a small smile. "Now, you know. Chalk it up as something else we have in common: maternal abandonment."

Ri did not smile back. He watched in horror as her beautiful brown eyes grew watery. "What's the matter?" he asked.

She shook her head briskly. "Nothing!" she insisted, her voice choked. "Nothing." She plastered a smile on her face, then cut a turn too short at the intersection and bounced the truck up over a curb.

"You want me to drive?" Wolf asked, flummoxed. What the hell was wrong with her, now?

Ri swiped at her eyes with a hand. "No way!" she answered, sounding ridiculously cheerful all of a sudden. "I told you, I'm fine!" She smiled at him for real this time. "Um... you said you'd tell me sometime about your trip to the Pribilof Islands, remember? You said it was a long story. How about now?"

Wolf blinked. She was crying and then she was happy, and then she wanted to talk about fur seals and walrus?

He relaxed in his seat. He could talk about the Pribilofs the whole ride home, if that's what she wanted. He did enjoy putting a smile on her face.

Even when she did make no sense at all.

Chapter 27

Ri and Wolf walked side by side down the dirt track, lugging all
of the day's gear and two empty water bottles. The day had
been cloudless and hotter than expected, and despite her best
intentions, Ri found herself dragging. The views from the
southwest slope of Haleakala had been amazing, and Wolf's
quiet company contented her to the point where she found it
difficult to hurry. Most likely, she admitted to herself, she was
subconsciously stretching out the workday because she was
unsure whether she could lure him into spending a fourth
evening in her company.

The physical magnetism between them was now impossible
to ignore. They'd managed to beat it into submission today for
the sake of Wolf's work, but it had taken a mutual effort. At the
same time, he was opening up to her emotionally, and he
genuinely seemed to want her friendship whether anything else
happened between them or not. Ri was both ecstatic and
terrified. She had left the infatuation stage somewhere between
seeing his sleeping bag in the dog run and feeling his arm
encircle her shoulders in Kai's kitchen, and whether she liked it
or not, her whole heart was now hopelessly, irretrievably on the
line.

They'd been hiking all day, but the walk back down the dirt
road they were on now seemed endless. Ri was uncertain why
Wolf had instructed her to leave the truck at the road's far end,
since she could have parked it at any one of several pullouts
closer to the trail. But she assumed he had his reasons. She
focused instead on picking the most compelling invitation for
tonight. A picnic dinner on a beach in South Maui? Window
shopping in old Lahaina town? *No, he would hate the crowds.* A
drive up the cliffs northwest of Kahului? Since they were
running late, they would have less playtime before dark.
Perhaps she could alter her budget so that they could spend the
night hours dining at a real restaurant. That would mean peanut

butter sandwiches for her for a month after he left, but what did that matter?

Just as they turned the bend and the truck came into view, Ri's path forward was abruptly blocked by Wolf's broad back and the bulky equipment hanging off it. She braced her hands on his upper arms and stumbled to a halt, enjoying the feel of his firm biceps even as she opened her mouth to protest. But no words left her lips. She could feel the tenseness in his muscles. He was standing with his arms outstretched in a defensive posture.

"Ri," he said quietly, but firmly. "Do me a favor and call 911, would you?"

Her breath caught. She couldn't see around him to know exactly what he was looking at. But she knew better than to waste time being curious. She set down her own load, slipped off her pack, and pulled out her phone.

"Could you put it up to my ear?" Wolf asked. His voice was calm, but his wariness told her otherwise as he scanned the empty road and bushes around them. They were near a crossroads, and there was some kind of commercial building a couple hundred yards away. But there were no other people in sight.

Ri dialed the number and waited for an answer. Then she reached up and placed the phone where Wolf could hear. Only then did she get a good look at the truck.

The wheels were sitting in a pool of shattered glass. Every window had been smashed out. Jagged shards clung to the frames, and those on the windshield near the passenger door were smeared with blood. Red streaks ran across the front right fender. Red droplets spilled out onto the road.

Ri couldn't focus on what Wolf was saying. She stood frozen, holding the cell phone and staring around them. Whoever did this could still be here.

"Ri?"

"Yeah?" she squeaked.

"You can hang up the phone now. But keep it out."

Ri released her pent up breath, slowly, and lowered her arm.

Wolf gradually let his own arms fall to his sides, although he remained tense and alert. "Let's walk toward the main road," he advised. "But quietly. And keep a lookout."

They did. The building supply store near the corner was inexplicably closed, but its parking lot was exposed on three sides and in plain sight of any passing cars, and as they reached its center, Wolf relaxed slightly. He shrugged off his gear and set it down on the ground beside him.

Ri's pulse continued to race as she did the same. Vandalism was bad enough. But she could not erase the sight of the smeared blood from her mind. That part could have been an accident. But it could also have been a warning. Either way, whoever did this couldn't possibly be sane. There was nothing of value in the truck. It had been parked within sight of a fairly well-traveled road in broad daylight. There was nothing about that scenario that boded well. She looked with dismay at the splint on Wolf's right hand. "You know who did this, don't you?"

Wolf didn't look at her. He was still watching every tree, boulder, and clump of shrubs that could possibly conceal a human being. He nodded.

"The man who hurt Bella?" she pressed in a whisper.

The muscles in his jaw tightened. He nodded. "I reported him to the humane authorities. I saw him kick her and I didn't think he was feeding her right. But he told them she wasn't his dog. He said she was a stray — that she was dangerous." His features hardened into a scowl. "*Dangerous!* Bella! I was hoping that animal control would pick her up then, but they didn't. He hid her in the house or something. I don't know what he did. But they couldn't find her. And sometime after they left, he laid into her again — only worse. I didn't see her in the yard for days. Finally I just went over there. That's when I found her under the shed. I told him I was taking her and he said no. He would have left her there to die."

Ri felt herself begin to tremble. She didn't know why she would start now. They were almost certainly not in any danger here, and the police would arrive any minute. "That explains the broken hand," she said softly.

Wolf shrugged, still not looking at her. "He took a swing at me first."

Ri's desire to wrap her arms around him was close to overwhelming, but she managed to suppress it. She knew he wouldn't want the distraction. He would probably not welcome her consolation, either, although she was not above offering it again at a more opportune time.

"I used to have a pretty good uppercut myself, you know," she said instead. "Or so I've been told."

She watched as the corners of Wolf's mouth twitched a little. His gaze flickered toward her. "Yeah?"

"You don't believe me, but it's true," she insisted. "I know you think I'm perfect and all, but as a toddler I was a complete psycho mess. If you ask my mother about it she'll go on for hours about the spectrum of attachment disturbances and sensorimotor deprivation and coping skills and resiliency. But what she really means is that I was a holy frickin' terror with anger management issues who used to punch other children in the face."

Wolf's eyebrows lifted. "Thanks for the warning," he said dryly.

"You're welcome," Ri said pleasantly. "I'm mostly over it now."

"Well, if The Beard shows up before the police get here, I'll be sure to shove you out front."

Ri chuckled. "'The Beard,' eh? Well, I'm a little out of practice. But at least my hand's not in a splint."

Wolf held up his right hand and studied it speculatively. "I've been thinking this thing could do some pretty serious damage, actually."

Ri's brief feeling of levity faded. "Please don't joke about that. I mean, I know I just did, but—" She felt suddenly sick to her stomach. No cars had come by. There was no sign of the police. Every time the wind rustled in the trees, her gut tightened. "Tell me the truth. Is this man seriously out to get you?" She could feel herself trembling again.

Wolf noticed. His arms swept out immediately and pulled her to his chest. "It'll be all right," he soothed, rubbing his good hand gently along her back. "I'm sorry to get you involved in all this."

Ri's breath caught in her throat. He felt so good. So strong, so comforting, so... sweet. He had held her before in the grove, but it was not like this. This was a Wolf she'd never seen before. No, that wasn't true. This was the Wolf she'd *heard* before. In the dark and the fog. Comforting a lonely, wounded animal.

This was his nature, his instinct. The side of himself he usually fought not to show. She closed her eyes and relaxed against him. She could stay here all day. She could stay here forever.

The sound of a car approaching on the highway met her ears, and Ri greeted it with mixed emotions. Having the police arrive on the scene was good. Wolf's tensing up and releasing her was not.

"It's nobody," he said with fake cheer, rubbing her upper arm briskly with his good hand while he stepped away. A red minivan sped by them, and he looked at her with concern. "Seriously, are you all right? I really don't think there's anything to worry about. I'm being cautious in case this guy is still around, but the odds are he's long gone. He obviously cut himself up."

Ri looked back into Wolf's intelligent, alert eyes, and a light dawned. Not only had he told her to park the truck in an inconvenient location, but he'd insisted they take a questionable "shortcut" that bypassed the regular trailhead and cut cross-country instead. That wasn't like him at all. He'd preached to her before about how sticking to the trails minimized damage to the environment. "He's out for revenge and you know it," she contradicted. "This guy lives nearby, doesn't he? You've been leading us out of our way to avoid him."

Wolf's brow furrowed. "He does know my truck. I've been parking within sight of his place for months. And it's true that he probably hates my guts. In his mind, it's all my fault that he's up on animal cruelty charges. I'm surprised he took the risk of lashing out in such a public place, but there's nothing for you to worry about now. The truck's covered by insurance, and we just finished all the work that's anywhere near here. Bella's perfectly safe where she is — he doesn't know where I'm staying, and even if he did, he thinks the shelter took her."

For all his reassuring words, Wolf continuously scanned three-hundred-sixty degrees around them, and he was still visibly tense. Studying him, Ri began to believe that his words were true, even if he didn't look as confident as he sounded. He probably wasn't all that worried about himself. But he did seem to feel responsible for her.

He forced out a laugh. "He'll regret cutting himself for more reasons than one. Without that, I'd have a hard time proving it was him. Now, the case will be open and shut."

Ri imagined the man sitting in a dingy house somewhere with his arm wrapped up in a bloody towel. He'd need stitches, but he'd be afraid to seek medical help for fear of getting caught.

"Oh, no," Wolf said suddenly.

"What?" Ri barked, her head snapping around.

"I just realized," he said calmly, albeit sadly. "The truck. It's... there's no way you can drive it, now. Oh, Ri," he lamented, his face awash with guilt. "I'm so sorry. That's my whole end of the bargain! How can I—"

A commotion arose to their right. Leaves and branches rustled sharply.

In a flash, Ri found herself behind Wolf's broad back again, shielded from whatever was happening at the edge of the gravel parking lot. She grabbed for the phone in her pocket, her heart beating wildly.

She heard a loud squawk. Then a low, rumbling vibration in Wolf's chest.

He turned to face her. "Damn chickens," he chuckled. "They're lucky I don't have a shotgun."

Ri looked to see two roosters posturing as they moved their argument back into the bushes again. She breathed a sigh of relief, closed her eyes, and fell forward against his chest. "Please tell them not to do that again," she murmured. Her hands crept to his waist and felt their way around his back. She leaned in and held him.

"You heard her, guys!" Wolf called out in an admonishing

tone. "Knock it off back there!"

Ri smiled. His arms had come around her, too. He was holding her back. It felt so natural, so right. The world could stop turning now. Time could freeze in this very second and her life would be complete. Surely he could feel that same sense of primal, unqualified bliss. Of comfort. Of contentment...

"I wish you weren't leaving so soon," she blurted.

*Crap.* She hadn't planned to say that. The words had just slithered out.

She squeezed her eyes shut with angst. He had tensed up a little. But he hadn't let go.

"I'm sorry," she amended. "I shouldn't have said that."

A beat passed. "You shouldn't have to apologize for saying the truth," Wolf said quietly. "I wish I wasn't leaving so soon, either. I was just in such a rush to get that plane ticket..."

It seemed as though he meant to say more. But he did not.

After a moment, Ri raised her head. She looked in his eyes and tried her damnedest to get a read on how he was feeling. But the man's emotions were a multilayered jumble of nonsense.

"But I am leaving," he said even more quietly, his voice barely above a whisper. "I don't have any choice. Not anymore."

His gaze held hers, and Ri could see that he meant what he said. He did want to stay. And he did have to go. His time on Frosty Peak was nonnegotiable, as was the conclusion of her internship on Maui. But when, if ever, would he open his mind to seeing past the next three months? Why was looking beyond the immediate future so unthinkable for him?

She could point out the obvious. She had been tempted, more than once, to casually drop into conversation the fact that the University of Fairbanks had a fabulous grad program in marine science. But if they weren't on the same page emotionally, her hints would serve no purpose. If and when his feelings became as strong as hers, he would be wracking his own brains figuring out how they could be together.

She steeled herself for patience. What could she do besides give their relationship more time? Never mind how little time they had. Perhaps it was a good thing he'd taken the physical aspects of romance off the table. It would force them to communicate their feelings in other ways.

If only the prohibition weren't so painful. She wanted to reach up right this second and run her fingers through his wavy locks, cradle his head in her hands, and kiss those gorgeous lips of his until he was breathless and begging. But that would be cheating, dammit. And Sriha Mirini Sullivan always played by the rules.

Wolf Markov, on the other hand, did not. He'd been studying her eyes every bit as thoroughly as she'd been studying his, and although she'd made the mental decision to resist her impulses, her face was broadcasting unequivocal, raging lust. She could hardly fault him for accepting that invitation as his arms tightened around her and the lips in question lowered hungrily over hers.

*No. Stop. I can't.*

She said nothing. She only thought the words. Even silently in her brain, they were half-hearted. She was enjoying herself too much. Her one hand explored his solidly muscled back while the other lifted to twine her fingers around his soft, wavy hair. She had not exaggerated her memory of their time in the grove. Kissing Wolf was amazing. She felt as though both her body and her being were melting. She wanted to get closer to him. She could not get close enough.

He clearly felt the same. His kiss grew more heated. His muscles felt so firm, his skin so warm. He was beginning to sweat...

A siren sounded.

Wolf released her so suddenly she almost fell backward. "I'm sorry," he said immediately, reaching out and steadying her. He looked around them. "I forgot I was supposed to be keeping an eye out. Fine bodyguard I'd make."

Ri took a second to catch her breath. The siren was getting louder, but its source still wasn't visible. As soon as Wolf seemed satisfied that the coast was clear, he turned his attention back to Ri. He smiled at her and reached up to reposition her headband.

His smile was very happy, very sweet. The look in his eyes was tender and only a few pegs short of loving. But he also looked damnably smug.

Practically victorious.

"That didn't count, you know," Ri said obstinately.

He lifted an eyebrow. "What?"

"You know what I mean," she said playfully. "I was taken advantage of in a weakened state. But if your policy still stands, then nothing's changed."

Wolf appeared confused. "Taken advantage of?" he repeated. "Did I miss something?"

Ri took pity on him. "I don't mean—" She shook her head with a smile. "You interpreted my feelings correctly. But we're supposed to be following *your* stupid-ass ultimatum, remember?"

He stared at her.

"No strings or nothing?" she reminded. "I'll say it again if I have to, just to clarify. I want strings. Casual sex doesn't work for me. So by *your* rules, Mr. Markov, that means no making out in deserted parking lots."

He continued to stare at her, his face slowly reddening, as a Maui County police van at last pulled up the road and turned into the gravel lot behind him. Wolf stood still, not even bothering to look over his shoulder until the vehicle had parked. He said nothing else to Ri. But when he turned towards the arriving police officers, she could hear perfectly well the words he muttered to himself.

*Stupid-ass is right.*

# Chapter 28

"Here," Wolf said, pulling a square, lightweight tarp from his backpack and handing it to Ri. "You'll need to keep this handy. If there's a deluge, you'll need to throw it over the instruments I'm carrying. My poncho might not cover them and I don't want to take any chances." He glanced up at the solid gray sky with a grimace. The weather did not look good. Passing showers were a near-daily occurrence on Maui, and he could carry out his work in light rain without too much difficulty, although doing so was both tedious and slow. But risking a heavy downpour was usually a nonstarter, and he had known the forecast when he and Ri headed out this morning. He just didn't have the heart to put off finishing up the job till tomorrow. Not when she'd been planning all week to spend the entire day Saturday driving the road to Hana and back.

Ri looked at him speculatively. "If we get caught in a torrent, are your instruments going to be at risk?"

He smiled a little. He liked that she cared. He liked everything about her. He just didn't know what to do about it.

"They'll be fine as long as we're careful," he answered. "But we'll have to take a break whenever the rain gets too heavy or the wind kicks up, which could make for a pretty long day."

"So long as I can still get Maddie and Kai to the ferry on time," Ri replied, looking concerned.

Wolf nodded in reassurance. "You'll get them there on time, whether we finish the job or not. We'll come back in the dark with a flashlight if we have to."

Ri gave him a brilliant smile, and its effect was wholly unexpected. His gut felt like it was simultaneously twisting and on fire. And if that weren't enough, he felt sad, too.

He turned away from her and began moving silently along the trail again. He was exhausted, that was all. He hadn't slept well for days. He'd been tied up forever in Kahului last night, wrangling endlessly with the truck leasing outfit and the insurance company, not to mention the police. The damages to the truck would be covered, but there was no way to get a replacement vehicle for the weekend without paying market rate, which he couldn't afford. He felt terrible about leaving Ri short of the promised set of wheels, but thank God, Maddie had come through for them. She had picked Ri up at the scene while Wolf rode on the tow truck into Kahului, and after hearing their tale of woe Maddie had offered Ri the use of her own truck while the engaged couple spent the weekend with Kai's family on Lana'i, which they had been planning to do anyway. The only catch was that Ri had to drop them off and pick them up at the ferry port in Lahaina.

The whole arrangement worked out well for Ri and let Wolf off the hook completely. But that only made him feel worse. He felt like he'd taken advantage of her skills as an assistant. She'd never actually taken his truck anywhere by herself, and it turned out she could have driven Maddie's truck this weekend anyway.

The least he could do was buy her a nice dinner or something before he left. Right?

He felt a splat against the thin plastic poncho that covered himself and his gear. Then he felt another seventy. The storm had begun. He felt Ri throwing the tarp over his shoulders, and he grasped it in his own hands, then spun around. "We're not going to make it to the next site," he told her as the rain pounded down. "But Hosmer's right up the hill from here. Let's wait it out there, okay?" He had to shout the last words. The rain was pelting them violently and her ears were covered by the hood of her own poncho.

Ri nodded, and they headed toward the grove. A few minutes later, they tracked a hefty amount of mud into the small picnic shelter that sat on the other side of the parking lot from the Hosmer Grove campsite. The shelter was open on one side and not much wider than the two picnic tables it contained, but by huddling in its center Ri and Wolf could at least get themselves and their unloaded gear out of the rain. Wolf felt gratified that his habit of saving the easiest and most accessible sites for last had once again paid off. Everything they had left to do was within hiking distance of the field station; they wouldn't have needed his truck today anyway. Even the section they did yesterday was a leftover; he'd been giving The Beard some extra time to cool off. Too bad it hadn't been enough.

The rain was coming down in sheets. It hit the paved parking lot in pulses, creating multiple ripples that moved down the asphalt surface like waves.

"Impressive," Ri remarked. She pulled off her headband and shook her whole head forcefully, wringing out her sopping curls by shooting a spray of droplets everywhere, including into Wolf's face.

"Ugh! What are you, a husky?" he joked, wiping his cheek with his splint.

Ri laughed. "Whiner. You sound like Mei Lin. Except she just calls me a dog."

"I thought you were wearing a hood!" he chuckled.

"I was," she confirmed. "But the curls had other ideas." She smiled back at him as she replaced her headband. She was still wearing the poncho, but Wolf could see through it. It could be made of lead and his imagination would do the rest. Damn, she was gorgeous. He had always thought that Maddie was gorgeous; and objectively, the picture-perfect redhead still was. But looking at the two women side by side the other evening, it struck him that Maddie's star had inexplicably dimmed. Maybe the tall, big-busted ecologist was too perfect? He didn't know. All he knew was that he'd never wanted any woman as much as he wanted Ri.

And he was leaving her the day after tomorrow.

Ri made a sudden gasping sound, and Wolf tensed, expecting to see a bear or a moose popping out of the bushes. He'd been on Maui four months now and still couldn't kick the ingrained reaction, although at this point, he figured he should stop trying. He'd be back in Alaska soon enough.

"Oh! You know what I want to do?" Ri exclaimed.

Wolf was pretty sure they both wanted exactly the same thing.

"I want to go camping tonight!" she finished with a bounce.

Her dark eyes shone with excitement and her cherry cheeks dimpled to the max. "That would be so much fun!"

Wolf found himself speechless. He looked from Ri's glowing face to the sea of mud on the opposite side of the parking lot. They definitely did not want the same thing. "You want to go camping?" he repeated with disbelief. "In this?"

Ri made a face. "Well, maybe not in *this*," she clarified. "We'd need a dry spell long enough to get the tent set up, at least. But I love sleeping out and listening to a light rain pattering over my head. Your tent is waterproof, isn't it?"

"My tent?" he repeated hopefully. Maybe they were on the same page after all.

"If it's big enough for two sleeping bags," Ri continued, bursting his bubble. "And Bella, of course. We'll need a chaperone."

Wolf found himself speechless again. She was teasing him, but then again, she wasn't. She was playful by nature, but there wasn't a deceptive bone in her body. He couldn't complain that she was leading him on. She'd been clear as a bell. She wanted him, but only if they had a relationship with a future. He had no future to offer.

Did he?

No. He didn't. How could he? If he was staying on Maui, then hell yes, he'd go for it — his policy and his mantra be damned. He kept forgetting why he'd come up with them in the first place. But he had to go back to Alaska and she had to stay here. She had no idea where she was going after that — she'd said so herself. His own doctoral work would take him all over the state — it would be years before he'd settle down to a steady job, and even then he'd probably be traveling. How she thought any "strings" could fit into that picture was beyond him. Wasn't that why he'd sworn off relationships in the first place?

*No. Not really.*

Wolf diverted his mind. Whatever he was starting to think about, he didn't want to think about it.

The point was that he couldn't offer Ri a future. But if that's what she wanted, that's what she deserved. And he had no business pressuring her into accepting anything less.

"Would Bella run off, do you think?" he heard her say, as from a distance. She'd been talking for a while. "Maybe we could bring a stake out."

Wolf forced his thoughts back to the present. "We can't bring Bella here. Dogs aren't allowed. She can't leave the field station grounds or Kenneth will get grief from the park service."

"Oh, right," Ri said, disappointed. Then she smiled with mischief. "Well, we'll just have to behave ourselves, then. How big is your tent?"

Wolf tried to get hold of himself. The images in his head were way too vivid and he was developing a gnawing pain in his gut. "You're a smooth one," he praised. "But I don't remember agreeing to lend you my tent, much less join you in it."

She smirked. "Caught me. Can I borrow your tent?"

"Yes," he answered. "But it's a bivy-style. Strictly one person."

Ri's lips pursed. "Maybe Maddie or someone else at the Hilton has a real tent. Something big enough to stretch out and play cards in. Have a midnight snack. Make shadow animals with a flashlight. That sort of thing."

Wolf stared at her sparkling dark eyes and realized for the first time that they weren't completely brown. Although the majority of her irises were a rich coffee color, the outermost edges were a stunning emerald green. A little gift from her Russian mother, he supposed. Along with the crazy curls. But her Filipino father was to thank for her luscious lips and the smooth bronze of her tantalizingly soft skin. Whoever her birthparents were, wherever they were, the two of them had given the world a very precious gift, indeed. Not that he would ever leave her real parents out of the equation. They had taken the raw material and raised a woman who was as exceptional in spirit as she was unique in genetics.

He'd forgotten what they were talking about. "What?"

Ri cracked up. Her laughter was mellow and pleasing. "If I find a tent, will you join me?" she invited. "At least for a little while? If you get scared after dark, you can go back to the

Hilton. I promise I won't make fun of you."

Wolf tried to reset his foggy brain. The rain was slowing down. The sky was looking brighter. They should get back to the site as soon as possible. He didn't want Ri to lose any more of her promised free time.

"You want me to beg?" she asked. "Look, Wolf, don't overthink this. It'll be a Friday night, and I have nothing else to do. Maddie and Kai will be gone, and I hardly know anyone else on Maui. I'll camp out by myself if I have to, but solitaire isn't my favorite, and making shadow animals without an audience would be seriously lame. You think Kenneth is busy tonight? Maybe he'd—"

"All right!" Wolf broke in with a laugh. "Yes! I will... hang out in a tent with you. For a while, anyway. But I've got to get some sleep tonight."

Ri beamed in triumph. His last words hung in the air, striking an odd chord in his ear. Why exactly had he tacked on that last part? It was true that he could and would get no sleep in her presence, whether he tossed and turned three feet away or whether he was pleasantly occupied. But he had no reason to say so. And now she was smiling at him with that damnable sharing-a-secret look in her eyes again.

Over lunch he'd take some antacids. Maybe he was getting an ulcer.

A gust of wind blew his hair around his face, and the force of raindrops striking asphalt picked up again. He sighed. "We might be stuck here for a while."

"I love the rain," Ri replied. Her voice turned wistful. "There was a house some of my relatives used to rent for family reunions in Bar Harbor. It had the cutest little cupola at the top, and the kids would all pile in it when it stormed. Rain would splatter all the windows, and you could see lightning flashing out over the water. Sometimes the floor would even shake with the thunder. It was dramatic and scary but I always thought it was beautiful, too."

Wolf turned to look at her. "You sound like Frieda," he heard himself say.

"Who?" she asked with a smile.

"My dad's—" He paused for a beat as he searched for the correct word. Then he chastised himself. "Wife," he finished with some embarrassment, hoping Ri hadn't noticed.

Ri smiled. "I didn't know you had a stepmother. That's nice."

Wolf frowned. "She's not my stepmother."

"Oh," Ri said thoughtfully. "How long have they been married?"

Wolf thought about it. They'd had a small, no-frills, outdoor wedding at Frieda's sister's place in Moose Pass, beside Trail Lake. It was less than a year after Frieda had moved into the house with them. So how old was he then? Sixteen? "Coming up on ten years, I guess," he answered uncertainly. Had it really been that long? It didn't seem possible.

There was silence, except for the rain. Ri was looking at him with a puzzled expression. "So how do I sound like her?" she asked finally.

"Frieda always sees the beauty in things most other people don't," Wolf answered. "Like a dead limb lying in the snow. Or fireweed that's bloomed and wilted already. She's the kind of person who always appreciates what she has, rather than worrying about what she doesn't. She's very down-to-earth that way." He paused, then chuckled to himself. "And she makes damn good barbecue. I've missed getting free food at her restaurant almost as much as I've missed my dogs."

Ri smiled, but her lovely brow still bore wrinkles of confusion. "So, you and she get along okay, then?"

He thought that an odd question. "Sure we do. Why?"

Ri seemed to be choosing her words carefully. "Because you don't seem comfortable calling her your stepmother," she answered softly. "And I was wondering why."

Wolf tensed. "Oh," he replied, thinking quickly, "well, it's not like I was a kid when they met. I didn't need a mother." *You were fifteen, idiot. That's not a kid?* He stumbled mentally, trying to recreate his own reasoning. "I don't know," he continued, thinking out loud. "I guess it never actually penetrated my thick head that they were married. In the back of my mind, I always figured her being with my dad was more of a temporary thing."

"But why?" Ri pressed immediately. "Why would you think it was temporary?"

Wolf felt something squeezing in on him. His stomach was acting up again. He was uncomfortable where he was and he wanted to move. He got up from the picnic bench and walked to the edge of the shelter. He thought he could hear a muffled exclamation from Ri, but he didn't turn around. He wanted to change the subject.

Nothing new about that. But this time, he did stop to wonder why. Why did he have no answer for that question? Why *had* he always been so sure that his father's relationship with Frieda wouldn't last? Even now, if you forced him to place a bet, he'd wager that Frieda was bound to wake up some random morning and walk out of their lives without looking back. He had no evidence for such a belief, and plenty of evidence to the contrary. Yet his father's ultimate separation from her seemed every bit as inevitable to Wolf as fog rolling back over the field station.

Perhaps, when it came to women, he had been gifted with unnaturally good instincts.

"Cheerfully withdrawn," Ri said behind his back, her tone tongue-in-cheek. "Shall we talk about the weather?"

Wolf turned around. He did adore her sense of humor. And he loved how well she understood him. "I'm thinking it looks like rain," he suggested. "And you?"

"Fifty percent chance," she said, just as another gust of wind blew a spate of moisture onto his back and dampened his exposed hair. He returned to the center of the shelter and sat down next to her again.

"Do you really, seriously, want to pitch a tent out here tonight?" he asked.

She gave him the smile again. The one that made him feel like he'd known her his whole life instead of only a few days. The one that made him feel a bizarre, bone-deep sense of excitement and anticipation as well as a boundless, weightless joy that made no sense to him whatsoever. And the one which, at the same time, left him horribly, achingly depressed.

"I really, seriously do," she answered.

"Then so do I," he agreed, the words sliding straight from his soul to his lips without so much as a backhanded wave at his brain. "It sounds like fun."

# Chapter 29

Wolf circled his arms around his middle with a groan. His ribs ached. As much as his stomach had been bothering him lately, the shooting pains in his sides now were ten times worse. He couldn't remember the last time he had laughed so much.

"So then," Ri continued mercilessly, "just when I find the gloves, Mei Lin comes back and reports to me that the snake is no longer behind Mom's toilet. She says she doesn't know where it is. She also says that Dad just came home and wants to know why his wicker clothes hamper is sitting outside my bedroom door with leaves and dirt in the bottom of it. And by the way, Mei Lin says, Mom just went in to take a shower."

Wolf laughed harder. Ri was lying on her back on top of the insulated sleeping bag she'd borrowed, her legs drawn up and crossed at the knee with one foot swinging. She was dressed for the cold night in a long-sleeved shirt and sleep pants, but her lack of exposed skin didn't dim her appeal in Wolf's excruciatingly tired eyes. Her look might be more cuddly than erotic. But it was a deliciously soft, incredibly sexy kind of cuddly.

Which is why he was staying on his side of the tent. And why any minute now, he was going to get up and head back to the Hilton.

Really. He was. In five more minutes.

"What happened?" he managed to ask.

"Never found it," Ri said shortly.

"Never?"

"Nope. I confessed to my dad, and he got my mom out of the shower — now *that* was funny — and then we searched the whole house from top to bottom, but Festus was never seen again."

"Did you get in trouble?"

Ri's lips twisted. "The official story ends there," she replied. "It plays better to audiences that way."

The pain in Wolf's sides was unbearable.

Ri continued playing with her flashlight, moving it around on the tent ceiling in funky patterns. It was a small, dim light, glowing just enough for him to see her face. They'd used a brighter one to make the shadow animals. He'd thought Ri was kidding about that, but he'd discovered she was amazingly good at it. He had to wonder what other hidden talents she possessed.

They'd had so much fun tonight... and he had needed a laugh. Although it had rained on and off all day, dragging out their work, they had finished in time for Ri to complete her ferry run. What Wolf hadn't thought about until he watched his friend Maddie come outside to climb into the truck was that he would most likely never see her or Kai again. And when the thought struck him, he was surprised at how deeply it saddened him. Maddie had given him a hug, told him how much she'd enjoyed working with him, and mentioned again how much she wished he could make it to her and Kai's wedding. Unfortunately, the cost of airfare made that out of the question. Wolf hated the thought of losing their friendship, and he wanted to believe that their paths would cross again. He told himself that maybe someday he could do more work on Haleakala, or that maybe Kai would draw some temporary assignment at the law firm's Anchorage office and that Maddie could come along. But Wolf knew that was only wishful thinking.

Only after Ri returned from the ferry port did his spirits begin to rally. He'd borrowed a roomy tent and an extra sleeping bag from Kenneth, and she had been delighted. Between periodic downpours, they had managed to pitch the tent, grill hot dogs, and explore the nearby nature trail through the eucalyptus trees, complete with multiple sightings of the colorful Hawaiian *'I'iwi*, a striking red honeycreeper with a curved yellow bill. As always, Wolf enjoyed simply being in Ri's company, and she was quiet much of the evening, as was he. But as the darkness deepened and more sleepless hours ticked by, they'd both grown increasingly punch drunk.

"So what kind of trouble did you and Bear get into?" Ri

asked, rolling over onto her side and smiling at him mischievously. "Did you lead him into sin, or vice versa?"

Wolf scoffed. "I was always saving that boy's bacon. His name is a total joke, you know. There's nothing badass about Bear — he's magazine-cover handsome and wicked smart. Blond hair, blue eyes. Girls have been following him around with their tongues hanging out since kindergarten. Little bastard knows it too, but he looks so friggin' innocent... he could always get away with anything."

Ri chortled. "No jealousy, there."

Wolf rolled his eyes.

"Tell me a story," Ri begged. "Tell me about some time when Bear did something stupid and you felt like you had to cover for him. Did that ever happen?"

Wolf scoffed louder. "Are you kidding me? Like, all the time!"

"Tell me!" Ri pleaded with a giggle. "I've told you all sorts of embarrassing things."

Wolf let out a tired, yet somehow contented, sigh. He really should get up and head back to the field station. It had to be well past midnight already.

"Come on!" she taunted, drumming her heels on the ground like a four year old. "I can picture it all so clearly. The totally innocent-looking chick magnet finally hits puberty and decides that girls aren't so icky after all, so he gets his loyal big brother to play the wingman—"

"Wingman!" Wolf protested hotly. "I am nobody's *wingman!*"

Ri cracked up hysterically.

Wolf threw his pillow at her head.

Ri caught it and kept laughing.

"I'll have you know," he said with mock indignation, "that neither of the Markov boys needed any help in the attracting-females department. Bear's only problem was that he couldn't so much as hold a girl's hand without falling madly in love with her. And Bear really, *really*, likes holding girls' hands."

"So why was that was a problem?"

"Are you kidding?" Wolf exclaimed. "Have you ever heard a teenage guy cry? He's always been a sensitive little twerp, and every time the girl moved on, he fell apart. But he just kept going back for more, beating his head into the proverbial brick wall." He shook himself at the memory. "Geez, those years were a nightmare. It started late in middle school and it didn't end till..." Wolf thought a minute. "Well, hell, I don't know that it has ended. The periods of agony just get spread further apart the longer his girlfriends last."

Ri sat up. "Wolf Markov!" she chastised, "that is *such* a negative way of—"

He lost the rest of her sentence as his pillow sailed back over and smacked him in the face.

"Did it ever occur to you that your brother may think the occasional pain is worth it?" Ri continued with annoyance. "That he might have weighed the pros and cons and come to the perfectly reasonable conclusion that, on balance, falling for every girl he holds hands with is a *fun* thing to do?"

Wolf pulled the pillow off his face and stared at her. "No," he answered honestly. "I think it's just his nature that he falls into the same trap every time."

Ri groaned out loud and collapsed flat on her sleeping bag again. "If I didn't like you so much, I would sentence you to quality face time with my mother."

"What?" Wolf asked, confused.

Ri flipped back on her side. "Never mind. *Rewind.* You were about to tell me a funny story about you and Bear. But let's go back before puberty this time. Before you became such an insufferable romantic. Tell me about Halloween. What were your favorite costumes?"

Wolf stuffed his pillow back underneath his head. He was lost again. The output of Ri's creative brain was hard enough to follow when he wasn't exhausted. But a flash of memory did stir at her question, and the long-buried thought made him laugh out loud. "The moose! The moose and the pile of moose poop!"

Ri's angel face smiled at him again. "Tell me," she urged.

Wolf relaxed on top of his sleeping bag. He could tell her one more childhood tale. Then he would hike back to his own bed. The story would only take five minutes, max. She would like it. It would make her laugh.

"Well," he began, watching with happy anticipation as her dark eyes twinkled in the glow of the flashlight. "At first, I wanted to be Spiderman. But Bear really wanted the two of us to do something together…"


Ri opened her eyes to the dim light of first dawn, and the air that touched her face was damp and cold. But when she realized she had been awakened by a chorus of birdsong near the top of an ancient volcano, her lips softened into a smile. She flipped over in her sleeping bag, and her smile broadened till it warmed her to the tips of her toes.

Wolf was still there. He lay nestled in his own bag just two feet away, his hair wild and tousled over his pillow, his muscles relaxed, his face serene. Ri squirmed closer to get a better look at him, being careful not to jar him awake. No unshaven mountain man could ever have looked more beautiful.

She had a feeling he wouldn't make it back to the Hilton last night. For a practiced hiker like himself, the distance was nothing, but that didn't make the cold, dark, potentially wet walk any more enticing to a tired man in the wee hours of the morning. Particularly not when some heartless villainess kept tempting him to stay "just a little longer."

Ri grinned to herself. She knew that he hadn't wanted to go. He'd had every bit as much fun as she had, even if he did suck at making shadow animals. And even if they had — by unspoken agreement — made a point of staying on their own sides of the tent. Their mutual attraction was as explosive as ever, but the campout wasn't about that. They'd spent the night hours together for one simple reason: because at no given moment had either of them preferred to be alone.

*One day left.* Ri felt the weight of that reality hovering, threatening to crush her dreams with a sickening thud. But she forced such menacing thoughts away. Wolf did have feelings for her, she was certain of that now. Somehow, some way, things *would* turn out right.

But not one second of the precious twenty-four hours they

had left together on Maui could be wasted. Today, at last, she would drive the road to Hana, and Wolf would go with her. He absolutely had to. She pulled one arm up out of the cozy sleeping bag, then reached over to twirl a lock of his shaggy hair around her finger. Slowly she withdrew her hand again, not wanting to wake him. He looked so precious, so vulnerable. His lashes were long and feathery, and in the dim light, they seemed a lighter blond than his hair—

"Bwwaaaa!!!" Wolf shouted as his eyes flew open and his arms popped out of his bag and grabbed her.

Ri shrieked and pulled away, folding up in her tapered, mummy-style sleeping bag like a caterpillar and accidentally rolling over backward. By the time she caught her breath and righted herself, Wolf was bent over into a ball, laughing hysterically.

Ri was glad she didn't have a heart condition. She swung her bagged legs over and began to kick him. "You are terrible!" she complained.

He could barely speak. "Oh, no..." he gasped, edging away from her blows. "You did... You started..." He was half out of his much looser bag, but Ri was a good kicker and he was laughing too hard to move fast. "You *so* deserved that!" he coughed out finally.

"I thought you were asleep!" Ri said indignantly.

"Well, duh!" he replied, still laughing.

Ri's legs were getting tired. She still hadn't wriggled out of her bag; the darn thing held her legs fast. She had only her arms out, and her last kick had tilted one of the tent poles. A few more direct hits and she would suffocate before she could free herself. She reached down to try and unzip the bag, but the top of it was caught in folds and the zipper side was underneath her butt somewhere.

"You need help with that?" Wolf chuckled. He was completely out of his bag now and attempting to fix the slanted pole.

Ri responded with another kick and immediately wished she hadn't. Her feet hit the bottom of the pole and knocked it out of his hands. "Hey!" Wolf complained as half the ceiling came down on top of him.

Ri wasn't listening. She was too concerned with getting the heavy, wet canvas off her face. She squirmed across the floor until her head was out in the relatively open space beside him. "Are you trying to suffocate me?" she griped.

"Me?" Wolf retorted with amusement. He popped the tent pole back into place, looked down at her tangled predicament, and laughed. "You're just lucky we didn't have a fire in the middle of the night."

Ri's face flamed. She reached down and peeled the still-zipped mummy bag off her legs like a sock, then tossed it to the side. Immediately, she was cold. Sitting on the tent's ground cloth was like chilling on a refrigerator shelf. It had to be in the lower forties outside this morning. She shivered.

Wolf threw her a knowing smile. "I'm, um... going to get some fresh air," he said cheerfully, opening a tent flap. "You might want to put some warmer clothes on before you head out." He reached for his boots and began to lace them up.

"Wolf, wait," Ri called, not sure when he would be returning. He'd slept in sweats and a hoodie — he could go back to the Hilton now if he wanted and strike the tent later. "You're coming on the road to Hana with me, aren't you?"

His expression looked blank for a moment, and Ri felt a flutter of panic. She hadn't phrased that right. "I mean," she revised, "I've been hoping you would come, even though I haven't specifically invited you yet. I'd love your company, even if you were horribly mean to me just now. It will show how forgiving I am."

"Ha!" Wolf scoffed. His eyes twinkled at her briefly, but then his smile faded. "I don't know, Ri. I have a lot of work to do today. I have to organize all my stuff and get my gear packed up and ready to ship before my flight."

Ri felt cold all over. How stupid of her. She hadn't considered that. "We can head back whenever you want," she proposed. "I doubt it will be my last chance to see Hana. But it will be my last chance to drive the road with you."

Dawn was breaking now, and light poured through the tent flap. The pain in Wolf's face was both deep and obvious, and

Ri's heart suffered a mixed reaction at the sight of it. He would miss her. He was sad to be leaving. She was as sure of that fact as she was of her own name, and that knowledge should make her glad.

But she couldn't rejoice at the hurt she was causing him. Not when she felt it so keenly herself.

# Chapter 30

Wolf opened the door of his room, closed it behind him, and slumped against it. He stared at the ragtag assortment of gear, empty duffels, packing materials, and equipment cases he'd hauled out of the storage cabinet yesterday. He blew out a breath of frustration, irritated by the continued ache in his stomach. He was definitely working on an ulcer again. Besides which, he was bone-weary. He'd barely slept last night, or the nights before that. He glanced at his watch. His plane took off in exactly eight hours.

Something was seriously wrong with his brain. How could he have goofed off with Ri *all day*? He should have spent that time getting ready. Should have eaten every scrap of food he'd left in the kitchen, made an unhurried round of goodbyes, given Bella a nice farewell rubdown, then turned in early for a good night's sleep. Instead he'd taken off early and come back later than expected, setting himself up for a heart attack when he'd returned to find the dog gate open and Bella missing. Twenty minutes later he'd found her, happy as a clam, sprawled on the hearth rug in the cabin of her proud new owner, Kenneth. But the panic had taken a year off Wolf's life.

He'd managed only a quick round of goodbyes to his co-workers and a passable ear massage for Bella before handing her off into Kenneth's capable hands. His uneaten groceries would be left to public consumption because he'd bought Ri both a picnic lunch and a nice dinner in Makawao instead. And since he hadn't packed a damn thing since hauling out all this stuff, the good night's sleep would be a hopeless cause.

He bucked himself up and reached for the first of his equipment cases. If he was going to get sloppier as the night wore on, he'd better do his own belongings last. Ri had offered to help but he had refused, claiming that packing was a one-man operation, and that he wanted her well-rested when she drove him to the airport. They were valid reasons, both of them. But mainly he'd wanted time alone to think.

Now he had it. And thinking made his gut ache.

He'd never admit it to Ri, or to anyone else on Maui. But he hated the road to Hana. He'd driven it once by himself — or part of it — and found it a living nightmare. The vistas were breathtaking for a passenger, but when it could be fatal for the driver to enjoy the same scenery, Wolf had trouble maintaining his enthusiasm. He preferred to relax and enjoy nature, not attempt to enjoy it while white-knuckling through blind hairpin turns around sheer cliffs in sometimes single-lane traffic with no guardrails. But apparently that was just him. Ri had lapped up every second of it. The drive hadn't unnerved her, nor had she seemed frustrated that she couldn't see everything she might have seen if she wasn't behind the wheel. When he'd offered — at great personal sacrifice — to spell her, she'd turned him down flat. Ri had *wanted* to drive. She agreed that the experience was nerve-wracking, given that any mistake could send their truck careening several hundred feet down onto the black rocks below. But she'd insisted that was also what made it "so exciting!"

Wolf was still trying to wrap his head around that one. Some things about Ri would always befuddle him, but overall, he felt he was coming to understand her better. Looking back on their first misunderstanding in the grove, he felt uncomfortable that he'd even suggested a casual fling. If he'd known her better first, really comprehended where she was coming from and what she valued, he could have saved himself the awkward rejection — and her the disillusionment. They could have just stayed friends.

*Oh, really?*

Wolf frowned to himself as he methodically deconstructed his equipment and replaced the pieces in their packing slots. Okay, perhaps not. "Just friends" sounded wonderfully evolved, but there was no way he could ever look at that hot little body of Ri's and not want her. Adamantly. Desperately. Ferociously.

*Stop.*

Still, he sought out her company. He tempered his desire

because he knew that either coercing or tricking her into more than she wanted would hurt her. He spent time with her anyway because being separated from her mesmerizing eyes and her warm, mischievous smile would hurt him.

They had fun together, regardless. Their two painfully innocent, abbreviated make-out sessions had put them out of the friend zone without leading anywhere more satisfying, but he'd enjoyed them anyway. As free samples went, he thought with a smirk, no woman had ever presented a more compelling advertisement for herself. His smirk waned as he remembered he had no way of taking her up on that advertised offer. He would say goodbye to her tomorrow, thank her for a fantastic week in her company, and then forget about her. Preferably, as soon as possible.

What else could he do?

He would like to believe that they could be together again someday. But he couldn't base his life on an expectation so improbable. Not when mourning over what he couldn't have would make him miserable every day he spent alone in the meantime. Maybe Ri was free to move around the globe, but he was not. He had to stay in Alaska and finish his doctorate, and that would take years.

Still. What if Ri came to Alaska?

The ache in Wolf's stomach receded a bit, and his heart skipped a beat. What if they *did* have the chance to try a real relationship? His hands stopped their mechanical actions and his teeth began to grind. Could it happen? The University of Fairbanks had a graduate program in marine biology, with research facilities all over the coast. But she couldn't even start that for a year. She said she had to work first, to save some more money. And she wanted to get a job in her field.

He growled to himself. Plenty of marine biologists found work in Alaska during the summer tourist season, but Ri wouldn't even be looking until fall, when nearly everything shut down. Besides, who the hell wanted to work in Alaska over the long, dark winter? With marine anything?

He was talking fantasy again. Even if Ri could find a decent job, housing costs in Alaska were almost as bad as Maui.

Besides, his research kept him moving around all the time —
there was no one place she could go where they could always
be together. He wouldn't want her to make a bad choice for her
own career. And this was all supposing she even wanted to
follow him to Alaska in the first place!

He was thinking crazy.

All his life he'd avoided so much as a steady girlfriend. He
didn't know how all the couple stuff worked, and he still wasn't
sure he wanted to. He was the last person in the world any sane
woman would move across an ocean to be with.

He closed the first equipment case and moved to the
second. He tried to think about something else, to plan out
what he needed to do when he got back to Fairbanks, but his
brain was too tired and the thoughts too boring. It was easier to
think about the time he would spend in Anchorage first,
visiting with his dad and his brother and the dogs. Bear had a
couple days at home before his new job started, and his dad
was taking off work so the three of them could hang out and
relax for a few days. Frieda would bring home Wolf's favorite
barbecue, and they'd sit around the family room and
reminisce...

He smiled to himself. Frieda would like Ri. Ri would like
Frieda, too. He wished the two of them could meet.

*Dammit!* He was thinking about Ri again. He picked up the
pace of his packing. If he didn't get some sleep tonight, he'd be
a walking corpse when he stepped off the airplane. It would be
cool again at home, at least. That would be nice.

His mind flashed with an image of Ri in her bright yellow
bikini. She'd looked incredibly sexy in Hana yesterday. She'd
never been on a black-sand beach before, and she was
fascinated by the look and feel of the dark, crushed lava crystals
squishing between her toes. Under ordinary circumstances, the
beach's unique geological properties would have intrigued Wolf
as well, but he was far more interested in the contrast between
the warm yellow of the bikini fabric and the cool bronze tones
of her skin. She'd found the shell of a Hawaiian spiny lobster
and insisted he take her picture with it, adding a splash of
brilliant blue and red to the image. They had frolicked on the

shore like kids, explored the funky beach caves, and eaten their picnic lunch in the lush jungle shade on the cliffs above.

No wonder they'd lost track of time. No wonder he couldn't stop thinking about her. He might as well stop trying.

Wolf moved to the next packing case, thinking about how happy it had made Ri when he'd let her snap selfies of them both by the waterfalls. She'd insisted they make goofy faces for Mei Lin, and he surprised himself by going along with it. He chuckled at the ghastly result. No, he wouldn't fight the memories. Maybe they could help him get through this long, miserable night as painlessly as possible.

The forgetting could start tomorrow.


Ri kept blinking. Her eyeballs felt strangely dry, almost burning. The drive down the mountain had been dark, and they had passed a million pairs of headlights going the other way. She would have loved to be in any one of those vehicles headed uphill to see the sunrise. Instead she had been driving downhill into Kahului, where she would watch Wolf walk onto an airplane and out of her life.

*For a little while, anyway*, she corrected. She was trying very hard not to think negatively. But the way she felt this morning, even "a little while" was bad enough. Yesterday's journey to Hana had been amazing. Every hour she spent with Wolf was amazing. But all those hours had come and gone, and now their time together was up. She didn't know what else she could do. She didn't know what else she could have done.

Wolf had tried to smile and be pleasant when he loaded up the truck in the frigid pre-dawn fog, but he had looked both sleep-deprived and miserable. She was hoping they could talk during the drive, but as soon as the truck started moving, his body had slumped against the window. And every other time she glanced at him, his eyes were shut.

Now, it was past time for speeches. She was pulling into the departures lane, and although Wolf was fully alert, he was hardly in the mood for a heart-to-heart. They'd run into a minor accident two miles from the airport that had traffic at a dead halt, and he had awakened to spend the next half hour in a state of high anxiety. They were both so tired and so depressed that they'd hardly said a word to each other all morning. And now he had to hop out and unload right away.

Ri spied an open stretch of curb and parked the truck. As she expected, Wolf set to work immediately. Within seconds, he had commandeered a wheeled cart and loaded his variously sized duffels, equipment bags, and instrument cases on top of it. Then he swung around to find her standing beside him.

He didn't say anything. He simply reached out, pulled her to him, and held her tightly.

Ri breathed in the intoxicating scent of him. It was the smell of their Haleakala — the cool air, the fog, the pine, the earth, the man. She relaxed into his muscled form and reminded herself that this was chapter one, the beginning, and not the end. She'd hoped that he would come to care for her, and she was certain now that he did. His mind was still a mess, probably. But that didn't mean there wasn't hope. There was still a way it could all work out. She was sure of that, even if she couldn't quite picture how. Sriha Mirini Sullivan was nothing if not a dreamer.

Wolf began to pull away from her, and her body tensed. She knew he had to go, or he would almost certainly miss his plane. But pulling away from him voluntarily required willpower she didn't have.

"I'm sorry, Ri," he whispered, raising a hand to caress her cheek. "And... Thank you. I..." Watching him search for words was painful. An announcement came over the PA system about some flight or other, and he visibly tensed. "I really need to—"

Ri reached up a hand to his lips. She wanted to kiss him again, but she decided against it. Better to leave him with the memory of her last, more enthusiastic effort. She felt too wretched now. "I know," she whispered back. "But don't say you're sorry. Nothing's over until it's over, Wolf." Her fingers moved up and tangled themselves in the wavy locks above his ear. Her eyes met his, and when she noticed the fine trace of moisture brimming at his base of his lids, she bagged her own resolution and kissed him softly on the lips.

"I could love you, you know," she said as she pulled away. "I think I might already. Remember that."

He stared back at her a moment, his face frozen in the same mask of conflicted agony she'd hoped her confession might ease a bit. But her words seemed only to stun him. He said nothing. He didn't move.

Ri took a few steps backward toward the truck. "Goodbye, Wolf," she forced out. Her voice was still quiet. But she said it with as much cheer as she could muster.

He snapped out his trance. "Goodbye, Ri," he said in a muted voice. His face contorted into something that was probably meant to be a smile, but fell short. He turned around and wheeled the cart into the airport.

Ri stood on the curb a minute, watching him. He did not look over his shoulder.

# Chapter 31



Wolf lay collapsed on the family room floor. He was starting to feel light-headed. Not only did his dog Suka have the whole front half of her body lying directly on top of his chest, but Tog was panting some seriously foul breath right over his face, contaminating what little air he had access to. Wolf laughed and rolled over onto his side, then broke into a fit of coughing. Suka barked pitifully and flopped off him onto the floor, then squirmed over to lick his face.

It felt good to laugh. Seeing his dad and his brother waiting for him in luggage claim at the Anchorage airport had been a much-needed pick-me-up, and being greeted so enthusiastically by the canine half of the family was another salve to his soul. Still, his laughter rang hollow in his own ears. It seemed forced somehow, and fake. Like spreading a layer of fresh paint over a rotting board.

"Guess they missed you a little bit," Wolf's father said with amusement.

"Just a little," Bear agreed.

Tog barked in outrage; Suka was monopolizing Wolf's face and the less dominant dog couldn't get a lick in. Tog stretched out his muzzle and shoved his nose into the back of his master's neck instead. Wolf was still laughing and coughing at the same time when Frieda came through the front door. "Good Lord, they've killed him," she said cheerfully, walking past the spectacle with a huge bag slung over her arm.

The aroma struck Wolf the same moment it struck Suka and Tog. In a flash, the air cleared and Wolf was suddenly able to breathe again. The dogs had left him. They were following Frieda now, tails wagging and tongues lolling, as she made her way to the eat-in kitchen and set the bag down on the table.

The other men in the family room laughed out loud. "You

lose!" Bear teased him. "They do love you, bro — just not quite as much as Frieda's beef brisket."

"And they're not getting a bite of it," Frieda said sternly, her hands planted on her hips. She was a plump woman with dark hair, bright blue eyes, and a ready smile, and as Wolf rose from the floor to greet her, he realized he'd missed her as much as her barbecue. "Good to see you, Frieda," he said warmly, wrapping her in a hug.

"You too, Wolfman," she returned, hugging him back. They'd come to a nice place eventually, he and Frieda, although it wasn't like they'd ever been in a bad place. Wolf had always treated her respectfully and politely. But he knew that he didn't treat her like Bear did, and that he never had, and that she noticed the difference. He treated her like a nice lady who made his dad happy, and over time he'd come to see her as a friend.

Bear treated her like a member of the family.

"What happened here?" Frieda exclaimed, looking at Wolf's splinted hand.

"Don't worry, he says the other guy looked worse," Bear quipped.

Frieda tilted her head at Wolf with concern. "What? Fighting's not like you! I don't believe it."

Wolf felt no particular need to defend himself, but apparently his brother did. "Now Frieda," Bear cajoled, "he was defending a female, after all."

Her blue eyes lit up instantly. "Really?"

Wolf threw his brother an eye roll. "A female dog," he corrected. He'd let his dad fill Frieda in on the details later. As far as he was concerned, he and The Beard were done. Wolf had been concerned that his inability to get back to Maui to testify would let the vandal off the hook and put the pit bulls' safety at risk, but it turned out he needn't have worried. When the police confronted The Beard about the smashed truck windows, not only did they find their suspect with a lacerated hand, they found themselves the victims of an assault. Wolf's testimony would not be required to bring the man to justice, and the pit bulls had been reclaimed by an ex-wife.

"Let's eat!" Nels broke in smoothly. "I'm starving. But you'd better feed those dogs first, Wolf, or we won't get a minute's peace."

"We won't anyway," Bear chuckled, watching as Suka and Tog circled the table with excitement. "Not after they've smelled barbecue."

"We'll eat fast," Frieda suggested, pulling some plates out of the cabinet. "Close the back door after them, Wolf. I don't want them clawing up the screen."

Wolf lured the dogs outside to their dinner bowls, fed them an extra helping of kibble — it was a celebration, after all — then shut the door as he was bid. Suka and Tog would be finished and whining in a matter of seconds, but the rest of the reunion would have to wait until after the human food was gone. His dad wasn't the only one starving.

They ate in record time. Once Wolf was settled back onto the family room floor, his back leaning up against the couch with his stomach full and two dogs fighting over his lap, he felt as content as he had in days. The flight from Maui to Honolulu had been rough, but he must have slept soundly on the second leg to Anchorage because he remembered nothing of it. His spirits were slightly higher and his gut didn't ache quite so much. It was nice to be home again, particularly with his brother around. They'd spent precious little time at the home base together since Bear had gone away to college.

Wolf relaxed as the family asked him a litany of questions about his time on Maui, and he surprised himself by answering all of them. He was in a talkative mood, for whatever reason, and he felt bad about how infrequently he'd called or texted. They knew he'd never been one to chit-chat on the phone, but still, he could have set a reminder to call every couple weeks. As much as he loved his family, he'd always sucked at long-distance communication.

Yet another reason to forget about Ri.

But that process would have to wait until after his debriefing on Maui, evidently, because her name kept popping up. He'd thought about omitting her from his report altogether, but decided against it. Besides being dishonest, it would require too damn much effort. He knew that the sooner he managed to forget about Ri entirely, the better off he would be. But at the same time, he accepted that purging her from his system would not be easy. Better if he didn't censor himself, perhaps, but let his thoughts flow where they might until he got over them.

"Tell us more about Ri," Frieda suggested. She was sitting next to his father on the loveseat, snuggled in comfortably with her feet drawn up underneath her. There was a teasing tone in her voice that made Wolf tense. "What does she look like?"

Wolf found the question odd. But he didn't object to answering it. Once his mind had conjured an image of Ri, he couldn't help himself. He started with a glowing physical description and found himself struggling to keep it G-rated. Her features led to an explanation about her background, which in turn led to a lot more than he'd originally intended to say about her search for her ethnic heritage and her discovering a distant relative on the island who happened to be engaged to one of Wolf's co-workers. But it was an interesting story and they were all looking at him as though they were fascinated... so he kept talking. He told them how excited she was about her internship and how she could have stood all day staring at the sleeping monk seal. He told them about how fabulous she was at reading out gas flux measurements and how nice it was to be with someone who appreciated the quiet. He told them how funny she was when she told stories about her childhood antics with her sister, how much she enjoyed his own ridiculous stories about himself and Bear, and how much fun she was to be with under any circumstances. And then he realized that no one else in the room had said anything for quite some time.

He decided he would stop talking. But still, no one said anything. They were all looking at him with bizarre, unreadable expressions on their faces. Wolf leaned down and buried his face in a dog.

"Is she coming up to Alaska for a visit sometime?" Frieda asked finally.

Wolf's chin snapped up. "A visit? Not that I know of. Why?"

Frieda's thin eyebrows lifted. She turned her head to look at Bear. Bear caught his stepmother's eye and shook his blond head sadly, sighing with an obnoxious, knowing smirk.

"What?" Wolf demanded, feeling an unwelcome heat rise up in his chest.

"You have no plans to see this woman again?" Bear asked with disbelief, his tone ever-so-slightly patronizing.

"Why would I?" Wolf answered, his voice rising. His know-it-all little brother excelled at pushing his buttons, but he was in no mood. Not with Ri as the subject.

Nels Markov looked confused. "Now, wait a minute. Calm down, Wolf." He sat forward and looked from his wife to Bear. "What are you two getting at?"

As far as Wolf was concerned, he *was* calm. "Yes, please," he said calmly. "What are you getting at?"

Bear smiled a smile that was aggravatingly smug. "Nothing at all, big brother. Nothing at all. Obviously, this Ri isn't *that* special a person. Just one woman among many. One more notch—"

"Bear! Stop!" Frieda said firmly, interrupting the statement just as Wolf became uncalm. She turned to the older brother with a conciliatory smile. "I'm sorry if I misread you. It just seemed like, the way you've been talking about this woman all evening, that maybe you had real feelings for her. That's all."

Wolf's face felt like it was aflame. He had been talking about Ri a lot, yes, but... Frieda couldn't know how he felt. *What* he felt. And Bear... who did they think they were?

*"Oh,"* his father exclaimed.

"Way to catch on, Dad," Bear stage-whispered.

Wolf had wanted to kill his little brother many, many times. But the urge had rarely been stronger than now.

"Well, obviously, you were wrong!" Wolf heard himself say. He was pulling words straight out of his hind end now. "If I was in love with her, I wouldn't have left her there, would I? But it's not like that. I only knew the woman a couple of days! I don't know what you think you're seeing or hearing, but it's all in your own minds. We said goodbye and I left and that's the end of it! Can we talk about something else now?"

Three stunned faces blinked back at him. Only then did Wolf realize he was shouting.

"I'm sorry," he said hastily, moving the dogs off his lap and scrambling to his feet. "I need a walk."

He strode toward the front door, the dogs at his heels. He grabbed their leashes and banged outside.


Forty-five minutes later, Wolf quietly let himself and the dogs in the back door. He was cold. He'd left the house without a coat. May in Anchorage wasn't winter, but the evenings weren't what you'd call balmy, either, particularly not with cloudy skies and occasional drizzle.

The dogs' tails wagged amicably despite his foul mood, and he smiled at their unconditional acceptance. This is why he loved dogs. He never had to answer to them. They never asked any questions.

He could hear the television blaring in the family room. Frieda had trouble hearing in one ear, and the volume was always a little too loud for everyone else. *Perfect.* Perhaps if they were absorbed enough in their show they'd let him slip up the steps without waylaying him.

All he wanted now was to take a hot shower and go to bed. He felt badly for shouting at them earlier and he did plan to apologize — at least to Frieda, whom he knew hadn't meant to upset him. But despite the brisk walk in the wet and the cold, his head was as muddled as ever and he had no idea how to explain himself. It would be best for everybody if he slept first.

He made it up the steps and into his room. But just as he grabbed his stuff and headed for the shower, Bear's lanky silhouette darkened his doorway.

"Hey, there," his brother said mildly. "How was the walk?"

Wolf let out a gruff exhale. "Fine. I'm tired."

"I can see that." Bear stood with his hands in his pockets, leaning against the doorframe with his legs crossed at the ankle. He studied Wolf with a pensive expression.

Wolf straightened as if ready to leave the room, but Bear made no move to get out of his way. "Did you want something?" Wolf grumbled, getting irritated all over again.

"I shouldn't have made fun of you," Bear replied, looking

his brother straight in the eye. "That was a mistake. You caught me off guard, and I was happy for you, that's all."

Wolf was on the verge of feeling dizzy. Bear had lost his mind. "*Happy* for me?"

Bear nodded. "I was beginning to think no woman would ever get through that mile-thick hide of yours. But it sounds like this one did. And you've only known her a matter of days, you said? That's some pretty impressive stuff, bro. I'd say she's worked a miracle."

Wolf looked at his brother's smile with disbelief. "Did I miss something? Was I passed out for part of that conversation? I told you I met a woman and we had some fun together. But I'm here now and she's there and I'm never going to see her again!" He realized his voice was rising again, but he didn't care. He threw his stuff back down on the bed. "How the hell do you get 'happy' out of that?"

Bear kept standing there, staring at him. "Did she end it, or did you?"

Wolf raised his hands in the air with a groan. "End what? There was nothing to end!"

"So it never really got started, then," Bear yapped on.

"Get out of my way," Wolf growled, grabbing his stuff again. "This is a pointless conversation. You're not listening."

Bear stood up straight. "I heard you say you loved her."

Wolf stopped short. His heart thudded painfully in his chest. *No. He had not said that.* "I did not!" he protested.

"Oh yes, you did," Bear argued. "When you weren't thinking about your words, it slipped right out. You said, 'If I was in love with her, I wouldn't have left her there.'"

Wolf closed his eyes and breathed out slowly, the way he used to when he was a teenager contemplating fratricide. "I *did* leave her there," he reminded.

"You had no choice about leaving her," Bear replied, undeterred. "But you do love her. That's why you feel the way you feel right now. Like you want to yell and pound and scream and cry and grab me by the shirt and beat the frickin' crap out of me. Because it hurts so damn much."

Wolf's reaching hands stopped in mid air. Something inside

him crumpled. The heat of his anger morphed into a hollow, aching cavern. His gut burned.

"It's not the end of the world, though," Bear added gently. "Doesn't sound like it has to be the end of anything. But you've got to get real. You've got to quit running scared."

Wolf looked his brother in the eye. Bear had wound up an inch taller, which was irritating. Usually the younger brother slouched so much that their eyes were level, but right now Bear was standing tall and forcing Wolf to look up at him. "I'm not *scared* of anything."

Bear crossed his arms over his chest. He shook his head slowly. "Not much. Just giving some woman a little power over you, that's all."

Wolf was genuinely confused. "Power?"

Bear sighed. "You want me to say it? It's hard to do without sounding sappy, but fine. What you're scared of is getting your heart broken."

Wolf's muscles tensed. He couldn't help but notice that Bear stiffened also, obviously in defense. The kid had a lot of nerve acting scared. Wolf had never hit him. Ever. No matter how much he deserved it.

"You think it's the worst thing in the world, but it's not," Bear continued quickly. "It's happened to me too many times to count, and I'm still standing! Dad had it rough for a while, but he survived. We all survive."

"You just said it hurts like hell!" Wolf railed.

"It does!" Bear shouted back. "But it's worth it! Don't you get that? You'll never get to the good stuff if you're too much of a coward to face the bad!"

Wolf's anger roared back. Heat rose in his chest like a boiling cauldron, pulsing outward. "What good stuff? Where's *your* loyal woman, Bear? Everything you've been through, and what have you got to show for it? Nothing! And as for Dad, women made his life miserable, and you know it! Or at least, you ought to know it!" His mind flashed with images of a little boy in pajamas, crying in his bed.

*"Wake up, dammit!"* Bear thundered, using a commanding voice that was completely unfamiliar. Wolf's little-boy

memories were replaced with a real-time image of a strong, passionate young man determined to make a point. "Open your eyes and look around you! Dad and Frieda have been happily married for ten damn years! Longer than our own parents ever even knew each other! Frieda isn't going anywhere, Wolfie! *Frieda is staying!*"

Bear's blue eyes seem to pierce all the way through Wolf's brain and out of the back of his skull. The heat in his body dissipated. All at once he felt laid bare. Ignorant. Bested.

And he was still angry.

"You handle your life however you want," he said in a low voice. "I'll handle mine. Now, *move.*"

Bear let out a breath. His stance relaxed. "Okay, big brother," he said easily, withdrawing from the doorway. "But I'm going to ask you one more question. And you can think about this one for a while."

Wolf pushed past him and stomped toward the shower.

"Do you really think Dad would be happier today," Bear called out to Wolf's retreating form, "if he'd spent the last ten years screwing around with women he didn't care about?"

# Chapter 32


*Maui, Hawaii, 2016*

Ri was walking out of her office and toward the Ma'alaea marina when her phone buzzed with her sister's ringtone. It was Friday. Ri had put in long hours all week at a rented computer indoors, and though she enjoyed the work, she missed the sun on her face and the breeze on her skin. In the few minutes she had after work and before the bus came, she'd taken to leaning up against a palm and enjoying the ocean view. Living in the moment and relishing the sensory experience of Hawaii was what kept her going these days. Being near the ocean, admiring its creatures, and marveling at its vastness could always buoy her spirits.

She pulled out her phone and answered, settled against the nearest palm. It was a camera call. "Hi, Mei," she said cheerfully.

"Hi," her sister answered. Her voice was strange. Ri looked down to see that Mei Lin was in her childhood room at their parents' house, lying on the bed. That was odd, since Mei Lin still lived with a roommate in an apartment only twenty minutes away, near the hospital where she worked in Portland.

"Are you sick?" Ri asked quickly. This weekend was her sister's big move to Texas. The whole family should be frantically checking tire gauges and taping up boxes. It was a long drive, and they were caravanning with the family car, a rental trailer, and Mei Lin's car, as well as with Josh and all his stuff.

"No," Mei Lin said quietly. She pulled the phone close to her face and looked into the camera. "Let me see the ocean."

Ri turned her phone so that the camera took in a sweeping view of the harbor, then across the bay to the heights of Haleakala.

"It's so beautiful," Ri heard Mei Lin say, her voice

melancholy. "You must love it there."

Ri pulled the phone back and looked into her sister's face. Much passed between them without explanation. But Mei Lin had called to talk. "Tell me," Ri said gently.

Mei Lin's beautiful, dark eyes watered. "Yesterday I got a call from the hospital in Texas. The starting date on my contract has been pushed back from June until September."

"Oh, no," Ri sympathized, knowing there was more.

"I called my boss here right away and asked if I could stay on through the summer, and she said yes, they'd be glad to have me. The lease on my apartment runs out at the end of the month, but I figured I could just commute from home until September. That way I could still help Josh with the rent on the place in Texas."

Ri watched miserably as a tear slid down her sister's cheek.

"But when I told Josh, he totally flipped out. He said I needed to be in Texas, that he needed me to cook and take care of the apartment and everything. And that if I couldn't find a nursing job down there, I could work fast food or something over the summer. And then he said that all that really mattered was that we were together."

*And he said it in that order*, Ri surmised. Her stomach threatened to heave, but she refrained from saying anything.

"He went on and on after that," Mei Lin said in a dull voice, "about how much I meant to him, and how much he would miss me, and how sorry he was about the way he made everything sound. But you know what?"

The question was rhetorical, and Ri said nothing. But her fingers were crossed.

"I didn't believe him."

*Yes!* Ri wanted to drop-kick the phone and do a victory dance, but once again, she managed to refrain.

"I think he was telling the truth the first time," Mei Lin went on. "He was mad because he was losing a cook and a housekeeper and a bedmate. He couldn't care less about what was best for me. Whether *I* wanted to flip burgers for three months, take a pay cut, screw up my resume, lose my professional momentum. It was all about him. It's always all about him.”

Ri could contain herself no longer. “I think you’re right.”

Mei Lin frowned at her. “You think the same as Mom and Dad, don’t you? That he’s changed over time. That’s he gotten complacent and that he’s taking advantage of my good nature. That he doesn’t appreciate me. That he doesn’t love me for who I really am, because he hasn’t made the effort to — wait, let me make sure I’m quoting Thera-Mom correctly here — ‘know and embrace the whole width and depth of my unique character?’”

Ri chuckled softly. “Ah, yes. That sounds familiar.”

Mei Lin sighed. “She’s right, Ri. I know she’s right. She’s been right all along, and Dad too, but it’s just so irritating, you know?”

Ri nodded. “I know.”

“I’ve been aware of what’s been happening with Josh. But you know me — I always want to see the best in people.”

“I really thought you were happy with him, Mei,” Ri admitted, feeling a little confused. “You never said a word otherwise.”

“I’m a happy person,” Mei Lin said with glum irony. “Easy to please. Which is usually great, but when it comes to picking a guy...” She paused and chuckled at herself. “Well, I guess I set the bar too low. Everything was good in the beginning. But once I had that ring on my finger, it was like he thought he didn’t have to be nice to me anymore. But I was happy *enough*, and I told myself that things would get better in Texas. I had so much time invested in the relationship... so much of my heart... I wanted to give it the summer, at least.”

Ri crossed her fingers again.

“But I can’t,” Mei Lin said with finality. “There is no hope. Marrying him would be a disaster. Even moving to Texas and seeing how it goes would be a mistake. I’m cutting my losses, Ri. We’re done. That’s it.”

Ri turned her face to the sky. It seemed as though a chorus of angels had broken forth into song.

“Oh, my God!” Mei Lin squealed.

“What?” Ri asked, concerned.

"Do you have to look so freakin' *happy?*"

*Uh-oh.* Ri forgot she was on camera. "I'm sorry," she said sheepishly. "I'm sorry he hurt you, Mei. But I'm not sorry you broke up. He treated you badly and he didn't begin to deserve you and I know you'll be happier with someone else. Does that make me a horrible sister?"

To her relief, Mei Lin smiled. It was her regular, dimple-making smile. "No. You're the best sister ever, weirdo."

Ri's eyes watered. "You too, scumbag."

"So hey," Mei Lin asked more brightly, swiping a hand across her cheek and sitting up. "You heard anything else from Alaska?"

Ri's heart turned instantly to lead. "Not since Wednesday." She looked at the time. "Listen, I've got to get to the bus stop. Call me again in about an hour and a half, okay? Or text anytime."

Mei Lin eyed her knowingly, and Ri fought back another wellspring of emotion. She'd been managing all right this week, day by day. Sunday through Tuesday had totally sucked, but on Wednesday Wolf had texted her a picture of his dogs. He was lying on a carpet somewhere and Suka and Tog were both on top of him, kissing him to death. He had typed one word along with it. "Reunion."

Ri had promptly sent back a picture of herself wedged into her new workstation behind the printer in the HR department, to which she added the caption, "Rehired." But she had not heard from him since.

She had been ecstatic to receive the message, but she knew better than to hope for an ongoing conversation. In all the time they'd spent together Wolf had hardly ever used his cell phone. And he would soon be in the Aleutian Islands, where his access to reception would be intermittent at best.

"Okay," Mei Lin replied. "You should text him again, though."

Ri felt another blanket of sadness weighing upon her. "Maybe I'll send something tonight. Something funny."

"Don't be so careful!" Mei Lin advised, sounding more like her old self, now that she was the one giving advice. "Go for it!

Go for him! You *cannot* give up!"

"I'm not giving up," Ri said sharply. She was trying to talk while she jogged toward the bus stop. "I'd follow him to the ends of the earth if he asked me. But he hasn't asked me, and I'm not going to stalk the man. I won't go where I'm not wanted."

"You know he wants you!" Mei Lin insisted.

Ri didn't answer. She did know it. But he didn't.

She reached the bus stop. An older woman with skin, hair, and eyes just like Ri's stood waiting. Ri smiled at her, and the woman smiled back.

*Hanging with my peeps.*

"I really have to go now," Ri said. She didn't like talking on the phone in public.

"Yes, yes," Mei Lin answered impatiently. She talked on her own phone constantly, anywhere, anytime. "Some men are just dense, Ri," she said sternly. "You have to be clear. I know that one week together is a little quick for the L word, but couldn't you just tell him flat out that you feel like you have a real shot together?"

Ri's eyes moved to the other woman at the bus stop, who could hear every word Mei Lin said. How embarrassing.

"Goodbye!" Ri said pleasantly, shutting the phone off. She stuffed it in her pocket and stared out at the nearby windmills.

"Sounds like a good idea to me," the woman murmured with amusement.

Ri's head turned.

The woman threw her a motherly smile. "My grandma always said to me, if you love somebody, tell them. Can't nobody else do it for you."

Ri felt a sharp pang in her middle. She knew the woman meant to be helpful, and so did Mei Lin. She didn't disagree with their advice. The problem was that she'd already taken it.

"I did tell him," she said softly. "He just hasn't answered."

The woman's eyes widened. But her face remained sympathetic as she smiled again. "It'll turn out all right," she said with a knowing wink. "You just wait and see."

# Chapter 33



*Anchorage, Alaska 2016*

Wolf pulled out his key to his dad's house, then realized the front door wasn't locked. It was stuck slightly ajar, as it had a tendency to do, and he could hear the dogs frisking around inside. Perhaps his father had come home for lunch. He rapped his knuckles on the door and swung it open. "Hello?"

He stepped into the entryway and was immediately accosted by two boisterous dogs. Soon afterward, Frieda rounded the corner from the back hall.

"Nels, what—" She stopped short. Her eyes widened and her face broke into a smile. "Wolf! I didn't know you were coming today!" She stepped forward and gave him a quick hug, which was improvised somewhat due to dog interference.

Wolf held up his right hand and flexed all his fingers. "Got the splint off," he announced happily. "Doc said the x-rays look good." He did not add that if the doctor hadn't removed the splint today, he was very likely to trash the thing regardless. The device he'd had applied by the orthopedist in Anchorage was less bulky than the one he'd gotten at urgent care on Maui, but it was no less annoying. Getting full use of his hand back had put him in a good mood. Not much else had done that the last few weeks.

"That's great!" Frieda congratulated. "Your dad should be here in a little while, and you can have lunch with us. I'm making a chicken potpie."

She moved off towards the kitchen and Wolf followed, petting two dogs' bobbing heads as he went. "I didn't expect to find you here on a Tuesday morning," he admitted.

Frieda chuckled. "Well, I don't haunt the restaurant quite as much these days. I have more staff to take care of things, now." She peeked in the oven, then adjusted the temperature. "You want a drink or something?"

"Thanks, but I'll get it," Wolf offered, grabbing a can of cola from the refrigerator. He made a point of using his right hand, enjoying the feel of the cool metal against his newly naked fingers. He watched with admiration as Frieda puttered about, doing whatever incomprehensible things an expert cook did in her own kitchen. He had always admired Frieda's talents, as well as her ambition. She had been only twenty-four years old when her first husband had been killed in a boating accident. But instead of curling into a ball and dying herself, she had used the life insurance settlement and her newly minted community-college business degree to open up a barbecue grill.

Wolf was glad she was home. The truth was, he had been wanting to talk to her.

"Can we sit down a minute?" he asked.

Frieda stopped puttering and looked at him. She pulled out a kitchen chair and sat down, and Wolf did the same. Unfortunately, now that he had her attention, he wasn't quite sure what to do with it. Seconds ticked by, and he said nothing. The moment turned awkward.

"You don't look so good," Frieda said gently.

Wolf looked away. He took a swig of cola. "Is it that obvious?" He could tell that she was nodding.

"You haven't talked to Ri, I guess?" she asked.

Wolf's breath caught. Even the sound of her name on someone else's lips set his nerves on edge. He was supposed to be forgetting about her. Every day was supposed to be getting easier. Frosty Peak was as good as on the other side of the world from Ri's sunny ocean bay — yet it made no difference. His assistant Justin read out gas flux measurements, and Wolf thought of Ri. The sun rose and set over banks over clouds, and Wolf thought of Ri. It rained in the middle of the night and the tent poles collapsed, and Wolf thought of Ri. A frickin' dog barked, and Wolf thought of Ri. There was nothing in his daily existence, not even something as simple as making a sandwich or turning on a flashlight, that did not remind him of Ri. And it was not getting easier. If anything it was getting worse, because he accepted now that he'd been wrong. He wasn't going to be able to forget her.

And he had no idea what to do about that.

"No, I haven't talked to anyone." He shrugged. "We've been camping most of the time. I can only communicate from Cold Bay." He dared a look at Frieda and found her caring blue eyes boring into his own. He expected her to say something else, to give him some unsolicited advice, but she didn't. She didn't speak for a long time.

"Was there something you wanted to ask me?" she inquired finally.

Wolf tensed. But Frieda's voice was mild, her expression friendly and approachable, as always. He had been the one who asked her to sit down. He needed to spit it out.

"I wanted to thank you," he offered.

She appeared surprised. "Thank me? For what?"

Her shock made Wolf feel even worse. Had he never thanked her for anything before? "For being here for the last ten years," he said firmly. "For making Dad happy. For taking care of Bear. And for taking care of me. Even though I refused to acknowledge that it was the slightest bit necessary."

Frieda grinned at him. "You were never any trouble, Wolfman. You did take care of yourself."

Wolf shook his head. "I was a jerk to you, and we both know it. I treated you like a houseguest, not like my father's wife. Certainly not like a stepmother. You deserved better than that, and I want you to know I'm sorry."

Frieda's smile broadened, even as her eyes moistened slightly. She reached a hand across the table and pressed it briefly atop Wolf's own. "It means a lot to me to hear you say that. But it isn't necessary. I understood what you were feeling. I know what you went through before I came along. And I don't blame you for being cautious about accepting another woman into the family."

Wolf felt that awful "laid bare" feeling again. Had Frieda really known? "If it means anything at all to you to hear me say it, then it was absolutely necessary," he corrected. "And it's not— I mean, you make it sound like—"

Frieda cocked an eyebrow. "Yes?"

Wolf's protests died on the vine. He didn't know why he

was bothering to defend himself. He had done exactly what she claimed throughout his entire childhood. He'd been constantly on guard, trying to keep all three men in the family from getting hurt. Specifically, sexist as it was, from getting hurt by a woman. And even more specifically, selfish as it was, he'd been guarding his own precious behind... never mind the cost to his dad.

Sheesh. He really was a jerk.

"I told myself I was looking out for Dad and Bear, but I was only thinking about myself," Wolf admitted, thinking out loud. He looked Frieda in the eyes again. "I never saw how much Dad loved you, much less how much you loved him. It's so obvious to me now, it's hard to understand that kind of blindness. But I was always so sure you'd leave, just like my mother did. Just like all the others did. I didn't *want* to care about you. I wanted to be vindicated."

"I know that," Frieda said mildly.

Wolf blew out a breath and hung his head with embarrassment. He rose and whirled away from the table. "Good God, Frieda. You should have just thrown my butt out of the house."

Frieda chuckled. "Don't be so dramatic. You might have been thinking mean thoughts, but you were always sweet to me. I knew you'd grow up sometime and I knew what kind of heart you had. What kind of brother you were to Bear. Or should I say, what kind of mother. I couldn't help loving you for that."

Wolf turned back to the table. The dogs had started whining and prancing about his legs again, angling for a walk, but Wolf ignored them. He moved back to his chair and dropped down heavily. "Mother?"

Frieda nodded at him with a smile. "Now don't go blaming your father for betraying a confidence, if that's what you're thinking. He's never said a word to me on the subject. But I care about you boys, and there are some things a woman just knows. Even though I never had kids of my own, I practically raised four siblings and two little cousins to boot — and good Lord, my cousins were so messed up they each counted as five." She shook her head at the memory, rolled her eyes, then forged on. "What I'm trying to say is, I've got a pretty good idea what went on when you boys were little. I know how old you were when your mother left, and *how* she left, and how that must have felt to you. And I know how old Bear was, both then and when he got attached to your father's other girlfriends."

Her blue eyes drank Wolf in with affection. "And I know from firsthand experience what a wonderful man Bear is now. He's well-adjusted, happy, and emotionally secure. He has a warm, beautiful, open heart that isn't afraid to love. And you know why that is?"

Wolf did not. He shook his head slowly.

"It's because of you," Frieda answered. "Your father did his share, don't get me wrong. Your father's a good, loving man and he certainly helped hold *you* together. But he's not exactly the nurturing type, not when it comes to comforting a small child who misses his mama. After what Bear went through at that tender age, you might expect he'd be an emotional mess. But Bear's just fine, Wolf. When your father thinks about the bad times, all he remembers is a blur, because it hurt him, too. That's why he can't see your role in it, even now. But I know what happened. You stepped in, Wolf, and you made yourself Bear's mama. You gave that little boy the affection and the coddling he was craving, because you knew it's what he needed."

Frieda's eyes looked moist again. "And you did a wonderful job. I've always wanted to thank *you* for that."

Wolf felt odd. Hollow inside, yet heavy. He barely remembered the awful time when his mother had left. He had always tried not to think about it. "Bear doesn't remember any of it," he heard himself say.

Frieda shook her head knowingly. "If he doesn't, that's to your credit. You smoothed over the hurt. He might have lost his mother figures, but he always had his dad, and he always had you. He was okay. He *is* okay." She rose. She stepped to Wolf's side of the table and laid a hand on his shoulder. "You did that for him, Wolf. That's why I'm so glad you've finally found a woman of your own to care about. I'm happy for you.

I'm happy for her, too. She's got herself a real keeper."

Wolf felt dizzy at the change of subject. There was that word again. *Happy.* Had his entire family gone insane? "I'm not happy," he objected.

They heard a noise on the front porch, and Suka and Tog raced toward the door.

Frieda gave his shoulder a squeeze, then blew out her breath with a sigh as she moved toward the oven. "You could be."

Nels Markov stepped into the kitchen. "Wolf!" he said with surprise. "You didn't say you were coming home today!"

Wolf repeated his explanation about the splint removal. Frieda finished pulling her potpie out of the oven, then walked over to his father. Nels greeted her with an arm out, and the two embraced affectionately, complete with a soft kiss on the lips.

Wolf watched the couple as if he'd never seen them before. Perhaps he hadn't. Nels bore little resemblance to the painfully thin, stressed-out single father of Wolf's childhood. That man's forehead was always creased, his hands in seemingly constant, nervous motion. His clothes were untidy and his hair was unkempt. This man's forehead bore no creases other than a few crow's feet, he was always ready with a smile, and he was on the verge of growing a potbelly. His clothes were stylish and neat and his hair was clipped and feathered with gray over the ears.

"Since when did you start coming home for lunch in the middle of a work day?" Wolf asked. When Wolf was living at home, Frieda was always working at the restaurant, and his dad used to pack a lunch. Although their house was only a few minutes from Nels' office, he'd only come home over the noon hour when the boys were on break from school.

Nels and Frieda shared a look. "Ever since Frieda's been here to come home to, of course," Nels answered with a smirk.

Wolf got that distinct "third wheel" feeling. It was like Maddie and Kai all over again. Only this was his *dad.*

He couldn't decide how he felt about that.

Frieda giggled as Nels kissed her again.

Wolf decided he was okay with it.

*Frieda isn't going anywhere.*

"Um... I guess I'd better be leaving." Wolf rose.

"What?" Frieda looked horrified. "You are not going anywhere until you eat some potpie. Now sit back down!"

"Yes, sit down," his father ordered. "Rob flew you in?" he asked, referring to a friend of the family who piloted regular trips to the Aleutians. When Wolf nodded, Nels gestured to the chair once more. "He can wait half an hour. I want to catch up with you a bit."

Wolf sat down.

Frieda served them a delicious lunch. Wolf's father asked questions about his work, and Wolf answered them. It was all very nice, very pleasant. But Wolf's mind was not on the conversation. Although he'd been telling people for years that Frieda made his father happy, he realized that only now did he actually believe what he'd been saying.

His dad *was* happy. Fully, deeply, genuinely content with his life.

Just like Kai.

And that was no freakin' coincidence.

# Chapter 34



*Lana'i, Hawaii, 2016*

Ri ran her fingers lightly around the edge of a giant yellow hibiscus blossom. The flower, part of a live arrangement near the rear of the seating area, was perfect. Everything was perfect. She had only seen Dole Park in the center of Lana'i City once before, but she couldn't imagine that the community greenspace had ever looked lovelier. Maddie and Kai had kept things simple with borrowed chairs and tables, and they had decorated the wedding canopy mostly with live plants and flowers that were already on the island. Perhaps that was why it all looked so lush and inviting. There was nothing synthetic, here. Nothing cut or pasted or dyed. Just living flowers, friendly people, and abundant good will.

Ri signed the guest book, then moved over to a patch of shade underneath a Cook pine. She looked around the assembling crowd, and a smile spread over her face as she caught sight of her cousin near the canopy. He looked amazingly handsome in a tuxedo, as she knew he would. They'd known each other only a little over a month, but it felt like so much longer. If she ever got more confirmation of a blood tie between them that would be fabulous, but if she didn't, she wouldn't care. She had been adopted into Kai's family tree, past and present, without question or reservation, and that was a privilege she cherished regardless.

The two teenage boys standing near Kai, also in tuxedos, Ri assumed must be Maddie's twin brothers. They were handsome devils, both of them, a fact which was obviously not lost on Kai's youngest sister Gloria, who buzzed around them in a stunning strawberry-colored gown. Another young woman, wearing a similarly styled gown in bright peach, stood nearby, and Ri assumed she must be Kai's other sister, Chika. Where Maddie was being cloistered, Ri had no idea. The wedding wasn't due to start for a half hour, and there was no music yet. Ri heard only the happy chattering of the milling crowd and the soft trill of doves overhead. Then she heard herself sigh.

*Please... Stop.*

She couldn't help it. Her eyes began to water. She'd been doing all right the past few weeks. Well enough. Decent. Fair. Things could be going so much worse than they were. She could have heard nothing at all from Wolf. But instead, she had gotten texts from him. *Twice.* That wasn't so bad, considering that he was primitive-camping at the ends of the earth. He'd sent her a picture and he'd sent her a text. He was still thinking about her, and that was what mattered. The waiting was harder than she'd expected, yes. But she had no reason to feel sad on a day like today. Today was Maddie and Kai's day. She would be happy for them.

She searched the crowd for someone she knew and caught sight of Lachland. He had a pretty blond woman standing next to him whom Ri assumed was his wife, and he was having a jovial conversation with Ben Parker, the oceanographer Ri had met her first day on Maui. Ben had a smartly dressed brunette on his arm whom Ri certainly *hoped* was his wife, because the way the woman looked at him, he would be in trouble if she weren't. Ri took a step toward the group, then stopped herself. They all looked so happy.

A middle-aged giant of a man walked up to Kai, said something in his ear, and clapped him on the back. The two men laughed loudly and their deep, mellow voices rumbled all the way to Ri's ears. Maddie's father, no doubt. And that would be Maddie's stepmother smiling beside them. Kai seemed to get along well with his future in-laws. That was nice.

*Mom and Dad would like Wolf, too.*

Ri turned abruptly and walked away from the crowd. She was ashamed of herself, but her tear ducts were nearing the fill line and she couldn't be seen. She found a large tree near the far corner of the park and sat down on the ground, heedless of getting her nice slacks dirty. She leaned against the tree trunk facing away from the revelry and lowered her face to her phone. Before she even knew what she'd done, Wolf's last text was back on her screen again.

I miss you.

Ten days. It had been ten days since those three beautiful words had popped into her life in the middle of a dolphin watch, nearly causing her to somersault overboard in her excitement. Her immediate response was still there right below it.

I miss you, too!

Since then, there'd been nothing.

She assumed he's gone out of range again. She didn't know what else she could assume. He missed her, and he wanted her to know it. But... what?

She had already been searching online for job opportunities in Alaska. She was a dreamer, after all, and advance planning was her specialty. If Wolf wanted her to come, she would be there. If he wanted her to wait for him, she would wait. All she needed to pull the trigger was a clear understanding between them, some kind of commitment she could count on.

But he had to give her that. And it had to come from him, of his own free will. She thought she could wait as long as it took, but this slow drip of life blood was more painful than she'd imagined. She thought she understood him. She thought she understood how it would happen. He would leave, and he would miss her, and after he mulled it over a while, he would take some action. That's why, when the text finally came, she'd felt so giddy with joy. She'd been right all along! It was happening!

Then there was silence.

She didn't know what to think. But the other possibility, the raw, percolating fear that his feelings for her would dim over time, had slowly become her constant, gnawing companion. She refused to acknowledge that fear. She wouldn't accept it. But nor would it go away.

*I miss you.*

"He meant it," Ri whispered to herself, hugging her phone to her chest and fighting to keep her eyes dry. "He meant it just days ago. Now stop." She shut her lids and conjured an image of Wolf on the road to Hana. He'd been nervous as a cat the whole way. He kept trying to clench the door handle with his splinted hand, but he couldn't get his fingers around it, so he'd wound up sticking his left hand in the drink holder on the truck console, gripping it until his knuckles went white. And all the while he'd been pretending to be cool as a cucumber. Ri chuckled to herself. He was such a cautious soul. It was a part of his nature. She let out another sigh, then opened her eyes. "He's afraid," she said out loud. "He's a wuss, but you love him anyway, so deal with it."

"Who's a wuss?"

Ri's head shot up. It was Wolf's voice, but it wasn't Wolf. It was a man in a suit, nicely groomed and spiffed up for a wedding. He had crept silently behind her and was standing not two feet away, smiling at her devilishly with a twinkle in his clear blue eyes. "Surprise?" he said uncertainly.

It *was* Wolf. He was here. Ri's brain twisted itself into a pretzel. He could not be here, and yet he was. Her optimistic heart yearned to rejoice, but her rational side fought the impulse. He was here... but "here" was at Maddie and Kai's wedding. She could not necessarily conclude anything from that. Could she?

The conflicting thoughts flitted through Ri's brain at light speed. The doubt, the recognition, the joy, the caution. In real time she simply scrambled up, flung herself forward, and clasped her arms around his neck.

She said nothing. All she did was hold him. His own strong arms wrapped around her waist, molding her tightly to his chest. She felt both his hands caress her back and realized that no bulky splint was poking at her. He smelled of... well, he smelled like an airplane. But Ri didn't care. She didn't care about anything. She never wanted to let him go.

"You feel so good," she murmured after a while.

"So do you," he whispered back.

"I thought you couldn't afford to come back here," she

mumbled, still holding him.

"I couldn't," he answered. "The ticket was a gift. From my stepmother."

A pleasant warmth flooded Ri's soul at the sound of those words, though in her present happy haze, their significance wasn't clear to her.

"I've missed you, Ri," he said softly.

She smiled into his shoulder. "I was hoping you would."

He pulled back just enough to look at her. "You called me a wuss just now. Either that, or you were talking about some other guy. But considering what else you said... I hope you were talking about me."

Ri studied his face. "Do you? I'm a pretty scary woman, Wolf. I don't give my heart away easily. I never have, and I never will. But I always play for keeps."

He held her gaze levelly. "I know that," he replied, his voice low. Then his brow furrowed defensively. "And I am not a wuss."

Ri grinned at him. "No?"

"No," he growled back at her, tightening his grip.

Ri reveled in the solid feel of him. He looked handsome in a suit, but strange. She liked him better in his sexy work duds with his hair all shaggy. "Prove it," she taunted, her lips inches from his.

He smiled wickedly. "I would enjoy kissing you very much. But it wouldn't prove anything, except that you're the most incredibly desirable vixen I've ever seen and you've been driving me to distraction ever since I met you, which you already know."

Ri's grin broadened.

"So how about this instead," he continued, setting her back from him. She felt the distance between them like a cold wind, but when he took both her hands in his and looked at her purposefully, her body began to warm again. "You said you want a relationship. I want that, too. I don't know how to make it happen because my doctoral work means I have to spend long chunks of time out in the field. But whatever I can do, Ri, I'll do it. If you're willing to work with me, there's got to be some way."

Ri's soul overflowed with joy, and she closed the distance between them with a pounce. She pressed her lips to his and circled her arms tightly around his waist. Her hands began to claw eagerly beneath his jacket, and what happened after that got hazy. She couldn't begin to say how much time passed, and she suspected Wolf couldn't, either. But the next thing either of them knew, Ri was reclining against a pine tree with two shirt buttons undone and Wolf was standing next to her rubbing his biceps with a frown. "What the hell?" he snapped.

"Excuse me?" a female voice protested hotly.

Ri scrambled up to see a vision of loveliness straight out of a fairy tale. Maddie's gorgeous red hair cascaded from her head in a sea of bouncy curls, spreading over her bare shoulders and down around the bodice of a simple, yet elegant white satin wedding dress that looked like it had been plucked straight from the centerfold of a brides' magazine. Or perhaps, given Maddie's voluptuous figure, another magazine entirely. Her striking face stared at both Ri and Wolf with a mixture of fury and amusement that was impossibly confusing.

"What was that for?" Wolf said resentfully, gesturing to his arm. Ri blinked in surprise. Had Maddie actually hit him?

"Would you have preferred I throw a bucket of water on you?" Maddie shot back, barely concealing a laugh. "That was the leading suggestion."

Ri looked out beyond Maddie's shoulder, and all the blood in her body pooled at her feet. Only a couple hundred people were staring at them. Staring at them, grinning, and snickering.

*Oh. My. God.*

"This is *my* wedding day, you know!" Maddie continued, her mouth twitching with a smile even as she berated them. "In case you're not familiar with how it works, the honeymoon doesn't start till afterward. And it's generally a bride-and-groom thing."

"We're sorry," Ri and Wolf said at the same time.

Maddie's gray eyes flashed with humor as she looked from one of them to the other. "I'm not," she whispered conspiratorially. She turned away, then whirled back and hissed another whisper at Ri. "Button up!"

The bride strolled off to take her place. Ri buttoned her top and Wolf adjusted his jacket. "Is your arm okay?" Ri asked with concern.

"It's fine," Wolf assured. Then he chuckled. "You know, I always suspected she could be dangerous."

"She could have tapped you on the shoulder or something first!" Ri protested.

Wolf smirked. "Um... I think she probably did. More than once."

They shared a knowing glance.

Ri wondered how long weddings lasted.

"I suppose we should find some seats," Wolf suggested.

"I suppose so," Ri agreed.

Wolf cleared his throat. "But I do need an answer, still."

Ri lifted an eyebrow. "An answer?"

He eyed her sternly. "Don't toy with me, woman. I'm not cheap. If you want this hot bod of mine, I expect a clear commitment. *In words.*"

The corners of Ri's mouth drew up slowly. She laced her fingers through his. Standing next to him without touching wouldn't work anymore. "I do want you," she said softly. "And I do think we can work it out. Somehow."

"Come to Alaska, then," Wolf urged. "When your internship is over, I mean. You can find marine biology work there. I can help you."

Ri's smiled deepened. Strains of wedding music, played by an odd assembly of ukuleles and a harp, carried over the island breeze. Her mind filled with images of breaching beluga whales, orcas, Steller sea lions, and sea otters. She saw snow-capped peaks, dark lonely roads, and a tent with a super-insulated sleeping bag for two.

"Yes," she answered.

# Epilogue

*Anchorage, Alaska, February 2017*

"Frieda!" Ri bounced in the open back door with the dogs jumping at her heels. "Frieda! Are you here?"

She rounded the corner into the kitchen and nearly collided with a plump woman in a flour-spattered apron. "Oh, I'm sorry! But I'm so glad you're home! I'm losing my mind. The letter came!"

"Well now, calm down," Frieda said with good humor, wiping her hands on her apron and then pulling it off. "What did it say?"

"I don't know!" Ri exclaimed. "I haven't opened it yet. I can't! I need help for these things. I was going to wait for Wolf to get home today, but I don't know exactly when he's coming and I don't have that kind of patience."

Frieda laughed. She steered Ri to a chair and sat down opposite her. "Well, have you called your family yet?"

Ri met her friend's eyes with gratitude, then shook her head. Frieda understood Ri's need to stay connected, even as she forged a new life in a new place. "My parents are on a plane right now, going to the West Coast to visit my aunt. And my sister's at work." She set the envelope down on the table in front of her. Her hand trembled slightly as she pushed it toward Frieda. "I want you to open it."

"Me?" Frieda asked, surprised.

"Oh, please?" Ri begged. "I hate opening things like this. Mei Lin always used to do it for me. Particularly when the letter's thin, because that's usually bad news."

Frieda studied the envelope. "Oh, I don't think that necessarily means anything," she insisted. "You said before that they might let you know about the assistantship separate from your acceptance into grad school, right?"

Ri nodded nervously. Acceptance into the master's program

at the University of Fairbanks was all she had a right to hope for. She had saved enough money to start in the fall either way, thanks to a decent paying job with the state fisheries department and Frieda's letting her live over the restaurant. But snagging one of the highly competitive assistantships would be a goldmine for her. Not only could she be with Wolf most of the year in Fairbanks, but she could afford to visit him more often in the field as well. Having her savings as a nest egg would make their lives easier all around. Including advancing their wedding plans.

"Just rip it open and skip all the intro stuff," Ri begged. "Read it to yourself and then tell me the verdict. In plain English. Without the mumbo jumbo. *Please*, Frieda?" The women were holding hands across the table.

"Oh, all right!" Frieda relented. She gave Ri's hands an encouraging squeeze, then picked up the letter. Ri took a deep breath. Next to her own mother and sister, she'd come to care for Frieda Markov as much as any woman alive. They were alike in so many ways it was scary, and they had become friends almost immediately, with no need of urging from Wolf or anybody else.

Frieda tore open the envelope and pulled out the letter. She readjusted her glasses on her nose to read the print through her bifocals.

Ri's heart pounded.

Frieda looked away from the paper and smiled at her. "You got the assistantship."

"Oh, Frieda!" Ri shouted, scraping her chair against the floor and jumping to her feet. "Really? I really got it?"

"You really did!" Frieda jumped up with her and the two women hugged. The dogs barked excitedly. A door opened. "What's all this?"

Ri let go of Frieda and looked up. Wolf and his brother stood in the doorway, laden with heavy coats, backpacks, and gear. Ri flew into her fiancé's arms, just barely giving him enough time to drop his backpack from his shoulders and catch her. "Whoa!" he laughed. "What's happened?"

"I got the assistantship!" she cried. "It's a free ride!"

"Oh, Ri!" he exclaimed, hugging her tightly and giving her a spin. "That's fabulous! Congratulations!"

The dogs were going wild. Wolf kissed her soundly, then set her down. "Sorry. Just a second." He greeted Suka and Tog with his usual enthusiastic rubdown, then pulled Ri back into his arms again. "Now, tell me about it."

Ri hastily explained.

"That's awesome, Ri," Bear congratulated as he moved both his and Wolf's stuff out of their way. "Hey, bro, does this mean you're going to start paying me for flying your ass all over the state?"

"I already pay you!" Wolf shot back.

"Yeah, but now I'm thinking of asking for a raise," Bear replied.

"Knock it off, you two!" Frieda ordered. "This is Ri's day to celebrate. Bear, take my keys and go pick up your dad. His truck's in the shop."

Bear pretended a scowl. "I just flew—"

"Oh, quit your bellyaching," Frieda reprimanded. "Didn't I put out a nice spread for Amanda's folks last weekend?"

Bear smiled lazily. "Indeed you did."

"Then pick up some brisket too, while I finish this pie and make a salad. And hurry. We'll all be good and hungry by the time you get back."

Bear offered his stepmother a salute, then leaned in and kissed Ri on the cheek. "Good to see you, future sis," he said cheerfully. "Congratulations. You deserve it."

"Thanks, Cub," Ri returned, smiling back.

Bear grabbed a set of keys from a peg by the back door and walked out, and Frieda excused herself to go check on her pie.

Wolf took Ri's hand and pulled her into the far corner of the family room. Suka and Tog pranced circles around them with every step. "Together again," Wolf said in a husky whisper, drawing her fully against him. "And alone."

Ri laughed. "You call this alone?"

His beautiful blue eyes gazed into hers. Ri no longer had any doubt that he loved her. And as much as it was possible for anyone to know anything, she was certain now that he always would.

"Work with me," he suggested.

# About the Author

USA-Today bestselling novelist and playwright Edie Claire was first published in mystery in 1999 by the New American Library division of Penguin Putnam. In 2002 she began publishing award-winning contemporary romances with Warner Books, and in 2008 two of her comedies for the stage were published by Baker's Plays (now Samuel French). In 2009 she began publishing independently, continuing her original Leigh Koslow Mystery series and adding new works of romantic women's fiction, young adult fiction, and humor.

Under the banner of Stackhouse Press, Edie has now published over 25 titles including digital, print, audio, and foreign translations. Her works are distributed worldwide, with her first contemporary romance, *Long Time Coming*, exceeding two million downloads. She has received multiple "Top Pick" designations from *Romantic Times Magazine* and received both the "Reader's Choice Award" from *Road To Romance* and the "Perfect 10 Award" from *Romance Reviews Today*.

A former veterinarian and childbirth educator, Edie is a happily married mother of three who currently resides in Pennsylvania. She enjoys gardening and wildlife-watching and dreams of becoming a snowbird.

# Books & Plays by Edie Claire

## Romantic Fiction

**Pacific Horizons**

*Alaskan Dawn*
*Leaving Lana'i*
*Maui Winds*
*Glacier Blooming*
*Tofino Storm*

**Fated Loves**

*Long Time Coming*
*Meant To Be*
*Borrowed Time*

**Hawaiian Shadows**

*Wraith*
*Empath*
*Lokahi*
*The Warning*

## Leigh Koslow Mysteries

*Never Buried*
*Never Sorry*
*Never Preach Past Noon*
*Never Kissed Goodnight*
*Never Tease a Siamese*
*Never Con a Corgi*

*Never Haunt a Historian*
*Never Thwart a Thespian*
*Never Steal a Cockatiel*
*Never Mess With Mistletoe*
*Never Murder a Birder*
*Never Nag Your Neighbor*

## Women's Fiction

*The Mud Sisters*
*Soccer Mom in Galilee (as Rachel Stackhouse)*

## Humor

*Corporately Blonde*

## Comedic Stage Plays

*Scary Drama I*
*See You in Bells*

www.ingramcontent.com/pod-product-compliance
Lightning Source LLC
Chambersburg PA
CBHW050559190726
48283CB00007B/2202